ARCADIA

PALMETTO
PUBLISHING
Charleston, SC
www.PalmettoPublishing.com

Hardcover ISBN: 979-8-8229-3361-3
Paperback ISBN: 979-8-8229-3362-0
eBook ISBN: 979-8-8229-3363-7

FALLEN COLONIES II

ARCADIA

ASHLEY ASHFORTH

Table of Contents

Chapter 1

GARETH

Gareth leans up against the elevator wall with his arms folded, watching his large family fawn over each other, ensuring everyone is pristine for the ball. He catches his mother's eye, and she licks her fingers, tucking away the defiant wavy locks that have fallen into his eyes. Gareth brushes her hands away in disgust and presses himself further into the corner. They're technically a higher class, but their ranks won't matter here. There's always the hope of an advantageous marriage elevating the family to a higher class. Greed is what motivates them.

Gareth is perfectly content with being invisible. He's never left wanting. Everything he could ask for is at his fingertips, and he's grateful for his rank. At this level, he can pursue any position in any department that may interest him. Any higher class and he'd be stuck inheriting roles like his cousin.

The elevator doors open wide to the entrance of the Great Hall. Hundreds of people in gowns and sleek suits flood the doors. Gareth's family, overflowing with excitement, quickly forget about Gareth as they make their way into the crowd. Some stop for the flashing lights, hoping to be noticed by the media.

A vehicle pulls up, and the doors are opened, allowing a couple to join the chaos. Eustacia and her escort emerge. Her silver hair is slicked back, revealing the triangle tattoos on her cheekbone, the brand of the Nox heir. She looks as miserable as ever. Making himself as small as possible, Gareth weaves through the crowd, sneaking up behind her. "Crack a smile, cousin, or they might see the real you," he whispers in her ear. Eustacia whips her head around and a grin spreads from cheek to cheek. She squeals with excitement as she pulls him into a tight hug. A man with orange hair scowls at the affection she gives him. "Careful, I don't want too much attention tonight," he says as he pulls her away.

"I've missed you, you little rat. Where have you been?" she says, hunching over as if it would allow them a private conversation.

"Where have I been? You're the one galivanting with the bottom-dwellers," his eyebrows wag.

"Watch it. I searched for you, but you weren't home when I visited."

"Well, I may have been trying out an apprenticeship in the Security Department, allowing me access to other levels." He grins and lifts his wrist discreetly, jingling bracelets hidden under his cuff.

"Taking advantage of your freedom, I see." She raises a brow.

"I've found delight in exploring the other cultures of our development," he says merrily.

"Oh, you rascal. You better be careful. Don't get into any trouble. I won't be able to bail you out on certain levels."

"I wouldn't burden you," Gareth smiles, and with a kiss on her cheek he whispers, "I think your date is getting testy. See you later, sweet cousin."

Stacy rolls her eyes but gives his hand a squeeze before he disappears once more into the crowd. He has mastered stealth over the years and makes his way back into the elevator without anyone's notice. The doors shut and Gareth leans against the metal walls with a large sigh. He pulls his sleeve back and chooses a key card at random before scanning it. As the elevator jolts with movement, he places his hands back in his pockets and takes his place once again, leaning against the elevator's railing.

The people he left behind live for the invitations and excitement of daily gossip. Gareth, on the other hand, is bored of it. He's considered nearly an adult. Nineteen years old, and he has yet to choose a career path, yet they've already found him a life partner. The thought of living with a stranger for the rest of his life has never been appealing. Though Astrid is no stranger, he'd do anything to get out of that arrangement. Desperate to lead a more fulfilling life, he's asked to explore the many options of the Development. Delaying his career means a delayed wedding. He refuses to settle as a drone technician, as that's what his father has experience doing and can be passed on to his son.

The elevator comes to a halt, making his innards feel as though they're trying to catch up with the rest of his body, and the doors open to a whitewashed hallway. Making his way down the hall, he notices two men in black pass through the intersecting entrance: security. Gareth freezes. Deep in their conversation, the men don't see him in passing. On the wall, there's a directory of the entire station. He can recall the map in his mind in perfect detail thanks to his photographic memory as he moves along to the next elevator. Quickly he scans the bracelet that matches that of the elevator code. This elevator moves sideways, throwing off his balance.

The ride is short as the doors open to the great sunlight of the arboretum, level 8. His eyes adjust quickly. Stepping out of the elevator, the arboretum has acres of fields providing sustenance for the entirety of the Stratos Development. This is one of his favorite places to escape to. It would take days to walk around the whole of the cylindrical fields. Those working in the fields all wear a brown uniform of different styles. The fields are worked by hand, allowing the development to conserve energy and keep the air clean, maintaining the purity of the produce. The first field is all grain, and he walks through the tall yellow stalks in awe as he stares overhead. The glass ceiling curves up and over like a giant dome, allowing total exposure to the sun and other stars that would've been hidden at this time of day on the earth's surface. It may be hard work here, but after the last incident caused by the Cole family, they're not willing to risk using machines for this work. Perhaps the view makes up for the hard labor in this sector; it's something to behold. Though the fields are at an angle, the gravity levels have been manipulated, so it doesn't feel as though you're aslant. He doesn't wander far into the fields so as not to draw attention to himself, being fairly overdressed in his off-white suit.

The heat from the arboretum has him sweating. Wiping his brow with a silk handkerchief, he retreats to the elevators again. Returning to the halls, he recalls the way to Factoria, level 5. This time using a bracelet made of dark metal, the elevators descend further. When it comes to a stop, the heat spills into the elevator like a thick, damp cloud. Factoria. The doors open wide to a dark city lit only by the neon lights of the signs and advertisements. There's no natural light. Gareth rubs his hands in anticipation. Stripping his jacket off, he's left with a sheer white shirt that droops at the neck, and he rolls his sleeves up to his elbows as he makes his way through the corridor. The fragrance in the air is unfamiliar, with a sour, smoky aroma. The streets are filled with goods and those looking for a trade. The goods for trade include scraps of fabric and electronic parts, wires, plastic sheets, and tubing. Some of the scrapped parts have been turned into intricate jewelry and clothing.

Most people come to these levels only to hire those with skills they can't find above—maintenance and repair workers, carpenters, stonemasons, mass production of clothing through sweatshops. On the other hand, Gareth comes for the nightlife when those workers have finished their shifts, and they find recreation in their strange danceclubs. They're nothing fancy by any means, but they know how to enjoy themselves.

Gareth runs his hand through his unruly raven hair and walks the colorful streets, admiring the change of scenery. Crowds of people pile into trams as they head home from their shifts. They rush off with a gust of hot air. As he browses the street market, he overhears a couple of men as they pass. The boisterous group couldn't be much older than him, perhaps in their twenties. They're excited to visit a new club that has become popular as of late. He follows the group at a distance.

He's led down several dark alleys, searching for the right one with a red fire escape along the building's side. Finally, they come to one with muffled music, and the alley curves into a staircase sinking into the ground. The small, barred windows are blacked out. As the men open the door, the music screams into the silent alley before they disappear behind it. Gareth looks up and down the path before he follows. The door is heavy as he yanks it open—the noise of humans and music blasts into him.

The lights flash more colorful than the streets outside. A horde of people are on the dancefloor, some dripping with sweat. Their way of dancing is so different from that of the upper classes. The music is much louder and strange yet pleasing. Further into the club, on the back wall of mirrors, is the bar. He takes a seat on one of the stools. The bartender looks him over with a scrutinizing eye. "What can I get you?"

"Surprise me." Gareth smiles and hands over the coin. The bartender scans the currency with a large grin. Grabbing a pole with a hook at the end, he fishes out a bottle from the top shelf. The bartender hands the coin back, pouring a bubbling pink liquid into a glass before him.

"Would you like a booth?" he gestures toward a roped-off area further away from the crowd with luxurious velvet chairs. There are already a couple of people in one of the booths, one wearing an off-duty military suit and the other in a gray suit with a black leather collar, indicating a very high ranking. The other two in his company, one male and one female, look as if they eagerly anticipate an exciting night.

"No, thank you. I prefer not to mix with that kind."

"Whatever shoots your rockets," he says before moving on to the next customer.

Gareth watches the crowd of people bouncing in sync with the music. On the edge of the group, a girl sways to the music as if she hears a different tune. She's with her friends, but they can't match her rhythm as the music gets more energetic. He's curious after watching her for a couple of songs. Finishing his drink, he starts to make his way over to her, bouncing along and smoothly moving through the crowd. Gareth's isn't the only attention she's caught, as another off-duty officer cuts in before Gareth reaches her. He whispers in her ear. She nods her head before allowing him to escort her. The crowd parts for them as they head toward the booths. Her friends look after her with concern.

He quickly returns to the bar and taps the counter for attention. "What are those men doing here?" He nods in the direction of the booth.

"They're recruiters," the bartender says indifferently.

"I think I'll take that booth after all."

With a nod, a tall woman in red skintight vinyl appears and leads him to the booth across from them. The guards watch the crowd as the gray suit puts his arm around her and speaks into her ear. The girl folds her arms, showing no interest in the man pursuing her. Gareth can't hear much over the loud music but can make out some words by reading their lips, though what he catches doesn't make sense without context. After some time and what looks like a negotiation, she agrees to leave with them. Gareth follows as they make their way through the city to the elevators. Another group of civilians joins before entering the corridor.

Gareth waits a minute for them to arrive at the elevators before peeking through the door. He leaves the door slightly ajar and waits for them to file in. As the doors close, he peeks in to see which level they head to. The elevator drops two levels. Quickly Gareth scans his identification code, and another elevator opens. He looks through his ID cards until he finds one for the Department of Health and Scientific Exploration, the DHSE. He scans it, and the elevator begins to fall. The doors slide open and he enters the DHSE lobby. No one has noticed his presence, so he quickly hides behind a reception desk. Security is on guard as they watch the civilians fill out their forms.

Three assistants come out to take the applications. At least ten applicants are signing the paperwork. When they finish, the assistants scan it. "Thank you so much for joining us today," the attendant says clearly, her voice calm and sweet. "My name is Ella. I'm thrilled to be working with you all. You've been invited to the DHSE because we need your help. In return, we want to help you advance in your careers and society. Before you accept our offer, I would like to clarify what we expect of you. We're testing a serum intended to help you become stronger and healthier. You'll live in our facility until the trial period has ended. We need to see how it affects you physically and socially. We've chosen you because you're all very different in body type, blood type and personality. You may have a negative reaction, which is why you'll always be monitored. If you have a negative reaction, our doctors will correct it quickly and efficiently so that your experience has minimal discomfort. Before we start, would anyone like to decline and return to their original department?" Everyone sits quietly, looking at each other. "Then let's get started, shall we? If you would follow me." She turns to lead the way as the group follows.

Each volunteer is led down a hallway. The security guards begin to leave as they are no longer needed; one assistant stays behind. The brunette Gareth has his eye on watches warily but is the last to finish her paperwork. Approaching one of the assistants, she hands over her form. "Thank you, Ms. Pruitt," the assistant says. "If you'll follow me." The automatic door slides open, leading to the hallway. Gareth slides in before it closes and locks. They pass each applicant in their exam room. The strangest part is that each exam room has a two-way mirror. Most wouldn't notice, but if you look carefully, you can see movement behind the mirror due to faint lighting.

He follows as quietly as possible until Pruitt is shown to her room. "Just wait here, and the doctor will be in to see you soon."

"I have some questions," the woman says, raising her hand.

"Doctor Oric will answer all questions." She looks as though she's going to ask anyway, but the assistant closes the door behind her. He watches her as she nervously picks at the hem of her top. Just as he's about to enter the room and speak to her, there's a strange noise at the end of the hall. He hesitates, but curiosity always has gotten the best of him, and he ends up following the hall further. There are a few empty exam rooms, and one patient strapped to a reclining chair in the middle of another. The patient is a young male with blonde hair and very sharp features. He's breathing heavily and regularly flinches. Frames sit over his eyes, wrapping snuggly around his head. The frame has dark tinted glass so you can barely see his eyes. Gareth waves, trying to get his attention, but it's as if he can't see.

He backs out and investigates the next exam room. A female is in the same situation. She yells out and looks as though every muscle in her body is strained, a vein in her forehead protruding. Looking down at her clenched fists, he notices blood dripping. "Hey." Gareth touches her shoulder to get a response. She screams out as blood drips from her nose. He jumps back and watches as her body goes limp. He backs out of the room and starts moving back up the hallway as quickly and quietly as possible.

Just as he's getting close to the end of the hallway, he runs into someone coming from the intersecting hall. Gareth trips over him but is caught by a metal arm. "Hello," the man greets him curiously.

"Killian Grey?" He recognizes him from a program he had seen months earlier. Everyone knows Killian Grey.

"Yes?" Killian raises a brow.

"Hey, can you help? You work here, right?"

"Yes. Are you alright?"

"There's a girl back there bleeding. I think she's in pain. Something's wrong." Gareth points down the hall. Killian follows Gareth as he runs back to the room. He removes the visor over the girl's eyes carefully.

"How did you get in here?" Killian asks Gareth, eyes focused on the girl.

"I followed one of the assistants."

"Are you one of the volunteers?"

"No, I… Is she okay?"

"She'll live. What's your name?" Killian asks as he opens the girl's eye and checks her pupil with a light.

"Gareth Nox."

"Nox." Killian twists around to face the young man. "You're not supposed to be here, are you?"

"No, I'm sorry."

"You should go," Killian says in a low voice. "Now."

"What?" Bumps rise on his skin.

An assistant comes in to help Killian and Gareth begins to back out of the room, but he spins around to see Dr. Oric blocking his exit. "Good evening, Gareth Nox," Dr. Oric grins. Stunned, Gareth takes a step backward. "I know what you're thinking." Oric holds his hands up in surrender. "This is the end. I've been caught illegally roaming in sectors I don't belong to. A capital offense. I am dead." Oric says playfully, "Tell you what. I won't tell if you don't. In fact, I'd like to give you an opportunity of a lifetime. Walk with me." He pats Gareth on the shoulder before turning out of the room.

Catching up with Oric, Gareth steps into the man's path, bringing him to a stop. "I'll go back to the sky levels immediately," he says. "I apologize for my disrespect to you and the other sectors. I can wait for security to escort me back if you don't trust me to return on my own."

"Gareth, don't worry." Oric smiles. "You're not in trouble. I need your help. You've proven to be inquisitive, resourceful and intelligent. We could use someone like you on our team."

"Really..." He's skeptical.

Dr. Oric continues into the lobby and sits on the white couch facing the window, with a view of the storming clouds below. Gareth takes a seat next to him. "I know you've been struggling. Your parents have contacted me with concern. You've been 'rebelling against them,' as they put it. However, I consider it a healthy curiosity. You've been arguing about your right to choose your companion and your career. You have rights. If you know you won't have a satisfying life in that position, then you should have the ability to explore other options. The recruits you just saw, they've all joined our most recent experiment. I'd like you to join it, but not as a patient. I want you to be something of a placebo. We need someone to be our control subject. You won't be given any drug."

"I don't think so."

"If I may speak frankly." Oric doesn't wait for the approval. "I know of your arranged marriage. Astrid is a good girl, not very bright, but she does what she's told. Unfortunately, if you accept my offer, that arrangement would need to be dissolved."

"I'll do it," Gareth interrupts.

A large grin returns to Dr. Oric's face as he looks out at the clouds. "Now, don't be hasty. There's so much work in finding a new career, starting from the ground up, and we don't know how long this experiment may carry on."

"I said I accept. Void the arranged marriage."

Dr. Oric turns his head with a smile and holds out his hand. Gareth looks at his hand and beaming smile. With a firm grasp, they shake on it.

Chapter 2

STACY

Upon entering the grand ballroom, the tall arched ceiling echoes with the high-society guests chattering. Clothed in a white inverted V-neck gown, it flows elegantly as Stacy is escorted across the large ballroom. Her suitor, a copper-haired man, is dressed in an indigo suit with a white sash wrapped around his side and draped over his shoulder, symbolizing his pursuit of the Nox family. He's holding a conversation all on his own as Stacy feigns interest. Looking around the grand room, she searches for one person in particular. It's been three months since she's seen or heard from him. Finally, an event that includes all families is allowing her to reconnect. She's already searched the hall and is about to give up on the idea when Killian is escorted in by Ella, who's never out of arm's reach.

Seeing him in person has her heart racing. His mannerisms have her captivated. Killian smiles at everyone approaching and greets them with a slight bow with his hand over his heart. The hard, bitter exterior has melted away. It's bizarre to see strangers bring these foreign expressions out of him. Stacy is drinking Killian in when she's interrupted. "What do you think, Eustacia?" her companion asks.

"Hmm?" Stacy's attention is returned to the tall thin man standing before her. Though he has a prominent societal position, she finds it hard to keep attention on his boorish rattling.

"Would you be able to introduce me?" he asks.

"Introduce?"

"To Killian Grey. You are John Nox's daughter, after all. I know you've made his acquaintance already. You were on stage with him during the interview."

"Yes, I have."

"I've never met someone from the gutters," he says as he bites his knuckle in anticipation. "They must've been hiding footage of him."

"Why would you say that?" Stacy says nervously.

"He's murdered people in cold blood. What would keep him from murdering us all? They must've been hiding something."

"I suppose."

"Don't make me beg. Introduce me, Eustacia," he says as he walks off in Killian's direction.

"Of course, Elliot, why not." She follows the man her father chose to accompany her. She looks after him in disgust. He crosses the room, excusing himself as he pushes past people, not caring how many gowns or toes he stomps on along the way, eventually standing at Killian's back as he speaks with another guest. Stacy catches up with him just as he taps him on the shoulder. Killian turns to face him. Looking at Elliot indifferently, he waits for the man standing at least six inches taller than him to speak. Killian watches him curiously as Ella leans in to whisper into his ear. A wry smile crosses his face as he nods in acknowledgment. He tilts his head, looking down at Stacy. The contrast between Elliott, over six and a half feet tall, and Stacy, only reaching 5'2", has inspired a wicked grin on his face.

Elliot clears his throat impatiently. "Eustacia Nox, isn't it?" Killian says to her instead, grinning.

"It's good to see you again, Mr. Grey." She plays along with his facade. Elliot clenches his jaw. "Have you met Mr. Elliot Cole?"

"Elliot Cole, I've been waiting all evening to meet you." Elliot introduces himself and reaches out to shake Killian's hand.

"Well, I hope I can live up to your expectations." Killian reaches out with his metal hand. Elliot winces as the mechanical hand grips his tightly.

"Tell me, how did you come to be here?"

"I was recruited."

"Yes, but how did you get here?"

"I took a car." Killian chuckles. Elliot chuckles with him but is irritated as Killian avoids his probing questions.

"I'm surprised you've made it to this level of society with a history like yours. Do you feel guilty for what has passed?"

"Elliot..." Stacy tries to intervene, but Elliot holds his index finger in front of her face, silencing her.

Killian looks over Elliot once more before speaking. "The Cole family. I understand you're an heir to the agronomy."

"That's right." Elliot smiles with pride.

"You've been taking control of production as of late. I heard about the few who had lost their lives due to communication errors before initiating the reapers. It's a shame. Those families must be devastated. Tell me, with their blood on your hands, do you feel guilt for what's passed?"

"Those families were compensated." Elliot adjusts his suit as if it's squeezing him.

"I wonder what kind of compensation can heal the wounds of a lost loved one. Well, you did your best." Killian pats Elliot on the shoulder consolingly.

"I've answered one of your questions. Won't you respond to my own?"

"Of course I feel guilt." Killian pauses for a moment. That answer apparently wasn't enough for Elliot. He waits for more insight. "Though some of them deserved to die." He steps closer to Elliot as if to tell him something in secret. "In the end, I did what I needed to survive. I'd never question anyone's motives if it meant choosing your own life over someone else. Let me ask you a question..." Killian looks up into the man's eyes as he rests his right hand on Elliot's shoulder. "Tell me, what do you hold most dear to you? What's the most important thing to you? What would be the most devastating thing to lose? It could be your mother, a sibling, a lover..." Killian glances at Stacy. "A favorite blanket?"

"I would say it'd be myself and what I've built for myself," he says, looking down on Killian with his chin raised. "Nothing's more important to me than myself." He grins.

"So, if someone..." Killian gestures to the room filled with those occasionally glancing at Killian with admiration. "If any one of these people, including myself, threatened to take everything from you, possibly even your life, would you not do everything to remove that threat?" Killian asks, tightening his grip on Elliot's shoulder.

"I would." Elliot's grin is muted as he pulls Killian's hand away. "Are you threatening me?"

"Absolutely not," Killian says with a kind smile.

"Your grip would say otherwise."

"Oh, Mr. Cole, I'm so sorry," Ella interrupts, stepping in between them. "As you may know, Killian lost his arm. We replaced it with a new mechanical piece, which he's still getting used to. I can assure you he has no ill intent towards you. I take full responsibility and will adjust the settings immediately."

"See that you do."

"I'm sincerely sorry, Mr. Cole," Killian says, bowing his head as Elliot storms off in the opposite direction. "I'm sorry for scaring off your suitor, Miss Nox."

"On the contrary, it relieves me of driving him off myself. I'm in your debt, Mr. Grey." Killian flashes a devilish grin. "So, how have you been? It seems you've been quite busy working for Dr. Oric."

"I've been well. It's easy to feel at home when everything's handed to you on a platter."

"I suppose so." Stacy steps closer. "I was wondering if you had any plans for your future here?" Stacy hopes he gets the hint as to what she's inquiring about.

Killian looks at her, and then something catches his eye behind her and he smiles, but she doesn't notice. "Not in particular."

"Perhaps we could make arrangements for an engagement next week?"

Killian becomes more distracted and looks around Stacy. "One moment, please. Ella?" Killian touches Ella's wrist before excusing himself and moving quickly past Stacy.

"Ms. Nox, would you like to make an appointment with Mr. Grey?" Killian's personal assistant glides around behind him, saying "Currently there are no available opportunities to meet with him next week. The next available time is three weeks from now. Would you still like to set a date?" Stacy doesn't hear a word as she watches him walk away.

He approaches Danit Sinai. Sinai is one of the most influential families in the Stratos Development, tall with olive skin and long dark brown hair slicked back into a neat ponytail. She wears a sleek black satin gown, and her left sleeve has been replaced with silver satin. When Danit sees Killian walking toward her, she smiles with excitement. That's when Stacy notices the black satin sash draped over Killian's shoulder. Danit reaches her hand out to Killian with a smile. He takes it and, with a bow, kisses her fingers before wrapping them around his elbow.

"Ms. Nox?" the secretary says again. A fire burns in Stacy as she watches them disappear into the crowd.

"Make the appointment for the earliest convenience and send me the details," she growls before storming off just as Elliot had done.

Chapter 3

ALAN
AND VIOLET

Alan jolts from a deep sleep, blood pounding like a drum in his ears as he wakes up to Violet's distant screams. He looks around the dark sleeping quarters. Lilly and Ember are still asleep. Alan is out of bed with a second scream from Violet. The patter of his bare feet on the cold cement echo as he runs through the hall to Stacy's old room. Violet had to move into a private room when the nightmares were causing the children to become distressed. Without knocking on the door, he slips in, closing it behind him as softly as he can. Violet is thrashing and whimpering in the large bed.

"Violet," Alan whispers. She continues. Alan crosses the room to the bed. Carefully he reaches for her. "Violet," he says firmly, gripping her wrist as he strokes her arm. "Shhh."

Violet jerks awake with a sob. Covering her face with her arm, she twists her wrist out of Alan's grip and holds her palm out to him. Alan takes her hand. She holds him so tight that he bites his lip to distract himself from the pain. Looking at Violet and her petite frame, it's easy to forget her inhuman strength. The mutation of her blood has given her the power of the creatures that have hunted humanity for some 100 years now, the mavens. Alan strokes her arm, soothing her until her unsteady breaths calm. When Violet loosens the grip on him, the blood rushes back to his hand. He gets to his feet and presses his lips to her forehead in what's supposed to be a sweet show of endearment. He isn't expecting the slick sweat that meets his kiss, and he spits and sputters. "Sorry, that was gross."

Violet can't help but laugh at her friend as she peeks out from under her arm. "I'm sorry, Alan," she says in a shaking voice. Alan knows she's not apologizing for the sweat.

"It's all right, sweetheart." He squeezes her hand before leaving the room. Shutting the door behind him, he leans up against the gray cement walls of the shelter inside a cave hidden by a hundred-foot waterfall. Usually, the sound of the falls is comforting, but as the winter months have come, the falls have frozen, trapping them inside for the season. Though the soothing rush of water has become silent, it's created a much-needed wall of protection. After the Stratos Development had invaded the cave to take possession of his closest friends, Stacy Nox and Killian Grey, he wasn't sure if they'd be back for the rest of them. Violet, Jack, Clara and the kids are the only people he has left. Living on his own for so many years, always in hiding, he never wants to return to that life. Though he's not as close with them as with Killian and Stacy, he considers them family. Watching Violet lose Killian, and have Nathan taken away from her as well, has been difficult. He understands her pain, having lost his entire family in the past. Though she hasn't lost them completely, it's still tough to watch someone struggle to return to life. A normal life.

Alan rubs his face, wiping away the tears that threatened to spill from his eyes. With a deep breath, he pushes himself away from the wall. He walks to the end of the corridor and crosses the mess hall to the corridor leading to the infirmary. The door swings closed behind him as he checks the EEG and ensures the feeding tube still nourishes Nathan. He's been in a stable coma for two months now, and they have no other choice but to wait until his body's ready to wake up.

"Morning, buddy," Alan says as he rubs Nathan atop his head. "Ready for your exercise for the day?" He lifts the blankets and folds them back. Alan gently applies pressure to Nathan's scalp, neck and shoulders, helping the blood flow. He massages his arms, wrists, hands and fingertips. He then lifts his arms and gently helps Nathan roll his shoulders and move his arms, flexing and stretching the joints. Then he moves on to his legs, applying the same techniques to get the blood flowing. He's careful as he helps the sleeping five-year-old with his morning routine. "All right, Nathan, imagine you're getting ready to go for a walk," he says as he curls and stretches Nathan's toes and makes circles with each ankle.

"It's a beautiful day in the woods. The sky is a bright blue, and strips of white clouds are painted across it. The air is cool, but the sun is warming your skin. You can hear the river gushing with water on your left, *krshhhh*. Birds are chirping happily in the trees. You're walking along the river now." Alan holds Nathan's heels in his hands and slowly moves them back and forth as if he's walking in the air. "You can smell the pine sap and the wet moss as you take a deep breath of cool air." He takes a big breath for Nathan and breathes out dramatically as they walk through the forest together. "Oh, did you see that? There, over there! A rabbit just skittered off. You spooked him, Nathan. Should we chase after him?" Alan moves Nathan's legs a bit faster but not too fast, careful not to jostle his little body. "Oh, there he is. Let's get him! Aw, he was too fast. Ran straight into the prickle bushes. Let's slow down now and enjoy the quiet as we walk." They walk together a little while through the forest Alan painted before returning to bed. He tucks the blankets around him and kisses him on the forehead, checking the machines to make sure everything's working as it should before leaving.

He watches Clara help Jack cross the mess hall to the leather chair he's favored since his arrival. He's recovering, but it's a slow recovery given how old the man is. Broken ribs have always been the worst kind of wound. Clara leaves him in his chair and heads to the kitchen to start breakfast. Jack catches Alan's eye and signals for him to come closer. Alan's wary as he watches the old man's face turn stern. He's heard plenty of stories from Killian about how Jack had taken him in when he was only nine. They had spent two years stocking the shelter they now call home with everything they could possibly need. The only reason to leave is to hunt for meat or medical supplies. Jack is a fantastic engineer who built their atrium, which provides enough fruit and vegetables year-round to feed at least 30 people. It was a surprise to them all when Jack revealed the truth about his past and the fact that there's a society hovering above an abandoned city, allowing everyone below to live in squalor, forgotten. A society Jack left behind out of guilt.

Alan leans against the wall beside Jack with his arms folded. "I wanted to tell you this a month ago," Jack begins, "but neither you nor Violet had seemed to be in a good head space after the burial."

"What is it?" Alan urged him to get to the point. As many good things as Jack's done for the people he loves, Alan still isn't sure if he can forgive him for building the weapons that have turned the world into what it is today.

"Stacy contacted us. She wanted to speak to you or Violet."

Alan pushes himself away from the wall to kneel, to be at eye level with Jack. "Why didn't you bring us in when you got the call?" Alan says, fury burning in his eyes.

"We didn't know where you were burying the dead and if it was safe for us to contact you. Anyone could be out there, even in the woods, and we could've given them your location by doing so." Jack's reasoning was sound, but his heart sank knowing they'd missed the chance to heal some open wounds with Violet.

"What did they say? Are they all right?"

"Stacy says they're safe, but something's wrong with Killian. She says he's not himself."

"In what way?" Alan clenches his hands into fists.

"Killian is telling people Violet hid Nathan from him. That's why she erased her memory of him. He claims she was an irresponsible parent and blamed her mutation."

"Why would he do that?"

"I don't know." Jack rubs his face and beard. "The boy could've lost his mind after the accident, not knowing what happened, or he may be playing the game. I can't be sure without speaking to him directly. We don't know when she'll be able to contact us again, so I need you to keep this with you wherever you and Violet go from here on out. She'll do her best to get him to contact us when Killian can speak freely." Jack presses the communication device into Alan's hand. "I want you to take Violet hunting. We're running low on meat, and this winter will be a hard one."

"I'll see if she's willing. I won't force her to leave Nathan if she doesn't want to." Jack presses his lips into a line but nods once.

Violet stares at the dimly lit ceiling sticky with sweat from the nightmare Alan saved her from. A fire burns in her veins. It's been smoldering since she buried the dead a month earlier. Alan won't allow her to blame herself for Nathan's condition, but she wrestles with herself daily. If not his mother, then who? Killian, for not listening to her? Stacy, for coming here when she doesn't belong? Development 6 and their warped society? The fire burns hotter and she kicks off her sheets. Her feet smack against the cold cement floor as she rips the door open. An echo of the door slamming against the wall has whatever whispers were in the mess hall silencing. She crosses the hall, thankful Ember and Lilly are still sleeping in their bunks.

Bright lights in the bathroom have Violet glaring. She turns on the faucet and cups the icy water in her palm. Bringing it to her lips, she slurps it up until she feels the cold in her belly. She stares at herself in the mirror. There are dark shadows under her eyes. She bites her lip in frustration. I can't stay like this. *I can't sit here thinking about what I could've done or who's at fault. I have to do something…I need to be in control. What can I do?* What can I do? Her shoulders are weighed down, and her chest aches. The cocoon that is her skin holding her body together tingles. Clenching her jaw, she rubs at her skin violently, leaving red marks. If she could crawl out of this cocoon, she would.

Turning to the cupboards, she rifles through it until finding a pair of scissors. Yanking the long thick braid of hair to the side with one hand, she holds the scissors ready. Cold metal glistens in the mirror as she hesitates.

Her lips are white from clamping them together so tight. Closing her eyes, she inhales deeply until her lungs ache. Not long ago, she couldn't have taken such a deep breath, as her left lung was filled with metal and blood. She had no control, brought still by a paralytic forced upon her. She'll never forget the feeling of cold metal piercing her skin, slicing through her rib cage, and ripping a hole in her lung. Though her hybrid system heals faster than any human, the memory of pain and fear is not something that'll ever heal. The air from her lungs releases in a sigh as the scissors cut and cut and cut. There's a release. The weight lifts as she hears the heavy braid drop to the tiled floor with a flop. Opening her eyes, she can't help but smile. The weight is gone, and though her hair is shorter on one side, she likes how it looks, matching the unbalanced feelings in her heart.

Violet hits the shower, keeping the water on the cool side, allowing it to chill the fire in her veins. It feels strange and invigorating as she washes her short hair. When she returns to the mirror, she notices her hair beginning to curl with new life now that the weight's gone. Satisfied with her new asymmetrical bob, she cleans up and gets dressed. She can already smell breakfast wafting in the air. Fresh biscuits.

Ember and Lilly begin to stir. "Good morning, lovelies," she says as she rubs Ember on the shoulder to help her awaken.

She opens one eye slightly and smiles warmly. "Morning," Ember says. She stretches her limbs and yawns.

Lilly is sleeping face-down with her knees brought to her chest, her bum sticking straight into the air. Violet crouches next to the bunk and rubs her warm little back. "It's time to wake up, my flower," Violet whispers. Lilly turns her head to face Violet, but her eyes are still closed, and her position squishes the side of her face, giving her fish lips. Violet chuckles and continues to rub her back. "Come on, little flower, it's time to bloom for the day."

Lilly opens her eyes one at a time and stretches, arching her back like a cat. A sweet smile spreads across her face. Blinking again and again, she frowns. "Your hair is gone."

"I cut it."

"I liked it long. You were like a princess. Rapunzel." She sits up and rubs her eyes.

"Ah, well, even Rapunzel cut her hair eventually."

"Why?" Lilly reaches her hand out, pulling on a curl. When she releases it, it bounces back into a coil.

"She wanted to be free, so she escaped the tower, but how can you run free when your hair is always catching on branches and bushes? Her hair was holding her back. With it gone, she could run free."

"Okay, I like it," she says, pulling another curl.

"I like it too," Ember says with a grin.

"Thank you. Me too."

Violet assists the girls in getting dressed and brushing their hair. As they gather at the table, Jack and Alan watch as Violet makes her plate, and the food quickly disappears. Feeling eyes on her, she looks up. Jack smiles at her and begins eating. The others follow suit.

Looking around the table, she studies their faces. Clara and Jack seem thinner. Alan has the same dark shadows under his eyes. This past month has been hard on everyone, especially the girls.

"I noticed we're low on meat. We should go hunting and get some supplies," Alan says, staring down at his food. Violet rests her chin in her hand, propping her elbow on the table. "We shouldn't be gone long, and we can keep the coms on in case there are changes with Nathan." Violet looks at Jack and Clara. They're avoiding eye contact. She glares, and the girls look back and forth between them.

"Fine," Violet agrees, clasping her hands together. Alan stuffs the last of his biscuit into his mouth and leaves the table to get ready.

"Violet, be careful, please," Jack says, looking at her with glossy eyes.

"I promise to come back with Alan safe and sound." She stands up and, rounding the table, kisses him on the top of his head. Clara smiles up at her, and Violet squeezes her shoulder. Lilly reaches out, taking hold of Violet's hand. Her warm little hand has her frozen, and she turns to face them. The girls both have tears in their eyes, ready to overflow.

Crouching down between them, she asks, "What's wrong?" They wrap their arms around her neck, holding her so tightly that Violet can barely breathe. Her heart cracks. The tears overflow. Lilly pets Violet's short hair. Violet kisses the top of their heads with a deep, shaking breath. "Don't you worry your pretty little heads. We'll be back before you know it. I love you very much, and

I'll bring back lots of yummy things." She pulls away a little to wipe their tears away. "Let me see those smiles," she says, willing her tears to hold back. They both try hard to smile, but the gestures are weak and quickly fade. She pets their heads before nudging them to finish their breakfast.

Over the past few months, the girls have grown very attached to Violet and vice versa. They don't entirely fill the whole caused by Nathan's accident, but they've patched it up in a way. They've become family.

Alan joins Violet in the cargo bay while she's packing Killian's blue rusted skyrider. He gives the bleach-stained spot on the ground a wide berth. Violet can't help but notice. He stashes away his belongings in his forest-green rider. When he turns to face her, she's leaning against the rider with her arms folded, staring blankly at the ground, at the spot he avoided. He comes around to stand in front of her. "Are you sure you're ready for this?" he asks as she looks up into his eyes.

"Yes. It'll be good to get some fresh air." Violet tries to smile, but the muscles on her face don't show the expression she has in mind.

Alan nods with his lips pursed. "It looks nice," he says, looking away from her.

"Thanks," Violet responds, self-consciously bringing her hands to her hair.

Alan fluffs the royal blue scarf around her neck. "Maybe we should pay him a visit too. Might be good to see an old friend."

"Not this time," she says with uncertainty.

"He should know what happened."

"Not this time," Violet says with more force. Alan nods and says nothing more. Climbing into the riders' seat, they start up with a roar. Sliding on the helmet Stacy once used, Violet buttons her cerulean blue coat.

With Alan's nod and the roar of the engines, the riders rise off the ground. Violet, having never driven the vehicle before, carefully follows Alan out of the cargo bay and into the larger opening of the dank cave. Though the waterfall is a solid wall of ice, the water inside the cave remains liquid. The tree at the center of the cave with its strange luminescent orange leaves catches her eye. Alan pulls alongside the wall of ice and kicks it, breaking down the thinner parts to create a hole to escape. After some work breaking down the ice, they're greeted by a bitterly cold wind. The river is frozen, and the ground is blanketed with thick snow. The only color left is the dark green pine peeking out of the white fluff, and a spot of blue sky when the clouds clear.

It doesn't take Violet long to get the hang of the sky-rider. They take off down the mountain. Alan, leading ahead, signals they'll be landing soon. As they come to a stop, he gracefully lands while she comes down a little rough, sending a flurry of snow into the air. He laughs. She takes her helmet off and takes a deep refreshing breath. Better than the stale air of the shelter. "We may be here a while. If you have to go, do it now," he says before ducking behind a tree. She heeds his advice.

They come together again to walk a couple of miles into the woods, to a tree with notches cut into it. Looking up, they see a small wooden shed hidden by the tree's limbs. The shed, more like a glorified box, can fit three people if you get cozy. Brushing away the cobwebs, they unpack their gear. Alan pulls out a crossbow from his duffle bag along with several arrows, gets it ready, and sets it aside. He leans back into the corner. "Let me know when something comes," he says as he closes his eyes and folds his arms.

Violet sighs and stares out the large open porthole. She gets into a comfortable position and waits. For a long time, there's not much of anything crossing the path but a few birds. She admires the light, though it's brighter than she's used to. When she's bored enough to start counting the visible trees, she notices movement. A rabbit is cautiously lurking about. "Oh, oh, a bunny," Violet hisses to Alan.

His eyes open, but he sighs, handing her the bow. "Get it yourself. Wake me when something better comes. Don't waste all my arrows." He turns over on his side. Violet smiles, aiming at the furry white rabbit. One shot and the arrow hit the ground above, sending the rabbit into a speedy escape. Before she can even look to reload, the little critter has disappeared. Violet sighs and Alan snickers, knowing she missed. She reloads the crossbow and waits once more.

A few hours pass. The sun has eaten away the clouds, making the snow a blinding white. The snow on the trees is melting and giving way, dropping to the ground. It sounds like a load of laundry is being dropped onto the floor. Violet gulps down some water and sets the canteen down. "How long do you think this'll take?" she whispers.

"Could be an hour or the whole evening. Could be a couple of days," Alan says, not opening his eyes. "If they smell us, they'll stay away. That's why it's important to relieve yourself far away from here."

Violet takes that as a hint and settles into silence again. She begins to ease into a light sleep as nature becomes quiet and comfortable. She isn't entirely comfortable enough to get deep sleep, but when she opens her eyes again, the sun has risen to its highest point and begun to drop. The birds are still chattering in the treetops, but Alan's sudden movements draw her attention. She looks out the opening and then back at him when she finds no game to warrant the abrupt movements. "I gotta pee," he finally says. Violet rolls her eyes as she tries to move out of his way so he can escape. "You should come too. Probably best not to go out too far alone, especially since you don't know the woods."

They hike about a mile from where Alan thinks the elk might come from. Violet walks a bit further for more privacy, as it's more difficult for a woman to squat in the snow. Though the cold bites at her exposed flesh, there's something refreshing about going in the woods. The trees sway with the breeze, dropping more snow to the ground with a plop, and the birds chirp happily. The blue sky barely has a whisper of a cloud. The pine scent seems more robust, with the cool ice smothering the other plants around it.

Violet buttons her trousers as a chill runs down her spine. Suddenly the happy chittering has silenced and it's eerily quiet, as if the air itself has stilled. She turns slowly, surveying her surroundings, readying herself for anything that might be hunting. A stick cracking nearby seems to echo in the otherwise silent landscape, and it has her twisting around. Though she has killed many maven, the sight of this one facing her now has her screaming internally. The sheer fear has her frozen stiff. Not even a squeak or a shuttering breath escapes her. She stares into the onyx almond-shaped eyes, looming at least nine feet tall. She pales almost to the same shade as the maven's ghostly white exoskeleton. How he snuck up to her with such stealth has her baffled. *Alan. Where's Alan?* Violet refuses to take her eyes off the maven a mere five feet from her.

"Alan." Violet's voice comes out in a whisper. The maven tilts its head and blinks. Violet assesses the maven's stance. It's standing still with its arms at its sides. Though its back is hunched over, it seems more curious than combative. Violet realizes too late that she's taking such shallow breaths that her head has become light. She watches as she drops to one knee as the creature crouches instantly to match her stance. It blinks and tilts its head in the other direction, silently waiting, watching.

Taking slow deep breaths, she looks down at its claws. No sign of blood. Though with that left arm, it could've shot a bone shard at Alan and killed him instantly. Her mouth becomes dry at the thought. Watching the maven study her, she's reminded of the night in the city when the maven attacked their group and she killed so many of them. However, one stood at a distance, watching her kill its kind. With another deep breath, she gathers her strength. As she stands slowly, the maven remains on one knee.

"I have a son. Nathan." The maven tilts its head in the other direction. "I need to live. Do you understand I need to be here when he wakes up?" Another tilt. Violet slowly takes a step toward the creature. "I could kill you easily if I wanted to. I'm not like the other humans. I'm stronger. I'm like you." A slow blink comes from the maven as it stares into her eyes. "I'm like you." She closes the distance between them. "We are the same," Violet says as if she realizes it's the truth as she speaks it. She slowly reaches her hand to its sleek, sharp face and stops a few inches away, hesitating, questioning herself. The maven blinks its onyx eyes and slowly tilts its head toward her, pressing its beak into her palm.

A sharp breath in the form of a hysterical laugh escapes her. The beast has its eyes closed as he leans further. She strokes the white bone between its eyes like you would a horse. It somehow feels warm under her touch. A smile reaches cheek to cheek as she pets the creature that's been hunting her and all of humankind for as long as she's lived. A strange rumbling emits from its chest, similar to a cat's purr. It rumbles so loudly that she can feel it reverberating in her body, making it hard to swallow, yet calm washes over her. It's strange, but she finds comfort in what's considered humanity's enemy. It'd be easy to kill it, but she feels pity for the creature making itself vulnerable.

"Violet?" Alan can be heard in the far distance. The panic in his voice is palpable. The relief at hearing his voice has her sighing. She didn't realize how far she had wandered from him.

"We're hunting elk," she tells the creature. "We need the food, so you go. You're scaring them off." The purring stops and it tilts its head once more with a slow blink.

"Violet! Where are you?" Alan comes closer.

"Go away so we can hunt," she says, pointing up the mountain. "Go." The maven rises and walks a couple of steps in the direction she points, but pauses and turns back to her, ticking and grunting as if speaking to her. "Yes, go so we can hunt, and don't kill any humans," Violet says, pointing to herself in emphasis. The maven turns and walks up the mountain as it's told.

"Violet!" Alan's voice has become desperate.

"I'm here!" Violet says, keeping her eye on the maven as it moves away without turning back. She moves towards Alan, looking back at the maven until it's out of sight.

"Violet!" Alan cries as she comes into view. She meets Alan as he stumbles up the path, weapon drawn. He runs to her and, pulling her by the arms, yanks her into a hug that crushes the breath out of her. "I think maven are in the area. We need to get as far away as possible."

"I don't think we need to leave. Are you sure it's maven?"

"Listen." He holds his breath so she can hear the silence, but the birds have come back to life, and the air is no longer still.

"What is it?" Violet smiles at him.

Alan breathes heavily as he puts his hand over his heart. "Thank you," he sighs. "Let's go. I thought it strange for them to be up in the mountains, but that's the worst scare I've ever had, aside from our last encounter. Thankfully I had already relieved myself; otherwise, I would've had a mess in my pants."

Alan rambles on and on as they make their way back to the shack, and Violet occasionally glances behind her, hoping the creature understood and would stay away. Now that the silence is gone, the birds seem almost too loud as they return to their usual chatter. As they come closer to the shack, Alan falls silent once more and walks as stealthily as he can. Soon enough, they settle back into the corners of the hut and snack on protein bars and jerky while they stare out into the woods.

A vibration buzzes on the floorboards, waking Alan and Violet with a jolt. Violet quietly scrambles to the window. No maven could be seen. The pale blue sky is faintly speckled with stars. The air is bitter cold. She shivers despite the heat provided by the heating pads in her gloves and boots. She scans the earth below again, but the buzzing continues. Alan is searching his bag for the culprit. Finally, he rips out the small device buried at the bottom of his pack.

"What is it?"

"It's Stacy's communicator."

Violet crawls over to Alan, crushing him into the corner as she presses in. Alan answers the call. Stacy's face comes onto the screen. Her silver hair is slicked back into a tight ponytail, making the white triangle tattoos on her cheekbone more prominent. Violet frowns at the sight of her. "Where's Killian?" she demands. Alan winces at the ice in her voice.

"He isn't here," Stacy says nervously. Violet takes in the way Stacy speaks, and her heart skips a beat as the cold of the winter air sinks into her bones.

"What happened to him?" Violet asks, holding back the feral emotions running through her.

"That's why I'm calling. I assume Jack told you everything?"

"What does Jack know that I don't?" Violet says to Stacy but turns her icy glare to Alan.

He shrinks into the corner further. "I only found out this morning."

"Found out what?" Violet asks through clenched teeth.

"Killian and I were separated upon arrival for a couple of weeks. When he was introduced into society here, he wasn't the same. He acted as if he didn't know me at all."

"Perhaps he did that on purpose."

"Maybe, but he lied to everyone about you, Violet."

"What kind of lies?" Violet says, turning her attention back to Stacy.

"He told people it's your fault Nathan died, that you were a neglectful mother and that it's probably because of your mutation. People fear you, Violet."

"As they should, but my son isn't dead," Violet says in a low voice.

Stacy visibly swallows. "I know. He also told them that you hid your pregnancy from him and wiped your memory of him on purpose."

"I don't believe you," Violet says, crossing her arms and staring out the window at the trees. Stacy glowers.

"Why would he say that?" Alan asks.

"I'm hoping he has his own plan and is playing the game, but we were separated for so long, and he was in the health and experimental department. They could've done something to him. I have plans with him this evening, and I'll find out the truth. I want you both to hear our conversation. Please tell me I'm wrong. I'll call you when I arrive and leave the communicator in my bag. Just listen to our conversation."

Alan nods in agreement. "And then what?" Violet snaps.

"You tell me. If you think he's acting normal, I'll leave it alone, but if you agree then we need to make another plan."

"Anything else?" Violet asks.

Stacy gulps again and looks around her bland whitewashed room. With a lowered voice, she says, "If Killian has a plan, it has to do with the magistrate's daughter. He's made it clear to the public that he's…" Stacy's throat bobs. "Pursuing a relationship with her."

"Well then, I look forward to your conversation with him this evening," Violet says indifferently.

Alan's at a loss for words as Stacy waves goodbye with a weak smile. The screen turns black. The rising sun smears a rosy hue upon the sky, kissing every surface it faces with its lovely light. She can tell Alan's searching his mind for comforting words. Though the sun warms everything around them, she remains cold and still as she stares out the window. The only thing that will comfort her is knowing the truth—knowing Killian's plan—hearing it from his mouth. For the time being, they can only wait. Alan gives up on searching for words and hands her food and water. They eat in silence as the stars wink out of sight.

The afternoon is quiet, and the air seems colder as the blue sky exposes them to the full brunt of winter cold. The previous cloud cover was a blanket holding in the earth's heat. Their breath seems to crystalize as it floats out the hut's window into the open air. Alan picks his teeth of jerky with a shard of wood he had whittled down with his knife.

Violet is beginning to drift off when she notices movement in the distance. It looks like moving branches until it bows its head to smell a patch of grass the snow so kindly melted to reveal. About 50 yards out is a giant elk, its antlers like bare branches of trees in the winter. Violet hits Alan's foot. He raises his hands in question, but she points excitedly. Alan looks out to see the elk and carefully, silently positions himself as Violet hands him the bow. He waits patiently for the elk to move out from behind a tree. He releases an arrow. It hits the elk in the chest. The elk starts but freezes in shock as blood gushes from the wound. The pure white snow now has a puddle of bright red. Violet feels the blood pumping in her ears as her heart races. Her mouth becomes dry. As the elk falls face-first into the ground, Violet turns, letting her breakfast come to greet her. Alan drops the bow and pats her back as he attempts to keep her short hair out of the way.

"Are you okay?" Alan asks as the heaving subsides.

"I will be."

"Here, drink some water." He hands her a canteen.

Violet gulps the water as he climbs down from the treehouse, waiting for her below. She attempts to clean up the mess she made with water before collecting her pack and climbing down herself. They stretch out their stiff joints before making the trek to the elk. No sign of any other prey loomed, so they get to work. Violet avoids looking at the puddle of blood beneath the creature. Alan ties its hind legs together before throwing the rope over a thick maple limb. Hoisting the carcass up into the air, he ties it off so the buck hangs at his level. He kicks snow and dirt over the blood that pooled from the kill. After removing his coat, he lays out a large tarp. "Are you feeling all right?" he asks as he begins to skin the creature.

"I'm fine. Do you need help?"

"Once I get the hide off. Can you handle it?"

"Yes," Violet says, nodding confidently.

Alan is skilled with his blade as he quickly removes the skin from the buck. Within 15 minutes the skin is free, and he drapes it over another low-hanging limb. The icy air keeps the animal fresh as Alan guts it. With Violet's help, they make quick work of deboning the creature. An hour and a half later, they have the animal quartered, and all the meat has been placed on the tarp. Violet helps wrap the meat up and fits as much as they can into their packs. It takes three trips to haul the meat back to the riders.

Golden yellow beams spike through the trees as the sun begins to set. They head back to the elk for the last haul and clean up. Alan cleans off the tarp as best he can and folds it up when the communicator goes off. Violet's stomach drops, and she worries she might lose the contents of her stomach again. Alan pulls it out of his pocket and answers. They sit down on a log that is relatively dry to listen in. For a long while it's quiet, other than the shuffling and clicking of shoes as someone walks. Then there's a knock and someone opens the door. "*Ms. Nox, my apologies,*" they hear in a tinny voice. "*Mr. Grey has not returned from work yet. He sent me ahead to make sure you were taken care of.*"

"*When is he expected to return?*" Stacy demands.

"*I will inform you when he has left the facility, but he shouldn't be long.*"

"*I'll wait inside for him, then.*"

"*As you wish.*"

Alan and Violet lean back against some branches and do their best to be patient. Alan bites at his nails as he waits. Violet stares up at the sky as it changes color with the sunset. The cold begins to set in, and they both break out the hand warmers.

"*What's taking so long? You said he'd be available at 4:30. It's almost 5:00.*" Stacy's abrupt voice brings their attention back to the communicator.

"*Killian's on his way. He sent me ahead of him because he had some work to finish.*"

"Didn't she already say that?" Alan whispers to Violet. Violet holds a finger to her lips to silence him, though she frowns in concern. There's silence for a while, then movement. Quiet voices in the background have Alan and Violet leaning in close to hear. There's rustling and then what sounds like liquid pouring, then a sigh.

As clear as day, they hear Killian say in a distant voice, "*Ms. Nox, it's a pleasure to see you again.*"

Chapter 4

EUSTACIA

Stacy waits in the parlor room in Killian's new home. It's open and bright. The glass walls allow a perfect view of the scenic manufactured landscape in the upper-class living facilities. The landscape curves with the disc shape of the Stratos Development. Beyond the landscape is the protective dome allowing the natural light of the sun and a full view of the arboretum levels below. Stacy's knee begins to shake as she becomes impatient and anxious. Ella enters the room with a tray of tea and a bite to eat. "What's taking so long? You said he'd be available at 4:30. It's almost 5:00."

"Killian's on his way. He sent me ahead of him because he had some work to finish," Ella says respectfully. Stacy sighs as she nibbles on a piece of dense honey cake. Ella pours a cup of tea for Stacy and sets it in front of her. Ella turns her head as if she hears something and leaves the room. Stacy straightens her posture and grasps her shaking knee, holding it in place. She hears Killian speaking to Ella in a low voice in the other room. Ella reminds him of his visitor, and he sighs. Stacy clenches her jaw. Killian enters the room as he unbuttons the cuffs on his gray shirt, rolling the sleeves up to his elbows. He runs his fingers through his hair, leaving it disheveled before he sits opposite her. Seeing him so clean-cut has her heart pounding. Killian makes eye contact with her for only a second before pouring himself a cup of tea. It gives her goosebumps, unnerved by the lack of connection. He takes a sip and sighs once more before pasting a smile onto his face.

"Ms. Nox, it's a pleasure to see you again."

"Killian," Stacy says sternly.

"How is Mr. Nox fairing? He's been frequenting the medical facilities often."

"He has?"

"You haven't noticed?" Killian raises an eyebrow. Stacy bites her lip as she thinks of how often he's been leaving for unscheduled meetings. She had thought he was having secret rendezvous with Kat, which is still likely. Now she's put to shame once more by Killian. "So, Ms. Nox, what brings you to my humble abode," Killian says as he looks out at the forest of trees and modern homes.

"I had some concerns," Stacy says, eying Ella as she comes to sit in the seat nearest the hall. "May we have some privacy, please?"

Killian turns to Ella and nods. Ella removes herself from their sight. "What concerns might you have, Ms. Nox," he says with another sip of his tea.

"Since when am I 'Ms. Nox?'"

"Ever since I was introduced into society. Isn't this what you wanted? I was invited here; I became part of the community. It would be inappropriate for me to call you Stacy, as it is not your given name but a nickname you gave yourself. Am I mistaken?"

"No…you're right."

"What else is on your mind?"

Stacy repositions herself, fidgeting as she tries to make eye contact. "What have you been working on with Dr. Oric? Anything exciting?"

"I have been assisting him with some of his experiments. Occasionally I work in the sick ward. It's never a dull day."

Stacy smiles and fiddles with her teacup. "It must be a nice change of pace."

"I will say, it's more gratifying to save people rather than destroy them." He didn't mean for it to come out so cold.

Stacy drops her hands to her lap and picks at her fingernails. Her chest becomes heavy from the guilt. There is an awkward silence as she searches for something to say to keep the conversation going. Something comes to mind, but she pushes it off. "My father has given me more responsibility with broadcasting," she says instead. "You'd be amazed at the amount of information that surfaces."

"I doubt that. Based on the footage they've shown me of Violet, I'm sure it is limitless."

"You have footage of Violet? I thought I destroyed the cameras." Stacy becomes pale. Killian stares at her with a blank look. She can't tell whether it's anger or indifference. "I can arrange for you to speak to Violet. I know she wants to hear from you," she says in a low voice.

"That is unnecessary." Killian brushes off her offer, looking out the window once more.

With little self-control, Stacy blurts out what she's trying to hold back. "What are your intentions with Danit Sinai?"

Killian looks into her eyes then. She can't tell if he's glaring or squinting because of the sun setting on the horizon. "I do not wish to discuss my personal life with you. Please don't misunderstand. I agreed to come here with you, but if you intended for a relationship between us to finally blossom with Violet out of the way, you'll be disappointed."

"That's not my intention! I only ask you while keeping your relationship with Violet in mind." Killian nods but seems lost in thought as he looks out again. Another awkward silence. Stacy clears her throat, trying to bring him back to reality gently.

After a moment, Killian looks back at her. His eyes have glazed over. He reaches his hand out to her. She takes it without a thought, and he squeezes it gently. "I'm sorry. I think I should be thanking you," he says.

"For what?"

"If you hadn't brought me here, I wouldn't have as much time with him."

"Who?"

"Nathan."

Stacy rips her hand out of his. "What do you mean?"

"I have so much more to look back on now. I have a lifetime of memories with my son, thanks to you. Before coming here, you could say I barely knew him. Now, I know him better than Violet ever had. They've given me many gifts and have asked for nothing in return. They've accepted me and forgiven me for my past. Violet saw me as the monster I was. She'll never look at me as she once did. Here I have a second chance, a new life."

"Don't be deceived by the gifts they've given you. They'll ask for your soul in the end." Stacy looks at him in disgust.

"My soul in exchange for a lifetime of memories with my only son? How can I say no, when they've given me everything I never thought to even ask for?"

"Have you lost your mind? What about our plan? I thought you were going to help me destroy this place. How can you let the rest of the world be destroyed? And Violet, the love of your life, included?"

"I don't see it that way, and I'd be careful of whom you speak to regarding treason. You may have gotten away with it on the surface, but up here I don't think they'll be so lenient," Killian says as his eyes darken with a furrowed brow.

"They've brainwashed you."

"Whatever helps you sleep at night."

"How would that help me sleep?" Her voice wavers.

"Brainwashing can be undone. If these are my true feelings, what can be done about that?" Killian says indifferently.

Stacy's throat becomes dry as she feels the urge to heave. "Nathan is alive," she says, but it comes out in a whisper.

"My son died in that cave, and so did I. This is all that's left." He gestures to his body. "Whether you choose to move on as I have or not, it is no concern of mine."

"So you won't help me."

"With treason? Absolutely not. I would like very much to live in peace for once. Though, I will do you a favor and not inform the authorities if you still plan to proceed. That is, if you don't try to involve me again. Do I make myself clear?" he says with a cold stare.

Stacy's chin bobs, unable to find the words as she watches Killian finish his tea peacefully. She takes to her feet and nods once before leaving the room. Ella is waiting in the hallway with Stacy's wrap. "I hope your visit was pleasant," Ella says as she helps Stacy into it. Stacy can't yet respond, still in shock.

Stacy's car waits for her outside. As she slides into the back seat, she takes a breath through her nose and out her mouth. The driver waits patiently for orders. Too many thoughts run through her mind at once, and she is at a loss. She can feel the tears coming, and she takes deep breaths. *No. I must find a way. I owe Violet this much.* With a new focus, she looks to the driver. "Take me to the club, please."

"Mr. Nox won't like it, Ms. Eustacia."

"Don't worry. It'll be a short visit. I'm looking for someone." The driver shakes his head but drives on.

Chapter 5

VIOLET

They're barely able to fit their goods in the compartments. Once they're packed up, they take a break to eat a meal. Alan watches her as they eat. She looks around as if admiring the scenery. She seems calm and collected until her eyes become glossy, and the tip of her nose turns a cherry red. Violet takes a deep, shaking breath. Fighting back the tears, she gets herself under control. Looking at her food, she no longer has an appetite but continues to eat, knowing she needs the nutrition. Alan stands up, brushing off the snow when she 's finished her meal. "Let's head back."

Violet doesn't argue. They climb onto the skyriders once more and head home. The ride was as quiet as the one when they'd left. Violet scans the land below for the maven that had met her in the woods, but there's no sign of it. It's a relief but also an aching emptiness.

Ember and Lilly are waiting in the cargo bay in thick sweaters. Smiles cross their face when both riders come into view. "We got a welcome wagon!" Alan yells over the roar of the riders as they echo through the cave.

Violet smiles as she watches the girls jump for joy. She lands a little more gracefully this time. Alan climbs off the rider and swoops both girls into his arms, swinging them in circles until they squeal. After a tight hug, he sets them back on the ground. The girls run to Violet for a hug. She's careful not to hug them too tightly. Though they'd only been gone for two days, Violet didn't realize how much she was missing them until they were in her arms. Lilly landed a warm, soft kiss on Violet's cheek. She's left gushing with love as they run back inside to tell the others they've returned. She wipes away the tear that threatens to spill down her cheek. Alan holds out his arms to her when he sees her tears returning. She huffs a laugh but never declines a hug when offered. He squeezes her into a bear hug but releases her when Clara and the girls return. Everyone helps unpack the meat and portion it out into meal-sized cuts.

Violet visits Nathan during dinner. There'd been no change while she was gone. Lilly falls asleep after dinner on the cool leather couch in the pentagonal commons area, bundled up in a thick blanket, her light curls crowning her face. Violet, leaving the library, notices the sleeping child. Lilly's brow furrows, and her breath catches. Violet stops, crouching beside her. Gently she smooths out her forehead and brushes away the fair-haired curls sticking to her eyelashes. Lilly's breathing settles. With a kiss on her forehead, Violet moves on, swallowing the knot in her throat.

Alan notices Violet struggling to hold herself together. She rushes to the restroom to splash water on her face. He waits for her outside the bathroom, sitting cross-legged on one of the bunks. She's startled when she notices Alan sitting in the half-lit room. "Why are you waiting outside the door like a puppy?" she asks.

"Hey, I'm not a puppy. I was just waiting to talk." Violet crosses her arms and glowers at him for a moment. She sits next to him on the bunk, and the mattress squeaks. "I want you to know you can talk to me about anything. If you need some time to yourself, I get it, but you're my family now, whether you like it or not."

"Thank you," she says, resting her head on his shoulder. He wraps his arm around her, hugging her into his side.

"Do you want to talk about Killian?" he says with a squeeze.

"Not really, but you're affected by this too, so…let's talk," Violet sighs.

"What are we gonna do?"

"Nothing." Violet shrugs.

"We have to do something."

"When it comes to Killian, we do nothing. When it comes to us…I've already been making a plan. It's not something I want to do. It'd mean leaving Nathan behind. Again. I don't know if I can do that." She bends down to hold her face in her palms.

"If we need to leave, we can still talk to Nathan through the communicators. We could always come back if there are any changes," Alan reassures her.

"I hope so."

"So, what is your plan?"

"Stacy left us a mission in the atlas before they were taken. She says Yoojin can't be trusted. According to her, he's from a place called Arcadia. The Stratos Development protects this city. She claims the Arcadians are the ones responsible for the bombings. We need to find out if it's true. If it is, we must destroy it."

"That's a tall order!" Alan gets to his feet and paces in front of Violet. "How big is this city?"

"I don't know." Violet clasps her hands and presses her knuckles to her lips.

"Where is it hidden?"

"I don't know."

"You think Yoojin was going to betray us?"

"I don't know." She feels the weight of all the questions on her shoulders. "But I don't think so. Yoojin invited Nathan and me to his home before he left. Maybe he was talking about Arcadia. Maybe the offer still stands if he was willing to take us before."

"So, where do we start?"

"First, we find Yoojin. We'll leave for Aelborne in early spring. That is, if Nathan doesn't wake up." Violet rubs her face.

"Ok. Spring." Alan and Violet nod in agreement.

Chapter 6

PIPER

Piper wakes feeling drowsy and sluggish. Opening her eyes in a flutter, she doesn't recognize her surroundings, unsure of how she got there. The last memory she could recall was arguing with her aunt. After her parents died in an accident at one of the factories, she moved in with her beloved Aunt Josephine. She was only seven years old when she lost her parents. Their faces have faded from her memory, but Aunt Josephine's love for Piper has always compensated for that loss. Though orphaned, she's grown up never feeling lost or alone.

"I'm doing this for you!" Piper yells.

"It's not worth selling your body to them to save mine. I'm dying, Piper." Josephine says. Her pale skin and frail body struggle to emphasize her worry.

"I know that! They can save you! They'll have a cure, and it's in the contract that you'll get the care you need

and be moved onto a farm in the arboretum as you've always wanted. You'll have everything you've ever wanted!"

"Piper, at what cost? I love you and don't want you to throw your life away to be some lab rat. I've lived my life. Don't miss out on yours."

"I'll join you on the farm when I've served my term," Piper says, turning away from her to hide the ache in her chest.

"How long is that term, Piper? Was that disclosed in that contract?" Josephine has always kept calm due to the lack of energy, but she could hear the fire in her voice coming through.

"I...I'm not sure."

"Don't sign it, Piper. I could never live knowing my beautiful baby girl sacrificed herself for me." Aunt Josephine's voice is weaker now. Piper faces her, knowing how much this conversation is taking out of her. Josephine's eyes are glistening with fresh tears. Piper feels a knot in her throat as she comes to stand in front of her. She takes her aunt's thin callused hands and swallows hard.

"If I don't take it, I live the rest of my life in the factory, in hell, without you. How could I ever be happy without you?" Piper's voice cracks as she breaks down and sobs.

Aunt Josephine pulls her in and wraps her arms around her as tightly as possible. Her breath catches between sobs. "Oh, my girl. My sweet girl. You are so strong. You're a fighter, like me. I know you'll find your happiness."

Piper closes her eyes tightly, pushing back the guilt for going against her aunt's wishes. Rubbing her hands over her face, she wipes away the tears and sniffs away the snot threatening to drip from her nose. She sits up, careful not to hit her head on the bunk above. Swinging her legs off the lower bunk, her bare feet are shocked by the cold cement floor. She rubs her eyes to remove the fog while focusing on her surroundings. She gets to her feet and feels somewhat like jelly. She turns to find a girl in the top bunk still sleeping. There are 15 bunks, each bed occupied by a young girl, all looking close in age to her. None of them look familiar, but all wear the same white tunic and loose-fit pants.

Measuring up the room, she's disappointed with their quarters. The walls match the cold cement floor with no windows. On the opposite end of the room, there's a heavy metal door, currently open. She finds a large room with white tiled walls and floors. There are stalls and toilets. Opposite the stalls are a first-aid cabinet, sinks and mirrors. Along the wall with the first-aid cabinet is a door. She pulls it open to find more bunks. She closes the door quietly when someone's snoring gets interrupted.

Around the corner is a communal shower, with each spout separated by 5-foot tiled walls but no doors or curtains. No privacy. Lining the adjoining wall are compartments labeled with names and numbers, 60 in total. Each of them contains a blue and black jumpsuit. She finds her name and pulls out the suit. It's a thick fabric, stretchy yet sturdy, heavier than the fabric they make at the factory for the security department, which has her questioning what kind of experiments they'll be undergoing.

Shoving the jumpsuit back into the compartment, she notices another door at the other end of the room.

Walking across the room, the sound of her bare feet smack on the tile. She tries the door, but it's locked. The lack of windows has her on edge. Coming back to the room with the bunks, some of the girls begin to wake up. She comes to the one with her hair cut short to her ears. "Hey, hey, do you know where we are?"

"What?" the girl groans as she stretches and sits up.

"Look around. Do you know where we are?" Piper wrings her hands, already regretting her decision to sign the contract without asking more questions.

"Ella said we'd be put in a facility." She sighs.

"When she said 'facility,' did you think it'd be like this? It's like a prison."

The girl sighs, plopping her head back onto the pillow. "It's only for a few months."

"I'm trying to sleep," another girl growls.

"I'm just trying to figure out what's going on."

"Shut up!" another girl yells and throws her pillow at her.

A loud buzzing alarm sounds off, jolting some out of their sleep. Others groan and hide their heads under their pillows. A voice comes out over a speaker in the ceiling. "Good morning, and welcome to those who have just joined us. By now, you may have noticed you are in the designated facility for the trials. Beyond the doors are showers, toiletries, and your uniform. Please be clean and dressed within 15 minutes." The alarm sounds off once more.

Piper, impatient for answers, heads first into the showers. Disrobing, she chooses a stall and hits the silver button on the wall. The water shoots out hot, immediately dispersing steam into the air. The water burns her chilled skin, but she fights through it. One after another, young men file into the communal showers. She ducks low, trying not to be seen as the girls file in. The new girls shy away, but the rest ignore the young men coming in. Some look the girls up and down as they undress, and others avoid it. There's a dispenser for soap, and she quickly washes up. She realizes too late that there are no towels to dry off. She cringes at the thought of air drying with dripping wet hair in the cold room.

Hitting the silver button once more, the water shuts off, and warm air gusts from the ceiling and floor, causing her skin to ripple under pressure and her mid-length hair to whip around her. Within two minutes, the air shuts off and she is dry, though her hair is still somewhat damp. Piper leaves her stall, picking up the tunic and pants to hide her body as she grabs her jumpsuit and runs into the sleeping quarters to pull her jumpsuit on in a hurry. It fits snuggly, holding everything in and helping the room's chill subside. She folds the tunic and pants into a neat pile and puts them in her designated compartment.

To avoid the awkward stares from the guys, she hides away in one of the stalls to relieve herself. When she comes back out, most people are clothed save for one boy who walks around naked, winking at anyone who makes eye contact. Piper does her best to keep her eyes aimed high, avoiding him altogether. He stops next to her while she washes her hands. "You're new," he says with a charming smile as he tussles his wet blonde hair, flicking water on her face. She ignores him. "Name's Jasper Price," he says as he leans against the mirror, looking her up and down. "Looks like I found my new partner. What's your name, doll?" he says in a silky voice.

"Piper Pruitt," she says, glancing at herself in the mirror. She notices another guy standing against the back wall with his arms folded, glaring through dark wavy hair hanging over his eyes. If looks could kill. The color drained from her face as she shook the water off her hands and moved back toward the sleeping quarters.

Piper could hear the two guys arguing after she left, but she didn't understand what they said as the alarm buzzed again, causing her heart to jump. Those still getting ready hurried into their suits as if their life depended on it. Taking a breath, she listened attentively.

"Please exit to the commons for your meal."

Piper looks around for the exit noticing a girl still hiding in one of the bunks. She spins around to see everyone filing through the door that was once locked. She stops when she hears a scream and returns to find the girl in the bunk convulsing. She starts to check on her, only to be caught by the wrist. The guy with dark hair and deadly looks grips her tightly and pulls her back into line with such force that her shoulder burns and her arm aches. He lets go, only to shove her forward to follow the line of people. She rubs her wrist and aching shoulder. Anger burns through her as she glares back at him. "Move." He shoves her again, looking just as angry.

What's this guy's deal? What happened to that girl? Why does no one try to help her? They all migrate down a dimly lit empty hallway that echoes the shuffling of their feet and those who quietly talk. They enter an open room with several stainless-steel tables and benches, and at the center of the room is a pillar with an opening. As people make their way through the line, they collect a food tray from the pillar and sit down to eat. The angry one cuts in front of her as she's distracted by the room. She watches as her meal rises from within when she reaches the pillar. She takes the tray and turns to find a seat.

Price is beside her in an instant, with his arm wrapping around her waist. She tries to move away from him, but he holds tight, and with her hands full she doesn't have much choice but to follow. He leads her to a table full of girls, and they all watch her with narrow eyes.

"Sit with me," he says as he leads her to the table with only enough space for one more, and his tray is already there. He tries to shoo away one of the girls already mid-meal, but she doesn't budge.

"I can eat somewhere else. This table is full." She twists out of his reach and sits at an empty table, or so she thought. The dark, moody one was at the other end, across from her. He glances up from his food briefly. Piper's heart leaps, unsure if she should move again. Price moves his tray and plops down with the bench between his legs. His knees brush against her backside and her thigh. She ignores him as she tries to eat the bland meal. Price rests his head on his knuckles propped up on the table. He gently tucks her brown hair behind her ear with his free hand. Electricity shoots down her spine as he drags his hand down her neck and back.

"Can you please stop?" Piper cringes.

"I don't think I can. You're tantalizing."

Piper looks at him then, somewhat stunned by how handsome he is, with high cheekbones and full lips curling up as he finally receives his desired attention. A contagious smile brightens his features, revealing perfect glistening teeth. His blonde hair falls into his crystal blue eyes as he moves in closer, taking her awkward smile as an invitation. "Thank you, but I didn't come here to play," she says, pulling back.

"This place can get pretty intense. There is no harm in lightening the mood," he says as his hand slides over her leg to her inner thigh. Piper drops her fork and catches his hand. Her blood pulses hard. She's never received this kind of attention in the past, so she's unsure whether she likes it. Her cheeks flush and, looking around the room, the guy across the table catches her eye again. He's finished eating and is watching her from under a furrowed brow. His shoulders are hunched slightly like an animal that's found its prey. The look on his face screams hatred, yet she can't break eye contact. She becomes embarrassed, turning her cheeks and ears a deeper red, and heat rises through her body.

Price is intrigued as she doesn't push him away but merely holds his wrist. He looks up at her and realizes she isn't looking at him. He turns his attention. "Gareth, do you mind? You're making her uncomfortable."

Gareth breaks the tension, locking eyes with Price. He pushes his tray forward and mounts his elbow on the table. Tilting his chin up, he rests his temple against his knuckles. His eyes move from Piper to Price with scrutiny.

Price tightens his grip on her thigh. She jolts her attention back to Price, ripping his hand away. "Looks like you're the one making her uncomfortable," Gareth says. His scowl deepens with her movement.

Price looks back at her with a seductive grin and bites his bottom lip. "In a good way?"

"On the contrary, you're both making me uncomfortable. I want to be alone, thank you." She picks up her tray and moves to another table. Price says something unintelligible to Gareth before returning to his gaggle of girls. Piper watches as he touches their waists, arms and hair as if it's second nature. Glancing back at Gareth, he has both elbows propped on the table with his hands clasped, pressed against his lips which have a ghost of a smile. He looks up at her, and the smile vanishes. Piper can't look away fast enough and returns to finish her meal. She leans her head into her hand propped on the table, letting her hair fall, acting as a curtain.

The alarm sounds once more. Everyone stands and dispenses their tray at the pillar in the center of the room. Piper shovels the rest of her food down her throat to follow their lead. Just as the last tray is parted, the voice returns. "New partners have been assigned. Please find your matching number and stand in line side by side." People start partnering up quickly, and Piper looks around the room, trying to find her partner, until she notices some of the girls from Price's table scowling her way. They watch Piper as she walks to the front of the line where Price waits for her. He leans against the archway with a smug look. He taps the number over the chest of his suit. She looks down, and her heart sinks as she sees the matching number 327 over her heart. Her hands clench into fists as she takes her place in line next to him.

"Proceed to the testing environment," the voice speaks. They walk into a rounded corridor, brightly lit by white ceiling lights. They stop at a pair of doors as the rest of the group moves on through the passage in both directions. The doors are marked 1 and 2. Piper tries the number 2 door closest to her, but it's locked. Price watches her with a severe look.

The voice returns. "Ladies first." Price curses at the ceiling. Taking hold of her arms, he moves Piper to face door 1 and takes his place in front of door 2. A tray comes out of the wall between the doors. Price takes the two devices and sticks one in his ear before turning to her. He gently tucks her chestnut hair behind her ear and presses the earpiece into place. His hands, once radiating heat, are now cold and clammy; he stares at her with crystal blue eyes as if he were trying to read her. The earpiece has a very faint, high-pitched tone every few seconds. There is a loud click, drawing their attention back to the doors.

Price stops with his hand on the door. "Do your best, Pruitt," he says, and it echoes in her ear. He opens the door to reveal pitch darkness. He steps into the shadows and the door closes behind him. The door clicks, and it is locked once again.

With a deep breath, she opens door number 1 and goes inside. The room is cramped and dark, but a faint glow emanates from the screen embedded in a desk. A swivel chair invites her to take a seat. "Can you hear me?" Price asks in her ear.

"Yes. Do you hear that faint beep in the earpiece?"

"Yes, it's always there. You'll get used to it. Take a seat and tell me how to get out of here." She does as she's told and sits, swiveling to face the desk. "What do you see on the screen?"

"A grid system. Each column's numbered, and the rows are letters. What do you see?" Piper winces as the high-pitched tone begins to irritate her.

"The floor is tiled, probably to match your grid system. Across the room is the exit door. On the wall, it says four times five is twelve, four times six is thirteen, and four times seven is...oh dear. That doesn't make any sense."

"Oh dear?"

"It literally ends with the words 'oh dear.'" Piper can hear the frustration in his voice. She repeats the sentence to herself and snorts with laughter. "What's so funny?"

"It's *Alice in Wonderland.*"

"It's who?"

"You've never read *Alice in Wonderland*?"

"Why would I? It doesn't matter. What am I supposed to do? I'm assuming I'm supposed to walk on certain tiles."

"How big are the tiles?"

"12 by 12, maybe?"

"Maybe if we multiply the columns correctly, that'll show where to step."

"That wouldn't tell me which column—"

A loud buzz cuts him off, and column A4 flashes red on her screen. "What did you do?" she asks.

"4 times 1 is 4. Uh...I was wrong. Where do I go? Tell me quickly."

"What's wrong?"

"The walls are crying." Piper could hear the eerie sound of a small girl crying through his earpiece, and rushing water. "Where do I go?" he barks.

"I don't know."

"Figure it out!" he yells, causing her ear to ring. "The floor is filling with water, Piper!"

"What kind of trial is this?"

"A life and death one! I'd rather not drown here, so tell me where to go!"

Piper looks her screen over once more and notices some numbers in the row are bold. "four times five is twelve..." she said under her breath.

"What?"

"Shush, I'm thinking."

"Can you think faster? I'm ankle-deep in tears."

"Go to B4."

"Which one is that?"

"One row to your right and three toward the door."

There's a splash. "Okay, next?"

The grid turns green where Price has stepped. "Stay in this column and step on the 4rth tile from where you stand now, B8." She waits for another splash.

"The water's stopping," he laughs. "Next?"

"Count two tiles from yours, B10, and straight on from there you can step on one tile at a time."

"You sure?"

"No, this is my first trial…"

She can hear Price sigh as he gingerly steps on the next couple of tiles across the floor. "Got it." The door behind her buzzes. Piper gets out of the chair and, as she reaches for the handle, it swings open, and Price is waiting there with a toothy grin. She steps out of the room, and he swoops her up by the waist and spins her. Her breath is stolen from her as he kisses her lips before releasing her. He sighs, "I'm so glad I got a good one." Piper wipes her mouth, feeling the heat spreading through her chest and into her face.

"Hope you don't lose this one," Gareth says with bitterness as he walks past them with his arms folded. His partner, a lean girl with a mop of red hair tied atop her head, scoffs at Piper and eyes Price in passing.

He returns the look with a wink as he bites his cheek. As if he suddenly remembers his partner, he turns to Piper. "How did you figure it out?"

"The numbers were bold, and I figured it was the B column because the only way for 4 times 5 to equal 12 is if you change the multiplication base." Price looks at her as if she's spoken another language. Gareth's words ring in her head: "Hope you don't lose this one." How many partners has he lost? How did he lose them? The earpiece beeps again, causing her head to ache, so she digs it out and places it back on the tray.

A few other people returned from their trial, distracting her from her thoughts. Some of them burst out, gasping for air. Others vomit water as their partner begs forgiveness for their mistake. As she watches those who struggled with the trial, she feels a chill run down her spine. The conversation with her aunt haunts her now. "You were right," she says under her breath.

"Hmm?"

"Nothing," she says as she follows his ginger stroll down the hall, stepping around those struggling for air on the ground.

Chapter 7

VIOLET AND ALAN

The air still has quite a chill, but new growth has begun, a sign of spring. Since the accident, this will be the first time venturing back into the abandoned city called Aelbourne. Back at the government building, they could locate a database unlocking the locations of many former colonies. However, Stacy had hinted at which colony Violet needed to look for. Looking back at the note Stacy had hidden in the back of the atlas, her chest grows heavy.

Violet,

I know you have no reason to trust me, but I need you to believe me. You cannot trust Yoojin. He comes from Arcadia. A colony that remains protected by the Stratos Development. They destroy smaller colonies when they are discovered. He is extremely danger-ous. Find Arcadia and destroy it if you can.

Stacy

Yoojin had only been threatening to her once, when they had first met. He'd always been a comfort to her since. From past experiences, she's beginning to lose trust in her judgment of character. Even Jack had been hiding his past their entire lives. Everyone has their se-crets and agendas. If Yoojin had only been helping her to learn the location of her colony, she'd be to blame for its destruction. To have that much blood on her hands would be a weight she couldn't bear. Though, she had never mentioned Safe Haven to him. He must've as-sumed she was a wanderer. Neither one divulged infor-mation about their homes. Even if he had followed her home, he wouldn't have taken years to attack. The many unanswered questions have her on edge.

Stacy's note has nagged at the back of her mind for the past three months. Killian's words still set fire to her chest when she recalls their secret call. She and Alan had agreed to wait until winter's end, giving them enough time to recover from the past experiences. Their last venture to Aelbourne has Alan overthinking. Nathan's condition has been stable, but no change. Violet worries about his condition being permanent but pushes that thought to the furthest corner of her mind. His stability brings her enough comfort to allow her to do what needs to be done.

It took some convincing, but Alan agreed to park closer to the underground garage entrance beneath the government building. The seven maven corpses scattered around the lot act as a warning to others. Violet's confidence in that puts him at ease, though she knows it doesn't actually keep them away. One, in particular, will always follow. It keeps its distance when they leave the cave, but when she sneaks out for some fresh air and alone time, that time is spent with the rogue maven in secret. Lowering the gate behind them, Violet follows Alan as they make their way to the control room. No sign of Yoojin. It's strange to be here without him. He was always there to help her, every evening in the past. It's better not to have him questioning her search for his home.

The pangs of anxiety send a prickly sensation through her skin, hoping he won't walk in on them. Trying to distract herself, she gets to work. They've been scanning a relatively large portion of the maps available. Only halfway through, there's still plenty of ground to cover. Though how she's to locate Arcadia, she's unsure. She doesn't even know what she's looking for. Researching the name, she realizes it could be a mountainous region, a hidden garden, or another ghost town. It could be an old city. She starts with the mountainous area but falls short of any progress. From there, they search sections at a time, being as thorough as possible so as not to miss any signs of life. Alan takes note of the activity they do find. If Arcadia is hiding bomber ships and has high-tech equipment such as Yoojin's speeder, it will be a large colony and difficult to hide. They've come across small colonies, but nothing that would amount to massive airships that could destroy a town. Most of them have very little to no technology. It's safer. Technology attracts unwelcome attention from seekers…and humans. A shiver runs through Violet when she remembers the seeker that had run her through the day of the explosion. The day her life was turned upside down.

It's late in the evening now, though you'd never know it in this room with no windows. A flickering candle and the many screens blanketing the wall light up Violet's face, making her look ghostly. Though she used to be very pale, her skin has darkened, thanks to her many walks with the maven and hunting. The darkened skin has assisted in hiding some of the dark veins that Jack couldn't hide with surgery. Her dark auburn hair hangs in loose curls, curving around her face. Violet has kept it short, finding it more manageable.

A couple of rows of desks behind her, Alan's snoring softly as he reclines in the leather swivel chair with his feet propped up and arms folded. His short, light brown hair, always in disarray. One snort and he wakes himself up. Stretching his stiff limbs, he watches the back of Violet's head. He can see the dark lines tracing the back of her neck. She usually has it hidden away, but she's becoming more comfortable with Alan. Her head dips, but her shoulders twitch, and she slaps her cheek to keep herself awake.

"All right, it's my turn. Take a break."

"I'm fine."

"Not if you're resorting to slapping yourself. Take a nap. I'll continue the search. Besides, if you keep working like this, you'll likely miss something important."

Violet gets up and takes his place in the warm leather chair with a sigh. She stretches her arms into the air. Her back pops loudly, and she yawns. "I'm going to call Nathan." Alan nods in response. She rummages in her bag and finds the radio. Putting the batteries back into it, she twists the switch. "Come in, Jack." A bout of static and silence. "Jack, Clara, come in."

"We might be too far," Alan says.

"It works off satellites." Alan shrugs off her rigidity.

"Violet, is everything okay?" Clara's voice comes in, clear as day.

"Everything's fine. We're safe. Can I speak to Nathan, please?

"Of course." There's a moment of silence. "Here's your boy, my dear."

"Hello, my love, it's your mom. I miss you so much." Silence follows. "I can't tell you where I am, but I wanted to tell you what I saw today. There was a large cat bigger than I had ever seen. It had large eyes and a white mouth. Its coat was a tan brown, and the tip of its long tail was black. We flew over it and spooked it so badly that it jumped and screeched at us. It looked fierce but so cute at the same time. Maybe you can tell me what kind of cat that was when you wake up. I can't stay on

much longer, so I'll let you sleep. I love you, little man."
Silence.

"Be safe, Violet dear." You could hear Clara's sweetness as she said goodbye.

"You as well, Clara. Hug the girls for me. Tell them I'll try to call again soon."

"I will."

With that, Violet switched off the radio and took out the batteries. Taking after Alan, she reclines in the same fashion with her arms crossed. Alan hums a tune to himself in his search, lulling Violet to sleep.

The candle next to Alan has its last lick of wax as it goes out in smoke. He bends down into Violet's pack to grab another. Yoojin enters the room with a slight limp, quietly closing the door behind him. Being half-Korean, he has delicate features but is built tall with broad shoulders like Alan. When Alan sits up to replace the candle, he jumps with such fright that the candlestick drops out of his hand, knocking the candlestick holder and the hot wax across the desk. Yoojin jumps out of the way before the hot wax can splatter on his coat. He tries to hold back his chuckling with a snort. Alan hits him in the arm. "Scared the daylights out of me, Eugene," he hisses.

Yoojin sighs while wiping a tear from the corner of his eye. "YOO-jin," he corrects.

"Shh…don't wake her up." Alan plops down in his chair, replacing the candle.

Yoojin sits next to him and swivels around to watch Violet sleep. "What's going on? Where's the rest of your group?"

"They're gone."

"What do you mean?" Yoojin asks with concern.

"There was an accident. I'm not going to get into details…" Alan pauses, glancing at Violet. "Her son is in a coma," he says in a choked voice. "Nathan won't wake up, and Killian and Stacy left."

"He left her?" Yoojin growls.

"Yes," Alan says in barely a whisper.

"After she'd been searching all that time for him, he just up and leaves?"

"It's not my place to discuss their choices. They're doing their own thing right now." Yoojin leans forward onto his elbows, shaking his head. "After everything that's happened… She seems to be handling things well. We have a good support system. I think it helps that the girls are there to keep her grounded."

"How many people are in your group?" Yoojin asks.

"Jack, Clara, Nathan, and two young girls, Ember and Lilly."

"Jack Wiseman?"

"You know him?" Alan turns from the screens to look at Yoojin, but he only watches Violet as she sleeps.

"Violet mentioned him a long time ago. I'm glad she still has him. From what I gathered, he was like a father to her."

"Yup. Killian too. They all grew up together." Alan turns back to the screens.

"I see," Yoojin says, deep in thought. "When did all of this happen?"

"The day after we separated," Alan sighs.

"That was months ago. How long have you guys been here?" he said in shock.

"We got here early this morning. She wants to stay a couple of days. She's looking for colonies. It's a good distraction for her." Alan looks him over. "It'll be good for her to see you too."

Yoojin pats Alan's shoulder, hearing the sadness in his voice. "Has Killian made contact with you since it happened?" he asks.

"Kind of. It's complicated."

"I don't care what the circumstances are. Violet was already in such a fragile state. Everything she'd gone through last year. He just up and leaves her."

Alan shakes his head, knowing Yoojin doesn't know all the details, though he agrees.

Violet's shoulder twitches. Yoojin stands up. Removing his coat, he drapes it over her. Alan knows better than most what Violet's been through. Violet had come out of a coma with bits and pieces of her memories. After locating her family, she found out she'd been living a lie with Charlie, who'd taken advantage of her manipulated memories. Her five-year-old son Nathan was the only thing keeping her feet on the ground. They

fled from a sudden attack on her hometown by an un-
known fleet. They escaped in Jack's ship, only to crash
later due to a cyborg in human disguise. She helped the
children escape but was trapped in a corner by maven.
Nathan, Ember and little Lilly were lucky to have Violet
with them. Even though she has a petite frame and
looked much more fragile than she does now, she can
destroy maven. Killian found them and took them all
to the shelter. Recovering her memory was torture of
its own. The long-lost family was reunited, but it was
cut short when Stacy came out about her past. While
they ventured out to get information, the maven caught
them at the worst time, resulting in Yoojin's limp and
the corpses scattered outside.

Stacy, Killian, Alan and Yoojin owed their lives to
Violet when she took out the seven maven that'd threatened them. Escaping with their lives, they took shelter
in an old water tower. Violet separated from the group
only for a moment for privacy when she was kidnapped
and put under a paralytic by Charlie, who now had a
vendetta against both Violet and Killian. Killian's true
nature came out when he found Charlie torturing her.
Forced to watch his brutal murder of Charlie, she ended
up with mixed feelings about Killian. He's the love of
her life, and yet he's become a different person. She was
relieved when he told her he was leaving with Stacy.

In sleep, Violet begins to groan. Yoojin looks down
at her sympathetically. She opens her wet eyes. He looks
away, pretending he'd been looking at the screens the
entire time, but she knows him better. Her eyes widen
at the sight of him, but a smile creeps across her face as

she watches him feign disinterest. Her chest becomes heavy as she wants nothing more than to take comfort in his appearance. She wants his arms wrapped tightly around her as he once did when she struggled. She wants to hear him say everything will be all right, but it will never be so. Tears fill her eyes as she watches him stare intently at the monitors. Then, she remembers why they came here.

"What are you doing here?" Violet rasps.

"Hello to you, too."

Violet realizes she's being rude and probably a little suspicious. "Sorry." Getting to her feet, she hands him his coat back.

He stands holding his arms out to her. "Hey, Kitten," Yoojin says solemnly.

She buries her face into his chest with a slight smile that doesn't reach her eyes. "Hey, Woof," she responds halfheartedly. His warm embrace releases the tension in her body. How can this man have betrayed her? It's just not possible.

"How have you been?" Yoojin asks as he pulls her away to look down into her eyes. "You cut your hair. I like it," he says with a soft smile.

"Thanks."

"Sorry if I woke you."

"It wasn't you," Violet says, averting her eyes. She opens her mouth, but no words come, so she shuts her mouth and hugs him tightly. Thanks to Stacy, she doesn't know whom to trust, and she's now questioning whether she really knows Yoojin after years of friendship. How well can you know someone in any case? She pulls away from him and slips into her coat. "Excuse me."

"Where are you going?" Alan shouts after her as she leaves the room. "You only got maybe an hour of sleep!"

"I need some fresh air. I won't go far."

"Would you like company?" Yoojin asks hopefully.

Violet shakes her head with a weak smile before closing the door behind her. She walks down the empty hallways and takes the stairwell to the underground garage. She avoids the cameras so the boys can't watch her as she makes her way out to the street. It's very dark except for the glistening stars freckled across the sky. It's silent as she makes her way down the dark empty road. Usually, the silence is a sign of danger, a warning that she should find shelter and be cautious. Since her first hunting trip, she has welcomed this silence.

A couple of blocks down, she sees the maven waiting patiently. She smiles at the way it stands, awkwardly still, like a statue, as it waits for attention. No human would dare approach these creatures without a death wish. It towers over her. Its fierce bone structure is harder than stone. Its head is sharp in shape, like a cockatiel on alert. Its eyes are as black as onyx. When a maven finds humans, it attacks without warning. With their right arm built as a weapon, they shoot bone shards at their victims. If maven blood is spilled, it acts as a poison, destroying its victim's blood cells. Violet is not seen as a mere human in this maven's eyes. It watches her approach in anticipation.

Violet stands before it, looking up at the creature. The maven bows its head. Nudging Violet's shoulder, like a horse wanting attention from its caretaker, it begins to rumble like a cat's purr. It echoes down the empty streets. Violet rubs the beak between its eyes. As she pets the creature, she closes her eyes. The vibration from the animal drowns out her surroundings. When she opens her eyes, several maven have gathered, watching. Her maven's purr changes to a deep reverberating hiss. Another maven responds similarly hostile.

Tucked into her belt, hidden in her coat, Violet pulls out the maven spike taken from her previous victims. With the sharp end, she cuts her hand open. The adrenaline pumping through her veins dulls the pain, painting the tips with her hybrid blood. Her blood is one of the only weapons against them, a poison. The other maven prepares to attack. When a loud screech escapes her ally, it becomes silent. The others stand straight, turning their heads curiously. The other maven talk amongst themselves in clicks and chirps she cannot understand; she puts away her poisoned spike and watches as they communicate. After a moment, the maven begin to disperse one by one, occasionally turning, watching their backs. Turning to face her ally, it is staring down at her. She reaches up to touch its beak, but it takes a step back. Violet had forgotten the blood on her hands. "I'm sorry." Clenching her hands into fists, she shoves them into her coat pockets. The maven bends down, touching its forehead to hers briefly before taking its leave.

As she walks down the dark empty street, she can hear a faint call. Alan is looking for her, and he's heated by the sound of his voice. Picking up her pace, she makes her way back. Yoojin is waiting at the end of the lot, staring into the darkness. When he sees movement, he pulls out his katana, ready for a fight. "It's me," Violet assures him.

"Where did you go?"

"For a walk."

"You said you wouldn't go far," he says, sheathing his sword.

"I lied."

"You shouldn't lie to your friends." Yoojin looks at her with disappointment.

"Friends lie to each other all of the time, Yoojin." Alan can be seen at the gate with his hands on his hips, preparing his words for a good scolding. She walks past Yoojin. He can't help but feel that that comment was directed at him.

"I've never lied to you," Yoojin says, following her back to the building.

"Only time will tell."

"What reason would I have to lie to you?" Violet shrugs. Yoojin grabs her arm, pulling her back. She stops to face him. "I will never betray you."

"Okay, then why don't I know everything about you? We've spent a lot of time with each other. How is it that I still have basic questions about you?"

"Maybe because you've never asked. Have I done something wrong?" he says, folding his arms.

"You're right. I should've asked you more questions. Where do you live?"

"Well, I spend most of my time—" Yoojin starts.

"No, where's your home? Where are you from?" Violet interrupts with a bite to her words.

"Arcadia," Yoojin responds thoughtfully. The blood drains from her face, and she finally feels the chill of the night. *At least he's telling the truth*, she tells herself and continues.

"Where is this place? I've been searching the database for a colony with high tech like yours, but I can't find anything."

"You've been searching for me?" A faint grin crosses his face. His smile makes her heart leap. All at once, she feels a fondness, longing, and Killian…the guilt dilutes the rest. She turns away, scrunching her face, trying to reroute her thoughts.

"I've been looking for your colony," she says as she continues walking. He follows behind with his hands in his gray wool coat pockets. Alan throws his hands up as they reach the gate in frustration. She holds a hand out to stop him as he's about to rant. "I know. I said I wouldn't go far. I'm a jerk, and I'm sorry," she says, ducking under the gate.

"What happened to your hand?" Alan's expression instantly changes to concern.

"I slipped and cut it on something." Her eyes dart away.

Alan sighs, grabbing her wrist. Dragging her inside, Yoojin closes the gate and watches them curiously with a smile. While Alan cleans up her hand in the control room, Yoojin sits beside her, resting his chin in his palm.

Violet watches him suspiciously. He smiles back at her scrutiny. "You are very fatherly, Alan." Yoojin grins. "It's cute."

"Shut up," Alan says coldly as he works.

"Why haven't I found your colony in the database, on the scanners, in the video feed?" Violet interrupts to put the conversation back on track.

"It's hidden away."

"Will you take me there?"

"I'd be happy to. I'll need to inform them of our visit."

"Take me now."

Yoojin raises a brow with a smirk. Violet glares at him, knowing he took her words for another meaning. "Nope, not happening," Alan says. "We're not going anywhere tonight. We agreed to stay out here for a day or two, not to explore foreign colonies at night." He ties a clean cloth around her hand.

Violet sighs. Having her hand back, she glares down at the bandage, picking at the frayed edges. Alan slaps her hand away. "Stop picking at it." Yoojin watches them, hiding his smile behind his fingers. Violet folds her arms, hiding her hands under her elbows like a stubborn child. Looking back at Yoojin, she notices him studying her. "What are you staring at?"

"You."

"Well, stop," she says, fidgeting in her seat.

"You've never acted so awkward around me. It's almost like you don't trust me anymore. I don't remember doing anything that would cause you to doubt me."

Violet glares at him.

"After our conversation with Killian, you would be too—ow!" Alan receives a swift kick to the shin.

"I have been lied to and manipulated too many times by the people closest to me. I'm questioning all my relationships." She sends him a death stare. He's lucky she held back on that kick. She could've easily fractured his leg. Controlling her strength hasn't been too tricky except when feeling certain emotions.

"You didn't need to kick me," Alan complains, as entertained as Yoojin is.

"I can inform them tomorrow," Yoojin says.

Violet and Alan look at him and then at each other. "Fine, but we shouldn't stay for very long. The kids will worry." Violet nods in agreement.

Chapter 8

YOOJIN

Yoojin sits against the wall, envying the others as they sleep. With Alan chainsawing away, Yoojin has gotten very little sleep. He's amazed at how easily Violet sleeps through it. Reaching over her carefully, he plugs Alan's nose. With the change in his rhythm, Violet's eyes open wide. Like a deer caught in headlights, Yoojin is frozen, staring into her wide hazel-green eyes. "What are you doing?" Violet asks.

"Nothing?" He releases Alan's nose, and he gasps with an enormous snort. Smacking his lips, he rolls over and continues his snoring. Yoojin presses his lips into a line as he glares at Alan. Returning to Violet, he is closer to her face than expected. He can't help but look at her lips and back to her eyes, noticing the flush on her cheeks.

"Were you trying to suffocate Alan?" Her eyes narrowed.

Yoojin sits back against the wall. "His snoring kept me up all night!" he points out. Violet smiles, listening to Alan's snore catch for a second, and he continues, "How can you sleep through that?"

Violet shrugs. "When he's snoring, I know I'm not alone. It's become a comfort. How do you know I was sleeping, anyway?"

He watches her as she yawns and stretches her arms overhead. "You were talking in your sleep. Unless you were talking to *me*, in that case, I might blush."

Sitting up, she clears her throat. "What did I say?" she asks hesitantly.

Yoojin leans close with a teasing look in his eye. "I love you," he whispers.

Violet looks away with a flush. She remembers her dream very vividly, as if not just a dream but a memory. *Running in a lace dress, she tromps through the forest laughing. She glances behind her. A younger Killian is chasing after her playfully. "I'll get you for that, you little imp!"*

"You have to catch me first!" she laughs.

"Just you wait!" he calls. They weave through the trees, knowing the forest like the back of their hand.

They come to the old shed covered in ivy. Violet reaches the door and goes for the handle, but Killian is closer than she expects, grabbing hold of her. She squeals as he turns her to face him. "Well, I've caught you. Now what to do with you?" Killian grins as he holds her tight to his body.

Violet smiles up at him mischievously. As he leans in to steal a kiss, she turns the handle on the door and jumps back as the door swings open, letting Killian fall in after her. She bursts into laughter as he catches his balance.

"Oh, you are going to get it," he threatens before leaping at her. He grabs her waist as they both fall onto the small mattress against the wall. Violet screams and giggles as he holds her down with his weight. Looking into his eyes and his beautiful grin so close to hers, she couldn't resist any longer. Pressing her lips to his, he is surprised and delighted. He kisses back with passion. Pulling away, he looks down at her adoringly. "Marry me," he says, breathless.

"Is that my punishment?" she jests.

"Indeed, for marrying me would surely be torture."

"Undoubtedly," Violet says playfully. Killian, exasperated with her games, tickles her sides until she gasps for breath. "See, it's torture already!" she gasps. Killian takes her breath away with another kiss. When he leans back, she looks up at him with twinkling eyes. "Marriage is just showing the public our commitment to one another. Who cares?"

"I care! I want to show the world that I am yours, and you are mine," he growls, leaning in to nibble her shoulder. A burst of laughter shakes the little shed. He sighs, pulling away once more to look at her warmly.

"I love you," she says with a shaky voice. The ache in her heart is not out of sorrow and emptiness as it once was. This ache is from the overflow of love she feels toward Killian. Her heart is so full that it feels as if it could burst if she loved him any more than she already does.

Upon hearing those words, Killian loses his mind. As if they had no time left in the world, they pull at each other's clothing.

"Earth to Violet." Yoojin waves his hand in front of her face.

Coming back to reality, her face turns a deeper scarlet. "I need to get some air," she says, jumping to her feet.

"Ah…okay?" he says, though she had already left the room before he could respond.

Alan wakes to the commotion. "What? What happened?" Alan sits up, looking around the room, sleepy-eyed.

"I'm not sure," Yoojin says awkwardly. Alan rubs his eyes and squints at Yoojin with one eye. "I think I scared her away."

"Did she bring her coat?"

"No?"

"She'll be back," Alan says, fluffing the bundled coat he's using as a pillow and going back to sleep.

Violet runs out of the dark room through the office floors and down three flights of stairs before escaping through the garage. One of the abandoned vehicles sits with a thick layer of dust but is otherwise in perfect condition. Glaring at it, the tingling feeling in her skin becomes unbearable. With a kick of her heavy boot, the bumper dents, rocking the heap of metal. Unsatisfied, she swings her clasped hands down like a sledgehammer onto the hood. It crumples pleasingly. She continues to take out her anger on the vehicle, shattering all the windows and denting the sides. Dropping to her knees, she is out of breath, and the vehicle is completely destroyed.

Sweat and tears drip down her face as she breathes intensely, staring at the pavement. She hears footsteps coming closer. "Did I do something wrong?" Yoojin stops ten feet away, watching her.

Violet looks up at the ceiling and wipes her face and nose on her sleeve, shaking her head. "I hate him."

"Who, Kitten?"

"Killian. I hate him." Her face crumples, and fresh tears come as she pulls her knees to her chest. "But I still love him. Regardless of what he's done, I love him."

"Then you don't *hate* him. You just don't like him right now."

"He says what happened to Nathan was my fault. He blames me."

"Well, now *I* hate him," Yoojin says in contempt. Violet snickers, shaking her head at him. "Alan told me what happened. It wasn't your fault. He's an idiot if he thinks you're to blame." He steps closer until he's standing over her.

"I think he's right." Her voice cracks and her shoulders shake as she looks down at her swelling, cut knuckles.

Yoojin crouches, pulling her into his chest. "Why would you think that?"

"If I hadn't stopped them from shooting Killian, Nathan would never have gotten hurt. I should've let him die!" She sobs. "I could have saved Nathan. We could have run away." She cries into his coat.

"You don't know that. You don't know what the outcome would've been if you had let Killian die. If the roles were reversed, you'd blame yourself for Killian's death. You did what you could and can't beat yourself up over it. If you'd done nothing, you might've lost both of them. Don't let this eat away at you." His words, though kind, are far from comforting.

"But I *have* lost them both," she says in a low tone. He is speechless as she continues to quake from her sobbing. There's nothing more he can say to soothe her, so he waits patiently, stroking her short bouncy hair. In time, her breathing becomes regular. She takes in a deep breath and lets it out slowly. "I'm sorry," she says.

"Don't apologize. I feel sorry for that car over there, an innocent bystander." Violet rolls her eyes with a weak smile. Yoojin wipes away the hair sticking to her tear-stained face and rests his hands on her cheeks. Staring into her eyes with such fondness and longing, for an instant he thinks he sees the same look in her eyes. His face comes closer. Violet looks down at her bleeding knuckles with a frown. Her hands have already be-gun to heal, but the cuts reopen as she flexes her hand. Yoojin looks away, dropping his hands. Violet's stomach growls. Yoojin chuckles.

"Alan's going to get mad at me for this. I should clean myself up before he sees it," she says as she gets to her feet. Yoojin smiles with a sigh but follows her back in. As she climbs the stairs, she beats her chest with her fist as her heart tries to break free. The thoughts of Nathan and Killian neutralize her stumbling feelings.

Chapter 9

ALAN

The sun is shining bright in the morning sky with minimal cloud cover. Despite the cold breeze, the sun warms them. As they gather their belongings, Yoojin collects his speeder and meets them at the front of the facility. He doesn't like the cold attitude she's taking on. There's something important she's keeping to herself. He sees the fresh pink scars on her knuckles as she lifts the heavy gate over her head. Alan locks it in place so they can come and go with ease.

"Are you sure we should leave it open like this? What if maven or seekers get in?" Alan asks.

"We won't need to come back here," Violet says indifferently.

"All right, what's going on? You've been acting strange since Yoojin showed up."

She looks around and listens for the speeder before turning to answer him. "The message Stacy left us in the atlas says we can't trust Yoojin, that he's dangerous. She says they're responsible for destroying discovered colonies, which would mean Arcadians destroyed my home."

"You think Yoojin destroyed Safe Haven?"

"If not him, his people. If it's true, she says we have to destroy them." Violet scowls at the sun shining in her eyes as she checks her pack to ensure nothing's missing.

"Stacy…she always spoke like it was as simple as that. It's not that simple, and it's not your responsibility to do something about it. Don't think you can manage this on your own."

"I can try."

"It's a suicide mission, Violet. Don't forget your priorities. You're a mother first. Don't put it in your head that you can save the world just because you're stronger than most." He storms off to his skyrider. As if on cue, Yoojin pulls up in his speeder.

Yoojin leads the way, and Violet and Alan follow, heading southeast toward the Dark Sea. Violet keeps their eyes on Yoojin and pays no mind to the lush forest they fly over. Alan becomes more anxious as the horizon turns from lush green to charred and ashen. They've been flying for an hour in the direction Killian once led him, where he lost his arm. He can feel his blood pressure rise as they reach the charred landscape.

His skyrider begins to cough and sputter. He kicks it and curses. "Don't you dare start this now, not here," he says as they draw closer to the desolate place. Violet looks at him as he falls behind and his engine begins to smoke. She speeds up to get ahead of Yoojin and signals him to land. Alan's skyrider sputters several more times and finally gives up about six feet off the ground. It crashes with a crunch, and a plume of ash and dust fills the air. Alan jumps off and kicks the machine as the other two land safely.

Violet hops off and runs to him. "Are you okay?"

"I'm fine!" Alan growls. "I'm so sorry, Vi." He looks behind her.

"Why are you apologizing to me? It's not like you killed it on purpose. You can ride with me." Alan sighs as he begins to unload his pack. The engine starts to hiss as more smoke billows out. "Alan, leave it and step away," she says as she hurries toward him.

"Let me just get the supplies."

"Leave it! It's going to explode!" she yells as she grabs his sleeve and pulls him ahead of her. The force of the explosion shoves them both to the ground a few feet from each other. Violet receives the brunt of it. Their ears are ringing as they slowly lift themselves off the ground, spitting ash and coughing. They try to catch the wind that had been knocked out of them. Yoojin skids to a stop to help Violet to her feet, causing more dust to fly. "I'm fine," Violet groans as she reaches for Alan.

"No, you're not!" Yoojin exclaims, but his voice is severely muffled. He takes hold of her arms.

"Ow, stop fussing over me. Alan needs help. I'm fine." She shoves Yoojin's hands away. Alan opens and closes his jaw as if that would help his ears clear. "Ow." She scrunches her face as she dusts off her coat. As she reaches behind her shoulder, she turns, allowing Alan to see a thin metal bar no thicker than a pencil protruding from her back. "Dang it," she complains.

"Don't touch it!" Alan and Yoojin yell in unison.

Before they can stop her, she rips it out of her shoulder and tosses the metal behind her. She hisses as she cranes her neck, attempting to see the damage. "Dang it!" Violet growls again. "My coat…" She shrugs out of the coat as she walks back to her vehicle to get a bandage, holding it up to inspect the hole.

Alan rubs his face in exasperation. Yoojin shakes his head in disbelief as he helps Alan to his feet. Violet mumbles as she removes her blouse and crumples it into a ball in frustration before shoving it into her bag. She sprays her wound with disinfectant and removes the packaging of an adhesive bandage, slapping it on crookedly. She pulls a fresh shirt out of her pack. Turning around, she buttons the new blouse and adjusts the collar. "What?" she asks louder than necessary.

Alan looks at Yoojin, standing there with his mouth slightly open. Violet rubs her ears as her hearing slowly adjusts. "Hey!" Alan punches Yoojin in the arm and glares. "What's your problem?"

"Nothing. I just never took her for a tattoo type of person."

"I don't have any tattoos," she sighs as she shrugs back into her coat, brushing her hand over the hole in the shoulder.

"What are you doing?" Alan says, giving him a look that tells Yoojin to back off.

"Okay, I'm sorry." Yoojin surrenders, his hands up.

Alan begins mouthing to him, "Don't make it weird, man…" Yoojin shrugs in confusion. Alan turns to face Violet, but she's standing very still, facing away. "Don't say anything," he mouths to Yoojin while pulling his thumb across his throat threateningly. Yoojin looks at him incredulously. Alan cautiously closes the distance to Violet. "Hey…so…how you doin'?"

"Yoojin said we could make it by evening," Violet says in response. "We won't have enough fuel if you and I ride together. We should see if there's anything here we could use to replace it."

"You sure? We can go a bit further and see what we can find."

"There's nothing beyond this town in our direction," Violet says, not making eye contact.

"We could backtrack a bit?"

"Don't be stupid. It's fine."

"Are you sure? Because it's okay to—"

"I said it's fine, Alan! Stop wasting time and let's get what we need to move on."

Alan bites his lip. Never has she turned her fiery temper on him before, and he feels a bit like a child being scolded. He takes a step back and awkwardly bows his head before turning back to Yoojin. He knocks his forehead with his knuckle in embarrassment. *Why did I bow?* he says to himself.

Yoojin tries to avoid laughing at Alan by biting his lips. "Something wrong?" he whispers.

"I just don't know how to approach…this." He waves his hands toward Violet.

"I don't understand."

"This is her home, or it was. It was destroyed the day they came to stay with us."

"This is Safe Haven?" Yoojin has become serious now.

"What's left of it," Alan sighs.

Yoojin gulps air as he takes in the landscape. The land is leveled with fallen, charred trees surrounded by new growth. A gust of wind sends dust and ash swirling into the air.

There's a strange whistle just as an arrow plunges into the seat of Violet's rider beside her. They turn to find a group of people moving in on them. Yoojin and Alan take cover behind the speeder. Violet rips the arrow out of her seat and peers at the strangers. At least ten people are racing toward them. Another arrow is let loose and lands at her feet.

"Violet, get over here!" Alan yells as Yoojin draws his sword. The people begin to shout, hoping to intimidate them into submission. Violet ignores Alan as she opens the compartment with her pistols. Another arrow is shot through the lid, snapping it out of her hands. She rips the arrow away and pulls the gun out before another arrow can be discharged. Aiming at the horde of humans, she yells at the top of her lungs, "Stop now or I'll shoot!"

Alan's head whips back to Violet. The voice she used, he'd never heard it before, and a chill runs down his spine. The others are about a hundred feet away and drawing ever closer. Violet walks towards the group of people, still yelling their battle cry. "I don't know why

I left that shelter," Alan complains as he closes his eyes and waits for someone to end Violet's life. "Every time we get too far away, something bad happens."

Violet yells once again, and this time her voice breaks through their battle cry. Some look at each other, but they continue running at full speed. Alan and Yoojin peer around the speeder. Several more arrows are shot. Violet snatches one out of the air and fires her pistol. A man falls to the ground screaming as he holds his shin.

The battle cry gets louder but in an unnerving way. It seems to reverberate. Hundreds of birds swarm out of the woods and flood the open field, whipping past the group of people. They're caught off-guard and their battle cry stops, but the strange sound continues. The birds beat past as Alan and Yoojin take cover.

"Oh no." Violet lowers her weapon.

"What's happening?" Alan yells, but no one answers him. The birds have cleared, and an eerie quiet follows.

The people once screaming to intimidate now scream in fear as, one after another, maven emerge from the woods at full speed. The people run for their lives in Violet's direction. The color in Alan's face pales as the maven comes into sight. He becomes frozen, incapable of looking away from the creatures that destroyed his entire family.

Violet drops her pistol and races towards the man she shot, now abandoned by his people. She reaches him just in time to snatch a bone shard intended for the man's head. He lies there, screaming, as the creatures draw closer. Violet holds the bone shard up to her hand.

"STOP!" Violet's voice rumbles and echoes through the clearing. The maven slow down until they stand before her, hissing and clicking twenty feet away. More maven emerge, and the hissing sounds like ocean waves as they gather.

Violet still holds the shard to her hand as one of the maven steps forward until it's within arm's reach and slowly drops to its knees. Again, there's a silence that would allow you to hear a pin drop. Some of the people have stopped running and hide behind the speeder and skyrider. Violet drops her arms and the shard falls to the ground. She smiles as she steps forward and lowers her head to press her forehead to the maven. It begins to purr. One maven after another begins to respond in the same way.

"Good boy," Violet croons as she strokes the sides of the creature's face. Each maven begins to kneel, and tears come to her eyes as these cold creatures show submission to her. She walks around the first maven and stands in front of the others, slowly reaching her hand out to the closest. It cautiously leans away at first but then allows her to stroke its beak. She greets the next one in the same manner, then another.

Violet then turns her back on the beasts, turning her attention to the man who was shot in the leg, lying limp on the ground. He recovers as she approaches and begins to whimper as he crawls away. The maven closest to him gets to its feet and slowly moves toward him. Violet catches up with it and strokes its arm as she stands between it and the man. She turns to the stranger. "Let me help you."

The man whimpers as he eyes the beast behind her and its onyx-black eyes. Violet kneels and pulls the man up by the arm. He cries out as he puts pressure on his wounded leg. "Can you help me?" Violet asks the maven with a smile, petting its arm once again. The maven offers its arm to the man. The man hesitates. "It's all right. It won't hurt you," she tells him. The man swallows hard and carefully touches the beast.

As the two bring the wounded man, the rest of the maven stay put. Violet leaves the man with the maven as she runs ahead of them. He whimpers as the maven scoops him up into its arms. She approaches a woman with long brown hair, wearing a dirty, hooded wrap tied at the waist. She's one of the archers but stands out from the rest. "Are you the leader of this group?"

The girl nervously laughs. "No," she says, unable to take her eyes off the maven holding one of her own.

"They won't hurt you." The woman looks at Violet in awe. "What's your name?"

"Nova—"

"Don't tell her anything!" a tall, gangly man yells. His hair is short but messy. "Nova! Get behind me!" Nova looks at him in horror as he approaches with one of Violet's pistols. He tightly grabs Nova's shoulder, aiming the pistol at Violet. "Nova!" he barks. Though Nova glares at him, she does as she's told, ripping her shoulder away from his grasp.

The maven holding the wounded man drops him next to Violet, crying in pain as he plops to the ground. The creature rumbles in anger, Violet rests her hand on it. Throwing caution to the wind, Alan snatches the sword out of Yoojin's hand and holds it over his shoulder, ready to swing it like a bat, as he approaches the thief with Violet's pistol as quietly as possible.

"And you are?" Violet questions the man with her pistol, trying not to bring attention to Alan coming up behind him.

"*I* lead these people."

"Okay, then I recommend you stand down for the safety of your people."

"I will not," the man says sternly. Violet can't help but laugh at this man who doesn't look much older than herself.

"Look, you can shoot me and let everyone die or give my pistol back and live to see another day. These maven like me for reasons I can't figure out, so if anything happens to me, everyone here will die, including my friends."

"Put it down, Mathias," the girl, Nova, says behind him.

"Shut up," he says as he tightens his grip on the trigger. The maven hisses as it tenses up. The others that stand at a distance imitate it.

"Don't be a freaking idiot. Put the gun down, Mathias."

Alan moves in close enough to rest the sword on his shoulder against the man's neck. Mathias flinches and drops the gun. Alan glances at Nova next to him. The corners of her mouth curve up instantly as she folds her arms.

Violet crouches down to retrieve the pistol but makes eye contact with Alan with a worried look.

Mathias stomps his heavy boot, crushing her hand beneath. She yells out in pain. There's a screech from the maven, then they all begin moving in on them. Alan jumps back, lightly cutting Matt's neck. Violet throws up her free hand to stop them, but the maven, once behind her, now has a grip on Mathias' throat. A screech escapes Nova before she clasps her hands over her mouth, and tears well up in her eyes. He desperately claws at the stone-like hand.

"Don't kill him!" Violet yells. Mathias removes his foot, releasing her, but the maven doesn't loosen its grip on his throat.

Nova crouches next to Violet as she rubs the feeling back into her fingers. "Make it stop, please." Nova's hands hover over Violet, too afraid to touch her physically.

Violet nods. She pulls on the maven, and he releases him. Mathias coughs and gags as he gasps for air. The maven falls behind Violet once more. "Nova! Get behind me!" he yells.

The fury rages in Alan. "Who the hell do you think you are? You don't speak to women like they're dogs, you worthless piece of…"

"Alan?" Violet looks at him with wide eyes.

"Don't 'Alan' me! How long has this—" he waves his hands at the horde of Maven— "been going on? How? After everything, how could you, Vi?"

"I'm so sorry, Alan. It just kind of happened. This is why I kept it a secret."

"This is why you'd go out on your own, isn't it? Wait…at the shelter? Were they there too?

"Alan, now's not the time."

"Well, I don't see why not, given that we're surrounded by a horde of them that do whatever you say and have no explanation. I'm sure this psychopath in front of us is also curious. How about you, Eugene? Are you curious how long these things have been following us, and why they've somehow become Vi's new pet?"

"Uh, yeah?" Yoojin calls from behind the speeder.

"Answers." He points the katana in Violet's direction. "Now." He drops the katana when the maven hisses, throwing up his hands in surrender.

Violet sighs. "This one found me while we were hunting. I think it's the same one I saw in the city when we were attacked, but he just watched from afar. He must've followed us home." She says it with endearment as she pats its arm.

"And you trust them."

"With my life…well, this one I do."

"Well, that's great." Alan shakes his head in frustration.

"You can put your hands down," she says. "It seems like this one's respected, like in a wolf pack. Stay on his good side and he won't harm you." Alan runs his hand through his hair and bites his lip before picking the katana off the ground.

"I'm bleeding!" Mathias announces as he holds his hand to his neck with pressure.

"You're fine," Alan sighs as he looks the blade over. He turns back to Violet. "Why does he submit to you, though?"

"Probably because I'm the first person he's come across who can destroy his kind easily."

"How do you know it's a he?"

"I don't know. I feel like it's a he," Violet shrugs, looking up at her maven.

"Well, now what? Are they just going to follow us wherever we go?"

"I guess. There weren't this many last night. I don't know why they're gathering, but when they purr they show submission."

"Well, that's nice." Alan continues to look at Violet and the maven. "Eugene!"

"What?" he calls from behind his speeder. He eyes those taking cover with him, and they watch him and his vehicle in return.

"Will you come out here, please?" he says in exasperation.

Yoojin sighs before removing his key and locking the door shut. He cautiously comes out with the other katana unsheathed. "What?" he grumbles.

"Look, I'm not used to being the one in charge. I don't know what to do in this situation. If Killian were here, he'd know what to do, but he isn't, and I don't know what we are doing...will you please stop staring at me!" Nova jumps as he raises his voice at her. "I'm very uncomfortable right now, and I feel Like you're piercing me with those....mesmerizing eyeballs." Alan waves the katana in her direction. She looks away quickly and directs her gaze down at the ground with wide eyes.

"Don't be rude, Alan. She's probably in shock," Violet interjects.

"I'm not...rude. I just...Eugene, please. Help!" Alan turns to Yoojin for guidance.

"Ask Violet. I don't know why you think you're in charge. Violet's the one with an army of monsters."

"Oh, so you're okay with all this? You don't think this weird bond is unhealthy at all?"

"I don't think we have a choice, Alan."

"I think it's amazing," Nova says in awe.

"What about these guys?" Alan calls attention to Mathias and the other man moaning on the ground. "Punish them for attacking innocent people? Take them captive? What would we do with prisoners? How would that work?"

"We're not prisoners. We'll fight," Mathias growls, still holding his neck.

"I surrender!" Nova retracts her bow with a flick of her wrist and throws her arms high. "He can fight, but I surrender. I'll do as you say."

"Seems like your girlfriend just threw you under the bus."

"Ew, no, he's my brother," Nova says in disgust.

"You don't have a boyfriend?" Alan asks in confusion. Nova shakes her head no as she looks away with a blush on her cheeks.

"Alan, what does that have to do with anything?" Violet scolds.

"It's okay," Nova says nervously.

Mathias looks up at her in disgust as she speaks. "No one will want you if you act this desperate," Mathias grumbles.

Violet seethes at his comment, but Alan speaks first. "Does he always talk like this?" he shouts. He squats in front of Mathias, looking down at him. "Do you always have this much garbage spilling out of your mouth? Can't you see the hurt in her eyes as you said that? Are you cutting her down to make her feel as worthless as you? Not sure if you're aware, but I saw this woman shooting arrows with precision while you were hiding behind her. How can a piece of trash like you be considered a leader?" Alan continues to rant and belittle him.

Nova wipes at the tears spilling down her cheeks. That's when Alan turns his attention to Nova. "Don't ever let anyone talk to you like this. You stand up for yourself. They think they can walk all over you if you don't stand up. Be confident. You're a beautiful, strong woman, and you should never take this treatment, you understand?" Nova nods vigorously while hiding the blush on her cheeks behind an oversized sleeve. "Nor anyone else! Don't let this psycho treat you like trash when he's the scum of this earth!" Alan stands, pointing his sword at others in their group. Coming back to Nova, he continues, "This guy's your biological brother?"

"Yes," Nova responds timidly.

Alan crouches back down so close to Mathias's face that he can feel the spit as he screams, "She's your family! Your blood! Show respect for your siblings. Don't treat them like animals you own! You don't own her! Got it?" He pants as he looks around at the many confused faces.

"Well said," Violet says with a pleased smile on her face. "Now, are you finished?"

"Yeah, if he keeps his mouth shut," Alan sighs. He stands up and straightens himself out.

"Agreed. Take a seat and breathe for a minute." Violet laughs. "Nova."

"I'm sorry I blew up your skyrider," Nova blurts out.

"Oh, that was you?"

"We've been watching you since you arrived in the city. I rigged it to explode after you took off so we could ambush you. I'm sorry."

"Traitor," Mathias scoffs. Alan responds by kicking him in the groin, and he cries out in pain.

"Alan." Violet shakes her head as Mathias rolls on the ground in hysterics. The maven ticks in a way that shows its approval, almost as if mimicking a laugh.

"He started it."

"Nova, do you have shelter nearby?" she asks as she eyes Alan.

"We've been using an underground facility near here."

"In Safe Haven?"

"Under the town that was destroyed last year."

"Lead the way."

Nova turns on her heels. Violet begins to follow, but Yoojin catches her arm. "We can crowd into my speeder. We don't need to go with them to Safe Haven."

"I know that."

"We can't trust these people," he whispers close to her ear.

"That's probably true, but I trust these people as much as your people, whomever they might be." Violet pulls away, ending the conversation.

Alan walks off as some members watch Mathias whimpering, still rolling in the dirt. Yoojin collects his sword from Alan. He and Alan collect their things and follow slowly in the skyrider and speeder as the rest make their way on foot. The maven keeps its distance but follows behind the crowd, cautiously ticking and hissing.

They're led along the outer skirt of the town. Alan drives near enough to Violet and her maven to send a gust of wind her way. He's uneasy at first, but he sees how at ease Violet is with her maven next to her. She occasionally glances behind her with a smile as it follows silently in an eerily graceful way. Then Nova catches his eye. She was watching him. She looks away awkwardly when she realizes he's looking back at her. He scrutinizes her as she walks ahead of everyone. Her ponytail sways with her movements. She's slightly taller than Violet and looks much more robust. She has curves he can't help but notice. Her full lips curl. He sees the blush on her cheeks and realizes he's been caught looking for too long. Alan looks around, clearing his throat, and realizes Violet is staring at him with a raised eyebrow and a wicked smirk on her face.

Chapter 10

NOVA

Nova touches the back of her hand to her flushed cheeks. Her heart is pounding in her ears. *Why was he watching me like that? Did I step in something? Do I have something on my face? Did I do something wrong? Does he think I'm going to turn on them? This is Mathias's fault...or is it my fault?*

"Nova." Toby, a handsome dark-skinned man from their hunting group, catches up to her.

"Hmm?" Her thoughts fizzle away. She awkwardly stares ahead as she avoids the memory of her former crush.

"Are we really going to take them to our shelter? What if they want to see what kind of threat we are before taking us out, taking everything we have?"

"I know how you feel, Toby. I don't think we have a choice in the matter. But I have a feeling that Violet girl doesn't want to hurt anyone."

"You know I respect you, but I have a wife and children I need to protect. Can you guarantee their safety?"

"I'll do everything in my power to protect our people, even if it means my life."

With a stern nod, Toby hangs back to walk alongside his wife and reassure her. Nova's mind screams questions at her. *Am I doing the right thing? Can we trust them? Will they turn on us as soon as I lead them to our shelter? Should I lead them somewhere else? There's that house on the shore. What if the maven turn on us? What about the children? Would they kill children? No, they didn't want to hurt anyone. This is too much pressure. Why am I in charge all of a sudden? Because Mathias is an idiot, that's why. I can do this. It'll be all right.*

"Are you all right?" Violet is walking next to Nova with concern written all over her face.

"Yes, I'm fine."

"You've been biting your lower lip for a while now. I may not know you very well, but I'm usually pretty good about reading people."

Nova smiles at her nervously. "It'll be fine…as long as your maven stays outside."

"I don't let them into our shelter, so I wouldn't ask you to make an exception."

"I appreciate it."

The woods that should seem familiar to Violet are mostly turned to dust that gets kicked up with each step. A field with tall grass opens up with wildflowers here and there. Nova spreads her hands out and lets the grass and flowers hit her hands as she walks. Violet does the same and raises her face to the sun, enjoying the sensation. Weaving through the grass and hidden grave-stones, Nova reaches the large doors in the ground. An unusual place to find shelter in the middle of a cemetery. The scorch marks camouflage the chipping, rusted red doors. The entrance to the sanctuary they'd been searching for, for years. Her colony has finally found a safe place to stay, where the children can grow up without fear. She turns back to see Violet crouched in the grass. Her eyebrows are pinched together in a frown as she stares down at a gravestone. "Over here!" Nova calls. Violet meets her eyes, and her expression is wiped clean.

Alan has landed the skyrider and is gathering what's left of their supplies. Alan comes to Nova's side and glares at the large, blackened doors. They screech as Nova pulls them open. Alan looks down at the hole in the ground wearily. "This is a trap, isn't it?"

"No!" Nova tries to look as sincere as possible but realizes she's probably looking more suspicious.

"Last time we came here, my friend was shot up, and he lost his arm because of it," Alan says, folding his arms.

"You know this place?" Her stomach drops. Suddenly this sanctuary doesn't feel as safe. Alan only nods in response as he turns to wait for his friends. "We aren't going to shoot you." Nova feels it necessary to re-assure him at that moment.

He turns to look at her and smirks before turning his attention away once more. "That's what they always say."

Violet's come close enough to hear the conversation and looks back and forth between them. "If you're that uncomfortable, you can stay out here with the maven." Alan and Nova look back at the creature standing at the cemetery's edge. With a groan, he looks back at Violet with pleading eyes.

Yoojin comes up to stand next to Violet. "This looks like a trap," he says, scanning the dark entrance.

"Thank you," Alan says, throwing his hands up triumphantly.

"My goodness, you're a bunch of wimps," Violet says in exasperation as she clomps down the stairs and disappears into the darkness. Nova follows after her with a grin. Reluctantly, they join the women in the darkness. As they move deeper into the dark corridor, Nova flicks a small metal piece attached to her ear, and a light flashes. As the rest of her people file in, it becomes brighter with their verging headlamps. The corridor is lined with stone walls and arches leading to different tunnels.

Nova follows a path that's been marked with blue paint. Everyone is so quiet as they pass through that you can hear each breath taken. Nova can hear her heartbeat in her ears as they draw closer. After turning down another tunnel, there's a light at the end. Nova takes a deep breath before stepping into the large room. Supplies are lining the walls as some of the older people sort them. They stop and stare as the strangers follow close behind.

"This is where we bring the supplies we find," Nova says, waving her hands about. Alan nervously glances behind him as the rest of the group files in, blocking any escape. She leads them down a large hallway with several doors. "We have some rooms we've made into family homes." She gestures to them, some with doors and some with just a cloth curtain. Violet nods and smiles as she passes those staring.

At the end of the hallway, it opens to another large room with tables and chairs. Along the walls are washing machines with a large sink beside them. "Here we found a ventilation system so I could rig up a kitchen of sorts. Over there, we usually come together to eat or go back to our rooms. Most people go back to their rooms."

"How did you get electricity down here?" Violet asks.

"There was already power in this place. It was just disconnected. It was an easy fix. The plumbing was the real problem." Nova shivers at the thought. "It was a nightmare, but we finally got the showers and toilets working."

Nova leads them through a corridor with more doors. "What's through here?" Violet asks.

"A laboratory or something."

"You were able to get in?" Violet continues as she taps the glass screen beside the door. It lights up, waiting to scan a handprint.

"I was able to hack in through the panel below. I had to get through to access the water supply and the ventilation system. Something creepy went down in there, so we stay out." Violet nods.

"What's down that way?" Alan asks as he follows the hall down past the lavatory.

"The nursery. When we go on the hunt, all the children come here," Nova says with pride as she pushes past him. He follows her down to another large room with walls of books and tables, where children of all ages are gathered, whispering. There are a couple of adults helping some of the kids read, some draw, and others put parts together.

Violet enters after them and stops in place, staring at one of the newest members of the colony, a woman with long black hair and brown eyes who's standing as still as her. "Jenna, you're alive!" Violet smiles as her eyes fill with tears and steps forward, but Jenna takes a significant step backward.

"You know each other?" Nova asks.

"Why are you here?" Jenna growls. The children become silent.

"I could ask you the same thing." Violet laughs off Jenna's cold response.

"Where's Charlie?"

The smile immediately drops from Violet's face, as well as her color. "Charlie's dead," she says coldly.

"You killed him."

"No, Killian did," Violet says, folding her arms against her chest.

Jenna scoffs. Pain crosses her face. She does her best to wipe it away but fails. "Why is she here?" she asks Nova.

"I had to—"

"Where's Nathan?" Jenna shoots daggers at Violet.

As if Violet were stabbed, she steps back and tries to hide the hurt. "He's with Jack and Clara."

"And where are they?"

"In a hidden shelter like this one."

Jenna crosses the room to stand directly in front of Violet. "You took everything I ever wanted and left me for dead." Without looking away from Violet, she speaks to Nova. "Everywhere this woman goes, destruction follows. Destroy her before she can destroy you and everyone you love."

"Jenna, Charlie wasn't who you—"

Jenna slaps Violet across the face. "I could care less what you have to say." She knocks against Violet's shoulder as she shoves her way through the crowded doorway. Violet hides her face in her hands as she breaks down in tears.

"Everyone is excused," one of the helpers says as they usher the children out of the room. Nova's frozen in shock from the encounter. Alan pulls Nova out of it as he gently pats her arm. "Can we get some privacy?"

"Oh, of...of course." She looks back at Violet, who's crouched into a ball on the floor with Yoojin wrapped around her as she sobs.

Nova helps the children out the door as their families collect them. The rest of her people have already gone to their rooms. She asks one of the men to keep an eye out if they leave, then makes her way through the shelter and finds Jenna pleading with Mathias. "They don't belong here. It'd be best if you kicked them out. We're all in danger if they stay. She's the reason this city was destroyed in the first place."

"We'll take care of it," Mathias says.

"Mathias is no longer in charge. Talk to Nova if you have a complaint," Toby mentions in passing as he and his wife croon over their toddler. Mathias glares up at him.

"Seriously? Can't you see? She's already destroying what you've built," Jenna says as she holds her hand to Mathias's face. What could she possibly see in him?

Nova pushes her negative thoughts to the back of her mind as she crouches next to Jenna. "I think you need to tell me what you know about Violet. Who is she?"

Jenna turns her bitterness towards Nova. "I think I've said enough."

"Who is Charlie and Nathan?"

"Charlie was my fiancé, and Nathan was his son. Our son. She took my world from me." Jenna turns her attention back to Mathias and fawns over the cut on his neck. "I grew up with her. She was a miserable child, and when she saw others' happiness, she made it her mission to destroy it or steal it for herself." She presses a wet cloth to Mathias's wounds. He looks into her eyes with pity. When Mathias looks away to meet Nova's gaze, his compassion turns to disgust.

Nova knows there's no point in discussing this further. Returning to the nursery, she dismisses those standing guard. With a light knock, she peeks in. Violet's still quietly sobbing as Yoojin whispers something in her ear. Alan steps out of the room to speak to her. "Is she okay?" Nova asks him.

"She will be."

"I know this isn't the best time, but after that scene, I need to know what that was all about. Are we really in danger?"

"No, Violet would never hurt innocent people. It's all a misunderstanding." Alan leads her down the hall away from Violet and squats down to sit on the floor. "Violet's been through a lot, but you can trust her. Charlie was a bad guy. Her son, Nathan, feared him, and for good reason. If that woman knew what Charlie had done to Violet, she wouldn't be saying these things. Charlie deserved what he got." Alan becomes quiet for a moment, chewing his bottom lip. "I know she was trying to spare my feelings by hiding the stuff about the maven. Years ago, the maven took all my family from me."

Nova sits down next to him. "I'm so sorry. "

Alan shrugs. "It's in the past. It hurts to see her like this."

"You love her."

"I guess I do. When I discovered she was my best friend's wife, she became instant family. Not many people stand up to Killian and survive, but she held her own." He laughs.

"So you're not in a relationship with her?"

Alan shakes his head somberly. "I wish I had someone. It gets pretty lonely where we come from."

"I know how that feels." Silence falls on them as Alan smiles at her sympathetically. Nova begins to fidget as she tries to think of something to say.

Just as Alan opens his mouth to speak, Violet and Yoojin emerge. Alan and Nova jump to their feet. "I'm sorry for causing a scene earlier," Violet says softly.

"It's fine, don't worry about it."

Violet nods. "I feel like I need to explain."

"Look, I know how Jenna can be, and I saw how her words affected you. You don't have to explain anything unless you want to talk about it."

Violet's eyes glaze over as a weak smile comes to her lips. "Thank you, Nova." Nova smiles reassuringly. Violet gestures to the locked doorway. "So when you went through here, did you find any supplies you could use?"

"Honestly, I didn't look around much once I saw the lab."

"Well, we need fuel for my skyrider since you blew up Alan's," Violet smirks.

"I am so, so sorry, Alan," Nova says.

"It's okay. No one got hurt." Violet raises her eyebrow at Alan. "Well, not badly."

"Will you help us?" Violet asks Nova.

"Okay," Nova says reluctantly as she remembers the strange black stains and prints along the floor and walls. She crouches next to the open panel to pull out the wires. Before finding the wires she needs, Violet places her hand on the scanner, and the heavy door slides open. "Not even Jenna could get this thing to open," Nova says. "You know this place."

"Not really. I have access. There may be more than just a lab, so it's worth exploring." Violet waits, gesturing for Nova to lead the way. Nova looks at their faces.

Yoojin stands with his hands in his coat pockets, a very solemn look on his face. Violet smiles kindly as she rubs her sore shoulder. Alan is watching her with eyebrows raised, and awkwardly looks behind himself as if Nova might be looking past him, but there's no one there. No one from her group is waiting for her.

"Nova, I can tell we're making your people uncomfortable," Violet says. "I'm sure they think we'll turn on you since you guys attacked us. I want to assure you that we aren't holding it against you. You're just trying to survive. So are we. We want to get supplies to carry on with our business. As soon as we find what we need, we'll leave and never bother you again."

With a sigh, Nova turns to the dark corridor and flips the light at her ear back on as she enters. The door closes behind them. The little lamp barely has any effect on the thick darkness. The only sound breaking the deafening silence is their breathing and the sound of their boots clomping on the cement floors. The deeper into the tunnel they go, the shorter Nova's breath becomes. She pulls her oversized sleeves down for comfort and bites at her fingers, regardless of the dirt they've collected on her travels. The tunnel is long but doesn't branch off in any way.

Nova hesitates when she passes the scorch marks on the wall. Violet touches them, recalling the story Killian told about losing his arm. "Alan?" Violet calls. Nova looks at Alan, and he's frowning again. With a short nod, he answers a silent question between them.

"Around this bend is the lab," Nova says with a shaking voice. They follow as she slowly moves on. The blue light spills out towards them. You can see the smeared footprints on the floor, but it looks like ink. Violet walks into the room and rubs at the phantom pain at the nape of her neck as she stares at the open chamber that once held her. The room is much smaller than she remembers. The metal table at the center still stands, and glass crunches under her boots.

Nova shivers as she hugs herself. "Do you know what happened here?"

Violet looks at Nova and smiles. "I'm curious to know what you think happened."

"Jenna said a monster was born here."

Violet sighs but can't help but smile. She walks around the table and touches the chamber door. Her blood still stains the blue gel bed. The glass is caked with dirt. "The person who came from this room looked like a monster. She was weak, bone-thin, with dark hair that hung past her hips." Alan and Yoojin look through the cabinets, but find nothing other than strange medical tools and robes. "Her body and face were covered in so many black veins that you could barely see her natural features," Violet says, touching her arms and face to emphasize. "She was connected to this machine at the neck. It was what kept her alive. She woke up alone, without a memory of how she got here. She had to remove herself from the machine with what little strength she had, and make her way through those dark tunnels with no light and no knowledge of how to escape."

"STOP!" Nova flails her hands and covers her face as uncontrollable squeaks escape her. "Please tell me she found her way out and we aren't going to find a corpse in these halls. I can't...I can't handle it."

Alan and Violet giggle. "I made it out," Violet reassures her." You shouldn't find anyone in these tunnels."

"Violet! Why would you mess with me like that?" Nova yells, but she can't help but smile as they laugh at her expense. "Cruel," Nova pouts, but Violet laughs again.

"I'm sorry, I couldn't help myself," Violet says, standing before her. Nova fans her face as she overheats from the adrenaline pumping through her veins. "Violet O'daire, The Monster." Violet holds out her hand and Nova takes it. "Nice to meet you. I realize we've been very rude and never officially introduced ourselves."

"Nova Whitfield."

Violet releases her hand. Alan stands beside Violet and offers his. "Alan Andrews. Sorry I cut your brother, but not really. He's a dick." Nova laughs but shakes his hand. He looks into her eyes as her heart pounds against her chest. She nervously rubs the back of her neck when he releases her hand.

Yoojin comes up between Violet and Alan. "Yoojin." They clasp hands and quickly release before he returns to what he was doing.

"Can I ask you a question, Nova?" Violet asks with her arms folded.

"Sure."

"Why are you here with us alone? Why didn't you ask someone to come with you when you were nervous about going on your own?

"I can take care of myself."

"It's three against one. Not that I doubt your fighting skills, but these guys are bigger than you. You didn't even tell anyone you were coming in here. Won't they worry about where we went?" Violet asks.

"Honestly, I don't think they'll notice or even care that I'm gone. They won't need me unless the plumbing or electricity goes out."

"Do you think so little of yourself?" Violet frowns.

"I don't think little of myself. I know my worth. I'm smarter and more capable than any of them. In this group, being intelligent and capable means you don't need anyone else." She folds her arms.

"They're intimidated by you," Violet smiles.

"We should adopt her," Alan says as he looks around the dimly lit room. Nova's eyes dart to Alan and a smile reaches from ear to ear. "She obviously doesn't fit in with those people."

"I agree," Violet says, watching Nova's reaction with a grin.

"Thank you, but I can't leave my people behind. I can't just abandon them. They'd be lost."

"Loyalty is admirable, but not when others take advantage of you," Yoojin chimes in.

Nova lets those words sink in. Uncomfortable with all the attention on her personal life, she turns back out to the hallway. The group follows silently. They move past the facility where the junction boxes and the ventilation system are. Avoiding the path marked by Violet's bloody escape, they walk the halls until they find another corridor branching off. The hall connects to multiple empty rooms. They're meant to be stocked with supplies, but the shelves are empty. At the end of the hall, there's another door. Violet scans her hand, but access isn't granted. Nova gets to work on the electric panel. Inside her baggy sweater is a small toolkit with screwdrivers, wire cutters and strippers.

Violet sits next to Nova and watches her work. Alan and Yoojin lean against the walls, quietly chatting about Yoojin's speeder. "It's cool you know how to do this stuff," Violet says.

"I had good teachers and read whatever I could get my hands on."

"Smart. All I could think about when I was younger was boys…well, one boy." Nova and Violet laugh.

"Where's that boy now?"

"Saving the world, I hope."

"There weren't many boys to think about when I was growing up. The ones I knew didn't appreciate it when a girl would inform them that the cylinder wasn't firing because the fuel injector was clogged, which causes an imbalance in the air and fuel mixture."

Violet giggles. "So you're a mechanic, plumber and electrician. Is there anything you can't do?"

"I can't cook."

"Noted," Violet says with a shrug. "So, how did you come to find this place?"

"We saw the smoke and knew another colony had been destroyed. We went through the town once the fires died out to find anything salvageable."

"Did you check the outskirts?"

"Yes, but the houses that weren't destroyed didn't have much other than a small food supply." Violet nods.

"It took us a few days to go through it all, but on our way out of town, we walked through that cemetery and found Jenna. We followed her into the tunnels. She was scared at first, but when Mathias asked her to join us, she accepted. She showed us the tunnels and all the supplies stored in them. We moved in immediately. This place being underground is way safer than where we were. Constantly on the move due to the maven and seekers."

"Ugh, seekers." Nova watches Violet as she rubs her abdomen.

"We've lost many people, no thanks to them. The elderly just weren't able to keep up."

"I'm so sorry. That must've been hard."

"Thank you, it was."

The doors slide open. Everyone gets to their feet. The room echoes with the sound of their breathing as if they're entering a large cave and the air is stale. Violet enters first, and as she moves forward, the ceiling lights up. "Motion sensors," Yoojin says as the others look up in surprise. Violet can see something in the distance as the large room lights up. She presses on, allowing the lights to reveal their secrets. Alan gasps, and Violet looks back with a toothy grin.

"Oh wow." Nova's jaw drops. They're in awe as they behold a large ship. It's smaller than Jack's cargo ship that was docked at sea behind his home but large enough to carry a large group of people at once. The sleek body resembles a creature that lurks in the sea. At the tail are two engines. The boarding hatch is already open, awaiting its passengers. They take their time admiring the craftsmanship as they walk up the ramp.

Inside, the walls have smooth white panels. Nova steps past the others as they marvel at the pristine interior, heading toward the nose of the ship. The cockpit has enough seating for a pilot, copilot and four passengers. A giddy squeal escapes her as she takes a seat. She grabs hold of the controls and drinks in the eye candy, searching the panel full of meters, screens, buttons and knobs. On the left side she locates the electrical control panel. Flipping a toggle and turning one of the knobs lights up the cockpit and corridor. Turning the other knob lights the way to a second level overhead, and another lights the cabin.

Nova hears Alan's excitement as he climbs the stairs, and she's out of the chair instantly, not wanting to be left out of the exploration. On her way up, she notices Yoojin smiling at their excitement but unimpressed, his arms folded. Nova ignores his lack of excitement as she climbs the narrow stairway to a cabin with a small lounging area and table. To the back are built-in bunks for the crew. What has them in awe is the panoramic roof. From the outside, it looks as though it's the same metal as the rest of the ship, but on the inside you have a full view of what would be the sky if the ceiling of this shelter wasn't barring their vision. As Nova takes it all in, tears fill her eyes from the excitement and pure joy of witnessing this beautiful ship.

"Let's start her up," Alan says, grabbing Violet's hands. Violet returns the excitement with a quick nod and races him down the stairs. They all make their way back down and into the cockpit. Alan takes a seat as the pilot, and Nova sits in the copilot's chair. Violet lingers behind the pilot's seat while Yoojin leans against the door frame.

Alan exhales slowly as he caresses the controls. "Any day now, Alan," Violet says impatiently.

"Okay." Alan looks over the many panels and starts flipping switches.

"What are you doing? Stop!" Nova yells.

"I'm trying to find the engine starter."

"You can't just start flipping switches. It's on that panel on the left," Nova says. Alan flips a toggle on the left. "That's radar." He presses a black button on the next panel. "Nope, that's the radio." He moves to the next panel. "No." His hand moves again. "Navigation…no… no. Are you even a pilot?" Nova complains. With his last attempt, he reaches far back and flips a switch. With a sigh, Nova climbs over him to hit the button. She feels him become rigid underneath her and quickly sits back in her copilot seat. They make eye contact for a second, and it feels like electricity in the air.

The engines rev up, groan, and sputter before tiring out. In unison, they groan in disappointment. "Too good to be true," Alan says, folding his arms.

"I can fix it," Nova says, and all eyes are on her. "I like fixing things."

"You think you can get it working?" Violet asks.

"Yes, and I think he can help me." She points to Yoojin.

All eyes turn on him, and he stands straight. "I'm not a mechanic."

"But you know what kind of ship this is, which means you have some knowledge of how it works."

"I think we should press on." Yoojin folds his arms.

"I think we can spare some time. What do you think, Alan?" Violet asks.

"Absolutely!"

"But I already informed them of our arrival this evening," Yoojin counters.

"Why?" Violet asks with a glare.

"So they wouldn't be on guard when they saw two vehicles following behind me," Yoojin says.

Violet folds her arms. "Well, you can inform them of your delay, but I'd appreciate it if you wouldn't give them any detailed information as to why."

"What am I supposed to say?"

"Let them know you wanted to explore the ruins of Safe Haven before returning home."

Yoojin looks to Alan in hopes he'll give him another option. Alan shrugs. "It's not untrue." Yoojin sighs and walks down the corridor and out of the ship.

"Why don't we start work on it tomorrow?" Violet says.

"Yes, please." Nova claps her hands together in anticipation. Violet nods and tries to catch up with Yoojin. Nova looks at Alan with his hands hovering over more buttons. "Don't touch anything," she says as she gets up to follow after them.

"Hey, I'm a good pilot. Self-taught!" Alan says, keeping up with her.

"That explains a lot."

Yoojin and Violet wait at the end of the hall for Alan and Nova to catch up before venturing into the dark hallway. Nova reaches into a pocket inside her loose sweater wrap. She pulls out a small canister and marks the wall with blue paint. "What else you got in there?" Alan asks.

Nova awkwardly folds her sweater tighter. "That's none of your business."

"Oh, I didn't mean…"

Violet snorts with laughter as she watches the awkward interaction.

Chapter 11
KILLIAN

Windows to each test subject are displayed on the wall. Killian is at the desk with Ella at his side. They work silently in unison. Dr. Zane Oric saunters in and rests his hip against the desk nearest Killian. His arms are folded, and his body twists to allow him to watch his patients. Multiple subjects have crumpled to the floor, screaming silently on the screen. Killian's face remains neutral as he watches the patients writhing in pain. The headphones allow him to hear all the happenings on the screen. Zane rests a hand on Killian's shoulder. Killian removes one of the earpieces to hear him. The screaming is so loud that Zane can hear them from the earpiece placed on the desk. "You know you can mute them," he laughs, reaching across the desk to silence their cries.

"It doesn't bother me. If I mute them, I might miss something they say." Killian smiles.

"The transcript is saved in the database to review later."

"Yes, but sometimes the tone in their voice can change the meaning of what's being said."

"You take this position very seriously. I like that about you, Killian. I think it's time for them to have a mental break. Let's schedule a visitor day." He glances over his shoulder at the screens again, and one patient in particular catches his eye. "He seems to be doing well."

"Yes, he's brilliant and empathetic."

"Very unexpected, knowing where he comes from," Zane smirks. Killian looks up at him, matching his grin. "All right, I'll leave you to it. Killian, Ella." He nods to each as a goodbye.

"Doctor," Ella responds with a bow of her head, returning to her work.

Zane saunters out of the room with his hands in the pockets of his white coat and whistling a tune. The duo works away, collecting data and notes on each patient. Each movement. Each interaction, verbal and physical. Even the looks they give others when their backs are turned. All of it is taken note of. Ella interrupts her task as her hands hover over the keys. "Killian, you have a patient waiting."

"Thank you, Ella." Killian stands up and stretches his arms overhead. He crosses the small room. Pressing his hand against the wall, a hidden closet slides open, allowing him to collect his white coat.

"Would you like assistance?"

"No, continue your work here. Get them ready for the visit."

"Yes, doctor."

Killian leaves the room, glancing back at the subjects before closing the door. Walking down the sterile halls, he flips his wrist. His mechanical arm activates a holographic screen the size of his palm. He scrolls through the information about the patient, pausing at the entrance of the patient's room. With a sigh, he flicks his wrist, deactivating it. "Mr. Nox, it's a pleasure to see you again, though I wish it weren't under these circumstances," he says upon entering.

"Dr. Grey. It's been a while."

"It has." Killian gets to work, activating screens on the wall that scan the patient, allowing him to see Mr. Nox's vitals.

"I wanted to thank you."

"Oh?"

"You've kept your distance from my daughter, allowing her to focus on her career. I've never seen her so dedicated to her work." Killian smiles in response. "I also wanted to thank you for being discreet regarding my health. I haven't told my family about my condition and don't wish to alarm them."

"I'm sorry if I'm overstepping my boundaries, but your condition hasn't improved with treatment. In fact, it's become worse. The cosmetic manipulation will hide it well, but I feel it's necessary to inform your family of your impending...departure. Speaking from experience, it's hard to lose a family member suddenly." Killian says it solemnly.

"Yes, I understand. I've tried to tell my wife several times. It's harder than I expected it to be…to let go."

Killian nods as he prepares the table for the cosmetic restructure. "If it'd be easier on you, we could meet with you and your family to discuss your health. Dr. Oric can do most of the talking for you. It's your choice, of course."

"Thank you, I'll think about it."

Killian nods again and invites Mr. Nox to lie down. He does so with a deep breath. Killian begins the procedure.

Chapter 12

PIPER

The door opens, and billows of steam spill out. Piper steps out into the hallway, wiping the sweat from her brow. Her skin is pink from the heat, and steam rises off her. Her partner Jasper Price hops out of his room laughing, trapping her in his arms as he lifts her off the floor and swings her around. She can't help but laugh with him. He sets her down and wraps his arm over her shoulders, escorting her down the hall. It's been almost three months, and Piper's become accustomed to Jasper's excessive physical contact. She takes a deep breath as he wipes damp hair away from her face. Though she has no interest in a relationship with this compulsive flirt, she's enjoyed how he makes her feel that no one else exists in the world. That is, until someone else gives him more attention.

Others finish their trials and begin to fill the hall. Jesse, a tall thin girl with a short pixie cut, ends her trial and confidently pulls him away. Piper snickers as she watches him go. She's found that Jasper is not known for self-control. When it comes to people of the opposite sex, he's there no matter what. Their body shape, skin color, height or personality doesn't matter. If they're interested in him, he has an interest in them. Piper looks at it as commendable. She walks on with a roll of her eyes as Jesse fawns over Jasper, him melting in her hands.

One of the doors swings open, and Piper sidesteps as one of the new girls falls out of the room, screaming in pain, gripping her leg. Piper only gets a glimpse of the charred nub that once was her foot before Jasper reclaims her, using his hand as a blinder to shield her from seeing the grotesque scene. Piper pulls his hand away, hearing the blood-curdling scream. The girl's companion stands at her side with horror on his face, hands over his ears. His face pales as he turns away, and the contents of his stomach splatter on the floor.

Jasper drags her away, avoiding the commotion she can't resist, but she looks back. The girl's smoking leg, reeking of cooked meat, makes her sick to her stomach. She watches as Gareth runs around the corner, ripping the sleeve of his suit off and soaking it in the nearest drinking fountain. Quickly running over to her and dropping to his knees, he slides to a stop at her side. He tries to calm her but can't be heard over her screaming. He wrings out the sleeve over her leg, and at first she screams louder, but then faints. Her leg steams and drips with blood and char. He attempts to peel the suit from her leg but struggles without lifting the skin with it.

Piper gags and Jasper attempts to drag her away again. She shoves him away as she gags again, but this time the contents of her stomach come back to greet her. She crouches on the floor, heaving and wiping her mouth on her sleeve. She looks up to see Gareth staring at her from under a furrowed brow. It feels like he's boring holes into her soul before he finally looks back at the girl's leg and begins peeling again. A crowd is forming now, and Jasper grabs Piper around the waist, pulling her to her feet and dragging her back to the dormitory.

He pulls her into the communal bathroom. Leaving her on the floor crumpled in on herself, she cries, unable to remove the images and smells of burnt flesh from her mind. He turns on one of the showers, testing the water to ensure it's on the cooler side. Piper whimpers as he drags her back to her feet and pulls her under the running water. She's in shock and doesn't notice. He unzips her suit and peels it off her body. She comes back to reality when he kisses her wet forehead. Turning away from him, she shivers, though she doesn't feel the temperature. He turns on the shower next to her, and she quickly glances at him. He's removed his clothes and watches her as he soaks his blonde chin-length hair. The look of concern is written all over his face. She quickly rinses her body and mouth before turning off the shower. After being blown dry, she uses her wet suit to cover herself as she grabs fresh clothes on her way into the girls' side of the dormitory.

Piper gets dressed in the same white loose-fit drawstring pants and a wrap top. Peeling the thin blankets back, she climbs into her bunk and pulls the blankets overhead. Her hair soaks the pillow. Fear and regret fill her with despair. She hears the rest of the group file in to take showers. Some of them are talking, but she doesn't listen to what's said. She feels someone approach her and rests a hand on her hip. The heat of their hand seeps into her skin. She holds as still as possible, trying to keep a steady breath. When they finally leave, she cries and doesn't stop until she feels herself drifting off.

She is jolted back into existence when the announcement for their evening meal rings out over the speakers. At first she doesn't move, but someone sits down at the end of her bed, and she peeks out from under the blanket. A girl is sitting there with one knee pulled to her chest, the other dangling off the bed. Over the past few months, she has kept to herself but has memorized most of the girls' names, except for this one. She's seen her before, but the girl keeps to herself for the most part. Her curly hair always pulled into a messy bun, held together with elastic from one of the mattress covers she mutilated. Ginger red curls that can't be contained frame her heavily freckled face. She looks over at Piper with her beautiful doe eyes that match her hair color. She doesn't smile but looks away and pats Piper's leg. "Don't worry. You seem to have a good head on your shoulders. Even if you were partnered with the most unreliable companion in the group."

"Pardon?"

"The trials are going to get hard. Choose your company wisely. Plenty of people are waiting for an opportunity to screw you over," she says while eyeing one of the other girls walking by. The one walking rolls her eyes and continues on to her meal. "I'm Reese."

"Piper," she says from under her blanket.

"You should eat while you can."

"I'm not hungry."

"You will be." She pushes herself up off the bed. "Keep your head down, get through your trials, and you'll be fine."

"Thanks?"

Reese looks back at her with a smirk and then walks out of the nearly empty room. Piper drops her head back on her pillow and pulls the blanket back overhead. The shuffling feet fade down the hall. When she's alone, she throws her blanket off with a huff. With her limbs splayed out, she takes a deep breath and sighs. Sitting up, she puts her bare feet on the cold cement and rests her face in her hands. She groans as she tries to rub the images out of her eyes.

"Are you not going to eat?" a deeper voice asks. Piper all but jumps out of her skin. "Sorry, I didn't mean to scare you," he says, trying not to let a smile take over his lips but failing. Piper peeks through her fingers to see Gareth leaning on the bathroom doorframe with his arms folded. Even though he smiles, he seems to have a permanent frown. His dark hair, contrasting his white robes, is wet from showering, and it falls in front of his eyes, giving him a menacing look. This is his first time addressing her directly. Piper doesn't respond, paralyzed by the thought of being alone with a person who's only shown hostility since her arrival. "Are you coming to eat?"

"How can you eat after that?" Piper says into her hands.

"I do what I need to do. To survive. To go home." She looks up at him as he pulls himself away from the wall, stuffing his hands in his pockets and slowly walking out of the room.

With a sigh, she reasons out loud to herself, "For Aunt Josephine." She slowly gets to her feet and walks out of the room and into the cafeteria. As if on autopilot, she grabs a tray of food, finds the table with the least number of people, and begins eating without seeing or tasting anything. Suddenly the room becomes silent. Piper looks up to see two men in white coats enter the room. All eyes are on them. She looks around the room at the wide eyes, watching them approach. Gareth is the only one giving them a menacing look.

"Good evening," one of them says to the group. "You may know me already, but for those that don't, I'm Dr. Oric, and this is my assistant Dr. Grey. You're doing a great job with your trials. I know they can be challenging." He clasps his hands in front of his chest and gives what looks like a genuine smile. "Rest assured, those who have received injuries are being well taken care of, and will return shortly. Or they won't." His grin seems to widen from ear to ear. Dr. Oric's mannerisms brings chills down her spine. His assistant remains silent and stoic.

"Tomorrow you'll have a day of rest. You'll be allowed visitors the entire day. I hope you have a pleasant one." Piper has butterflies at the thought of seeing Aunt Josephine. Dr. Oric clasps his hands behind his back and quickly turns away, his white coat flaring like a cape. Dr. Grey glances beyond Piper before turning away to follow Dr. Oric out. Piper looks behind her to see what had caught his eye. The only thing out of the ordinary is how Gareth seems to be seething in his seat.

This is the first visitor day, a privilege Piper wasn't aware she would have. She sleeps very little. The anticipation of seeing her aunt, and the nightmare images that haunt her whenever she closes her eyes, holds her sleep hostage. She rolls onto her side, making the bedframe squeak. The only other sound in the room is deep breathing and quiet snoring. It's not unusual for her to be the first awake, but she had hoped she would sleep in so she'd look well-rested for Aunt Josephine.

She yanks the blanket off. The cold cement floor has become a comfort, the only thing she can count on around here to stay consistent. Entering the communal bathroom, she notices the doorway to the male's domain is open. Quiet as a mouse, she peeks her head in. There's plenty of snoring but no movement. Most of them have limbs hanging off the bunks, as if they're too small to contain their bodies. No one seems to be up yet, so she proceeds as quietly as possible to get changed. The provided garments aren't the standard skin-tight suit but another set of loose-fitting linen items. A white three-quarter-sleeve wrap tunic, drawstring pants, and charcoal-colored robe with pockets. It was very comfortable, though the wrap was loose, allowing the neckline to plunge deeper than she'd prefer.

After folding her sleepwear neatly, she goes to the sink to brush her teeth. Looking in the mirror, she sighs. As she suspected, she has dark circles under her chocolate brown eyes. She'd never found the need to scrutinize her looks, but she wants to ensure Aunt Josephine won't worry when they meet again. She splashes her face with cold water until it bites at her skin.

Now finished with her hygienic routine and with nothing to do, she sits on the bench in front of the lockers. Pulling her knees up to her chest, she wraps her arms around them and begins picking at her fingers. The silence is starting to drive her mad. Piper's heart seems to gain speed the longer she sits. Trying to distract herself, she braids her hair, but the little wisps framing her face refuse to cooperate.

Her knees had begun to shake restlessly when someone finally enters the room. When she sees it's Gareth, it feels like all her organs shut down at once. Gareth's permanent frown seems even more profound. His expression doesn't change when he sees her sitting there alone. Ignoring her, he goes to the shower and turns on the water. Piper watches him as he removes his shirt. She expected him to be on the scrawny side, but that isn't the case. She's surprised to see a toned body beneath the loose clothing. Gareth looks over at her as he throws his shirt in her direction, his dark hair falling over his eyes. Her complexion turns beet red when she realizes she's staring, and she slowly turns her entire body in the opposite direction. She hears another garment drop near her. Facing the wall, she holds her legs tight to her body as she drags her eyes along the grout lines between each tile as if it's the most exciting thing she's ever seen.

More people begin to stir, and Reese is the next to come in. Piper watches her as she looks Gareth up and down before winking at Piper with a toothy grin before joining him in the showers. One of the shower heads turns off, and she hears footsteps coming toward her. They continue past her and she sees Gareth collecting his clothes. She watches as the many muscles in his glistening back tense with the slightest movement. He glances over his shoulder, catching her once more. She turns her body away to give him privacy, rubbing her hands over her face to remove the embarrassment.

"Are you feeling better?" A dripping Reese slides onto the bench next to her.

"Not really. I didn't sleep well."

"I can tell, you look like trash."

Piper looks up at her, dropping her hands. "Thanks…" she laughs when she sees the grin on Reese's face. She drops her eyes once more when she realizes Reese is still naked.

"What are friends for?"

"Is that what we are?"

"If that's what you want. You seem like you need a friend. People might think you're unapproachably mean and scary if you're always alone." She emphasizes the last word by leaning towards Piper with her fingers splayed out like claws.

"You're one to talk," another girl says as she enters the room. Piper recalls that her name is Adah. Her cropped kinky brown hair frames her face well, drawing attention to her contrasting teal-blue eyes and full lips. Piper decides she's the most beautiful and intimidating of all the girls.

Reese's face screws up as she turns her attention to Adah. Adah rolls her eyes as she continues her stride to the showers. Reese turns her attention back to Piper and shakes her head as if she always gets that reaction. She smiles and gets up, grabbing her clothes. After pulling her pants on, she sits back down next to Piper as she slips into her wrap. "We can be friends, right?"

"Of course." Piper smiles.

An arm slides over her shoulders and around her neck, resting its hand on her chest. She looks down at the hand. The fingertips tuck themselves just inside the collar of her tunic. Only one person would be so bold as to rest their hand so dangerously close to her breast. His skin warms her chest, and she revels in the warmth for a moment before grabbing his pinky finger and dragging it back to her shoulder. Looking over the opposite shoulder, she smiles into his grinning face. "Good morning, Price."

"Morning, doll. Did you sleep well?" She shrugs, growing tired of the question when they know the answer based on her looks. "Well, sleep or not, you still look gorgeous," he says as he runs his fingers through her hair, sending a tingle down her spine. Reese has a knowing smile as she looks back and forth between them.

"So, where do you come from?" Piper asks Reese, ignoring Jasper's flattery.

"You can't tell by my grease-stained hands?" Reese rubs at her blackened fingertips. "Mechanical Advancement."

"Hey, Level 4 comrades!" Jasper announces, reaching around Piper to bump fists. Reese reciprocates with a grin. "You must be in transportation. I had the pleasure of being in the biomechatronic department."

"If it was such a pleasure, why did you leave it for this?"

"Who wouldn't want to upgrade to a higher society?" Jasper reveals a toothy grin.

Reese rolls her eyes. "What about you?" she asks Piper.

"Textiles," Piper says.

"Oh, from a level above," Reese purrs. "What's it like?"

"It's dark, and I didn't know how dirty it was until I left. I didn't know lights could be so bright. I've never seen daylight, but I assume it's like the lighting here."

"This is nothing like daylight," a voice chimes in from behind them. They all turn. Gareth stands, looking down at them with furrowed brows and arms folded across his chest. His raven hair is still wet and slicked back. For the first time, Piper notices that his eyes aren't as dark as she thought, but silver with flecks of gold. "Nothing compares to the warmth of the sun." Jasper snickers at that, facing away from Gareth once more.

"What level are you from, Gareth?" Reese asks, staring up at him with the corner of her mouth turned up.

Piper waits for his answer but he shifts his weight from foot to foot under scrutiny. "Why do you want to know?"

Reese climbs off the bench to stand in front of him. He stands his ground, even though she's so close to him. Piper watches as he looks into her eyes while she speaks. "You speak as if you've seen the sun. Where are you from?" she repeats, matching his stance with folded arms. Looking from his eyes to his full lips, she waits for an answer, biting her bottom lip in anticipation.

Jasper turns his attention back to Gareth to hurry him along. Gareth looks down at Reese's lips and quickly looks at Piper. To Jasper. Back to Piper. His mouth opens as if to speak, but an announcement suddenly begins. "*It is Visitor Day. Please exit the main hall and follow the floor-lit path to the lobby. Your name will be announced when your visitor arrives. If you don't have a visitor, feel free to walk the grounds.*"

Jasper is pulling Piper to her feet before Gareth can utter a word. She glances back at Gareth as she's dragged to the exit. He seems to ooze gloom as he shoves his hands into his robe pockets, staring down at the spot where she once sat.

As they gather in the main hallway, a doorway she'd never noticed before is open, and everyone files into a large room with a very tall ceiling. Panels that make it feel bright and warm, and trees with long trunks varying in height, their perfectly round tops reaching for the ceiling, are peppered throughout the room. Lounge chairs made of clear plastic are limited, but it's not long anyway before names are being called. A brown breakfast bar had been provided, though most avoid it.

Before too long, the room becomes quieter. Piper watches as one after another fellow...*what would you call them*, she wonders. She pulls her legs in and wraps her arms around them. Fellow testee? Test subject? She shakes her head in disgust. They aren't friends. Associates? Comrades? What if Aunt Josephine doesn't come? What if she's still angry? What if she's too sick? Is she getting the treatment she needs? Whom could she talk to? How can she find out? No, she'll come. She distracts herself by eating the block of nutrients provided. It's dry and bland. She watches as another person gets called, and they disappear behind swinging wooden doors.

Piper looks around the room. There's only one person left besides herself, Gareth. He sits with his elbows on his knees, his hands clench into fists in his raven-black hair, then sits up and leans back, resting his head on the chair. Gone is the glare she thought permanent. In its place was the look of grief. Wiping his blotchy red face with his sleeve, he stares up at the ceiling and breathes. Before she can think, she's up and walking towards him. He notices her approaching from the corner of his eye. In the blink of an eye, his sour expression returns. She hesitates before sitting down next to him. The silence between them seems to drag as she watches him glare up at the ceiling, occasionally peeking at her through the corner of his eye. He hides his hands in his robe pockets.

"Are you okay?"

"I'm fine." His voice cracks and he clears his throat. "Why do you ask?"

"It looked like you were upset about something."

"I was expecting… I was hoping someone would come. I thought for sure my cousin, at least, because we're close. It's fine." He presses his lips together to silence himself.

"I'm sorry," Piper says, pulling her legs back to her chest.

"Who are you waiting for?"

"My aunt, but we got in a fight before I left. We never fight. She's also sick, so she might not be able to come. They said she'd get the care she needs, so it should be okay." She stares at her knees. Her throat tightens, and she swallows the knot lodged there.

Gareth opens his mouth to speak but is interrupted by an announcement. "*Gareth Nox. Please come to the exit to greet your guest.*" His eyes widen as he straightens his posture, and his mouth hangs agape. Hopping out of his chair, he walks to the exit but then stops and turns. He looks at Piper and then at the door. She doesn't know what he sees, but it must be pathetic, because he walks back to her and holds out his hand. "Come with me. You don't have to be alone."

Piper looks at his hand and the sincerity in his eyes. "What if she comes and I miss the call?"

Gareth tilts his head. "It's been two hours. She would've been here long ago if you were as close as you say. This place has a way of denying you the things you need most." Her eyes prickle. Placing her hand in his, she is pulled to her feet and they exit together.

She can see people walking amongst foliage outside through a long hallway of windows. True light. He pulls on her as she slows, distracted by the new scenery. They reach the front desk, and a man there instructs them that his visitor is at the entrance. They move towards the door, and it slides open. They both cover their eyes from the light. Her hand is released, and she steps out onto a wooden patio. It feels warm compared to the cold cement inside. She spins around as she takes a deep breath. The air is thick with mist. The sky is gray and overcast, but she doesn't mind. She can finally breathe and feel the fresh air. In the distance is heard a rumbling roar that fizzles in and out.

Piper steps off the stairs and her feet sink into the damp, cool sand. She stops next to Gareth and notices his hands are balled into fists. The assistant who accompanied Dr. Oric is leaning against a sleek white vehicle that hovers above the ground. His hands are in his pockets as he observes Gareth. His brown hair is slicked back, and his perfectly trimmed beard gives him a stern look. His eyes are so dark brown that you can't tell where the iris stops and the pupil begins. He is tall, lean and handsome. She notices he and Gareth are similar in height now that he's standing straight with his head high.

"What are you doing here?" Gareth growls.

"I thought you might like some company this time."

"I don't need your company," he grumbles, shoving his fists into his pockets and looking off indifferently. Piper feels the tension and moves in close beside Gareth.

"I can see that," he smirks as he looks Piper up and down. "Dr. Killian Grey." He holds out his hand, but Gareth pulls his hands out of his pocket and adjusts his position to obstruct the doctor's view. Piper frowns as her extended hand is bumped away from his body.

"If you aren't going to help me, then leave. I don't need company from a bastard like you."

"Ouch," the doctor frowns, apparently not fazed by Gareth's words. "Walk with me." He flicks his fingers in the direction that he begins walking.

Gareth looks over his shoulder at Piper before grabbing her hand again and pulling her behind him. Piper notices the others watching them as they attempt to catch up with Dr. Grey. Reese catches her eye with a tilt and a questioning look as she speaks with her guest. Piper shrugs. Reese's eyes seem to linger on Gareth before turning her full attention to her guest.

Piper tugs on Gareth's hand. "Why are we following him if we don't want his company?"

"He's supposed to be my cousin's friend. She trusts him." Gareth sighs.

"Why is he a bastard?"

"Because he let Dr. Oric put me in here, knowing full-well who I am and what these trials would be like."

"Who are you?" Piper asks curiously.

"Not now." Gareth shakes his head. They catch up with Dr. Grey's long strides. "What do you have to say, Killian?"

Piper doesn't hear anything further as she's released and walks past both of them toward the most beautiful thing she's ever seen. Her long brown hair whips around her face with the breeze. She holds her hair back to watch dark gray water roll and crash onto the sand with a rumbling roar. Piper's drawn to the water as she walks to the edge, where the water stops and begins to recede. Another wave crashes against the beach and rushes towards her feet. She gasps as the cold water runs past her, bubbling and pushing at her ankles. She giggles as the water pulls away from her, drawing the sand around her feet, causing her to feel like she's sinking. She loses her balance and falls onto the damp sand, landing on her bottom. The laughter bubbles out of her as she turns her hands repeatedly to look at the sand. Another wave crashes onto the earth, and she squeals as arms reach under her shoulders, pulling her to her feet just as the water rushes her again.

Piper turns with a larger grin, giggling. She looks up at Gareth's serious face and can't help but squeal as the biting water splashes around their legs. She grabs his sturdy arms as her head tilts back with laughter. Though she holds tight, the water dragging at her ankles pulls her off-balance. His hand catches her lower back and pulls her to him to stabilize her. She's laughing so hard that tears are welling up in her eyes. Looking up at him through her tears and laughter, she notices the subtle humor softening his features. Her giggling dissolves as his gaze into her eyes lasts longer than expected. He lowers his head briefly to break eye contact.

Before another wave can attempt to drag them in, Gareth swiftly bends down, wrapping his arms around her legs, and lifts her to hang over his shoulder. Piper grunts from the pressure in her gut. She tries to pull away, but there's no escape unless risking a fall into the wet sand. Gareth carries her back to Dr. Grey and sets her down. The doctor watches them curiously with a tilt of his head. Piper smiles awkwardly, then looks away. Gareth grabs hold of her hand with both of his behind his back before returning his attention. She tries to pull away, but his grip tightens. She sighs and draws shapes in the sand with her toes as they talk. "So, doc, you were saying?" he asks Dr. Grey.

"Your parents have been informed of your transfer, but they've been instructed not to discuss your whereabouts with anyone outside your immediate family."

"Why?" he growls, tightening his grip on Piper's hand. She squeezes his hand in return, and his grip loosens.

"We know how close you are with Eustacia. She can't be trusted not to have another bout of rebelliousness. Dr. Oric doesn't want this study interrupted."

"What exactly are you studying? What are these trials?" Piper asks.

"Psychology."

"I thought these trials were for gaining strength and stuff. Why did we get that serum?"

"The serum was to put you out. The trials test and train your cognitive processing and social behavior. We can see how individuals interact and work together by putting you in different trials with a companion. He's not getting the desired results, so things will change soon."

"People are getting hurt," Piper retorts. "What kind of results is he looking for?"

"I don't know, I'm sorry," he says sympathetically.

"These changes, will they be for the better or worse?" Gareth asks. Dr. Grey just shakes his head slowly in response. "Why are you telling us this?"

"I'm informing you because I know Eustacia wouldn't want you in the dark."

"You care about her," Gareth says matter-of-factly. Dr. Grey doesn't confirm or deny. "If you care about her, then you know she'll be hurt if you keep this from her."

Dr. Grey steps close and leans in as if to kiss his cheek. Gareth pushes Piper back with one hand. "By keeping silent, I'm protecting her. If you want to protect the ones you love…" The doctor looks into Piper's eyes as he continues. "You must play your part."

He is about to step back, but Gareth grabs him by the lapel of his jacket. "Help us out of this hell!"

The doctor isn't startled by Gareth's rough handling. "You got yourself into this mess." Calmly he takes hold of Gareth's fists and forcefully removes his grip from his coat.

"Please," Gareth's voice cracks. The agony in his voice sends pain through her chest.

"I'll do what I can. For now, play your part." He promptly turns his back on them as he adjusts his coat.

"Wait! My aunt didn't visit me today. Is she getting the treatment she needs?"

"What's her name?"

"Josephine Murray. They promised to give her the treatment we couldn't afford and relocate her to Level 8."

"I'll look into it," Killian says with a partial glance back at her before walking away.

As he watches the doctor leave, Gareth is as still as a statue, his arms limp at his sides. As soon as Killian's out of sight, a strangled cry escapes him as he grabs fistfuls of his hair, his posture collapsing in on itself. His legs dig into the sand. It looks as though he'll sink into the earth under the weight of his grief. Piper's lip quivers. His agony is so palpable that his pain pools with hers, and she can't stop the tears that fall down her cheeks.

Piper crouches next to him and rests her hand on his. Gareth's breath catches as if he'd forgotten she was there. Under her palm, she feels his grip on his hair loosen and fall away. Beads of water have collected on his hair from the heavy mist. She pets his feather-soft hair a couple of times and pats his back. His hands rest in the sand, palms up. The sleeves of his robe are rolled up to his elbows. She notices on one of his arms that there are stripes on his skin of a lighter tone than the rest of his forearm. Unconsciously she traces the lines on his arm with her finger. His fingers flinch at her touch. "What happened here?"

"Nothing happened. They're just tan lines," he says, a dejected smirk crossing his face. He adjusts his position to face her, sitting cross-legged. Swiping his hands together, he dusts the sand off before resting his chin in his palm, propping his elbow on one knee. His other wrist is limp on the opposite knee. He looks over her face as if searching for something with his glossy eyes.

"How did you get them?" Piper asks with concern.

A slow smile creeps onto his face. "One day, you'll see the sun."

Piper returns his smile. "What is this then?" She tilts her face to the sky and holds her palms up.

"Where do you think you are right now?"

"Outside," she says with her eyes closed.

"'Outside' as in outside of the Development?"

"Aren't we?" She looks back at him with a squint.

"No," he chuckles. "This is just an imitation. An artificial beach. We're on the second or third floor, which is why you can't see the sun. The storm shield conceals everything below level 7.

"Storm shield?"

"As much as Price brags about how smart you are, I would've expected you to know more about the place you've lived your entire life." His grin becomes wide as he tilts his head.

Piper looks at him straight on without a hint of humor in her eyes. The flame is ignited. "And as sad and pathetic as you were moments ago, you sure recovered quickly." She gets to her feet so fast that sand flies in every direction.

Gareth laughs. "What did I say?" he sputters as sand flies into his mouth.

"I should have left you to wallow in your pity," Piper grumbles as she storms off.

"Piper, come on!" She almost turns to look at him hearing him say her name for the first time, but she shakes it off, continuing her tramping. "Piper," he says earnestly. Gareth catches up and yanks her back to him. Her hands tangle in his robe. She feels the heat of his hand on her cheek, and before she can blink, his soft full lips are on hers. Her eyes widen, and she freezes. Before she can react, he's pulling away. "Thank you."

"You're welcome," she says under her breath, unable to take her eyes from those lips still so close. Those lips curl into a teasing smile. Piper frowns, turning her back on him promptly. She takes a moment to shake whatever just happened off into the sand before storming off again, but the fire that was once raging has fizzled out, and she feels clumsy.

Chapter 13

GARETH

Piper is acting chattier with Reese and Jasper than she ever has before. It's good that she feels more comfortable and gets along with others, Gareth thinks, but her choice of friends is a cause for concern. He watches Piper laugh at something Jasper says, and he can't help but bristle at the thought of them becoming close. She laughs again with her head thrown back.

Gareth turns his attention back to his food. He feels the heat rising from his chest into his neck and cheeks. Her laughter summons the memory he's been trying to bury all day. That laughter, her smile, the glisten in her eyes; he couldn't help it. Of course, to avoid his feelings, he deflects by teasing her, but his desire only burns hotter when she gets angry. He unconsciously touches his thumb to his lips as he reminisces. At one point, he glances at Piper and catches her watching him. It's as if a bolt of electricity has run through him. She quickly looks away, but the flush on her neck and cheeks tells him she knows what he's thinking. Or is she thinking about it herself?

Looking down at his food, he fights the urge to bang his knuckles against his forehead like he had after she turned from his kiss and walked away...or rather, stumbled away. She looked as unsteady and lightheaded as he felt at that moment, though he couldn't help but feel like he'd made a colossal mistake. He followed her into this mess. He should stay away from her and focus on finding a way out of here.

Laughing to himself, he wonders how his feelings can change so quickly. At first he blamed her for getting stuck here, but it'd been a month now and he knew it was all his doing. If he'd gone to the ball like he was supposed to, he wouldn't be in this mess, but he wouldn't have met her either. Kissing her may have opened another can of worms. If she keeps avoiding him, then perhaps it'll be forgotten, and that'll be the end of it. Another glance her way and she's draped her hair around her like a curtain as she converses enthusiastically. Reese catches his eye, and a slight smile crosses her face as she keeps eye contact with him. He nods in acknowledgment and focuses on finishing his food.

Killian was serious when he said changes would be made, though not the changes he'd expected. There's now a common area with music, books and simple games available. The ceiling light panels are hexagon-shaped. How they can change these structures with cement walls so quickly baffles him. Maybe it's not out of the ordinary, knowing the types of machines level 4 has produced. As everyone gathers in the new recreation room, it becomes crowded. It becomes loud, too loud. Gareth takes this time to get to bed early. He can fall asleep before the others begin snoring. Maybe he can catch up on sleep. He doesn't bother changing his clothes before climbing into his bunk.

"Gareth," a voice whispers in his ear later. He groans and frowns. The warm touch on his hand stirs him. "Gareth," they whisper again.

His eyes flash open when he recognizes the voice. Seeing the shape of a girl with long wavy hair kneeling next to him, he asks, "What? What happened?" He sits up, hitting his head on the top bunk. Falling back on his pillow, he rubs at the now throbbing spot. She laughs through her nose at his expense. "What are you doing in he—"

Her hands cover his mouth to silence him. "Shh, you might wake someone up," she says as she looks around at the others snoring away.

Gareth pulls her soft hand away. "Piper, why are you here?" he whispers back.

"I couldn't sleep."

He rubs his hands over his face in exasperation. "You couldn't sleep, so you decided to rob me of mine? Are you punishing me?"

"I woke you up because I need to ask you a question. It's your fault I can't sleep, so yes, this is punishment."

Someone groans as they roll over, and Piper gasps as she quickly gets to her feet. At that moment, Gareth reaches for her, pulling her onto the bunk with him. They make more noise than he intended to, but at least she wouldn't be causing a scene in the boys' dorms. They hold their breath as they wait for the other's breathing to settle. They barely fit on the small bed, so he pulls her in close back to his chest. They both let out their breath and feel each other relax.

"What did you need to ask me that couldn't wait until morning?" he says into her hair, keeping his arm wrapped around her middle.

"I didn't want to ask with an audience."

"Hurry up with it so I can get back to sleep." He moves her hair out of his face and pulls her closer, her back pressing against his body, reveling in the warmth. His mind races with thoughts of how little separates them from being skin to skin. He tries to shove them away.

She audibly swallows before speaking. "Why did you thank me?" She pauses for an answer, but he doesn't know how to answer immediately, so she continues in a bitter tone, "Were you thanking me for the kiss you stole? Were you teasing me again? Or were you thanking me for trying to comfort you? If that's the case, that's a poor way of showing it. You can't just make someone feel like an idiot and then kiss them and think that's okay. You should—"

"Are you going to let me answer or just keep rambling?" Gareth interrupts. She becomes silent, and he hopes she can't hear or feel the drumming in his chest that seems to get louder in the silence. "I'm sorry I kissed you."

"You're sorry?" she says too loudly.

He clasps his hand over her mouth. "Yes, I'm sorry. I didn't mean to make you uncomfortable. I didn't think you'd lose sleep over it."

Her mouth moves under his fingers, so he puts his arm back around her waist. "You're sorry you kissed me," she confirms. "Why did you even kiss me in the first place?"

Gareth tries to bury his face in her hair. "I couldn't help it…" he says, turning his face into his pillow.

"Why not?"

"Because you drive me insane," he says in frustration.

"I don't understand," she replies with a pout.

"Me neither." He lets out a breath.

"Gareth, please."

Propping himself onto his elbow, the shifting weight causes her to roll towards him. They now face each other, but he can barely see her features. A light shining from the bathroom reflects off her eyes. "I already apologized. What do you want me to say? You want me to tell you how I couldn't take my eyes off you when I first saw you? How I got stuck in this hellhole because I followed you like Alice after that damn rabbit? How I want to tear Jasper into pieces every time he hangs all over you? How I can't stand the way he peels off your clothes with his eyes? Or how, more than anything, I hate the way you smile at him? The rage I feel when you laugh with him? You don't want to hear the rest of my thoughts, so what exactly do you want from me?"

Piper's breaths are fast and shallow as she stares at him from his pillow. Gareth searches her eyes, waiting for some response. "I'm your…white rabbit?" she finally says in a quiet voice, the sarcasm already starting to spread across her face.

"Yes," he groans.

"And so that makes you Alice?" The corner of her mouth curls up.

Gareth lets out a breath and rolls onto his back. "I'm glad you find this humorous," he says, hiding his face in the crook of his elbow.

Piper takes a deep breath and lets it out. "Where do you come from, Alice?" she asks, propping her head up so she can see him and smiling down at him.

"Upper levels."

"Which one?"

He peeks out from under his arm before answering. "Level 9," he whispers almost inaudibly.

Her eyes widen. "Why would you come down here?"

"I was bored."

"You saw me somewhere, like Alice did the white rabbit, and followed me here," she clarifies.

"I followed the rabbit to the hole but was shoved into it by the Mad Hatter."

"Dr. Grey?"

"No, he's more like the Cheshire Cat in this story. Dr. Oric is the Mad Hatter, or maybe he's the Queen of Hearts. He's the director of Levels 2 and 3. He controls who comes and goes. He doesn't like uninvited guests."

"Curiouser and curiouser."

"Curiosity killed the cat. Did I answer your questions to your satisfaction? Can I go back to sleep now?"

She lays her head back down on the edge of his pillow. With both lying on their backs, there's no room for movement without the possibility of falling to the cold floor. "When I first saw you, I thought you hated me."

"For a little while, I blamed you for getting me locked in here. Now I know I was wrong," he adds quickly before she can say anything. "Sorry if I made you uncomfortable."

"It's okay." Gareth and Piper share the pillow, bringing their heads close together. They become quiet, realizing how close they are to each other.

"Are you going to kiss now? I thought you didn't come here to play, Piper!" a voice calls from above. Gareth exhales loudly, turning back to stare at the bunk above him. Jasper's head pops into view, hanging upside down from his bunk. His head blocks the light from the restrooms, making his dangling blonde hair glow but his face all shadow. You can hear the laughter in his voice. "It's okay, guys. I only want to watch."

Piper hides behind her hands. "Go back to sleep, Price."

"If you don't want to kiss her, I'll gladly take your place. She has the softest lips. Any excuse to kiss them again." Though his face is shadowed, you can see the shine of his teeth when he grins. "Are you jealous you weren't the first to steal a kiss?"

Piper groans in embarrassment. "You should go back to bed," Gareth says, nudging her. She takes his advice, taking the warmth with her.

"It's not gentleman-like to kick a woman out of your bed, Gareth. Do you want to climb in bed with me, Pruitt? I can keep you warm tonig—ack!" Gareth smacks him in the face with the back of his hand. Jasper groans as he rolls back and forth on the top bunk, causing it to creak and moan.

"Sorry I woke you," she says as she tiptoes out of the room. Gareth settles back into the center of his bed with his arms folded.

"I like her, you know," Jasper sighs.

"You like everyone."

"True…but there's something about Pruitt."

"Yeah, she doesn't let you have your way when you give her a look."

"What look?"

"You tilt your head to the side like a puppy while tucking your stupid hair behind your ear and batting your pretty blue eyes."

"Aw, you think my eyes are pretty?" Jasper teases. Gareth rips the pillow out from under his head and whips it over the top bunk. Jasper laughs as he stuffs the extra pillow under his head. "I'm serious. I like her a lot, Gareth."

"I don't care. I'm trying to sleep. Give me my pillow back."

"Nah, I think I'll keep it. I'd rather not risk being smothered in my sleep by my competition."

"There is no competition," he growls.

"We'll see. You have a bit of a head start, though; I'll have to catch up. How did you do it? Catch her off-guard? Maybe I can catch her in the showers." Gareth could see in his mind the nasty grin on his face as Jasper spoke. He kicked the bunk above him, making it shake and creak more. Jasper snickers.

"Shut up!" someone grunts from the darkness. Jasper tries to stifle his laughter, transforming it into a snort. Gareth rolls onto his side, trying to get comfortable without a pillow. Jasper's laughter subsides, and it becomes quiet once more, besides the snoring. The snoring he'd been able to avoid when getting to sleep early on. Now it's at its loudest, and he covers his ears with his forearms. That muffles things enough to allow him to sleep, but now the cold is setting in. With a sigh, he curls into a ball and waits for sleep to take him out of his misery.

Chapter 14

ALAN

A song echoes in the air, giving the dark empty tunnels an eerie ambiance. Violet is sitting on the floor outside the door, singing to the radio in her hand with her eyes closed. Alan walks past her, opening the door with his backside as quietly as possible, and her singing fades as the door swings shut behind him. Yoojin is where Alan left him, at a desk with a lamp and tools, trying to fix a part they need. He drops off two of the plates balancing on his arms. Yoojin sits back, exhaling loudly. Alan grins wide as a greeting. Yoojin glowers at him before picking up his plate of food and eating.

Spinning on the heel of his foot, holding the remaining two plates of food, he heads towards the ship. Nova lies on top of a creeper beneath it, clanking away, but only her heavy boots can be seen. "Food," Alan says with a kick to her foot.

"You can leave it there. I'll eat when I finish," she grunts. Whatever she might be doing under there is clearly taking a lot of effort.

Alan sighs, sits both plates on top of a tool cabinet, and grabs a hand towel. Taking hold of her boot and pulling, she glides out easily. The look of shock and frustration is all over her face, as well as the grease from the parts she's been working on. With an arm on each corner of the creeper, he pins her there. "You've been working in here since before the rest of us even woke up."

"I like working on projects. I don't normally eat breakfast anyway."

"Doesn't matter. When I bring you a meal I put effort into making, you stop what you're doing and eat it."

Nova gulps. Alan looks down at her lips as she speaks and realizes just how close he is. "Okay, sorry." A flush warms her grease-stained cheeks. Clearing his throat, he corrects his posture and brings her the plate of food, avoiding eye contact. "Thank you," she mumbles.

Alan walks back to Yoojin and plops down into the chair in front of the desk, shoveling the food into his mouth. There isn't much for him to work with regarding food. Most of their food sources are dried or canned. He mentally kicks himself for making a big deal out of eating this mediocre meal.

Violet comes in to collect the remaining plate as they eat in silence. Yoojin gets to his feet, offering his seat. She signals for him to sit back down and sits on the ground next to Nova. Amongst the sound of chewing and forks scraping plates, there's a sniffle here and there.

It's enough to draw everyone's attention. Alan looks for the sniffler to find tears streaming down Nova's cheeks. Violet notices at the same time. Alan's face pales. The dread sinks like a rock in his stomach. *Did I make her cry? Did I scare her? Did I look angry? What have I done?*

"Nova, what's wrong?" Violet asks, placing her hand on Nova's knee. Nova clears her throat but struggles to speak as she fights to control her emotions. Alan is frozen and has difficulty swallowing the food he's been chewing. Nova points at Alan while trying to gather her self-control. Violet turns a death stare on Alan, and he chokes on his food. She set her food aside as she readies for a physical fight. "What have you done, Alan?" Yoojin is silent with a crooked smile.

Nova shakes her head, waving her hand. Alan is about to apologize when Nova gains control, though her voice shakes as she speaks. "He didn't do anything wrong." Taking a deep breath, she continues, "The succotash. It's delicious." She laughs with a bit of a sob. "It tastes just like my dad used to make it. He passed away three years ago." Alan lets out a breath, and all his muscles relax, making him slump into the chair.

"Oh, I'm so sorry," Violet says, rubbing Nova's back to comfort her.

"Sorry I'm so emotional. I've been trying to recreate this dish, but I'm a terrible cook." Nova and Violet laugh together.

"Alan's a pretty great cook," Violet says as Alan continues trying to clear his airway. "He makes most of the meals at home."

"Thank you again, Alan. It's perfect."

"You're welcome," he croaks. Yoojin roughly pats his back a bit late. Alan pushes away Yoojin's lazy attempt at helping. He collects the plates and returns to the make-shift kitchen once everyone finishes their food. No one is in the common area, but he can hear them in their rooms talking amongst themselves. The pot of food he'd made was picked clean. He'd made enough for others, but no one had asked for any, and no one thanked him for the meal. Maybe that's just the way they live. Leave food unattended and it's first come, first serve. He sighs as he begins the clean-up.

He can't help but eavesdrop when some speak louder than others. "I don't understand why you're letting this happen," he hears a man say from one conversation. "She shouldn't be spending so much time with them. She's completely abandoned her other projects. She's supposed to be helping us, not them."

"We don't need her," the other voice he recognizes as Nova's brother Mathias says.

"I disagree. She's important to our community. She's the only person who's kept things working around here. No one works harder than her."

"I agree, Mathias," a woman's voice joins in. It's the woman from earlier, Jenna. "I think you should end this and kick them out."

"We can't kick them out and risk an attack from the Maven," Mathias grumbles.

"What if she leaves with them?" the man asks.

"Then she leaves," Mathias responds.

"Why do you think no one fought that woman on deciding who leads our group? You may have some leadership skills in telling people what to do, but who really leads these people? Who provided a comfortable living for us? Who provided the kids with the means for an education? Who's the one that keeps finding the best loot? It's Nova." Alan nods in eavesdropping agreement. At least someone in this community recognizes her worth.

"If you're so desperate to keep her here, you should go to her yourself," he seethes. "If you keep insulting me, I'll kick you, your wife, and your children out to the maven, waiting to devour you all outside our doors."

"Fine, I will talk to her myself." The curtain is whipped around as the man leaves the room. Alan avoids looking at him until he passes through. He looks over his shoulder as the man goes through the kitchen into the hallway. It's the same man who approached Nova on their walk back to these tunnels. Finishing up, he rinses his hands and dries them on a rag before following the man.

Seeing how much these people need her, he feels a little guilty for wanting to take her away from them. The thought of bringing all of them back to the shelter in the mountains doesn't seem so bad, especially when the kids will have more people their age to play with. That is, until he hears Mathias's voice echoing down the hall, something about food. There's no way he'd allow that man into their home. The way Jenna speaks of Violet, it wouldn't work out. Leaving Nova to care for all these people's needs on her own makes him feel sick.

As he enters the room, he can hear the man speaking with Nova. He lingers outside the door, watching.

Yoojin and Violet are huddled together, pretending to work on a part already finished. They occasionally glance in Nova's direction.

"You haven't been around much this past week," he says, leaning against the panel as she works on the other side.

"I've been working on this. Where have you been?" she says in exasperation.

"I haven't gone anywhere. I miss you," he says with a tilt of his head.

Nova stops what she's doing to stand straight. She looks at him with narrowed eyes, the sleeves of her jumpsuit tied at her waist. The black tank underneath hugs her figure, and her skin glistens from working so hard. She puts her hands on her hips, and you can see the muscles in her arms flex. "How's Julie doing? I heard she hasn't been feeling well."

"It's just a cold. She's always complaining about something."

"So you say. Julie's a good mother."

"Yeah. So, is there anything I can do to help around here to move things along?"

"No, we've got it. You can go help Julie with the kids."

"She's got it."

"But she's sick," Nova counters.

"Look, I wanted to talk to you privately about something. Can we go somewhere? We could step out to the hallway."

With a sigh, Nova sets her tool down with a clunk and lets him lead her out. Alan moves deep into the shadows until he can't see his hands in front of him. "What do you need to talk about, Toby?" She stops abruptly just outside the doorframe. Spinning around, she faces him with her arms folded.

He comes to stand directly in front of her. "I just...I miss you. We used to hang out and talk all the time. Why have you become so distant?" he asks in a low voice as he rubs her arms.

"You got married and had children." Her grip on her arms tightens.

"I feel like you're distancing yourself from everyone," Toby says. "Others feel that way too. You know how important you are to us. To me." Alan is crouching in a ball, doing his best to keep quiet, even though his instincts are screaming at him to do something.

"First, you flirt with me and lead me on," she replies. "The next thing I know, you marry someone else. Now you have a family and flirt with me in an attempt at...what?" She pushes his hands away. "Am I supposed to be your sidepiece? I deserve more. I deserve better. I don't want to be an afterthought. Those people are strangers, yet they've treated me with more respect than any of you in all the years I've known you. With them, I'm respected for what I am, not for what I can do for them."

"You can't trust them."

"Oh, but I can trust you?"

"Of course you can."

"I can't do this." Nova tries to walk past Toby, but he grabs hold of her knotted sleeves at her waist, twisting her back to face him.

The shock on her face is all it takes to get Alan moving. Within two significant steps, he's right next to him. "Didn't your mother teach you any manners?" he says indignantly. He grabs Toby's hand, pressing deeply into a pressure point. Toby yanks his hand away, releasing Nova. "I don't think we've been introduced. Alan Andrews. And you are?" Holding his hand out to shake, a grin curls across Alan's lips as he stares down Toby.

"Tobias. We were in the middle of a private conversation." Toby eyes Alan's hand, not wishing to fall into that trap.

"Mmm, I disagree, seeing as she tried to walk away." He tilts his head and sharpens his eyes.

"This doesn't concern you."

"No?" he says, taking a step closer to Toby.

"Go back to your wife, Toby," Nova says, grabbing Alan's hand and pulling him back. Alan laces his fingers through hers, drawing her attention to their hands.

"Bye, Tobs," Alan waves with his interlocked hand, giving an amused smile. Tobias is silent but shakes his head in disapproval before turning away and stalking into the darkness. It's not long before his headlamp is flicked on, and the light slowly grows small as he returns to his family.

Nova grabs Alan's wrist, pulling him out of his head. "My hands are dirty," she says quietly.

"Sorry." Alan releases her fingers, and she wipes them on her pants.

"It's okay." She smiles timidly. "You didn't have to do that, you know."

"I'm sorry. I was trying to help. I don't mean to overstep,"

"No, I'm happy you did, thank you. I don't know how much of the conversation you heard, which is embarrassing, but I'm thankful you keep saving the day." She smiles awkwardly before speed-walking back to the ship. Alan's left with his mouth open. He wasn't sure how to respond without sounding cheesy. Instead, he scratches his head as he watches her go.

Chapter 15
STACY

"Where is he?" Stacy bursts through the front door. Her aunt and uncle are startled by the commotion. They'd been lounging lazily on the sofa, watching a program. The rest of the family has a free ride to success, thanks to her father's status, which entitles them to laziness.

"Eustacia, my dear, what in the world?"

"Where is he?" she demands.

"Who?"

"Gareth. He hasn't been to the club in weeks. None of his friends have heard from him. What happened?"

Her aunt exhales dramatically, slumping back into the sofa. "Silly girl. Gareth is fine. He was hired as an intern by Dr. Oric. Supposedly he's working closely with him and Mr. Grey. I don't know how that boy does it. He's had so many amazing opportunities. You know this is better than any position he would've received under your father." She laughs proudly.

"Since when?"

"Soon after the ball he started working for them. He didn't even take time to grab his things. Everything was provided for him and they put him right to work. I occasionally get a message from him telling me how much he enjoys his new position."

"Let me see these messages."

"Oh, I don't save these things. I hate seeing those little numbers. It gives me anxiety. I'll forward the message next time he sends one, if that will put you at ease."

"It doesn't put me at ease. You don't know Oric," she says in exasperation as she turns away from them.

"Close the door behind you!" her uncle calls to her. She walks back, only to slam the door as hard as possible. Though the door muffles him, he continues, "That girl has no manners. I'm so glad she hasn't been around to influence Gareth."

Stacy looks around at the neighboring houses. Some of the neighbors have come to the window to see what the ruckus is. She rolls her eyes, frustrated with the lack of privacy this place provides. Her heels clack on the ground as she stomps back to her vehicle. The driver is waiting for her inside. As she slips in, the door shuts behind her. She takes a deep breath and adjusts her suit, distracting herself from the thoughts rushing through her mind. The driver stares at her, awaiting instruction. "Take me to security."

"Ma'am?"

"Don't question me. Just do it."

The driver nods and the vehicle begins to move. It's a short drive through the neighborhood to the elevator.

Though the Stratos Development feels large, getting from one side to the next in the right vehicle doesn't take long. The door to the lift closes after them. As the elevator rises, gravity pulls at her body, then lifts her to weightlessness for a moment when it stops. They arrive at the highest level, and the lift opens its doors again. The sun beats down on the 10th level. Even with the large tinted glass dome separating them from the ice-cold atmosphere, it's still blinding when it reflects off the white ground and buildings. The vehicle speeds off to its destination.

With the security footage, she hopes she can determine if what her aunt says is true. If she can learn of Gareth's whereabouts, she might be able to get somewhere. Without him, she won't have access to the other levels she needs. That clever boy was her ticket to gaining access to the entirety of Stratos Development; that is, until he disappeared without a trace, and no one seemed to care. No one finds his disappearance unusual. Now that she thinks back, he often used to disappear, but not for days and weeks. Her cousin only wanted to explore his options. Never had he shown interest in the science or health industries.

Arriving at the security headquarters, she's welcomed. It was wise to play along as her father's successor. It'd taken time to gain enough responsibility for the others to respect her position, but working hard has paid off. Her father has been leaving early often enough that he isn't micromanaging everything she does anymore. Walking with determination, those working stay out of her way until she reaches the data library. There are many who work in this department. This is where they store all the digital recordings of security cameras throughout the levels of the Stratos Development, the ground seekers, and whatever's left of the old surveillance cameras below.

Looking around the room, only a few get distracted from their work. One curious mind does look up, and she locks eyes with him. He looks away, bowing his head, so it's hidden behind his cubicle wall. Stacy marches over and places a hand on his desk to draw his attention. "What is your name?" she asks with authority.

He turns to her nervously. "Elon Jenks, ma'am," he says, fidgeting with his hands.

Stacy looks him up and down with a charming smile. "I need your assistance, Mr. Jenks. Do you have a moment?"

"I'd be happy to help, ma'am."

Stacy smiles and sits on the corner of his desk, leaning in and putting her weight on her arm. "You can call me Stacy. Would you mind pulling a file from January 3rd?"

"Of course. Is there a specific location you were interested in seeing, Miss Stacy?"

"The ballroom entrance of the gala would be sufficient, around 7:15 in the evening."

Elon pulls up the file quickly enough. "Would this view work for you?" The file shows the guests stopping for photos and entering the building.

"Perfect. Can you skip ahead to the footage of me when I arrive?

"That was closer to 7:40," he says. Stacy eyes him curiously. "I, uh…I was working that day. I was privileged to work on this project that evening."

Stacy gives him a knowing smile as he avoids her eyes, then says at a certain point in the playback, "Right there. Gareth Nox. Can you follow him?"

"Shouldn't be too difficult." Stacy leans in closer as they follow him into the civilian elevators. "How did he get those?" Elon asks as Gareth reveals the access tags. Stacy stays quiet while they follow him to level 5, Factoria. There are not as many cameras on this level, so they wait for him to return to the elevator. When he does, the footage turns to static and ends. "That's strange."

"What happened?" Stacy leans in closer.

"I'm not sure. It looks like the file's corrupted."

"Can you restore it?"

"I don't know. It looks like there's a file missing as well."

"What floor did he get off on?"

"It looks like Level 2, but I can't be sure."

"I need you to search all elevator files leaving levels 2 and 3."

"Okay," he says hesitantly, but does as he's told, searching each file for any sign of him. The only people coming and going are the regular staff dressed in gray suits.

Stacy pulls a chair from an empty cubicle, sliding close to Elon. "Wait, stop there."

"That's just Mr. Grey," he says, trying to move on. Killian enters the elevator and turns to scan his tag. On the opposite end of the elevator, a woman in a sleek black dress with a high slit is turned away from the camera.

"Who's that with him? She's not regular staff."

He zooms in on the woman and pauses. "I don't think we should be looking through these files."

"You'll be compensated well," Stacy says, leaning over him to play the feed again. Elon leans back, covering his mouth anxiously. As the doors to the elevator close on the footage, Killian closes on the woman. Without warning, her leg wraps around his as his arms slip around her waist, lifting her into the air and pressing her against the elevator wall. Stacy looks away as a fire burns under her skin, and her lungs ache. She tries to keep her breath steady. "Skip ahead," she snarls. Elon quickly speeds it up.

Getting to her feet in a huff, she paces. "How large a sum would you need to go through the footage inside Levels 2 and 3?"

"There are no cameras on those levels."

"Why not?" She stops pacing to glare down at him.

"I don't know. We've never had camera footage for levels 3 and below."

She pulls out her datapad as she speaks. "Can you run through the elevator footage until you find Gareth? Even if you must go through to the present day?"

"That could take hours. I have to fill my quota of logs as well. I guess I could run through them on my breaks or work overtime, but—"

"I've already wired your compensation. If you find him, inform me right away. It's imperative that you keep this between you and me."

Elon picks up his datapad as a notification comes on the screen. He opens it to see the sum, and his jaw drops. "I, uh…okay. I'll get back to you as soon as possible, ma'am."

"Thank you, Elon," Stacy says as she pushes back the chair she borrowed. The blush on his cheeks from using his first name tells her he'll do whatever she asks—an ally to keep under her belt.

Chapter 16

PIPER

The addition of the rec room wasn't the only change. After breakfast, everyone lined up as usual to enter their designated door. Gentlemen first, their partner still acts as eyes on the other side, but no longer will they face the trial alone. The morning trials end with mild injuries, scrapes and bruises.

The afternoon trials are more menacing. When they enter the blinding, white-washed room, a handful of others enter from along the wall. They all look at each other with confusion. Some are excited to see a friendly face and wave at each other, but it's not long before their humor fades. They stand on a square three-foot platform. You can't see the bottom floor past the platform's edge. Though the room is bright, it's as if the ground is covered in shadow, and they're at least three stories from that darkness. There's no exit in sight. Her heart begins to race.

Piper spots her friend Reese on the other end of the room. Reese nods her head pointedly as she crouches down, as if ready to bolt at any moment. Piper looks up in that direction. Across the room, at least four or five stories up, is another three-foot platform and the exit. There's no other platform to jump across, and the opposite wall is at least 50 feet away—nothing to hold onto or climb. Jasper is quiet as he tries to understand the screen before him. Suddenly a burst of wind from the shadow comes, so intense it feels like it'll rip her from the platform. Piper presses her back against the door, hearing her heartbeat in her ears. Looking around to see who will make the first move, the wind suddenly stops for a couple of seconds, seemingly inconsistent. Piper watches Reese as she presses her finger to her ear and responds to her partner, Gareth. She nods and gets ready.

"Jasper, what do you have for me?"

"It's playing a song I don't know, and it's not in English, so I have no clue." The panic's evident in his voice.

Reese nods and is about to jump when she stops hopping at the edge and then bounces back, as another gust of wind pushes up. She shakes her head in frustration, but some other girls had been watching her and actually jumped when she only acted like she was going to. The girls scream as the wind pushes them high into the air but not high enough to reach the door, and then suddenly stops. They continue screaming as they plummet into the darkness, kicking and calling for help. As soon as the shadow engulfs them, they're silenced.

Piper looks back to Reese. She's covering her face with her hands. "Jasper, sing it to me!" Piper yells.

"It's already started! And I told you, I don't know it."

"Just repeat the hymn as you hear it!" she yells, drawing Reese's attention. He tries, but it doesn't sound like anything she's heard before. Reese jumps just as the wind begins to blow, timing it perfectly. She spreads her arms and legs, allowing the current to pull her higher. The wind dies down a little before pushing her higher, but not relatively high enough, and she begins to spin gracefully as if she has complete control. The other girls jump in now, following Reese's lead but not as gracefully, as some run into walls and others struggle to keep their arms and legs straight. The wind dies down again but then gusts even stronger, pushing them higher, and Reese is suddenly now above the exit. She glides over to it on her stomach, moving her arms in a way that allows her to flow from one side to the other. When she's positioned herself, her legs flip over her head and she lands on the platform with her arms out, as if to say, "And that's how it's done." She smiles as she turns around to help pull a couple of girls to the exit platform. The one who was struggling finally gets the hang of it and is gliding toward the exit too.

"Let's go, Piper!" Reese yells after the wind stops abruptly. The straggler grabs hold of the platform just as she loses the wind. Reese grabs hold of her wrist and hauls her up. She follows the girls out, winking at Piper before disappearing behind the door.

"The song ended," Jasper says.

"How long is the song?"

"About three minutes."

"Tell me when it's at the two-minute mark. We need to use the wind to carry us to the exit."

Piper waits as the gusts of wind begin to show a pattern in the breaks and strength. She's alone now, as the last girl has taken off and disappeared into the darkness. "Now!" Jasper yells in her ear, and she jumps, but the air isn't coming. She's falling. "Piper?" he calls as she screams. The darkness is getting ever closer, but just before she descends, a gust of wind hits her like a wall, knocking the wind out of her. "Piper!"

"I'm okay!" is all she can get out as she struggles to keep herself steady. Piper tries not to panic as the wind dies down and drops lower, before it rushes again with more force, bringing her higher, letting her touch the platform just as the wind dies down once more.

"You can do this," Jasper says under his breath again and again. She flails, trying to grip the platform, causing her legs to drop. She forgot about the last dip in pressure before it gusts at its strongest. As the wind rushes, her legs are pulled upwards, and she hits her head on the platform's edge. Her head throbs and she becomes disoriented as the wind whirls her around. Finally steadying herself, she realizes she's too high. She tries to move her arms and legs as if swimming to the exit, but the wind stops and she falls. Jasper still whispers encouragement as she catches the platform with her arms and chest. Her teeth clash together as she hits her chin on the floor. She struggles to take a breath after her ribcage hits the platform. She hangs there with her legs dangling, unmoving, for fear of losing her grip, but she can feel the strength leaving her. She attempts to swing a leg up. Searing pain shoots through her chest, which has her gasping.

Knowing there's no one to help her, she fights through the pain and swings her leg up, this time catching it on the ledge. She freezes there to catch her breath. A gust of wind blows, giving her that little push she needs to roll onto the platform. She groans in agony as she rolls onto her back, taking careful breaths. "I… made it," she cries as tears run down her face. Jasper sighs in her ear. Piper uses the door to ease herself up to her feet, and takes another breath before opening it. As she turns the handle, the door is pulled open. She moans as it yanks her arm.

"Piper." Gareth wraps his hand gently around her head as he pulls her through the doorway by the waist. "Are you hurt anywhere else?" He bends down so their eyes meet. He wipes away the blood dripping down her brow into her eye. She had barely noticed her head wound after hitting her chest.

"Piper, are you okay?" Jasper yells down the corridor.

"It hurts to breathe. I fell on my chest," Piper pants, only looking into Gareth's pale eyes as he wipes her tears and blood away.

"Are you okay?" Jasper skids to a stop, crowding them and supporting her lower back.

"Does she look okay?" Gareth straightens, giving Jasper a dirty look. He bends down again, gently pressing a palm to her cheek. "Let me see." He begins unzipping her suit down to her navel.

"Gareth, no!" She cringes with pain as she holds her suit closed. Her chest and face are instantly flushed.

"We need to check if you broke something," Gareth says sternly.

"It's fine. I didn't feel anything break. You can't just undress me in the *hallway*." Piper's eyes dart around the corridor as there are now many eyes on them. "Stop causing a scene."

Someone grabs Piper's wrist and pulls her out of the Jasper and Gareth sandwich. Reese drags her down the corridor. Piper looks back with stabbing pains that take her breath away. Gareth follows close behind, with Jasper at his heels. Reese is walking too fast for Piper to follow comfortably as she gasps for oxygen, tears streaming down her face. "Reese, slow down," she gasps.

Reese doesn't slow her pace but pulls her into the bathroom. "If you're hurt badly, they'll take you away. When you come back, you won't be the same. Sonja hasn't." Piper recalls the scorched body as Gareth peeled the cloth and melted skin from Sonja's steaming nub of an ankle. Though her foot was missing when she left, she returned whole without a mark on her body, but it was as if she'd lost her soul. There was no life left in her eyes. Piper shivers.

Reese retrieves a first aid kit hidden under a sink. Piper eases onto the bench as Reese opens the kit and rips open packages. Outside the door, Gareth and Jasper can be heard arguing about who should be allowed to enter. Reese rolls her eyes as she wipes Piper's forehead wound clean with an alcohol swab. It stings, and the smell makes her head spin. Reese works quickly and tapes the cut closed. "Stand up and we'll get you changed," she utters. Piper does as she's told as carefully as possible. She holds her breath as she gets to her feet and lets it out while standing straight. Reese unzips the suit further and folds it off her shoulders.

"You were graceful in the trial today. How did you do that?" Piper asks.

"I used to play in wind tunnels. It was a fun pastime. It's like flying." Reese's eyes brighten, her smile wistful. When she comes back to reality, her eyes turn cold. She yanks Piper's sleeves off and Piper yelps in agony. "Sorry," Reese says with an apologetic smile.

Gareth bursts through the door. Reese steps in front of Piper as she tries to cover herself with her swollen, bruised arms. "Are you okay?"

"She's fine. She doesn't need a bunch of boys staring at her right now," Reese grumbles. Gareth doesn't respond but moves quickly to the lockers and brings her a wrap tunic and pants. He unfolds the top with a shake and holds it open behind Piper. Reese watches him with narrow eyes. Piper looks up at him, turning slightly to see his eyes.

"Are you okay?" Gareth keeps his eyes locked on the wall beyond her.

"It's getting harder to move."

"Your body is stiffening up. Here, put your arm in." Gareth holds the sleeve lower and closer to the front, so she won't have to twist as much.

Piper slips her arm in. He reaches around the other side, gently easing her arm into the other sleeve and then carefully slipping the tunic over her shoulders. The pain is numbed slightly with the gentle touch of his fingers as he sweeps her hair over her collar. Jasper's words run through her mind: *I thought you didn't come here to play.* She hopes no one notices the flush that covers her body now.

"I can help her, Gareth." Reese folds her arms and raises a brow.

"You're being too rough with her," Gareth retorts as he comes around to tie the tunic for Piper.

"Seriously?"

"It's fine, Reese," Piper interrupts.

With another roll of her eyes and a sigh, she says, "Fine," and walks out the door. Jasper bends his neck, trying to see in before the door swings closed. Gareth unfolds the pants with a flick of the wrist and helps peel the rest of the suit off. Insisting she hold onto him for stability, he helps her into the pants. His knuckles brush her skin as he ties the drawstrings for her. The loose-fit clothes are welcome as she feels less confined.

"I know this might make you uncomfortable, but we need to look at your chest and ensure there's no major bruising, okay?"

The words catch in Piper's throat as she watches him drop to his knees, so she nods. Ever so gently, he lifts the bottom of the tunic. His warm hands gently press on her abdomen, glancing up occasionally. "Does that hurt?"

"Mmm," Piper shakes her head gently.

"I'm going to check your ribs now." He lifts the tunic a bit higher. Piper tilts her head back, squeezing her eyes shut as she chews on her lip. Gently he drags his fingers along her ribs. "Does that hurt?" Piper shakes her head. "You aren't breathing." Piper lets out a breath and flinches in pain. "Where does it hurt the most?" Piper points to a rib below her underarm. "Okay, it'd be easier to open your top."

"Mmm-hmm," Piper responds, unable to look him in the eye. The way Gareth is so gentle and slow with his movements is almost like torture.

He carefully adjusts the tunic so that her breasts are always covered, then takes a breath through his teeth as he peels back the fabric underneath. Her ribs are already turning purple. He feels them where it's turning colors. "Nothing feels out of place, but if it's that painful to breathe, it could be a fracture."

"Okay, what do I do?"

"Well, the good thing is, you just have to let it heal." He grabs a bottle from the first aid kit and sprays a cool mist over her ribs. Piper tries to take steady breaths, fighting through the pain. Taking a large patch, he peels the paper from the adhesive side and gently presses it around the wound. The patch releases a cooling sensation and eases the pain, allowing her to breathe better.

"That's helping," Piper says with her eyes still closed.

"Good, it should help you heal faster," he says as he adjusts her tunic and ties it.

"Thank you," she says breathlessly, looking back down at him still on his knees. With her hands resting on his shoulders, it's tempting to run her fingers through his silky black hair. She fights the thoughts running through her head, trying to remember the purpose of coming here, but those eyes. His eyes are drawing her in. And those lips. She doesn't realize she's leaning in until the pain from bending too far catches her breath. Still, on his knees, he stretches up, closing that distance and pressing his lips against hers. She threads her fingers through his hair in reaction. His tongue brushes her lips, parting them, intensifying their kiss.

Piper pulls away, gasping. "I'm sorry," Gareth says with a look of worry. "Are you okay?" His hands hover over her face and then her shoulders. He looks down at her chest as if seeing her wound through her clothes, and the worry in his eyes is evident when he looks back up at her.

"Too much," she breathes, pulling him in for another, but he pulls away. Her ears pound like a drum.

"What's too much? Does it hurt? I don't want to hurt you."

"Yes, I'm in pain, but that look in your eyes. That's too much. I feel like… Just kiss me." She presses her lips to his so forcefully, he sways back before matching her insatiable need. He holds on to her thighs to keep from falling backward.

Jasper clears his throat noisily. Piper breaks away, holding her side, gasping for breath with a groan. Gareth finds himself on his hands and knees, staring at the floor. He sits back on his heels, flipping his hair back with a jerk of his head to glare at the ceiling. "You might want to change," Jasper teases, looking down between Gareth's legs. "That suit isn't leaving anything to the imagination."

Gareth gives him a sideways glance with a furrowed brow. "Speak for yourself."

"This? It's always like this. It can't be helped when I'm around gorgeous women."

"You're so vulgar," Gareth growls.

Jasper crosses the room, wrapping an arm around Piper's shoulders. "I prefer the term 'naughty,' or…" He tilts his head closer to whisper in Piper's ear. "Erotic."

Goosebumps run down her back as she scratches her ear. "Gah, will you stop doing that?" The weight of Jasper's arm makes it harder to breathe comfortably, even with the pain relief patch. Gareth sighs as he gathers his clothes and begins changing behind them. She pulls herself out of reach.

"Is it too much?" Jasper says with a toothy grin.

A fire burns in her chest, hearing her words in his mouth, and her first reaction is to slap him in the face, but she hits him harder than she means to, leaving a red mark on his cheek. "Sorry," Piper breathes.

Gareth snickers as he ties the drawstrings on his pants. "Don't apologize to him. He deserved it."

"If she's apologizing, perhaps she meant it as a love tap," Jasper says, twisting his body to press against hers, slipping his fingers up her tunic.

"Oh my gosh, stop," she convulses, bringing up her knee to greet his groin. Jasper groans as he lurches forward. "Sorry," she grunts in pain from the quick movements.

"I think there's no doubt about what she meant." Gareth laughs, but there's no humor in his eyes. "Piper, you should go get some dinner. I'll be right out to help you."

Piper looks at Jasper with pity before taking her leave. She waits outside the doors, pressing her back against the cool cement wall, to hear what Gareth has to say without her present.

"You know, your partner seems a little agitated as of late," Jasper rasps.

"And?"

"Don't know if you've met many redheads. They aren't ones to cross."

"I can handle Reese."

"You're not the one I'm worried about."

"I'll take care of it. In the meantime, flirt all you want, but if you touch her like that again, I'll tear you open with my bare hands and strangle you with your intestines. Understood?"

"Jeez, Gareth, you're twisted."

"Do I make myself clear?"

Jasper rolls his eyes. "Perfectly. Now get out of my face. I can only take so much abuse."

Piper is slow to push off the wall. Gareth pushes the door open, and she moves out of its path just as it slams against the wall. He looks down at her and glances back at Jasper as he leads her away. She wonders what he looks like as he threatens her partner out of what comes naturally to him. She finds it hard to keep the smile off her face, knowing someone's being threatened on her behalf. Someone she could never imagine hurting anyone. The way he tried to look after Sonja when she was injured. The way he takes care of her.

Speaking of Sonja, she's sitting at a table staring at the wall, eating without seeing her food, almost as if eating is now merely a mechanical function. Several people act the same way, including some girls who had fallen into the dark shadows earlier. The others seem jittery and anxious, as if someone might strike them at any moment. Piper had stopped moving as she watched the others. Gareth gently moves her along as he grabs two trays of food for both of them. Something about their mannerisms has her ringing her hands.

Reese is already sitting at their usual spot, waiting for them. Gareth sets both trays next to each other. With a smile, Reese grasps the extra tray and drags it across the table to encourage Piper to sit next to her. Gareth helps her onto the bench and ensures she's comfortable before sitting across from them. Gareth eyes Reese warily. She doesn't seem to mind the attention as she stares him down with half a smile. Piper looks back and forth between the two as it becomes more uncomfortable, and the silence lingers on.

"You guys work well as partners," Piper says before filling her mouth with food.

"Best partner I've ever had, and I've been here a while," Reese responds.

"How long is your contract?"

"A few months, but the days have been a blur. I have no idea how long I've been here." As she watches Gareth ignore the conversation and eat, Reese adds, "Time flies when you're having fun."

"You're enjoying these trials?" Piper can't help but notice Gareth's eating very quickly.

"I make the best of every situation."

"You're a really positive person, Reese. I admire that about you."

"Thank you, Piper. That means a lot for you to say so."

Gareth jumps up abruptly, startling both Reese and Piper. "Are you finished?" He directs his question to Piper.

"No, I'm still eating," she answers.

He stalks away to deposit his empty tray and returns to sit next to Piper, leaning his back against the table with his elbows propped upon it. "Finish your food," he orders as he watches the crowd eat and chat.

Piper watches him with curiosity. His mood has turned from kind and worried to sour and impatient. She can't help but wonder what brings on these quick changes. Is it Jasper? Gareth's head rolls to the side to look at her as if he heard her question. He looks at her tray and back at her eyes. She had never noticed before because he was always frowning, but the skin under his eyes is puffy and darkened, making him look tired, which would explain why he looks so grumpy all the time. Is he getting enough sleep?

"Are you waiting for me to feed you?" Gareth smiles mischievously as he reaches over.

Piper instinctively pushes her tray away from him, hovering over it as she quickly stuffs her face. From the corner of her eye, she sees him flash his white teeth at her as he runs his hand through his wavy black hair.

"Do you want to play a game after this?" Reese asks as she picks at a bread roll.

Piper opens her mouth to speak, but Gareth cuts her off. "She needs to rest."

"Do you need to rest, Gareth?" Reese leans back to look around Piper.

"Yes," he says without hesitation.

Glancing down, Piper shoves the last bite of food into her mouth as he snatches the tray out from under her and drops it off before coming back to collect her. "I don't need to rest right away," she says. "We could play a little."

"Yeah, Gareth, you don't speak for her." Reese grins.

"True, I can speak for myself." Piper eases herself off the bench carefully, and Reese follows.

Gareth drops his head in frustration. "I'm not trying to. I just want to—"

Piper scoops his face into her palms. His cheeks squish and his lips pucker as he stares down at her with squinty eyes. "Don't worry your pretty little head," she says. Gareth involuntarily smiles, contorting his face further. Her heart swells at the way he looks at her. Reese tugs at Piper's arm to get her moving.

The game has finally ended, and she regrets not listening to Gareth. Her head is throbbing, her body is so stiff, and her chest feels tight from the swelling.

She looks over at Gareth sitting in a chair with his head propped in his hand, his pinky resting on his lips. His eyes are closed. He must've fallen asleep watching them play. Most of the others have already gone to bed.

"Aw, he's all tuckered out," Reese says.

"I should go lay down," Piper sighs.

"Okay, I'll get this lug to bed," Reese says as she runs her fingers through his hair. Stabbing pain in Piper's chest keeps her from moving. "Unless you need help."

"I think I do," Piper says quickly.

"Hey Jasper, you want to help your partner to bed?"

Jasper whips his head around. His blond hair falls into his eyes as he puts his book back and trots over with a smile.

"It's fine," Piper says.

"Don't be silly," Reese says as she tucks Gareth's hair behind his ear.

"Stop!" Piper yells louder than she expected, freezing everyone in their tracks.

Gareth is startled awake. He rubs the sleep from his eyes as Reese rests her hand on his shoulder. "What's your problem?" she scoffs.

"Stop touching him like that," Piper responds. Jasper continues walking straight out of the room, avoiding confrontation. Gareth, still half-asleep, looks at both of them in confusion.

"Fine." Reese drops her hands and marches off.

"What's going on?"

"Nothing," Piper grumbles as she holds her side. "I want to go to bed." Gareth gets to his feet without another thought.

He eases her into her bed and makes sure she's comfortable. As he tries to leave, she grabs onto his pant leg. He kneels, petting her head, careful to avoid the cut there. "I'm cold," Piper whispers.

"Do you want my blanket?"

"No." She feels stupid, unable to say exactly what she wants from him. Gareth seems to understand as he walks around to the other side. She scoots to the edge with difficulty. Gareth climbs in next to her and gently pulls her close. She fights the urge to moan in pain as she lifts her head to move her hair out of his face. He's so close; his warm breath caresses her neck.

He places his hand over her heart. "If my laying here will keep you from the rest you need, I'll leave," he whispers in her ear.

"Is that a threat?" she pouts.

"Yes. Your heart is pounding."

"It'll quiet when I know you won't leave after I've fallen asleep."

"I'll lie with you forever," he sighs.

"Promise?"

"I promise you the world if you'll go to sleep."

"I don't need the world…"

Gareth kisses her neck. "Goodnight." Piper takes as deep a breath as she dares to calm her drumming heart.

Chapter 17
VIOLET

Violet falls on her back, and dust plumes fly into the air. She grits her teeth as she slowly picks herself back up. A thick layer of dust coats her sticky skin and clothes. "What happened to going easy on me, Woof?" Violet gasps as she holds her abdomen.

"You've gotten a lot better. The only way to progress is to make it harder," Yoojin laughs. He's dressed in a white tank and trousers. His skin glistens as he walks circles around Violet.

"Yeah, okay, but that hurt a lot," she pants.

"In a real fight, you're going to get hurt. You should get used to it. And don't leave yourself wide open like that."

"I wasn't wide open. Just a little open." She emphasizes with her index finger and thumb. Yoojin chuckles. Violet braces herself by holding her knees and taking deep breaths.

"In a real fight, you wouldn't be able to take a break either." Yoojin comes around again.

"Yeah, yeah." Yoojin is beside her when she leaps upon him. Wrapping her legs around his neck, she drops upside down with so much force that she pulls him down with her. Yoojin is flipped onto his back, and she releases her grip around his neck. "You should listen to your own advice." They both lay on the floor, panting and coughing from the dust.

"You got me there, Kitten."

Violet sits up and twists around to rest her head on his shoulder, feet pointing in the opposite direction. "Calling it quits?"

"We can take a break," he says, lifting his head to rest on her shoulder. They both look at each other from the corner of their eyes and smile.

Violet remembers how she felt at that moment. Like they were the only people left in the world. Nothing mattered; the past she couldn't remember, Charlie and his lies. Then she would remember her responsibility as a mother, and the guilt would eat at her until she returned home. As she watches Yoojin work with Nova on the ship, those conflicting feelings still linger. Though now there's also that doubt about his character on the table. Looking back, there's no doubt about him being genuine, but how could he be that naïve if his people were responsible for destroying Safe Haven and so many other colonies? Or does he know the truth and pretend to be naïve?

She's been speaking to Nathan and the girls daily to keep herself grounded. Yoojin has been itching to leave this place since their arrival. It's been a week, and even Violet is getting restless waiting for this ship to be finished. The longer they stay, the more attached to Nova they become. Her sweet personality seems to have enraptured Alan. When she's not around, that's all he talks about, and when she is around, he's constantly shoving food and water in her face. If it's not nourishment, he's begging her to rest.

Violet observes that Nova is happiest when she works on a project or talks about something she loves. She and Alan speak for hours on end in detail about subjects Violet can't follow. It's as if they're speaking another language. When they get that way, it brings her joy to watch their interactions. There's a weight in her stomach, thinking about when they'll part ways. It could be more dangerous for Nova to leave with them. Ultimately it's her choice, as Alan's argued with Violet before.

Nova skips around the ship, wiping her hands on a rag. Alan and Yoojin are keeping themselves busy arguing about flying the ship. Violet catches her attention. "How's the progress?"

"The engines are running smoothly now. I need to make sure stabilizers and thrusters are functioning, which would require a test drive." Her excitement is palpable.

"Can we test it in here?"

"The stabilizers, yes, but the thrusters will need more space. And the roof does open. I need to find the access panel for that. Though, the ship may have remote access."

"You think you can fly this?"

"I know I can. My dad taught me to fly an old jet. It was hijacked and destroyed a long time ago, but you never really forget."

"That's amazing." Nova shrugs with a giddy smile. "Hey, Nova, I appreciate you helping us. It means so much. You're an amazing person." Nova blushes, and her words catch in her throat. "I don't know what you plan to do when we leave, but of course you're more than welcome to come with us. But I need you to be fully aware of what you might be getting into."

"What do you mean?"

"We're heading to Arcadia, a place we know nothing about other than it's a very civilized colony. That's where Yoojin's from. He doesn't know, but we're going there to investigate. We suspect they're responsible for destroying many of the colonies, if not all of them."

"What?" Nova's voice rises an octave.

Violet moves closer and lowers her voice. "Yoojin can't know why we're going there."

"What if it's true? What if he's the enemy?"

"Yoojin isn't our enemy," she says firmly but shakes her head. "If Arcadia's truly that dragon, I plan to cut its head off. Which means you and everyone with me would be at risk."

Nova nods. "Why are you trusting me with all this?"

Violet's caught off-guard by the question. "You…" She pauses. "I've been watching you…but not in a creepy way." She crosses and uncrosses her arms. "I just feel like I can trust you. You're different from most girls

I've met. I'm comfortable around you." Violet wrings her hands.

"I like you too, Violet." A bright smile lights up her face. "I'm going to hug you now."

"Okay," Violet laughs, opening her arms in invitation. Nova hugs tighter than she expects. Maybe she needs a friend as much as Violet does. She matches the tight squeeze.

"What did I miss?" Alan intervenes.

"Female bonding time," Nova responds.

"Do you feel left out, Alan?" Violet asks with a smile as they release each other.

"A little."

"Aw, poor Alan," Nova coos while holding her arms out to him.

"This is very patronizing, but I never turn down hugs, so…" Alan reasons with himself as he goes in for the hug. Wrapping his arms around her, he lifts her into a bear hug. The squeeze leaves Nova with a grunt.

"Oh my goodness," Violet laughs as Alan sets her down. She notices how Alan's eyes consistently linger on her face when Nova can hardly keep eye contact. A flush warms Nova's cheeks as she giggles.

Alan quickly turns his attention. "Eugene, you want in on this?"

"No," he replies curtly as he cleans up his workspace.

"Guys, I think Eugene is feeling left out too." Alan crosses the room.

"No, I'm not." Yoojin doesn't bother looking up but continues with his work. Violet and Nova make their way over as well.

"Denial is a sign of distress," Violet adds. Yoojin looks up at her with a furrowed brow.

"Don't worry, friend, I know what you need," Alan says as he draws closer.

"What kind of friend are you if you refuse to pronounce my name correctly?" Yoojin complains while slamming a drawer closed.

"What do you mean, Eugene?" Alan walks a circle around him. Yoojin drops his arms to the sides as he glares up at the ceiling. Alan comes in behind him and slips his arms around his chest, hugging Yoojin tight. Yoojin allows it for a second but gets frustrated when he lingers and tries to pry his arms off. Alan locks his hands around him. "Don't fight it, Eugene. Just embrace the love." Violet and Nova giggle as they join in.

"Poor Yoojin," Violet teases as she wraps her arms around his middle. A large sigh escapes him as he gives in and wraps his arm around Violet's shoulder. Violet looks up at him with a large grin. He gives her a sideways look, irritation still bubbling inside of him. His expression mildly changes as their eyes meet. A crooked smile catches on his lips, and he leans down slightly to kiss her forehead and rest his cheek there. A warmth spreads through Violet.

Alan's hands move to grope Yoojin's chest. "Ooh, nice pecs, Eugene."

"All right." Yoojin breaks free and walks away as they all chuckle at his expense.

"I think we got through to him," Alan says triumphantly with his hands on his hips. With a clap of his hands, he continues, "All right, let's get back to work."

Nova joins Alan back to the ship but glances back at Violet with a nod. Violet watches them anxiously. She's not worried that Nova will talk about what she confided. No, she worries that she'll join them, regardless of the warning. There's a sudden sense of dread, watching them laugh together and be happy. Her chest feels heavy and tight. Violet takes deep breaths to settle her nerves, but it's not working. The large room feels like it's getting smaller, and she needs to get out.

Running down the halls, she makes her way. Though many eyes turn to watch her, she ignores them and runs faster through the dark tunnels until she reaches the metal doors. They burst open with a loud clatter. Violet takes a deep breath as if breaking from the water's surface. She shakes her clammy hands as if this will remove the panic, like drops of liquid. Involuntary moans escape her as her tongue becomes dry and nausea hits in waves. A flood of tears streams down her cheeks as she starts to hyperventilate. She stumbles around in the field of tall grass like a lost child. She clasps her hands onto the sides of her head as she crumples into a ball.

The loud buzzing in her ears subsides as it's replaced with a vibrating hum. The rustling in the grass draws her attention. Blinking away tears, the maven stands over her with a tilted head. It kneels beside her, allowing Violet to lean against it. The sound reverberating from its chest rattles her body. The maven leans down, resting its head on her shoulder. Violet raises a shaking hand to its beak, resting her head against his.

In its own time, her heart begins to settle. Taking calm breaths, she caresses the creature that brings her so much comfort. Violet shivers, realizing that it's been raining and her hair and clothes are soaked. Pushing herself off the ground, she brushes away the mud from her bottom with little success. The maven rises with her.

"I should get back. They'll worry," Violet tells the creature. In response, it bows its head to brush against hers with clicks and purrs on its tongue. "You're such a good boy," she croons. Patting its beak, she moves away and heads to the doors sitting wide open. She closes one side, and the maven helps close the other.

Violet laughs and opens it back up. The maven moves in her way with a deep chirp, and presses its head against hers with more aggression than usual. "What are you doing? I need to go inside," Violet says with a smile as she pets him and moves away. The maven steps on the door, crouching low with that deep chirp. It presses its head against her chest and closes its eyes. "What's wrong with you?" she asks, hugging its head tightly. "Did you miss me?" The maven nudges her with its beak as it purrs with its loud clicking. "I'll take that as a yes." When she stops petting him, he nudges her and chirps again. "My goodness, you're so needy today. Let's go for a walk at least, so I don't freeze." The maven is pleased as she moves away from the doors.

They walk amongst the tall grass in silence. The maven watches her all the while with its large onyx eyes. "You're so different from the others, you know. You're intelligent and gentle. Well, when you aren't seeking attention." Violet laughs. The creature mimics it, which makes her laugh harder. They walk a while longer, moving past the boundaries of the cemetery. The field continues far as the eye can see. This must have been the grain fields. Violet stops and turns to face the maven with a grin. "I should give you a name." The maven tilts its head curiously. "You're not like the other maven," she says, tapping her finger to her chin. "Maverick? Rebel? Rogue?" The maven tilts its head in the other direction, chirping and clicking.

"Hmm, your mannerisms are similar to a bird." The maven looks up at the sky, looking for this bird she speaks of. "And you're smart... Raven. No, that's too similar to maven... Icarus." Violet scrunches her nose, unsatisfied.

The maven looks back down at her. "Rook. You look like a rook. You act like a rook. Therefore, I dub thee as such." The maven bows its head as Violet reaches for him. "You are Rook, and I am Violet. Rook. Violet." She places her palm on the side of its beak. "Rook." The maven places its taloned hand over hers and mimics the sound. Violet chuckles, bouncing up and down on the balls of her feet. "That's right. You are Rook."

Rook purrs as it places its taloned hand against her cheek, and a guttural sound she could recognize as "Violet" comes from him. Violet is hysterical with excitement as she pats Rook's claw. "Yes! You're such a smart boy!" He purrs in response to her emotions.

Violet's so happy, she doesn't notice the ground beneath them changing until Rook hisses and drags her away. The ground rumbles and shakes as the earth begins to open and the crevasse opens wider. Rook forces her to retreat further. Suddenly it stops. Dirt and grass continue to drop off into the opening. Violet carefully makes her way to the edge. Rook complains with a deep chirp as she gets dangerously close. Peeking over, she spots Nova three stories below, making her way out from under the ship. "Are you guys okay?" Nova yells.

Alan sputters as he struggles to stand up. He's covered in wet soil and crouched where the desk would be. "A little warning next time would be nice," he grumbles as he shakes off large clumps of dirt. Yoojin digs his way out from underneath the desk.

"I'm so sorry. I had no idea this would hap—AAAHHH!" Nova screams as she leaps a foot off the ground before clasping her hands over her mouth. She's spotted Violet creeping over the edge and Rook crouched next to her. Violet can't contain her laughter. Rook mimics her with a strange clucking sound. "Is it laughing?" Nova asks sourly, as if she tastes something bitter.

"Isn't it cute?" Violet smiles at the maven with admiration.

"No, it's creepy," Nova says, taking deep breaths to calm her trembling heart.

"I disagree!" Violet leans over to see Alan and Yoojin better, but the mound of dirt she leans on gives way. She has nothing to grab onto as she falls over the edge.

Chapter 18

YOOJIN

"Violet!" Nova's shrill voice cuts through the air like a knife. Violet's body hits the ship, knocking her unconscious. Yoojin catches her as she slips off the tail end to the ground. The maven screeches as it leaps down near Yoojin. Nova cowers behind Alan as he backs away with his arms in a protective stance.

Yoojin keeps his eyes on Violet. The warm, wet liquid coats his hand as he cradles her head. "Violet?" he calls as he lays her down as gently as possible. The maven moves in as soon as Yoojin turns his head to look for Alan. A low rumbling emits from the beast as it tries to pull her away from Yoojin.

"No! Don't move her!" Yoojin yells, crouching over her. The maven screeches, causing their ears to ring. It tries to pull on her arm again. Yoojin grabs hold of the beast's wrist. "You could hurt her!" The maven moves its other arm to aim at Yoojin's face. Yoojin pulls his hands away and holds them out in front of him, backing away slowly. The maven becomes silent as it stares at Yoojin's hands and looks down at its wrist, and something like a whimper escapes it. It releases Violet and steps back in a crouched position to rub its wrist in the mud. "Alan! Get over here and help me!"

Alan's ripped out of his frozen state and retrieves his pack from inside the ship. He scans her body for breaks. "She's clear. No fractures. Use this. Put pressure on the wound." Yoojin takes the clean cloth and keeps pressure on it. "It'll stop bleeding soon. Stitches are a waste of time on her." Alan sits back on his heels, rubbing his face in exasperation. "This woman's going to be the death of me."

"Stop exaggerating," Violet rasps. "What happened?"

"I'm not exaggerating. If anything serious happens to you, Killian will have my head."

"I doubt that." Violet winces as she tries to lift her head.

"Don't talk like that, Violet. You and Nathan are his world. Nothing will ever change that. I have faith in him, and so should you." Alan gets to his feet, swiping at the mud on his pants and stalking off.

Yoojin watches Violet's face crumble as she hides behind her hands. He feels as though they're falling apart. Alan and Violet are harboring feelings they aren't sharing, and it's eating away at their relationship, slowly but surely. Violet seems to be pushing everyone away lately. She trusts strangers over those she's known for years, which bothers him. They were so close before the accident. He was going to convince her to take Nathan and come home with him, before the maven broke in. His world was turned upside down when she was crushed in that explosion. The future he saw for himself was in jeopardy as he rushed to get to her, but he was too late. Charlie was there pulling her out of the wreckage. He had no idea how badly she was hurt or whether she'd survive.

Yoojin knew where she was, but he'd have to answer to her people if he went to her. He couldn't divulge information about his colony and refused to risk exposing hers. Reliving those memories of leaving her behind and returning home empty-handed without knowing if she made it, he wipes the pain from his face before lifting Violet into a sitting position and hugging her tight to his chest. The maven creeps closer with a growl.

"Rook?" Violet looks at the beast.

Yoojin sighs and brings her hand up to hold the cloth to her head. She sucks in the air through her teeth. "That thing threatened to kill me, and you're over here giving it a pet name."

"He did?" Violet looks at Rook sternly, and it hunches its shoulders.

"It did."

"Are you okay? Are you hurt anywhere?" Violet places her hands on his cheeks, tilting his head this way and that, checking his shoulders, arms and chest.

"I'm fine. He backed off when I got your blood on him." The maven looked at its wrist and rubbed it on the ground again.

"You what?" Violet was up in an instant, dropping the cloth on the ground. "Rook, are you okay?" Yoojin watches dumbfounded as she fawns over the creature as if it were the one that had fallen three stories and knocked itself out. It displayed its wrist to her as it chirped, clicked and eyed Yoojin. He had a feeling the creature was accusing him of something. "You have to be careful, Yoojin."

"Come again? I have to be careful of what?"

"If my blood had been exposed to his, it would've killed him."

"Shouldn't you be more careful? It's your fault I had blood on my hands. That thing would've killed me! Besides, there's a thousand of them."

"Wrong. There's only one Rook."

"There's only one Violet," Yoojin counters. "You need to take better care of yourself. If not for us, then for Nathan."

Violet straightens and marches back to Yoojin as he gets to his feet. "I made a mistake and slipped. I don't need all of you to gang up on me and make me feel guilty for it. I don't need you or Alan breathing down my neck."

"That's not what I was trying to do." Yoojin tries to show his sincerity by touching her arms, but she shoves him away.

"Really? It sure feels like it." Violet stalks off, leaving him with the maven.

"You're going to leave him here?" Yoojin calls after her.

"Yes!" she yells over her shoulder.

Yoojin sighs, picking up the rag drenched in Violet's blood. He shakes it at the maven. "You better behave. I won't hesitate to use this." The maven grumbles in response. Shoving the cloth into his back pocket, he allows it to dangle out as a warning.

Turning to walk out, he realizes Nova's been watching all this time. "It's true, you know," she says.

"What is?" He scratches the back of his head, hoping to hide his annoyance.

"Since we met, you guys nag her every time she gets even the tiniest nick."

"You can hardly call this a tiny nick."

"I agree that was a big oops, but she's not as fragile as you make her out to be. She's stronger than both of you combined, and she heals abnormally fast. Cut her some slack."

"You don't know her as we do."

"That may be true, but I doubt you know women as I do. Keep at it, and she'll keep pushing you further away."

Yoojin huffs on his way out. He knows she's right, but it's not so easy letting someone you love more than anything continue to get hurt. In the back of his mind, he worries that she's purposely hurting herself and playing it off as clumsiness. She wasn't always this way. Violet's changed so much since their past. His memories of her are filled with happiness and regret.

The ship had been cleaned off, and most of the dirt had been pushed to a corner of the large facility. The maven Violet kept calling Rook proved helpful with the clean-up. Though it seemed to love her, it didn't hide its distaste for Yoojin in passing. The first flight was a little bumpy initially, but Nova gained control quickly. It wasn't like the other ships she'd flown, so it was remarkable how quickly she could adjust. Yoojin was still wary of Nova and how close she and Violet have become in such a short amount of time.

Yoojin had contacted his mother, informing her of the delay in his arrival, but he'd yet to inform her of his guests. She was leery when he told her of his intentions with Violet, but he got her to accept it after some convincing. He's finally bringing her home four years later, but bringing two more than he'd planned on may complicate things. Nova hasn't made any indications that she'll be joining them, but given Alan's obvious attachment, it's unlikely she'll stay behind.

Nova lowers the ship into the underground base once more. She flips switches and gently lands the ship with ease. "That was an impressive landing," Yoojin says.

"Thank you!" Nova replies with enthusiasm.

"If you could shut the doors. We don't want to leave it exposed," Yoojin adds. Nova pulls up a screen and does as he requests. As they depart the ship with Rook in tow, they watch it slowly begin to close. All eyes point to the sky as a strange sound comes from the enclosure, waiting for it to break down halfway. The clanking sounds are strange and arrhythmic. There are two more feet before closing when spider-like legs peek over. The body of the mechanical spider comes into view for a split second before it explodes into pieces. Yoojin looks over to see Violet with her pistol, smoke swirling from the barrel. Bio-scouts.

"Seekers," Nova gasps. "They know we're here."

"They may not. Violet destroyed it quickly. It wouldn't have had the chance to do a scan." Alan rubs her back to comfort her. The enclosure is sealed tight, and the lights ease on.

"No, it's no longer safe," Violet insists. "You have to get your people out of here before they send more, or something much worse."

"Where are we supposed to go?"

Violet holsters her weapon and turns to face her. "Nova, tell your people it was my fault. I exposed us to the seekers. Instruct them to leave this place. You and Alan will take them to our shelter. It's well-hidden, well-stocked, and made for a group this size."

"But leaving with such a large group would draw attention," Nova says, wide-eyed.

"It'd take days to get them there," Alan interjects.

"You have a ship." Violet gestures to the beautiful vessel they've repaired. "If your group is too large, take the women and children first and return for the others. Those who have transport can follow behind."

"Violet, what about you?" Nova says in a lower voice. "I can't take Alan. You need him."

Violet shakes her head with a smile. "Alan's the only person who can take you to the shelter. I don't remember the way. I'll leave with Yoojin. Everything'll be fine. It's better this way." Yoojin watches them in silence.

"You're not going anywhere without me. What if something happens?" Alan folds his arms over his chest.

"I can protect her." Yoojin steps in.

Alan's about to say something but shuts his mouth and looks away. Yoojin can tell there's a lack of trust. They've all been nervous around him as of late. In Violet's case, he's been blaming her trauma. He'll earn her trust back, though he doesn't know how he lost it in the first place. This is his best opportunity. It'll be like it was, just the two of them—a second chance.

"Rook." Violet captures Yoojin's attention again. "Alan and Nova." She side-hugs both as Rook comes to stand before them. "Guard them, protect them—my family. You keep them safe. Do you understand?" Rook steps forward, touching its taloned hand to Nova's cheek and then Alan's. Alan closes his eyes, holding his breath until the maven releases him. "Yes, they need you to help keep the rest of them in line. Do not hurt anyone. None of this." Violet shakes her head as she pulls on his weaponized arm. "None of this," she repeats sternly. The maven purrs, bending down to press its forehead to hers. "Good boy, Rook," she coos as she strokes its long face. She turns to Yoojin with a severe look. Yoojin nods in understanding as they make their way out.

"Violet!" Alan yells as he runs after them. She turns as he slams his body into hers, holding her tightly. He whispers something Yoojin can't hear in her ear, but she hugs him tighter before parting ways. Tears stream down her cheeks when she turns back to Yoojin.

"Let's go," Violet says in a low voice.

Chapter 19

ALAN

Rook stands behind Alan and Nova as her people gather to hear what she has to say. They're silent as they eye the creature looming over them. The last group comes in with Mathias standing in the back, leaning against the wall with his arms folded in defiance. With all eyes turning to Nova, he can see her shoulders pulling in. She's taking shallow breaths. Alan steps up, touching his hand to her lower back, and says to the assembled crowd, "There's been a seeker sighting. You're not safe here anymore." The people begin to murmur in fear, some in frustration.

"How did this happen?" one calls out from the crowd.

"It's because of that woman who left yesterday, isn't it?" yells another.

"It's because of the maven!" a woman says in fear.

"Where are we supposed to go?" another cries.

"Yes, Violet went to the surface. The maven is here to protect us," Alan says.

"Why don't you leave and take your maven with you! We wouldn't have this trouble if you hadn't come here!"

"You attacked us, in case you've forgotten," Alan starts, but Nova presses a hand on his shoulder to silence him as she steps forward.

"The relevant fact right now is that none of us can stay. We have a place we can go that's hidden in the mountains. A shelter that's well-stocked and made for a family as large as ours. Alan will take us there, but we need to move quickly. Only take what's necessary. Clothes and supplies."

"And how can we safely move everyone into the mountains?" Mathias interjects sardonically. Jenna stands behind him, watching cautiously.

"We have a ship that should be able to carry all of us."

"I thought it wasn't working." Toby joins the conversation.

"We fixed it. Listen, we don't know how long before more seekers come. You need to gather your things to leave immediately."

"Why should we listen to you? We didn't see any seekers," Mathias contradicts. "We're comfortable here. We finally have a safe place large enough and secure enough to sustain us. Even if there were seekers, they wouldn't be able to get in."

"If you want to stay, stay. No one will be forced against their will."

"Everyone will stay. You're not going to take that ship anywhere. You don't lead these people. I do."

Alan watches Nova as her back straightens and her head raises a little higher. "I'll lead those wise enough to recognize a fool when they see one. No one wants to be controlled by a selfish, egotistical child in a man's body. This maven behind me is insurance. He acts on my behalf. If any of you try to keep me from doing what's right, protecting this family, you'll answer to him." Nova points at Rook, and he steps forward. The crowd steps back in fear as a rumbling emits from its chest. "Get your things, those who want to go. We're leaving in 20 minutes with or without you."

Nova turns and walks back down the hall. Alan and Rook follow. When they arrive at the entrance to the ship, she turns on the spot. "Was I too harsh? Should I go back? Should I have said something else? He always pushes me, and I just take it, but I simply want to ensure my people are safe. He doesn't have their best interests at heart."

"Whoa, whoa." Alan holds her shoulders steady to keep her from pacing.

"I'm not a horse, Alan." Nova huffs her breath.

"No, you're *not* a horse. You're a strong, intelligent, kind, beautiful woman. You said exactly what you needed to get through to your people."

"You think I'm beautiful?" Nova asks, eyes wide as she looks up at him.

Alan steps closer, their faces mere inches away from each other. "Is that all you got out of what I said?" he says with a tilted smile.

"Answer the question," Nova says breathlessly.

Alan tucks hair behind her ear so that he can see her eyes better. "Yes, you are beautiful. You are…" In his peripheral vision, he sees movement accompanied by a rumbling purr. They look over to find Rook hunched low enough to be face-to-face with them, only a foot away, watching with its head tilted curiously.

"So creepy," Nova mumbles as she pulls away from Alan and disappears through the entrance.

"Really, Rook? There's something called spatial awareness. There's a large bubble around me, Rook." Alan draws an invisible circle around himself. "You popped that bubble! Just moved right into that bubble." He steps closer to Rook and points an accusing finger at him. "We were having a moment," he complains, slumping his shoulders in defeat and running his other hand through his hair. Rook lifts one clawed appendage and touches it to Alan's finger. A large breath escapes Alan. The maven starts to purr once again. "Great. Are you trying to have a moment with me now? Of course you are. Why are you like this?" He pulls his hand away.

Rook follows Alan to the ship. He busies himself with cleaning up even though they'll be leaving it all behind, while Nova sits at the end of the ramp, her leg shaking impatiently. She keeps checking the time as if hours have passed. The longer she waits, the more nervous she gets as she bites her knuckles. Alan doesn't want to give her hope if they refuse to listen, but he hopes they're smart enough to follow her lead.

It's been 15 minutes and no one has come. Alan squeezes Nova's shoulder as he passes to start up the ship. Rook stays near Nova, sensing her unease. As the engine roars to life, he looks out the windshield, disappointed that people aren't taking this seriously. He makes his way out of the ship to collect Nova and Rook. Nova jumps to her feet as he makes his way down the ramp. Her shoulders relax as families start filing in. They move quickly when they realize the ship is ready to go. Nova guides them into it, filling the second floor first. Alan assists after asking Rook to stand guard at the ramp. Everyone has enough room if they sit on the floor and bunks, the smallest children on their laps. Even Mathias decides to put his pride aside, taking one of the four seats in the cockpit with Jenna taking the other.

Nearly every crevice of the ship is full, and they hope it won't be too heavy to take off. Rook is the last one on the vessel and stands in the corridor. Nova opens the ceiling once more, now that the sun has fallen below the horizon. You can hear murmurs and awe as the sky opens to them. Alan watches as she flips switches and checks gauges before taking a deep, shaking breath. Her eyes glisten with tears as the ship lifts off the ground, and they rise out of the underground facility.

Alan puts in the coordinates, and they take off at a greater speed than the skyriders. The ride is quiet. Alan glances back at Mathias and Jenna, looking in opposite directions. The only sound amongst the roaring engines is the cry of a baby and the babbling of small children. Soon the landscape morphs into mountainous forests as they reach their destination. "The ship is too large to fit inside, so we need to land elsewhere," Alan says. "There's a meadow up the mountain a short distance."

He points it out on the map, allowing them to see the terrain as if it were daylight.

"What's that?" Nova points out an unnatural hole in the mountain a short distance from the waterfall.

"I don't know. Get closer." A light flashes and waves as they draw closer. "Is that…" Alan recognizes Jack waving a lamp, leading them into a facility similar to where they'd found the ship. "It's Jack. He's showing us where to land. Violet must have told him we were coming." He smiles, removing his seat belt and moving towards the ramp as Nova carefully brings the ship down. When the ramp is lowered, he impatiently hops out, jogging over to meet Jack as he turns a winch to close the ceiling overhead. Alan helps him as Jack seems to struggle. Once the roof is closed off and Jack locks it, Alan pulls him into a bear hug. Jack becomes rigid and Alan turns to see what has him on edge. Rook is making his way off the ship. Alan reassures Jack that it is safe. He believes him when he watches the many people leave the ship after the creature. Rook watches curiously as men, women and children pass him by. He makes no move to harm them.

Jack leads the large group into the shelter through a tunnel that Alan had no idea existed. Alan wonders how many more secrets this man's kept from Killian, from everyone. He shoves the thoughts to the back of his mind when Ember and Lilly come running. Alan lifts Ember into a hug while kissing the top of her head. Scooping Lilly up with his other arm, he hugs the girls as they squeal with delight. They begin filling him in on what he's missed since he's been gone. They speak simultaneously at such a fast pace that he has difficulty following, and he can't contain the laughter that bubbles up.

As Jack and Clara begin the tour in smaller groups, Alan makes a beeline for the infirmary. Nathan's condition hasn't changed, but the girls inform him they've seen him twitch. Alan doesn't have the heart to tell them it may be false hope. He brushes the hair from Nathan's forehead and greets him with a kiss on the forehead. "I'm home, little man."

Chapter 20
VIOLET

The black ocean looks hungry to swallow her up as it chops beneath. No land in sight has Violet on edge. She's never been this far from land. If something were to happen to her skyrider now, she'd be lost to the sea and the formidable creatures lurking below. Her teeth chatter as she tries to fly a little higher. Though the air has warmed, her nerves are getting to her as she desperately looks for land. Yoojin forbade her to go too high, to avoid being caught on the radar. He flies on, and she follows close behind.

It hasn't been more than an hour after they left the beach before a frosted mountain appears to emerge from the ocean depths. As they draw closer, the mountain grows more prominent. She feels a wave of relief. The warm sun rises, painting a rose hue across the streaks of cloud amongst the expanding mountains. Dread flows through Violet as the mountains break free from the water and float higher into the sky, exposing the jagged cliffs of its belly. Waterfalls turn to mist as the liquid escapes the mountain. The mountain looms over an island below, overflowing with vegetation, no beach in sight. At first, she thinks birds are swarming the island and mountain, but she soon realizes they're aircraft. This is a city. Arcadia.

Yoojin leads her around the island to a harbor. Many are working to pull large fish out of nets and into steaming crates. They wave when they recognize Yoojin; as Violet passes, they look wary. Yoojin leads her to a wharf where he proceeds to land. Violet lands near his speeder. He's by her side as soon as she shuts off the skyrider. He holds his hand out to help her off it. She looks at him curiously but accepts. Where was this chivalry coming from?

The air feels thick and warm here. Violet peels off her coat and stuffs it into her bag. Hoisting it over her shoulder, she steps away from her rider. Yoojin takes her hand and places it in the crook of his arm. He still wears that knit hat, as he always does, but he left his gray trench coat behind. A blue blazer is draped over his other arm, matching the blue vest he's always worn. His sleeves are rolled up to his elbows, exposing his muscular forearms.

He leads her away from the wharf. Violet looks back at the exposed skyrider. "Shouldn't we conceal them?"

"Don't worry. Arcadia's the safest place you can be. No one will touch our things." Violet raises a quizzical brow but says nothing.

Walking deeper into the lush island, he presents different plants and foods as if she'd never heard of them. Granted, she had never seen most of them in person, but she was educated. It feels condescending, though she knows he's just excited. Many people are working in fields to get ready for planting. They all wear a uniform color, brown. They almost blend in with their surroundings. Everyone Violet and Yoojin pass greet him by bowing their head with a smile. He greets most in the same way. Others he greets by name, and they seem to glow with joy at being spoken to.

"These people seem to love you."

"And I love them. They're family."

"All of them?"

"Not by blood, but similar to your relationship with Jack." Violet nods. The terrain changes, revealing beautiful grass-covered terraced hillsides. People are standing on the tiers with their pant legs rolled up to their thighs; each tier is flooded with water. An old woman is tending the field some distance away. She holds her back, and Violet can almost feel the ache as she stretches. "Halmeonim!" Yoojin steps away from Violet and calls her again as he waves. The woman waves back, mumbling something as she makes her way over.

Violet hears her grumble as she approaches, "Aigo, Aigo." She pats Yoojin's arms. As he bends down, she places her palms on either side of his face and croons something in their language. Yoojin laughs and gives her a gentle hug. He continues to speak in Korean to her before she turns to Violet with a shocked look that eases into an excited smile. The old woman moves to her.

Grabbing her hands, she shakes them while speaking in her language. Violet looks at Yoojin for help with translation, but he's smiling down at the old woman with fondness. Violet nods and smiles, hoping she doesn't offend the woman. She reaches her calloused hand up to pat Violet's cheek. Yoojin says something and the woman nods, bowing her head several times as he guides Violet away with his hand against her back.

When they're a reasonable distance away, Violet turns back to see that the woman has returned to work. "What was all that about?"

"That was my *halmeonim*, my grandma. She's my favorite person in this entire world."

"What was she saying to me?"

"Halmeonim said she's been waiting to meet you, that you're a beautiful child, and to take good care of me."

"That's very sweet. I didn't think you would've told others about me."

"Of course I have. You're a significant person in my life."

"Am I?"

"You're very important," he says seriously, looking straight ahead. Violet feels uneasy as her heart begins to race. She doesn't speak more on the subject, and Yoojin becomes more focused on where they're going rather than giving her a tour of the island.

The closer they come to the island's center, the more people there are. There are dirt roads and many homes, all similar little huts exposed to the ground instead of having a sturdy foundation. They're generally the same size regardless of how large a family lives in them. As the village grows outward, the homes become more modernized. Several massive trees tower over all the houses in the city's center. Yoojin and Violet follow the road leading up to the trees, and Violet looks up at the aircraft swarming around them and the mountain above.

As they draw closer, she realizes they aren't just trees. They're so large that they've built high-rise buildings inside them. From these living buildings there are pods docked along the exterior. They look very similar to Yoojin's speeder and constantly come and go. It sounds as though they're approaching a giant beehive. Violet looks up when she hears a different sound. It's another type of ship, a sleek silver one, taking off from the mountain above. She stops and watches as it hurtles away, reflecting the sun into her eyes before disappearing into the distance. Her mouth becomes dry. She's seen that ship before, or one very similar to it.

"Come on, we're almost there." Yoojin presses his palm to her lower back. Violet closes her mouth and hopes that Alan and Nova have made it home safely. They walk up to the closest tree. At the base of the trunk is a triangular slit, and along that slit is a grey metal lattice framework built into it with glass windows. Higher above are the docks for the pods.

Yoojin leads her inside. The tree weaves through the building. Her mouth hangs open as she stares up at the tall ceilings. He approaches a desk with a woman in a black suit. She stands up and bows her head before him. Violet turns around in slow circles as she admires the multicultural community, and the architecture allowing nature and modern buildings to coincide. While her eyes follow a spiral staircase lining the boundary of the walls, a very handsome man locks eyes with her as he descends. He's tall with brown skin, and his dark hair is shaved close to his scalp. His clean-shaven face draws out his strong jawline. Though he has strong masculine features, his large brown eyes are soft.

Violet closes her mouth, knowing she looks like a fish out of water. She looks around to see if he's staring at someone behind her, but there's no one, and Yoojin is still talking to the woman at the desk. The corner of the man's lips curl. His expression turns from humored to mischievous as he slinks up close to her. "Hello," he says in a low rumbling voice while looking her up and down.

Violet tilts her head back to look him in the eye. "H-hi."

She doesn't have anything else to say as he steps closer, even though there's barely any space between them. His beaming smile is crippling. "You wear the color of the noble," he says, tugging gently on the blue scarf Yoojin had given her, tucked inside her blouse. "And yet you don't belong here, do you?"

Violet's cheeks flush as her brows knit together. "Colors don't belong to anyone," she replies as she stands her ground.

"We'll see what they have to say about that." Though his hands are clasped behind his back, he somehow makes her feel like he's engulfing her.

"Are you one of them?" Violet steps back, and he steps forward.

"Me?" He laughs. "I wear the colors of the militia."

"If the militia is responsible for taking lives, black is very fitting," Violet says, looking him over before bringing her eyes back to his lips as they spread into a wider grin.

"I only take the lives of those who don't know their place," he teases, stepping forward again, forcing her to step backward to keep her distance.

"I know my place," Violet says, though her voice comes out weaker than she would've liked.

"And what place is that?" he says, lifting a finger to carefully move a curl out of her eyes without touching her skin.

The hair on her skin rises, and a chill runs down her spine. Charlie's image flashes into her mind, and in reaction she grabs the man's hand, twists it around his back, and swipes her leg, pulling his feet out from under him. In a matter of seconds, he's face-down on the marble floor. Her left knee digs into his spine as she stomps her right boot mere centimeters from his face. "My place is wherever I choose it to be," Violet growls close to his ear.

Yoojin spins when he hears the body hit the floor. "Violet!"

The man on the floor begins to laugh. "Know your place," Violet says to him, releasing him to stand tall with her arms folded.

"I'm sorry, madam," he laughs while he gets to his feet and faces her. "Please accept my humble apology." He places his hand over his heart and bows deeply. "I now know that my place is…beneath this beautiful woman."

Violet snorts out a laugh, though she refuses to look at him. Yoojin steps between her and the man before her. "Leave us," he says. Violet looks at him sharply, only to see that he's speaking to the man.

"I can't, sir," he says condescendingly.

"Yes, you can. Walk away."

"I would, but your mother has assigned me as Ms. Odaire's bodyguard."

Violet moves around Yoojin to spectate. "That is unnecessary," Yoojin growls.

"I'm now well-aware." He winks at Violet before giving his full attention to Yoojin. "But Madam Kim was clear that Ms. Odaire is not to leave my sight."

Yoojin huffs and puffs in frustration as he glares the man down. "You're to keep your hands to yourself. Do you understand me?" he blusters.

"Understood." The man bows low.

Yoojin leads Violet around him to the large staircase the man came from. She glances back to see him following them. He winks at her as they climb the stairs in silence. "Who is that?" Violet leans in to ask.

"Dominic Powell," Yoojin answers.

"Yoojin's best friend," the man adds from behind them.

"You don't need to speak in your role as a bodyguard," Yoojin says in exasperation.

"True," Dominic says with a toothy grin.

Violet doesn't ask any further questions, since this entire subject seems to put Yoojin in a foul mood. As she begins questioning just how many more stairs they'll be climbing, they stop at one of the several doors they've passed. Yoojin enters a code and the doors slide open. He invites Violet in and begins to follow, but Dominic blocks the entrance. "These pods only seat two, sir," he says with a stern look.

"There are many other pods."

"Yes sir, and you are free to choose any other pod beside the one she uses."

"If you think I'm going to leave her in your hands—"

"My apologies. My orders are always to keep Ms. Odaire in my sights. Considering these seat two people maximum, I'd be putting my career at risk if I were to contravene."

"Yoojin, I'll be fine." Violet sits along the bench seat and fastens the belt over her lap. Dominic's mischievous grin returns.

"Don't flirt with her." Yoojin stalks off to find his pod before either of them can respond.

Dominic fights to keep the laughter contained as Yoojin disappears up the staircase. He then slides in next to her, fastening his belt and locking the doors behind them. The aircraft turns on with the flick of a few switches. With his hands on the yoke, he turns to Violet. "I want to make myself very clear. I'm sincerely apologizing for making you uncomfortable. I only wanted to get Yoojin riled up, but I didn't think about how it might affect you. So, again, I'm truly sorry."

"You're his best friend?"

"We grew up together. I've made it my goal in life to embarrass him anytime the opportunity arises."

"He's been pretty uptight as of late," Violet says, accepting his apology with a nod.

"Yoojin finally succeeded in bringing home his dream girl. I'm happy for him, but now comes the battle of persuading his family to approve. That'd put anyone on edge."

"Excuse me?" Violet stares at him wide-eyed.

"Did I say something wrong?"

"I didn't come here for that. He hasn't even told me of intentions along those lines."

"Then why did you come?"

"He hasn't even hinted at the idea." Violet ignores his question, staring out the window to the island below and the swarming pods.

Dominic tilts his head and gives her a sideways look. "I have a hard time believing that. When Yoojin likes someone, he's pretty obvious. The longing looks while pretending to be indifferent. The blush from accidental skin-to-skin contact."

Dominic would've kept going, but Violet stops him with a raised palm. "I'm aware of all that, but he knows I could never...we could never...for goodness sake." Violet's face lands in her palms with a smack. Dominic bites his lips, trying not to take the situation lightly. Violet looks up at him, and he relaxes his face to look more serious. Her cheeks are flushed, and she takes shallow breaths. "How long has he been planning this?" Violet almost weeps.

"Uh...I've known for at least the past five years or so."

"Five years he's kept this to himself?" Her voice raises in pitch.

"Not really. Everyone here knows all about you. He didn't shut up about you. There was no living with him when you disappeared." Dominic shivers at the thought.

Violet puts her head between her knees and takes deep breaths through her nose. "What do I do? What am I supposed to do?" she asks herself.

"Honestly, his mother probably won't approve anyway. She had someone lined up for him, and he's been putting it off for a while now."

Violet shakes her head, closing her eyes tight. "This isn't why I came here," she whispers to herself again and again. Dominic leans in to hear what she is saying. "No, focus on why you came here. Nothing else matters."

Sitting up abruptly, Dominic straightens up to match her. "So why did you agree to come here again?"

Violet looks at him in all seriousness. "I came here to learn about Arcadia and who Yoojin really is."

"That's it?"

"Yup." Violet folds her arms and hunkers down. "And then I'll go home to my son, where I belong."

"I thought he was coming here too."

Violet turns her head slowly to glare at him. "You thought wrong." She faces the window once more. "Let's get this over with so I can go home."

"As you wish, m'lady."

Dominic releases the pod from the dock and it immediately begins to plunge, causing Violet to cling to the walls before the engine turns on and it begins to rise higher and higher. The aircraft is a quiet ride. Like a bee from the hive, they move with the traffic's flow as they swarm around the cliffs of the floating mountains. As pods and other ships come and go, they wait their turn to land, signaled on the screen Dominic points out to her. As they draw closer to the mountains, she realizes they aren't just mountains. The mountain face is broken up geometrically, and within each crag lies a bustling city, unlike anything she's ever seen before. Somehow these people have managed to build a city that mimics nature itself.

They land smoothly on a large landing strip at the base of the snowy mountains. As the doors open, they're greeted by brisk air whipping around them. Violet shivers as she holds her hair in place so she can see. She barely hears Dominic as he guides her to where Yoojin is waiting. The noise from the wind and ships is unending as vehicles come and go. Violet digs in her bag for her coat as they walk. She notices the militia accompanying Yoojin as they come near. Dominic takes her bag, allowing her to don her coat without juggling. She focuses on Yoojin and her anger toward him as she takes her bag back from Dominic. The wind dies down, and it isn't as frigid as they move away from the landing strip.

Violet walks straight up to Yoojin with her head held high. He unfolds his arms, looking uneasy under her scrutiny. Before Violet can form words to speak her mind, a woman in blue walks down a path flanked by her guards. Yoojin turns to the woman, giving her all his attention with his arms at his sides. This must be the mother. The woman looks Yoojin over, a mild disgust crossing her face. "Why do you insist on wearing colors below your station?" she asks. Yoojin quickly removes the knit hat from his head, tucking it in his back pocket. He always wears that hat. He looks so different without it. His black hair falls past his brow as he averts his eyes. "Are you going to introduce us?"

Yoojin quickly collects Violet, displaying her in front of him. "Madam Kim, Eun-Ju, this is Violet Odaire. Violet, this is my mother."

"It's a pleasure." Violet sticks her hand out to greet her.

Madam Kim pauses with her eyes glued to Violet's hand. "And the boy?" She looks at Yoojin.

"My son will stay where he is, thank you," Violet responds for Yoojin as she glares back at him, a warning she hopes he understands.

Madam Kim snickers. "I would think you'd want to provide the best care for him in his condition. There's no better place for him to recover than Arcadia."

"I'll be the one to decide what's best for my son," Violet snaps. "And how do you know about his condition?" She steps forward and the guards counter.

"I told her." Yoojin pulls her back.

"Why are you telling strangers things that don't concern them?" Violet asks through clenched teeth.

"Violet, my dear, he was concerned for your well-being. You and your son have been on his mind for some time now." She says it in the sweetest voice, though the look on her face is patronizing.

"That's nice and all, but I've heard nothing of you or this place. And I've been burned before, so forgive me if I don't appreciate people deciding the future of my family and me behind my back."

Madam Kim smiles as she steps closer. She looks down at Violet's collar. Violet stares at her defiantly as Yoojin's mother slowly pulls the scarf from her neck and holds it up. "This color is reserved for nobility." She smiles kindly.

"I'm well-aware." Violet glances back at the straight-faced Dominic.

"Then I'm sure you understand if I return it to its rightful owner." Madam Kim holds it out to Yoojin.

"By all means, it would be an honor for someone of your...stature to return it to my neck." Violet steps forward with her hands clasped behind her back and bows to make it easier.

"I think there's a misunderstanding."

Violet keeps her shoulders stationary but lifts her head to look Madam Kim in the eye and speaks loud enough for everyone to hear. "If anyone is mistaken, it is you, Madam Kim. You see, I earned my nobility by saving your son's life. It was a gift. That scarf belongs to me." Violet raises her shoulders so their eyes are at the same level, and in a low voice utters, "I'd return it if you know what's good for you."

Madam Kim returns Violet's smile as she steps back. Violet bows once more but holds her stare as Madam Kim reluctantly wraps the scarf around her neck. "Her confidence is commendable, Yoojin," she says as she ties it too snuggly around Violet's neck. Violet doesn't flinch but sends her a wicked smile back. "You must be starving. Let's have lunch."

Chapter 21

PIPER

The blindingly white room echoes with screams as the girls jump from platform to platform. They're seeing something Piper cannot. Each white platform holds its secret, and she needs to avoid the ones that will cause her harm. Jasper's advice was to wait until they saw what the other girls do. One by one, the girls are swallowed into these thin platforms; most are too high to see how. Piper keeps a note in her mind of which ones to avoid.

Following those not affected by the platform works well at first, but she's shaken as she watches a girl fall apart as if she stepped into a pool of acid. Her cries are tortured as her skin bubbles and melts away like cheese in a hot pan, revealing muscle tissue and bone. Layer by layer, she dissolves until her screams become a gurgling groan. Piper loses her lunch over the side of the platform. Her weakness causes her to lose track of the rest of the girls as they get farther ahead. Looking back, there's one scared stiff at the entrance. She watches her go into a panic as a green gas slowly swirls around her feet. As she moves around, trying to kick it away, it swirls up, causing her to cough when it enters her lungs. She screams as she begins to cough up blood and her eyes start to bleed. "Help me!" the girl cries as she chokes on the gas. Five girls behind Piper start moving quicker, trying to avoid the gas.

"Jasper! This isn't working! You need to give me something! Each trial is a puzzle. There must be a way to figure out which platform is safe!" She looks at the three paths before her. The third is a death trap, so there are two options left.

"I can't figure it out, Piper! It's just a bunch of flashing circles ranging in color, and every time they blink it's a different color."

"What color am I on now?"

"I wasn't keeping track, and if there's an indicator for your current location, I can't see it."

"Jasper!"

"I'm sorry! I don't know how to help you!"

Piper quickly counts the platforms from her entrance to the current one. "Okay, from the entrance I'm five platforms up and twelve from the left. What color is that?" Piper waits for him to respond, but there is only a strange, muffled sound.

"What are you?" Jasper's voice sounds far away.

"Jasper." She looks at the two platforms to the left. It's a 50/50 chance of success, so she leaps to the one furthest to the left. The platform transports her into a jungle thick with vines and many different plants. As she shoves her way through, strange orange and red, bell-shaped flowers stick to her. As she pulls away, they spill their sap-like liquid onto her sleeves, making it harder to rip away from the plants. Finally, she finds her way to the platform's edge, with three more platforms to choose from.

"Jasper, I really need your help!" Piper screams in a panic. Nothing. No response, just the continuous sound of static and the always-present rhythmic beep in the background.

There are only two more levels before reaching the exit. One of the girls from behind her reaches the platform from the other side. They both must choose the correct one. The girl leaps ahead with a look of determination to the middle platform. She instantly turns to jump away but is caught by something, and her blood-curdling screams are accompanied by breaking bones before she crumples away and sinks into the platform as if it were a thick bath of cream.

The gas is still rising. Piper jumps to the platform on the right as another girl reaches the next safely. She quickly attempts the jump to the same platform but is yanked back by the ankle. She drops to her knees, clawing at the smooth platform as a slimy tentacle wraps around her waist. "Help me!" Piper screams to the girl, but she acts as if she doesn't hear a word as she reaches the exit and disappears through the door.

Piper unwinds the tentacle from her waist and ankle, leaving a slimy, stringy residue. She reaches the other platform, but another tentacle catches her by the wrist, slowly pulling her back. Piper tries to unwind the tentacle, but tiny hooked claws sink into her flesh, fastening themselves to her arm. She screams in pain. She crouches down to anchor herself and tries pulling away, ripping at her skin. "Let go!" she roars, but it doesn't budge. She's beginning to lose her grip as it slowly drags her back. In a panic, she sinks her teeth into the tentacle, filling her mouth with bitter slime. She gags but yanks her head like a dog ripping at a slab of meat. She rips it in half but it still holds fast. She spits out the mucus, sinks her teeth again, and yanks back, freeing herself from the creature. What's left of its tentacle is still writhing on her arm.

She gags as the mucus and slime spill out of her mouth. She quickly gets to her feet, jumps to the exit platform, and spills out of the doorway as she ejects slime and bile from her stomach, startling those who have made it out. She's gasping for air as she weakly gets to her feet and wipes her mouth. Her eyes water as she makes her way to Jasper.

She pulls the door open just as Reese saunters out. Piper's in shock as Reese walks past her without a word. Inside the room, Jasper pulls his suit over his shoulders and zips himself up. As he adjusts himself, he looks up to find Piper standing there with a look of pure hatred. He turns pale as he sees the state she's in. The tentacle writhes on her bleeding arm, and her hair is a mess of sap and slime. Jasper closes the distance between them, asking if she's all right. All she can hear is her blood pounding in her ears as her veins set on fire.

Piper backs into the corridor away from Jasper. He pulls at the tentacle, ripping her skin more, but she doesn't feel the pain as a burning rage blinds her. She pushes Jasper so hard that he falls back. Before he can react, she's on top of him with her hands around his throat. "I almost died because you were getting your rocks off! I would never have left you like that! Are you trying to turn me into one of those zombies? Is that what happened to your other partners? They don't screw you, so you screw anyone willing, leaving them to fight for their lives on their own?" Many hands grab hold of her. "Get off me!" Piper barks as they drag her back.

"Piper, I'm so sorry!" he rasps while massaging his throat.

"I don't want your apologies, you idiot!" She pulls free of those holding her back. Ripping the tentacle off her arm, she throws it at him. The tentacle slaps against his face, leaving streams of slime and blood. Piper shoves her way through the crowd of onlookers. Finally getting to the bathroom, she rips her clothes off, leaving them in the middle of the floor. Frantically she scrubs the slime and muck off her body. She takes shallow rasping breaths; her lungs feel like they're being squeezed and she can't get enough air. It may be the blood loss, but things begin to blacken around her, and she leans her back against the cold tile. Her head spins as she slides to the floor, letting the hot water pelt her while she cries hysterically.

Gareth bursts in, skidding to a stop, catching himself with his hands before falling to the ground. "Geez, Piper," he says as he punches the shower button, turning off the water and activating the drier. "You're bleeding." He lifts her, allowing the air to flow around her. She doesn't respond, crying as if he weren't there. The air stops and he lifts her into his arms, setting her on the bench. She sits there shivering as he drapes a tunic over her, wrapping her up. He quickly retrieves the first aid kit and makes fast work of cleaning up her arm. By now she's stopped crying but is instead now staring off into nothing.

He helps her get dressed and begins drying her hair with someone else's clothing. Her eyes fill with tears, and he kneels in front of her so she can see his face. At first, she doesn't see anything but a blur of colors. She closes her eyes, forcing the tears down her cheeks. When she opens them, she can see the worry written all over Gareth's face as he rubs the cloth over her head. "Gareth." Her voice is barely there. He leaves the fabric draped over her head as he wipes the tears from her cool cheeks. His hands burn her skin, and she feels her chest tighten again. She grabs hold of his collar as if he might disappear. "I can't do this anymore."

"I know."

"I can't do it."

"It's okay."

"No, Gareth, they were dying in horrible ways. I almost died. Gareth, I can't go back in." She pulls him closer, so their foreheads touch as she starts to hyperventilate.

"Okay, shhh, it's okay," Gareth croons. "I'll find a way out. I'll get you out." He speaks louder so that she can hear him over her grieving moans. "Take deep breaths." He sits beside her, breathing deeply, guiding her. It's not long before her breathing's calm once more. Her head lulls back on his shoulder with her eyes closed.

"Gareth?"

"Hmm?"

"I threw up," she rasps.

"Yeah? Do you need water? Do you want to brush your teeth?" Gareth asks. Piper lazily nods. "Here." He lifts her, leading her to the sink to brush her teeth and then back to her bed. Before she even hits the pillow, everything goes black.

Piper hears distant voices, and her ears begin to perk up. Her body feels heavy. She opens her swollen eyes and jolts awake when she sees Jasper sitting on the bed across from her. "Gareth," she rasps.

Gareth twists, kneeling at her bedside. "I'm here."

Piper clears her throat. "What's he doing in here?"

"He was just telling me what happened, and he brought us food," he says, setting the tray beside her legs.

"I'm not hungry." Piper avoids looking at Jasper and the food.

"You need to eat. I'll force-feed you if I must."

"I'll eat when he leaves," Piper says defiantly.

Jasper gets up from the bed, nodding. Piper glances at him as he leaves. His blonde hair is disheveled, his cheeks look hollow, and his eyes look puffy. Once he's out of sight, Piper begins eating as if she hadn't eaten all day.

"He feels bad, you know," Gareth says.

"Good," she says between bites.

"He promises it'll never happen again."

"Can't we switch partners? Just swap suits. I doubt they'd notice."

"I wish it were that easy." He smiles at her, watching her scarf the food down with a smile. When Piper finishes, she pushes the tray away. Gareth folds his arms on the bed and rests his cheek while he stares at her.

"Do I have food on my face?" Piper asks, wiping her mouth.

Gareth smiles. "No."

"Then why are you looking at me like that?"

Gareth doesn't respond immediately but searches her face as if he'll find the answer there. "I never thought I'd feel this way about anyone." A faint blush paints his cheeks.

"What way?" she says, picking at the bandages on her left arm. Her arm throbs, but she focuses on his voice.

"Like…" Gareth lifts his head and runs his fingers through his wavy black hair as if it's torture to speak his mind. "Like we're all jigsaw puzzles. We're almost complete except for that one piece missing. I could take a piece from another puzzle, but it won't fit. Even if it did fit, it'd be off. I feel like I've found my missing puzzle piece. Without you, my puzzle is incomplete."

"Are you saying you can't live without me?" Piper pulls the covers off and lets her legs dangle off the bed.

Gareth raises his head and balls his hands into one fist, pressing it to his lips. "I'm saying I love you…" He looks at her from the corner of his eye to see her reaction.

Piper pulls his hands down and pulls him closer so she can look at him straight on. "I came here to help my aunt rise out of the gutters. I didn't come here for love." Gareth looks down in embarrassment. Piper holds her hands against his cheeks to get his attention back. "But you have so many strings tied around my heart, it's constricting."

Gareth's eyes glaze as they rove over her face. "You make it sound cumbersome."

"What I'm saying is, I love you too."

Gareth gawks at her. "Sorry, I didn't hear you."

"I love you, Gareth."

Piper is silenced by his soft, pillowy lips. Gently his fingers trace the line of her jaw, down her neck and into her hair. His lips part as his tongue samples hers. Gareth tries to pull away slightly to look at her, but she doesn't allow it. His arms tighten around her waist, and her legs wrap around him as heat ignites in her abdomen. They melt into each other, losing themselves in their kiss, one that evolves from sweet to passionate and then greedy and desperate.

The sound of laughter pulls them back to reality as they reluctantly pull away, breathing heavily. Their breaths mingle as their foreheads press together. "If you're done, I'd like a word." Piper gasps in surprise. Killian leans against the wall, waiting patiently. Gareth glares up at him with that look of death she now adores.

"Your Aunt Josephine's being taken care of. She's undergoing treatment as we speak. According to your contract, we'll relocate her when she's in recovery."

"Thank you." Piper feels a weight lift off her shoulders, though she's in shock that they're following through.

Killian pushes himself off the wall to walk away, but Gareth stops him. Piper gets to her feet, unsure of what will happen. Killian's eyes roll before meeting Gareth's. "Is there a way out of this place?" Gareth asks.

"Of course there is. How do you think I got here?"

"Take us with you. We can't stay here."

"I can't help you. You signed a contract."

"I never signed any contract," Gareth growls.

"No, worse, you were caught snooping." Killian folds his arms indifferently.

"Please, you're the only one who can truly help us. Inform my cousin, tell my family the truth, or tell us how to get out and we'll find our way from there."

"Please," Piper begs while resting her hand on Gareth's arm.

Killian glances at her bandages and back at Gareth. He studies him for so long that they're about to give up. Finally, stepping close, he lowers his voice. "I'll tell you the way out, but it's imperative you're not followed. Do you understand?"

Gareth and Piper look at each other with renewed hope.

Chapter 22

YOOJIN

Sweat drips down Yoojin's collar as he watches Violet interact with his mother. Their introduction was not what he'd imagined. The look Violet gave him when his mother mentioned Nathan cut his soul to pieces. He hopes to never be on the receiving end of it again. Once their hackles settled, Violet was led into the heart of Arcadia. His mother had instructed her to clean up and change. He cringed at her commanding tone, hoping Violet wouldn't put up a fight.

Yoojin had a room prepared with her taste in mind, knowing she'd feel out of place. There's a lounging area and table separate from the bedroom. She had described the beach from Safe Haven several times, so he knew she'd appreciate the view of the ocean. He hoped it'd bring some comfort. Violet said nothing as she entered her room. He anxiously left her to get cleaned up himself.

Later, Yoojin wrang his hands under the dining table, waiting for Violet. He knew Dom would make sure
she was okay, but his nerves were still getting to him.
He wanted to be with her, to care for her. Instead, he
waits with his mother, who grows more impatient by
the minute. Yoojin gets to his feet as they finally arrive.
Dom leads with a knowing smile, and Violet follows,
wearing a mixture of her attire and the brown suit provided to her. The simple brown blazer fits her snuggly,
offsetting the worn black pants she came in. The blue
scarf is wrapped around her head in a display, pulling
her hair up and off her neck with a few loose curls framing her face. It brings a smile to his face as she walks in
with her chin held high, as if she owns the place.

Now he watches as his mother interrogates her
while Dom stands against the wall, eavesdropping.
Violet eats her meal and gives vague answers to her
questions. When she doesn't want to answer a question,
she takes her time chewing her mouthful of food and
deflects with a question of her own. "So, what exactly
are your intentions with Yoojin?" his mother eventually
asks. Yoojin freezes mid-bite.

"I don't see how that's any of your business," Violet
answers before taking a sip from the goblet. She makes
a face and puts the goblet off to the side.

"He's my son."

"That's irrelevant, seeing as he's an independent
adult. Unless you still nurse him when he's home."
Though the food hadn't yet made it into his mouth,
Yoojin chokes as she continues without missing a beat,
Dom snickering behind her. "In that case, I intend to

hightail it out of here, because I don't want any part of that."

"It's not necessary to be vulgar." His mother responds with a tight jaw as Yoojin recovers.

"You don't deny it. Should I leave?"

"I don't think I need to answer such a question."

"It'd make sense why he has such thick silky hair." Violet looks over at him with a charming smile. A chemical floods his veins, sending a tingling sensation through his body, and he can't take his eyes off her.

"I would never." His mother's voice pulls him out of his euphoria, tearing his eyes from hers to stare at his meal.

Yoojin doesn't hear anything from there. His mind races with thoughts of Violet. He'd planned to bring her here to show her what life could be like in the safety of Arcadia, not to give her over to his hostile mother and have her questioned to no end. When he's finally had enough, he gets up quickly, causing the chair to screech as its feet scrape along the floor. He slaps his napkin onto his food and turns to Violet.

"Sorry for my tardiness." A wave of relief flows through Yoojin as a tall, silver-haired man enters the room. "Though it seems I've come right in the knick of time." A soft smile warms his face.

"Violet, this is my father."

Violet gets to her feet when the man approaches her with his hand out in invitation. She gives him her hand, and her shoulders tense when he brings his lips to her knuckles. "Violet, my dear. My name is Robert.

It's an honor to finally meet you. We've heard nothing but good things."

"Have you? I don't mean to be rude, but I wouldn't have thought so with the amount of questioning I've received since my arrival."

"I must apologize on behalf of my wife. She can be a bit overprotective. Yoojin is our only child."

"Ah, I see. Well, it's a pleasure to meet you, Mister…"

"Just Robert. You're practically family at this point."

"It's kind of you to say so."

"Eun-Ju, you've been exaggerating. She's all manners," Robert says as he takes a seat across from Violet. "Yoojin, have you given her a tour yet?"

"I'm sure she's tired from her travels," Madam Kim answers for him.

"Not at all, Eun-Ju. I'd love a tour." She gets to her feet and watches the anger flood the woman's face hearing her first name out of Violet's mouth. "Will you be joining us, Robert?"

"I'd love to, but I haven't eaten yet, and it seems neither has my wife. Why don't you go on without us?"

"I hope to speak with you again, Robert. Enjoy your meal," Violet says, bowing her head to him and turning to Yoojin. Her face is aglow with smiles.

Yoojin holds out his elbow. Violet takes it after a quick bow of her head in the direction of his mother, as if an afterthought. He can hear his mother slam her utensils against her plate as they leave the room. Dom follows behind silently. "Did you see how disrespectful she is?" His parent's voices fade away as he rushes Violet out.

Adding more distance between his mother and Violet allows him to relax. As they walk through the halls Yoojin used to play in, he's overcome with joy at showing her where he grew up. That is, until she pulls away to turn to Dom. "How was that for keeping it cool?"

"That was much better." Dom smiles in approval, and she grins back at him.

"You two sure have become chummy for only knowing each other for a few hours." Dom shoots him a knowing smile.

"Is he not your best friend? Why would I make an unnecessary enemy?" Yoojin nods thoughtfully. Violet looks him over. "Dominic, can you give us some space to talk, please?" Without a word, Dom steps away out of sight. The frustration bubbles up in him. If he had asked for a private conversation with Violet, Dom would've closed in on them, but she asks and he does so without question.

Violet brings his attention back as she folds her arms and keeps walking. Yoojin is quick to catch up. A guard passes, bowing to them both. Violet bows her head in return. "How is it that everyone here seems to know almost everything about my son and me, yet I know nothing of Arcadia and its people?"

"You never asked."

"Yoojin, you let me believe you roamed the world alone. You let me think you were like me."

"It never occurred to me that we were different."

"You never thought, maybe since we were spending so much time together, you might tell me about your home, your family?"

"I wanted to tell you about it, but you had someone waiting for you in Safe Haven. I was respecting your boundaries."

Violet stops and turns to face him. "Are pet names your way of respecting boundaries? Besides, I don't remember establishing any boundaries to respect."

"I'm sorry. Honestly, I wanted to bring you here a long time ago. When the accident happened, I thought it was all over. When we found each other again, I did ask you to come home with me. I gave you that option."

"You did. Maybe I should've listened," she says as she grips her arms so tight her knuckles pale, and her eyes glaze over. "Or perhaps not. Bringing Nathan here to let your mother belittle us is not the environment I'd want to raise him in." She says it more to herself as she continues walking.

"That's my fault. She's taking her frustration out on you because I ran away when she tried to marry me off." Yoojin folds his arms to match her.

"Was her choice so bad?"

"She wasn't you." Yoojin looks down at her. Violet stops but stares ahead as she takes shallow breaths. Her neck and ears flush.

"You had so many opportunities to tell me your feelings, Yoojin. Instead, I hear of your intentions from a stranger. Can you imagine how I might be feeling right now?" Yoojin has no words. As she looks up at him, a tear falls. Violet's eyes shimmer, reflecting the hurt he's caused her. Something he never intended. "Had you told me early on…" Violet shakes her head as if to shake away her thought as she begins to walk off again.

Yoojin grabs her arm, pulling her back to him. "Had I told you, it wouldn't have changed anything."

Violet looks up at him with bitter anger. "It would've changed everything," she said through her teeth as tears raced to her chin. "I wanted a reason to leave Safe Haven. I wanted to take Nathan out of that toxic environment, but I had nowhere to go! I needed a way to escape Charlie. I needed you! You let me believe I had nowhere to go." Violet rips her arms from his grasp, walking away.

Yoojin's petrified. Dom appears next to him like a ghost. "A lot's going on in that head of hers."

"It's never been simple." Yoojin sighed. "I thought—"

"You've always liked a challenge," Dom teases.

"What would you do?"

"Be honest, Yoojin. She needs to know everything. If you hold anything back…" Dom turns to face him. "And I mean anything, you'll lose her."

"Where do I even start?"

"Start with this tour." Dom shrugs and trots after her.

Yoojin lies on his back, staring up at the ceiling. Violet asked more questions than he'd been prepared to answer. He had to rely on Dom to answer many of them. It was an eye-opener. He knew everything about the island below but only found interest in some of the ins and outs of Arcadia. Violet genuinely had an interest in his home and everyone in it. She greeted all who passed and introduced herself when the opportunity arose.

We didn't have permission to access several places, and Violet was visibly irritated by that. They'd explained it was for safety reasons, but she wasn't satisfied with that answer. Especially when it was regarding how the mountain floats. Dom explained the mechanism, but she yearned to see it up close. Both explained that it wasn't in their power to access certain parts of the island. Violet had looked at him like she'd caught him in a lie. Since reconnecting, she's made it clear she doesn't trust him.

Yoojin reminisces about the time he almost asked her. The night everything went to hell.

Violet sits against the wall, panting between gulps of water. Taking a deep breath, she closes her eyes, leaning her head back. Yoojin wipes the sweat from his forehead. This round of sparring was particularly draining. He could tell she had something on her chest she wasn't ready to speak about. He can't help but adore everything about this woman. She's tough as nails, with eyes that pierce your soul, brown hair that turns to fire in the morning sun, and tan skin from sitting on that dock she always talks about. He's so busy admiring her from head to toe that he doesn't notice her attention has turned to him.

"What are you staring at, Woof?" She has no idea the allure that name has on him as a chill runs down his spine. Or does she know? So many questions run amok in his mind. "You know I can see you, right?" Violet says, inching closer to him on her hands and knees. She must know what she's doing to him. Is she teasing? Does she feel the same way he does? All he can do is stare into her eyes as she creeps closer until she's mere inches away.

"Woofie," she drawls with a smile that emphasizes those dimples he loves so much, which draws his attention to her lips. Without thinking, he closes the distance between them, selfishly wrapping his hand around her head so she can't pull away. But she doesn't even try. Violet parts her supple lips, an invitation he won't waste a moment questioning. Her hand drifts over his chest and pulls at his collar as their tongues tangle. His head becomes light as she straddles him, and their bodies press together. "Wait," she gasps, pulling her lips away but keeping her forehead touching his. "Wait," she repeats, even though he's already frozen by her words.

Like an idiot, he says, "Charlie?"

"What?" Violet pulls back with a frown.

"Is it Charlie?"

"Is what, Charlie? What does he have to do with this?" Violet gets to her feet.

"You still live with him." It's as if he can't stop the words coming from his mouth. Is it jealousy? Somehow, he feels more defensive the angrier she gets.

"In separate rooms. You think I stopped because of Charlie?" Violet looks at him, repulsed.

"Why else—"

"Because of Nathan! I needed to slow down because I was thinking of my son. I can't just do whatever I please without affecting my child. I can't believe this." Violet says the end more to herself as she paces.

"I..." Yoojin starts to speak, but can't think of anything to remedy the situation. Stuck in his head, overthinking everything as always, he watches the woman he loves ignite into a pure rage. She gathers her things to leave him for who knows how long. He's about to stop and tell her to grab Nathan and come home with him, but that's when the maven breaches.

There's a knock at the door, and Yoojin reluctantly slides off the silky bedding. Before he can reach the door, it opens. A man wearing a golden-yellow uniform steps in with a tray of food. Yoojin's mother enters after him in an elegant blue robe. She stands to the side with her head held high, waiting for the servant to finish. The aroma reminds Yoojin's stomach just how hungry he is. Without a word, the man places a meal with various foods and drinks on the table, arranging it neatly before leaving. He closes the door with a bow.

Yoojin sits to eat his meal, knowing his mother has something to say. "What is it?"

"We're going to have a little soiree to welcome you home in seven days."

"I wasn't gone that long this time. Why do we need to celebrate?"

"Is it wrong for me to show my love for you?"

"No, I just question your motives."

"Will Ms. Odaire be joining us?" Madam Kim asks.

"I don't know. I'm sure she'd appreciate a formal invitation. As I'm sure, you've provided the other attendees." Madam Kim nods with a smile that doesn't reach her eyes before turning to walk away. "Mother." She turns back with a genuine smile this time. "You didn't invite *her*, did you?"

His mother stands before him and leans down, pressing a kiss to his forehead. "How can I say no to someone who loves you as much as I do?" she says before turning away and briskly leaving the room.

Looking back at the large amount of food, he realizes he's lost his appetite.

Chapter 23

STACY

Stacy collapses onto her bed, staring up at the ceiling. The grueling day has finally come to an end. She doesn't know how much more she can take of her father micromanaging her every move. Yes, she's training to take over when he retires, but it's as if she can't do anything right by him. It's a long while before he'll ever retire. Once he does, she'll never have to worry again about him breathing down her neck. She feels a bit morbid thinking of her father's end. Her mother will be devastated, but at least it'd end his disgusting affair with Kat. Retirement means you're incapable of working. Therefore, you're no longer needed by the community. When you retire, you're taken to Dr. Oric and never seen or heard from again.

The delicate bell resonating from her purse draws her attention. Ripping the bag open, she pulls out her datapad. Sighing, she scrolls through the messages from

Elliot informing her of the engagement she's missed once again. His frustration is palpable as he demands to be respected. Stacy rolls her eyes and is about to toss it when a new message pops up. She hesitates, dreading what else he has to say, only to find a long-awaited message from Elon:

Hello Miss Stacy, this is Elon Jenks. I regret to inform you that I have not successfully located Mr. Gareth Nox, but I think I have something else. I think it would be prudent to speak about it in person. I understand if you are too busy, but I will make myself available at your convenience.

Stacy's heart pounds against her chest. Why hasn't he been successful at locating Gareth? What could be so important that they can't speak about it over the comms? What if it's more news of Killian and that wench from the elevator? Knowing he has something essential to divulge, she can't let it go unheard. Stacy quickly asks him to meet at Gareth's favorite club. Though it's a very public place, it'd be difficult for anyone to overhear their conversation with the loud music. Elon agrees to meet her, and she quickly bounces off the bed, ripping her clothes off to change into something more suitable for the setting and to help her blend in. She pulls on a white skin-tight playsuit with a cropped jacket covered in iridescent feather sequins and her favorite platform boots that make her short legs look longer than reality. Glancing in the mirror, she stops to adjust her ponytail higher on her head and add a holographic shadow to her eyes and lips before sneaking out through Kat's hidden pathways.

The music assaults her ears as she makes her way into the building. Colorful lights flash to the beat, lighting up the otherwise dark building. Aerial dancers hang from the ceiling from hoops and long ribbons of silk in fluorescent clothing, providing entertainment to those lounging. In contrast, others crowd the dance floor, allowing them to escape reality. The air is thick with heat and sweat from the many bodies.

Stacy searches the many faces, looking for Elon. She doesn't have to search for long, as he must've come straight from the office. He stands out like a sore thumb in his modest white suit, prim and proper. He stands close to a wall with his arms folded and shoulders close to his ears. His shoulders release when he spots her. His jaw drops open slightly when he sees what she's wearing. She raises an eyebrow and smirks at him. "Not very good at blending in, are we?" Stacy yells over the noise. Elon looks himself over and realizes his mistake. "Come on." She shoves him into a dark corner. He stumbles, unsure of what she intends to do.

Stacy unzips his jacket and rips it off his shoulders. Elon holds as still as possible, and though he's uncomfortable with how close and personal she's getting, he's too scared to say anything. She turns the jacket inside-out, revealing its silk lining, and returns it to him. As he takes it, she unbuttons his shirt to mid-chest and rolls his sleeves to the elbow. Sucking air through her teeth, she looks him over.

"Come here," she says, waving her hands toward herself. He looks at her wide-eyed but hesitantly bends down so that his face is inches away from hers. She runs her fingers through his slicked-back hair and shakes it out, revealing a mess of wavy hair. "That's better. Now drape your jacket over your shoulder." He does as he's told but hits himself in the face with his sleeve in the process. Stacy snorts and motions him to follow her.

They make their way up a flight of stairs. She greets a bouncer and he smiles, gesturing for her to enter. Stacy leads him to one of the private booths on the upper floors where the music roars, but you can loom over those below. She sits, crossing her bare legs and resting her arms on the back of the leather seating. Elon awkwardly waits for her instruction to sit before he does so. Stacy tilts her head in amusement as he takes a seat far away.

As a server greets them, she turns her grin on them and signals them to bring drinks. She's visited this place often enough for the server to recognize her and know what she always orders. He nods before turning on his heel and disappearing. Stacy turns her attention back to Elon, who's distracted himself by staring at the aerial dancers in awe as they rise and fall in graceful movements. Seeing him in this colorful change of scenery, looking out of place like a child in a candy store, she realizes he's quite handsome. Elon catches her staring, but she doesn't concede. He mouths something while averting his eyes. Stacy slowly leans forward and cups her ear with her hand. He awkwardly scoots closer but retreats when the server returns with two glasses and a decanter filled with blue liquid.

When the server leaves, Stacy closes the distance between them. Leaning in close, she brings her mouth up to his ear. "Do I make you uncomfortable?"

"No, no. I mean yes, but not in a bad way," he says, flustered. Stacy smiles up at him before turning to pour the liquor into the glasses and handing one to him. He waits for her to take a sip before he gulps his down. He sets down his empty glass to rub his knuckles as his knee nervously bounces.

Stacy sets her drink down to place her hand on Elon's thigh. Instantly he stills and stares down at her hand. She leans close once more. "You said you have something for me."

Elon's throat bobs before he opens his mouth to speak. "Yes," he gulps again. "I finished going through all the files, but there was no sign of Gareth. Instead, I noticed someone else." His eyes shift as a server passes by.

This is taking too long. Stacy removes her jacket to allow her skin to breathe and draw his attention back to her, but he's busy staring after passersby. Losing patience, she pulls his legs toward hers and places her palm on his cheek, dragging his attention back. She leans in to hear what he says but doesn't remove her hand from his cheek. Anyone passing by would think they were being intimate instead of sharing secrets. "Your father, he, um, has been visiting the health department frequently. It's been more frequent in the past two months. The most recent was three days ago, and he collapsed in the entrance." A smile grows on Stacy's face as a plan finally begins to formulate. "Is Mr. Nox ill?" Elon turns his head to hear her answer.

"There's a good chance he is."

"He hasn't mentioned it?"

"My father's a very prideful and private man. He'd never let news of this kind spread. Especially to me." Stacy's grin turns diabolical. "Thank you, Elon." She kisses his cheek before reclining, resting her arms on the back of the couch. Elon's stunned by the affection.

Stacy sways and stumbles as she makes her way to her front door. It opens upon her arrival. She giggles to herself, thinking of Elon and his shy mannerisms. After providing the good news, she convinced him to celebrate with her. He argued, thinking himself beneath her, which of course irked her as well as endeared him to her. She poured him a drink and then another, and before long he was doing everything she asked of him without question. She's giddy, thinking of the way he touched and held her. They danced and laughed until the evening's end, something she hasn't been able to do for many years. A weight had been lifted, and she finally felt alive with a second chance.

She clumsily rips off her shoes and tosses them aside. Making her way through the darkened living room, she stubs her toe on a piece of furniture, bringing her to the floor, half-complaining from the pain but laughing hysterically, as it all seems too amusing. She snorts and sighs as she gets back to her feet when the lights come on, momentarily blinding her. She covers her eyes and groans in protest.

"You insist on making a mockery of our name," her father growls.

"Do I?" Stacy peeks through her hand to see her father sulking in his favorite chair.

"What else would you call this?" John taps a screen in his lap then flips it, allowing Stacy to view footage of her and Elon's night out.

"Oh, may I have a copy of that? I haven't had this much fun since that evening at the theatre. Do you remember? You caught me kissing that actor in—"

"Why do you insist on embarrassing this family? What am I supposed to tell the people, tell Elliot, to explain your behavior?"

"You can tell them to mind their own business, especially that idiot in blue." She laughs as she pulls her hair down from the tight ponytail, tossing her hair as she scratches her scalp.

John bolts out of his chair, clattering the screen to the floor. "That idiot will be your husband one day. I suggest you learn to show some respect," he spits in her face.

"I did learn some respect. I learned to respect myself instead of allowing others to belittle me. I recommend you learn to respect me if you know what's good for you." Stacy tries to hold a straight face by biting the inside of her lip.

The smile is wiped away when his large hand meets her face. "You will not disrespect me again," he growls.

Stacy rubs her stinging cheek. "I'll do as I damn well please," she says in a low voice as she wipes away the tears that defiantly spill down.

"I can't hear you."

"I will *do*." Stacy shoves his chest. "As I *damn*." She shoves again. "*Well*." Again. "*PLEASE!!!*" she shrieks as she pushes him one last time. He trips, falling onto the couch. She crouches over him. "Can you hear me now?" John is speechless as the fury wars over his face. She pushes herself away from him. The adrenaline is pumping through her blood, allowing her to have total clarity. "It's funny. I've always thought of you as this large, strong, intimidating man. I can feel your frail body beneath that tough-man costume. Could your health be failing you?" John doesn't respond.

"Seeing how often you've visited Dr. Oric, you must be in the advanced stages. The only disease Dr. Oric can't fix is osteomortem. You're dying, my dear father. I fear it's time for you to retire." She sighs. "I'll inform the press tomorrow. I suggest you spend this time with your loving wife." Stacy begins to walk away.

"I will not allow this!" He weakly grabs her wrist as she passes.

She stops, looking down at him in disgust. "What are you going to do? You can't slap your way out of this one." She rips her wrist out of his grip easily, retreating to her room with a triumphant grin.

Chapter 24

YOOJIN

Walking down the corridor seems to take longer than it ever has. His shoes clap against the marble floors and bounce off the walls, assaulting him with each step. It never bothered him before, but now that Violet's here, he notices how uncomfortable the home he's grown up in really is. The colors of the walls and floors are cold and muted. It's so quiet here that he can hear himself breathing as if amplified by the emptiness he resides in. Yoojin wonders if Violet would ever think of this frigid place as a home. A new Safe Haven. A home in which she could raise her son without worrying about the dangers of the outside world.

Muffled laughter drifts down the corridor. Yoojin pauses mid-stride. With that laughter, her laughter, the corridor is flooded with warmth and light. Hearing that sound in these halls, he can imagine Violet chasing their children down these halls, bringing a smile to his lips. Laughter echoes again. Seeing his reflection in the window, he adjusts the sleeves of his blazer and runs his fingers through his hair, ensuring everything stays in place before heading to see her.

Dominic isn't stationed outside her door as he should be, and he sighs. Yoojin knocks on the door and turns the handle. Upon entering the room, he finds Violet on the floor, holding her stomach as she giggles. Dom sits cross-legged on the floor next to her with a mischievous grin. When he notices Yoojin, he gets to his feet and clasps his hands behind his back respectfully, though he struggles to hide the smile on his face.

Violet's giggling subsides as she wipes the tears from her eyes and takes deep breaths. Looking up to find Yoojin sets her off as she bursts into hysterics. Dominic snorts, attempting to keep his composure. Violet gasps for air as she crawls to Yoojin. She reaches up, and he takes her hand, pulling her up to stand. Though she can barely stay on her feet, she looks up at him with tears streaming down her face and a smile reaching ear to ear. "Pew pew!" She shoots finger guns at Yoojin as she continues to laugh, and his jaw drops. Heat floods his cheeks as he glares over her shoulder at Dominic, who has now turned away with his hand over his mouth, shoulders shaking with laughter. It's a memory Dominic had always held over his head from when they weren't yet five years old. Yoojin used to play cowboys and bandits with Dominic and his older sister at the river. Yoojin didn't have swimwear, so Dom's sister gave him one of her old ones. At the time, wearing a girl's swimsuit didn't bother him. He thought nothing of it, equipped with his cowboy hat and belt around his waist, holstering his pistols made from broken sticks. It was a sight Dominic never forgot. He brings it up every chance he gets.

"I'm guessing Dom's been filling you in on all of my embarrassing childhood moments," he grumbles.

Violet nods vigorously as she exhales a long breath to control herself. Grabbing the lapels of his blazer, she clears her throat. "Don't be angry, Woof. I begged him to tell me. Also, Dom gave me coffee, and at first, it was ick, but then he made it delicious, and now I really like coffee," She rambled.

The warmth flooding him at hearing his pet name deepens the flush on his cheeks. The anger and embarrassment instantly wash away, and the joy emanating from her brings a smile to his lips. Her eyes twinkle as she looks up at him. "How have I never noticed?" Violet asks as she reaches for his face and pokes his cheek with her finger. "You have dimples."

Yoojin is speechless. Her suspicious, bitter personality has slipped away, revealing the old Violet. The Violet he fell in love with. He doesn't want this Violet to slip away. She begins to withdraw her hand, but he catches it before she can escape. She gazes at him, looking back and forth between both eyes, pupils dilating. Looking up at him with that smile, he can feel himself melting into a puddle before her. At this moment, he would give her the world if she asked for it.

Violet blinks, and the fleeting moment is over. She wipes at her dampened cheeks, but her smile lingers as she gently tugs her hand away. Yoojin releases her reluctantly. She tucks some curls behind her ear while clearing her throat. "What brings you?" she says light-heartedly but avoiding eye contact.

"I wanted to show you more of the island. If you'd like."

"Oh, yes, please!"

"Yoojin, I don't—" Dom begins.

"Whatever excuse you're about to give about why we need to stay put is a waste of breath. Besides, my father requests she be fitted for a gown for that *soiree*." Yoojin dares Dom to contradict him with a piercing look. Violet looks back and forth between them. Dom nods, keeping silent. Violet smiles up at him, bouncing on the balls of her feet. He relishes her excitement as he holds his arm out to her, and she eagerly takes it. Yoojin glances back at Dominic with a steely look. Dom smiles in return and follows them at a safe distance.

As Yoojin guides her to their destination, he answers Violet's many questions about the island. Though he's fond of the people, he never thought to ask the questions she does. *Why are they segregated? Why don't they have the right to choose where they live? Why does the color of clothing matter? Why aren't they provided with a more suitable dwelling if they have more laborious jobs? Why do you have such an advanced society in these mountains, yet your people break their backs to provide for you? What do you offer them?* Yoojin provides the answers he'd always been given when growing up, but as he speaks he realizes how naïve he's been. *They're segregated based on their income. They live where their work is, to make it easier for them to commute. The colors make it easier to distinguish their role in society. Their amenities are based on the material available to them. Why change what's worked for our community for decades? We provide them protection.*

"Protection from what?" Violet asks as Yoojin asks himself the same question. The maven have never crossed large bodies of water. The bioscouts are no threat. The only threat to humanity would be Arcadia, but she doesn't need to know that. As if she could hear his thoughts, she stops abruptly and turns to eye him. "What are those ships for?" She points her finger at the window. He steps forward to view the sleek silver ship returning from an assignment. He thinks carefully before answering.

"Those ships are sent to assess threats."

"And if they find a threat, what would they do?" Violet looks out the window as the ship touches down on the landing strip.

"They would eradicate that threat." Yoojin clasps his hands behind his back to keep from fidgeting. Violet glares down at the ship from above like a cat finding its new prey. When she doesn't say anything further, he looks back at Dom. Dom shrugs. "We're almost to my father's office. He's been looking forward to your visit." Violet glances at him from the corner of her eye as he moves past her. She follows tight-lipped and doesn't ask any further questions as she's led to a part of the mountain she hasn't yet seen.

Violet takes in her surroundings as if memorizing each step with a lingering eye. When she spots a camera, Yoojin takes note of her caution. As the doors open, they meet his father's assistant, Aadhya. As she turns to greet them, Yoojin's eyes are drawn to the small diamond nose ring linked to her ear by a simple chain with pearl beading. Her long dark lashes highlight her large eyes. You can't deny her beauty with her dazzling smile and dark skin. Aadhya bows her head in greeting.

"Hello, Aadhya. My father's expecting us."

"Of course. It's wonderful to see you again. How was your trip?" She nods to Dom and Violet in greeting before giving him her full attention.

"It was favorable." Yoojin glances at Violet, but she's too busy studying her surroundings to pay attention to their conversation.

Aadhya follows his gaze and smiles meekly before holding her arm out in the direction she'll lead them. "You must be Violet. It's so nice to finally put a face to your name. I feel we're already friends. I've heard so much about you."

Violet drags her eyes back to the person speaking to her. "That's very kind of you to say. Unfortunately, Yoojin wasn't as forthright regarding the people in his life. What was your name again?" Violet didn't mean for her words to come off as harsh, but there's an undeniable bite to them.

Aadhya smiles at Yoojin and then Violet with lackluster. "My name is Aadhya. I am Yoojin's-"

"Aadhya's a friend of mine. She works for my father." Violet's eyes drift between Yoojin and Aadhya, who's now blushing with a smile.

"Any friend of Yoojin is a friend of mine."

"Don't get on her bad side, though. My backside is still recovering from her wrath."

Violet gives Dom an incredulous look. Aadhya laughs, though it seems somewhat forced. "You probably deserved it, you philanderer."

Dom audibly gasps. "I never! I may love all women but never at the same time." The three of them snort laughter in response.

"I look forward to the little party your mother is putting together for you." Aadhya's attention returns to Yoojin.

"Ah, yes," he responds awkwardly.

"She loves you very much." Aadhya looks up at him in admiration.

Yoojin avoids eye contact. "Yes, I know."

He sighs in relief when they finally approach his father's office. Aadhya knocks twice before opening the door. "Doctor Kim, your guests have arrived."

Violet pops in behind Aadhya with a wide grin and waves at him. "Violet!" Robert calls with the same enthusiasm. "Thank you, Aadhya." She bows her head before leaving the office. Aadhya smiles at Yoojin. Lowering her head, he can't ignore the longing look in her eyes. He bows in return but avoids her eyes.

"No one told me you're a doctor! You're very modest compared to other physicians I've met, allowing me to call you Robert."

"Ah, that's very sweet of you, but you're like family," he says as he finishes typing something up on his screen and swipes his hands across, wiping away the view.

"You barely know me, sir," Violet says with a tilt of her head.

"On the contrary, I know you very well, my dear Violet. Yoojin spared no detail. Though your hair is very wild and much shorter than he described." Robert winks.

"Is there anyone in Arcadia who hasn't heard of me? I'm beginning to think he's conspired against me. I haven't had the pleasure of hearing about Yoojin's family and friends." Violet glares back at Yoojin, and he self-consciously bites the inside of his lip.

"Ah, don't hold it against him. He was strictly forbidden from divulging any information on his ventures into the world to keep our home safe."

"I understand." Violet smiles back at Yoojin. Muscles he didn't know were locked up begin to relax.

"So, Miss Odaire, how was your first night in Arcadia? Did you sleep well?"

"Very well, thank you. It's a very comfortable room you've provided. Arcadia is beautiful. I would love to explore every inch of it, but that'd probably take all year."

His father chuckles. "That's probably true. Even I haven't explored every inch. Though Yoojin probably has. He's never been able to stay put." Yoojin smiles but shakes his head.

"Is that why we're here? To explore more?" Violet asks innocently.

"In a way. I can give you a tour of my facility. Still, I wonder if you would permit us to do a physical exam." Violet shifts her weight and drops her arms to her sides. "Yoojin's informed us that you've sustained a couple of injuries while you've been together. Dominic mentioned some strange scarring when you were changing." Yoojin sharply turns his head to glare at Dom, but he keeps his eyes trained on the back of Violet's head.

"Did he now?" Dom steps back, dropping his eyes to the floor as Violet looks back at him.

"Of course, we'd only do so with your permission. We were only informed out of concern for you. You're a courageous woman to put yourself in harm's way to save your friends."

"Thank you." Violet's voice loses its enthusiasm, and her hands ball into fists.

Robert comes around from his desk to stand before her. He stands a foot taller than her, and she must tilt her head back to look at him. He gently grasps her upper arms. "Please know that you're safe here. No one wants to harm you. We only want to help ensure you're healthy and well taken care of." He smiles down at her kindly. Violet's hands relax, and she nods.

Chapter 26

ALAN

The shelter is abuzz with life. Babies cry, people chatter, music plays in the background, and the place finally begins living up to its potential. Alan checks room by room to see that everyone's needs have been met. He doesn't leave anyone wanting. The last person to check on would be Violet. Unfortunately, wherever she may be, there's been no contact. Nothing has come through over the radio, putting him on edge. Nova must've noticed as she seems to be on edge as well. He's caught her early in the morning, sitting nearby or ensuring she's close enough to hear anything coming through.

Jack doesn't seem worried. If he is, it doesn't show. He's too busy barking orders at Jenna. Though she wants to be helpful, she's been reorganizing and making unnecessary changes that have made things difficult for others. Since their arrival, she's shown no interest in Matthias, which has altered his mood from a control freak to just angry and bitter. He keeps to himself for the most part.

Alan keeps himself distracted by cooking meals with the help of Clara. He's stirring a large pot of beans when the bay doors squeak. "*Ckawlin!*" The strange sound echoes through the shelter. Most people jump at it, but Alan looks up at the ceiling in exasperation. "In the kitchen!" he calls.

People part to allow Rook to pass. A large doe is draped over its shoulders. "*Ckawlin,*" it calls again.

"What?" Alan looks over his shoulder at the beast. "Didn't I say to skin it before you bring it in?"

"*Ckawlin.*" Rook lets the doe slide off his shoulder onto the floor.

Alan slams the spoon onto the counter. "Rook, you need to skin and gut it outside. Take it outside and peel the skin like a banana." Alan tries to show rook by pretending to take off its skin. Rook tilts his head and clicks his tongue.

"I can do it," Nova interrupts. "Can you help me pick it up, Rook?"

"*Orva,*" he chirps.

"Yes, good boy. Can you help me take it into the garden?" Rook does as she asks. Grabbing a butcher's knife and platter, she turns to Alan. "After I'm done prepping this, can we talk?"

"Yeah. Library?" Nova nods with a smile on her way out. Alan returns to stirring the pot of beans. It's already begun to stick to the bottom. Then comes the crying. Looking through the window to the dining area, he doesn't see the culprit, though it grows louder.

"Uncle Alan!" He turns to find Lilly rubbing her eyes as tears stream down her cheeks. "Uncle Alan, day wone lemmieplay," she blubbers.

"Sweety, I didn't understand a word you just said." Lifting her, he props her on one arm so he can stir with the other. "Now, take a deep breath and speak slowly."

"They. Won't. Lemme. Play," she says between gasps of breath.

"Who won't let you play?"

"The. New. Kids," she hiccups.

"What are they playing?"

"Lords and Minions."

"Ah, I see." Alan turns off the heat to the pot and sets Lilly down. He heaves the pot onto a backburner and takes Lilly's tiny hand. "Lead the way, m'lady." Lilly's sad tears have dried up and are replaced with a look of fierce determination. She pulls Alan along as if his long legs aren't keeping up with her little ones. He enters the recreation room to find a small group of teenagers setting up the game. One of them is reading the rules aloud to the others. When they approach, Lilly drops her hand to place her fists on her hips.

"I hear you're denying this little Lady the privilege of playing this game. You only have four players, and it allows six."

"It says for ages 12 and up."

"She's fully capable of playing this game. She already knows the rules."

"Fine, she'll be an easy target." The kid rolls his eyes.

Lilly smiles triumphantly, taking a seat at the table. She picks out her favorite character and sets up her board while she waits patiently for the kid to finish reading the rules. Alan leaves her there, giving her a wink on his way out. She winks back at him with the sweetest grin.

As he leaves the room, he spots Ember holding a basket loaded with vegetables. He takes the heavy load off her hands. "Why aren't you spending time with the other kids? Get to know them."

"We have so many mouths to feed. I'm worried we'll run out of food," she says, tucking a stray hair behind her ear. He notices the dirt under her fingernails. Alan drops the basket and takes a knee so that she's looking down at him. She's changed so much in such a short period. Suddenly she looks so much more mature. She's growing into a woman.

"Ember." He takes her hands and turns them over. They've become rough from working the ground. "You're still a child. You don't need to worry about how many mouths there are to feed."

"But I—"

"No, you girls have had a rough start. You've had to grow up too fast. It's time to slow down and enjoy your youth. There are plenty of adults here, and we're quite capable."

Ember's eyes glaze over, and her nose turns cherry red. "I know, but—"

"No more but's. If we need help, we'll ask for it. Everyone will do their part here, but your only job is getting to know our new friends and having fun. You understand?" Ember nods, getting too choked up to speak. Alan pulls her into a hug. Her arms wrap around his neck snuggly. "I mean it, stop growing so fast, okay? I feel like you're a foot taller than when I left." Ember giggles and wipes away the sniffles. "Go have fun." She smiles and joins the others in the recreation room.

Alan takes the food into the kitchen and starts prepping it for storage. One of the women he hasn't met yet assists him. They make quick work of it as they seal the produce in bags and load it up in the freezer. Nova returns with meat to be packaged and frozen as well. Alan asks the woman to continue and asks another in passing to help as he and Nova make their way to the library. As the door closes behind them, Nova wrings her hands nervously. "What's going on, Nova?" he asks.

"Why hasn't Violet contacted us yet? It's been two days."

"It's been one day technically, and maybe she's too far for the radio to work."

"What if they're blocking the signal? What if they didn't make it? What if they did make it and something bad happened? What if she's being held captive?"

"Nova." Alan grabs her arms to keep her from pacing. "Deep breath." He breathes in and out. Nova takes a breath to satisfy him. "You know what Violet's capable of." Nova nods her head vigorously. "Do you think it's even remotely possible she'd be held against her will?"

"What if they drug her?" Alan cringes, remembering how Charlie had easily incapacitated her. He shakes the thought out of his head. Nova continues, "Think about it. She knew she was going somewhere dangerous. They could've prepared a trap if they knew she was coming to destroy it. What if Yoojin really is the bad guy?" Nova is spiraling, and her questions pull him down with her.

"What are you talking about? Did she say she'd destroy Arcadia?"

"She said the plan was to cut the head off the dragon." Alan starts pacing now with his hands on his head. "I thought you knew about this plan. She only said Yoojin wasn't supposed to know."

"I was supposed to be with her." Alan realizes he made a huge mistake leaving her alone with Yoojin. Though he trusts him with her life, he doesn't trust Violet not to do something stupid. She acts as if she's invincible, and it's going to get her killed. "I don't even know where she is," he says, more to himself.

"What's south of Safe Haven?"

"Nothing, just the Dark Sea."

"There has to be something." Nova's voice becomes higher-pitched. Alan looks at the large atlas on the desk at the center of the room. He begins his search frantically, flipping pages. He stops and runs his hands through his hair and rubs his chin. Nova looks at the page he glowers at. There are a considerable amount of islands peppered south of Safe Haven. "Can Rook track her down?"

"I don't know."

"Then we'll search each island." Nova folds her arms, daring him to contradict her.

Chapter 27

YOOJIN

"I can't believe you've been watching Violet change her clothes." Yoojin had held his tongue as long as he could, but the longer he held it in, the louder his inner voice became, until it was unbearable.

"It wasn't intentional. She asked me a question, and without thinking I looked over as she removed her blouse. I assure you I didn't linger."

"Yet you had enough time to take count of her scars?" Yoojin tightens his folded arms over his chest.

"Have you seen them? It's not something one easily forgets."

"I've seen it."

"Then don't question my intentions. I wasn't assigned to her just to make sure she doesn't cross any boundaries; it's also to keep her safe." Dom looks up at his friend, the worry clear in his expression.

Yoojin rubs his hands over his face and hair. "I know."

They become silent when Aadhya exits the exam room with several vials of blood. She doesn't acknowledge her audience as she focuses on her duties. Yoojin follows her into the lab, where the vials are labeled and stored.

"How much longer will this take? It's already been an hour."

"It won't be long now."

"Why did you need to take so much blood?"

"Have you seen it?" Aadhya holds it up to the light in awe. The purple hue contrasts as she holds up another sample. "I've never seen anything like it. We weren't sure if we could test it like any other human sample, so we took extra just in case." Yoojin sighs, crossing his arms over his chest as he does when he's anxious. "May I ask you a question, Yoojin?" He nods sharply. "You could've chosen anyone. There are so many people here who care so much for you. Why her?"

Yoojin chooses his words carefully. "Violet isn't like anyone else I've ever met. She's strong, independent, intelligent and loyal." Aadhya frowns, distracting herself with the vials, and realizes he would describe her with the same traits. He shakes his head before continuing, "She views life as a gift and always wants to make the best of any situation. Violet isn't afraid to take chances, though some consider that a flaw." Yoojin could feel her full attention on him now, though he struggled to look into her eyes for fear of seeing any pain he may be causing her. "She's also pretty cute." He looks down at his folded arms and picks off invisible lint.

"She's a lucky girl." Her voice is softer. Yoojin clears his throat. "You should go. She should be done very soon."

"Thank you, Aadhya," Yoojin says on his way out without looking back, though he doesn't know what he's thanking her for. Nurses and doctors bow respectfully as they pass him in the hall. Yoojin barely notices while thoughts swarm his mind like a hive that's been knocked around. Those thoughts settle into a whisper when he returns to find his father speaking with Dom. Dominic's face seems more severe than he's ever seen, and he nods in response.

When Yoojin comes to stand before them, his father turns to him and smiles. "So, what's your verdict?"

"Verdict? You'd think she was being interrogated."

"Is she not? She's been under tight scrutiny since her arrival. I'm surprised you asked Dom to wait outside."

"I think that's a bit overdramatic, but you're right. It was all with good intentions."

"If you say so." Yoojin folds his arms, leaning against the wall next to Dom so he can watch the door Violet is behind. Roger smiles fondly at his son. "There was some faint bruising on her back and head. She said she fell two days ago." Yoojin nods to confirm. "She heals incredibly fast." Yoojin nods again, keeping his eyes on the door. "My concern is the black scar stemming from her neck."

"It's a tattoo," Yoojin says, glancing up at his father and back at the door.

"That's what she said. Though I've never seen a tattoo look like that. It's not like ink-stained skin. It's something else…" Roger eyes his son with his hand holding back his white coat in his pocket. "She's had several breaks and fractures in her hands." He waits for a response but gets none. "She also has a lot of scarring on one of her kidneys and her liver. I can't tell if she's prone to accidents or gets in a lot of fights."

Yoojin snickers, thinking of all the injuries he's witnessed. "Both."

"Let's hope her fighting days are behind her."

"Unlikely…" Yoojin says under his breath.

"As far as I can tell, she's in good health. She's just changing back into her garments now."

"Good."

Roger steps into Yoojin's view and gently grabs his chin. "Relax, my son. She's here. She's safe. Isn't this what you've wanted all these years?" His father's eyes convey his sincerity, and he relaxes his shoulders, allowing his arms to fall to his sides. A smile curves his lips. He slaps Yoojin hard on the arm before walking away. "Don't forget to take her shopping. And inform your mother of the expenses when you're finished." Yoojin leans to the side, rubbing his arm. The thin blue jacket sleeve mildly softened the unexpected blow.

Violet adjusts the sleeves of her brown blazer as Roger disappears down the hall. The blue scarf is still boldly displayed on her head, which warms his heart. A brilliant smile crosses her face, and his whispering worries melt away. "What's next?"

Yoojin pushes away from the wall and holds out his arm. "Shopping."

"Oooh, shopping." Violet rests her hand in the crook of his elbow and allows him to lead the way.

Violet dramatically falls onto her bed with a groan. "I never want to go shopping again." The plush blankets muffle her, grumbling as she lazily kicks off her shoes. "Dom, rub my feet."

"Absolutely not." He places the three parcels in his arms on the table before dropping himself into the sofa, and Yoojin drops off some of his own parcels.

"Ugh, what's the point of keeping you around, then? Be gone with you!"

Dom chuckles at her light-hearted request. "I must get these expenses to my mother. I'll be right back."

"Would you ask her to remove her guard dog while you're there?"

"Hey, I'm not a dog," Dom complains but not lifting his head from the sofa or opening his eyes. Truth be told, he'd also like to be done with this assignment.

"Apologies. Is 'shadow' better?" Violet lifts her head for approval. Dom nods. "This talking shadow is getting annoying, and I'd like my privacy."

"I'll do my best."

"Thank you," they say in unison.

Yoojin laughs as he makes his way to his mother's building. It's still early in the afternoon, so she'll still be in her office. He should've had the parcels shipped to her room; his back aches from holding them for so long. He rolls his shoulders and pulls his arms backward, allowing his back to pop. He pulls at his collar. These clothes have always felt so restricting. Glancing toward the landing, he spots the sleek silver ships being cleaned and tuned up.

Finally reaching the lobby to his mother's office, she finds the assistant is away from her desk. He must've come on her break. Yoojin strolls past the reception desk and pulls the door open just an inch before freezing in place. A man is speaking to his mother.

"…there were no signs of life."

"Were there any bodies?"

"No, ma'am. They must've evacuated before our arrival."

"How could they have moved that many people so efficiently?"

"We don't know, madam."

"Did you not intercept any kind of communication?"

"Only one."

"What was it?"

"Someone requesting a check-in, but there was no response."

"I want bioscouts sent to this location. I want to know everything about this facility in the mountains. And be discreet. We don't need them relocating again."

"Yes, Madam Kim."

"Lieutenant."

"Yes, madam?"

"I've been informed we'll have several important guests arriving tomorrow. We must make a good impression if we aim to ascend to Stratos Development. Anything they need."

"Understood, Madam Kim."

"You're dismissed."

The lieutenant stands up and briskly walks towards the door. Yoojin quickly moves to the other end of the lobby and turns as the door opens. He tries to hold his composure as they walk past each other. The lieutenant bows his head as he passes. Yoojin looks back at him in concern as he leaves. The doors to his mother's office are left open wide. "My son, what brings you here at this hour?" she says when he arrives.

Yoojin turns to face his mother and hopes his smile is genuine. "Father requested I report my expenses for Violet today." He hands over a datapad, wringing his hands behind his back as she reviews it.

With a sigh, she returns it. "I suppose she has good taste." His mother looks up at him and places her hand on his cheek. "I'll never get over how fast you've grown. So handsome. I'm so proud of the man you've become."

Yoojin leans into her hand as he tries to hold back his feelings. His voice cracks. "Thank you, mother."

"I know you'll choose the right path for yourself," she says to reassure herself. "You know what's best for your family."

"I do," he says sternly.

CHAPTER 27

Madam Kim smiles up at him fondly. "Good boy. Now, go entertain your guest while she's here." Yoojin smiles in response, but it doesn't reach his eyes. He turns on the spot, and it feels as if time slows as he walks away. She'll never accept Violet as his match, but there's a more significant matter to worry about now. Yoojin knew it was possible their ships had been responsible for the destruction of Safe Haven, but to have it confirmed felt like the wind had been sucked out of his lungs. It could destroy his relationship with Violet, a secret that would cause more damage if she found out on her own. If she knew they were searching for Violet's shelter in the mountains, she'd want to do something about it. What can be done without betraying his mother? What's the purpose of keeping tabs on the shelter? They're no threat. Should he tell Violet? What can be done? An unending surge of questions floods his mind.

Chapter 28

STACY

Lights flash and several drones whiz by as they try to find the perfect angle to record from. Everyone will be tuning in to hear this announcement. Her speech was approved by the Magistrate himself. Stacy does her best to keep a serious composure. The news she's about to spill is not something to make you leap for joy, though her heart's doing just that inside her chest. When someone retires, it's not just the end of their career. If someone is no longer capable of continuing their work, they're of no use to the community. The Stratos Development may be a large facility, but it can only contain so many people. When you retire, it's a forever visit to the D.H.S.E. The long sleep.

Stacy takes a deep breath before stepping up to the podium. Thanking the audience for taking the time, she informs the public of the status of her father. There's an audible gasp when she reveals her father's attempt at keeping the deterioration of his health a secret. She carries on with all the information she was able to gather to bring him down and announce his inevitable retirement. She does her best to answer the many questions that follow.

"How long has your family been hiding the truth?"

"My father acted alone. He wasn't going to inform his wife or daughter until the end. He's a very proud and stubborn man." From her peripheral, she notices people approaching the stage as she speaks. Killian, with that cold look, is accompanied by her father. And Elliot. Stacy is stunned to see them line up behind her.

"This is not the first case of osteomortem. Should the public be worried?"

Stacy looks at the person asking the question, but her mind goes blank as she feels a sudden dread. *What's her father up to now?*

Killian approaches her and whispers in her ear, "I'll take it from here." He smiles warmly, and the heat from his hand on her lower back has her stepping aside. *Is Killian finally making a move?*

"Doctor Grey! Is he really dying? Is the disease spreading? Should we be concerned?"

Killian holds his hands up, and the voices come to a silence. Stacy steps back on the opposite end of the stage from her father and Elliot. Watching Killian's back intently, she holds her breath, waiting to hear what he will say.

"Yes, John Nox is indeed dying of osteomortem. There have been more cases in the past month, but I assure you Dr. Oric and I are actively working on a cure.

We've recently acquired a…substance. It was discovered by our allies in Arcadia. Mr. Nox has graciously volunteered for the clinical trials. We will work together to find the cure."

There is applause. Mr. Nox steps forward as Killian steps back to stand beside Stacy. "This has been a trying time," John says when the applause subsides. "I want to assure you I didn't want to keep this secret from you. From my family." He looks back at his daughter with that loving smile she knows all too well as a fake. "I knew we were so close to a cure. Perhaps I was wrong to have kept it to myself, but I wanted to do right by my people. I've served you for so many years, and I feared I'd let you down. Rest assured, I may be stepping down from this position, but my replacement will be quite capable by the time I enter the clinical trials. I will be training my son-in-law Elliot Cole to be my successor." The blood drains from Stacy's face, and her mouth becomes dry.

"Why isn't Eustacia stepping in for the position?"

"As you well know, Eustacia was ill for some time, and we fear she may be on a similar course. We wish for Eustacia to be able to provide us with an heir through this arrangement. Providing an heir while simultaneously taking over my position would be too much in her current condition." Eustacia looks up at Killian, hoping he'll stand up for her. He looks ahead, unfazed.

"Is she still ill?"

Stacy steps forward to take back control of this situation, but Killian catches her by the wrist, pulling her back.

"My wife and I don't wish to discuss the details of our daughter's health, but we're not willing to risk losing the opportunity of carrying on our legacy."

"Elliot Cole is already the heir to the agronomic industry. He can't possibly do both!"

Elliot steps forward, as John allows him to take center stage. "I understand your concern. I'll be stepping down from the Agronomic Industry. My younger brother is more than capable of taking over while I step in for Mr. Nox."

Elliot carries on answering questions and speaking of his planned-out future while Stacy wrings her hands. She was so confident; looking at the situation now, she knows she made a mistake by showing her hand too early. She can't take this any further.

Just as the pressure in her chest is becoming too much, Killian tilts slightly toward her. "Don't fight what you can't control. If you throw a fit now, you'll prove to them that John is correct in his decision to replace you."

"Tell them it's not true," she hisses.

"I suggest you find some damning evidence that he's not the replacement they need."

"Help me or I'll make your life a living hell."

"You have no power here. Your threats are rather lackluster." The corner of his mouth quirks up as he stares ahead into the flashing lights.

"You'll eat your words, Killian Grey."

"We'll see." Looking down at her, the quirk on his lips stretches.

"Violet knows," Stacy blurts. She never intended to tell him, but that smirk on his face has pushed her.

His eyes narrow in question; what does she know? Her brow rises as she waits for him to answer his own question. She can't help but smile as the smirk melts off his face and is replaced with anxiety. Her expression shifts into determination as she looks back to the crowd.

Chapter 29

VIOLET

Convincing Dom to allow her an early-bird walk will be like pulling teeth. Mostly because he doesn't like to be awake. When she sleeps, he's finally allowed a break. She lay in bed this morning, tossing and turning in those silk sheets in the most comfortable bed she's ever slept in, staring up at the arched ceilings, wondering how peaceful it'd be to grow up here. Yet, intruding thoughts weigh on her heart, making it feel like the room's closing in on her. Violet shoves the sheets away, pulling on a heavy satin robe, and swings the door open only to startle a stranger.

Violet can hear Dominic groaning as the guard wakes him. Instead of impatiently waiting in the foyer, she marches in after him and threatens to leave without him if he feels like sleeping in. That gets him moving. The other guard stands stiff, watching her, while Dom can be heard fumbling and cursing behind closed doors.

Tight-lipped and hands clenched into fists, Dom leads her to a park with manicured lawns and bushes dusted with ice. A river cuts the park in half with a large bridge allowing you to see a beautiful cascade of water running down the mountain. Mist beads on her skin and hair as she watches the water continue into a tiered waterfall, pooling into the river below before it runs off the island's cliffside. The cold air bites her skin as she watches the sky transition into a painted sunrise of pale yellows and pinks.

The tightness doesn't ease in her chest though the fresh air had always made her feel at ease. Violet picks at the dampened wood railing as she looks over at Dom. He's still frowning, arms folded in on his chest with his eyes closed as he leans against the rail behind her. She hopes he won't be too bitter for her interruption with no one else to talk to. "We passed several people on the way here," she says. Dom only grunts. "When I greeted them as you traditionally do, they frowned at me or ignored me. What changed?"

Dom opens one eye to look at her and closes it again with a sigh. "You aren't wearing the scarf." Violet had left the scarf on a dresser.

Looking down at herself in her brown satin robe, she scoffs. "I'll never understand how the color of your clothing can somehow put someone beneath you. All humans are human. Everyone should be treated equally."

"I agree, but that's not the world we live in."

"Maybe." Violet bends down, resting her chin upon her arms on the railing. Her chest tightens as the colors fade into a pale blue sky, knowing that all of Arcadia will soon be waking up. "Can I ask you a question?"

"Ask away," he sighs.

Violet pauses, questioning whether it's a mistake to ask. "Can you be in love with two people at once?" She holds her breath, waiting for his response.

Dom leans with one elbow against the railing next to her. "I don't think I'm qualified to answer these questions."

Violet lets out her breath. "You're the closest thing I have to a friend right now, and you can't expect me to speak on this subject to Yoojin."

Dom nods, turning to face the sunrise as the fog builds with the warm air. "I think you can love many people at once. Though I don't think you can love each person equally, there are many ways to love someone. You'll always have someone you love more deeply than others."

"How do you know which one you love more deeply? And what if they don't love you equally? What if one of them can tear your heart to pieces?"

"That's the trouble with love. Only you can decide whom to gift your heart to. You must trust that the person you choose is truly giving their heart to you in return. On one end of the scale, you could be entirely happy and content, and on the other could be regret and heartbreak. It's a choice we all must make. You have to decide if it's worth the risk." Dom looks over at her, feeling her eyes burning a hole in him.

Violet can't hide the look of disgust. "You're making this so much worse!" She clenches her chest as she tries to take deep breaths.

Dom laughs as he grabs her shoulders and straightens her up. "Take a deep breath. Don't think of the what if's. It just leads to fear and anxiety. Instead, think of the possibilities. Think of how you'd feel loving each person, having children, growing old together, whatever your ideal life would be. Then decide which life would hurt the most to lose?"

Tears begin to fill her eyes. "What if both break my heart?" Her voice wavers.

"If that's true, then I think you need to do some exploring before you make your decision." Violet raises an eyebrow and looks down at his arms, realizing how this embrace could look to others. "No, I don't mean explore other options. Get your mind out of the gutter, woman." He lets go and drops his hands into his pockets. "You should give Yoojin a chance, and if you really can't see yourself in his future, then you need to let him go."

"I don't want to lead him on if it's a possibility I could break his heart."

"That is what courtship is. It's spending time together to see if you can picture a future with that person. If you don't at least try, you might have regrets later on."

"It sounds selfish."

"You're choosing a future for yourself as well as your son. You're not being selfish; you're thinking smart. People who rush into relationships without dating others sometimes think of what they may have missed out on and then break up their families in pursuit of a future that no longer exists. Now *that* is selfish." Dom's voice rises as he slaps his hands onto the railing, looking out to the world's edge.

"Sounds like you do have some experience in this department."

"I watched my family fall apart because my father had regrets. He left us struggling while we watched him build a life with someone else. He always made it difficult for my mother."

"I'm so sorry."

"Thank you. Have you had enough fresh air?" Violet nods in agreement. Dom nods, moving back up the path. Violet follows but a glint in the sky catches her eye. At first she thinks it's a whale, but her logic corrects her. Whales can't fly. Pausing to look closer, she sees a ship she's not seen before. It's a large white one that moves like a blimp, slow and steady. Dom calls for her, and she drags her eyes away from the ship to follow.

The day had dragged on until suddenly it ended with no word from Yoojin. Meals were served in her rooms. Violet questioned whether Dom had secretly informed Yoojin of their conversation, but he assured her he had not. Violet was left with her miserable thoughts with only Dom for company, and though he was a teasing flirt, he wasn't much for conversation after their early morning chat. He kept leaving the room to take private calls. He would redirect the conversation to her personal life when she asked about them. Violet didn't come here to spill her life story, so she went to bed early.

Another day passed with no word from Yoojin or his family. However, she did enjoy a visit from Aadhya. Violet found it easy to carry on a conversation with her. Though it wasn't hard to miss the change in her demeanor when Yoojin was brought up. She admired the fondness when she spoke of him. The visit from Aadhya lasted only so long, and then she was left staring at the designs on the walls and playing cards with Dom to pass the time.

Now here on the third day, she refuses to remain in her rooms again. Leaving Dom sitting at the table with her breakfast, she storms out of the room. Dom quickly catches up with her but follows at a silent distance. Violet clomps through the echoing halls. She doesn't need to be led around by her guard anymore. She knows exactly where she's going. Hearing silverware squeak and clank against dishes, she knows they're still eating breakfast.

The doors slide open as she enters the dining hall. The mild chatter and clanking silence as she approaches the table. Violet notices a new guest sitting across from Yoojin as he rises at her presence. His mother and father are seated opposite each other. "Ah, Ms. Odaire, I didn't know you would be joining us for breakfast this morning," Madam Kim says with a pointed look toward Dominic.

"Yes, well, eating alone with one's thoughts can grow tiresome day after day." Violet raises a brow at Yoojin as she rounds the table to sit next to the stranger.

"Your choice of clothing is…interesting."

Yoojin smiles weakly before taking his seat and staring at his food.

"I grew tired of wearing the clothes you provided," Violet says as she checks the collar of her white loose-fit blouse tucked into her black skin-tight pants.

"You look like a character from a storybook. A pirate."

Violet looks at Madam Kim with wide eyes and a dropped jaw. "Madam Kim, I think that's the nicest thing you've ever said to me."

"Good morning, Violet." The humor in Roger's voice is evident.

"Good morning, Roger. I trust the results weren't alarming, since there was no word otherwise."

"We can speak of that later, my dear," he says with a smile. Though it's meant to be reassuring, it's actually the opposite. She suddenly feels her skin on fire as her pulse quickens.

Distracting herself from her nerves, she turns to the stranger. Her silky brown hair is pulled into a sleek ponytail on the crown of her head. The woman's features are pleasing to the eye, and her black attire, though very sharp, shows off her shapely body. "Hello, my name is Violet O'daire. Are you another one of Yoojin's many friends?" She extends her hand to the woman.

The woman shakes hands, and Violet notes how soft she is. This woman has never worked a day in her life. "Magistrate Danit Sinai. It's wonderful to meet you." Danit has a slight accent that she can't pinpoint. She can feel her smile is genuine, though, which calms her slightly. "I was told they had another guest visiting. I hope we can get along while I'm here."

The smile slips from Violet's lips as she distracts herself by filling her plate with food. "I don't see why not." Violet questions whether Danit struggles to get along with most people. She throws the thought away, determined to keep this day as positive as possible. Looking across the table, she watches Yoojin slowly picking away his food. He glances up at Violet as she's taking a bite but looks away quickly. Violet's eyes narrow on him. "Yoojin." His attention snaps back to her. "I'd like to visit Halmeonim today."

Yoojin drops his fork mid-mouthful and tries to catch it before it crashes onto the plate, only to knock it into his glass. "Halmeonim?" Madam Kim interjects.

"Yes, the sweet old lady who works in the rice fields."

"That sounds lovely. May I join you?" Danit adds with a wide grin.

Yoojin looks to his mother. "Are you sure? We wouldn't want to bore you."

"On the contrary, I'd love to meet the locals," Danit says with excitement.

"I'd be happy to escort you," Yoojin says with an approving nod from his mother.

"Wonderful," Violet sighs. She was hoping for alone time with Yoojin. He's avoiding her, and she's determined to discover why. With the addition of Danit, it won't be easy to have a private conversation. "I would suggest you change into something less formal, Danit. The grounds aren't suited for heels and gowns. I have something you could wear if you don't have anything suitable."

"Thank you, Violet. I appreciate it."

"That's not necessary," Madam Kim speaks up. "I'm sure we can find something for you, Magistrate Sinai." Violet smiles at her use of the formal title.

"I'm sure you have more important things to do, Madam Kim. Violet and I can work it out." Danit carries on eating after brushing off Madam Kim.

Violet smiles up at Danit. Beyond her, Madam Kim glares. Violet's grin widens. "Yoojin will show you to my accommodations after breakfast. Today will be fun." Danit agrees, smiling eagerly. Violet turns her attention to her food, attempting to hold back her delight in Madam Kim's frustration.

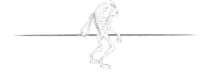

"They're brown." Danit holds up the clothes, feeling the texture between her fingers. Violet had chosen the set of brown slacks and a brown wrap tunic. Dom waits in the corridor to receive a pair of boots for Danit that will fit.

"Do you have something against the color brown?" Violet asks as she adjusts the blue scarf around her curly mop in the mirror.

"No, I just—"

"Good, get changed. I want to leave." Violet closes Danit in the bathroom before she can protest.

"I never paid much attention before, but you *have* always dressed kind of like a pirate," Yoojin says in a low voice. Violet turns around to find him leaning against the wall with his hands in his long cobalt coat pockets. His head is tilted back against the wall seeming bored, yet the quirk in his lips shows humor. Violet finds her heart trying to leap out of her chest as he focuses his narrowed eyes on her form.

"Hide your treasures, good sir. I mean to pillage," Violet teases, leaning against the door, matching his stance.

"The only thing of value I own is my heart, and you have stolen that long ago."

He says it so quietly that she questions if she misheard. Violet's jaw drops slightly. "That's a bold statement."

Yoojin looks up at the ceiling and pushes himself away from the wall. He glances around the room as he crosses the floor. Standing inches away, he towers over her. "This is the first time we've been alone, and I intend to take advantage of that," he says with an undertone.

"Okay." Violet can't decide whether to look at his eyes or lips. She leans her head back against the doors, holding the handle for support. How easy it'd be to close the distance between their lips with his head inclined towards hers. With determination, she locks eyes with him.

"Violet, I need—"

The door behind Violet opens slightly before Violet slams it shut, closing her eyes in frustration. Just as Yoojin's finally about to open up about his feelings, of course they're interrupted. The knock at the door has them both sighing as Yoojin steps back into place against the wall, staring up at the ceiling. Violet releases the door and steps aside. Danit comes out, adjusting the simple tunic. "That color suits you," Violet says, giving her a once-over. Danit scrunches her nose in response.

Dom returns with a pair of boots just in time, as Violet's eager to get off this mountain. She barely gives Danit time to pull them on before she's out the door. The flight back to the island is short. The sun's still low and things are just beginning to warm up. The air's thick with the moisture of the melting ice that falls like mist from the mountain. Violet doesn't allow any time to waste in the small markets as she heads to the terraced hills. Traveling through the island's jungle-like terrain was a much easier hike on the way in, as it's all uphill now. Danit gasps for breath and takes many breaks. Violet smiles as she watches sweat spilling down her face. Yoojin, who left his coat behind, rolls up his sleeves and unbuttons his shirt to allow more airflow.

"How much further?" Danit asks when she has control of her breath.

"Not much further," Yoojin answers before moving on.

Danit's long silky ponytail is beginning to look more like a horse tail from the moisture and frizz. She seems more frazzled, and her composure falls further apart the further they go. When they reach the top, they're led to a well where many farmers take a water break. Danit jogs to them and begs for a drink. They look at her curiously. When they see Yoojin, they're all smiles and greetings. They provide him with a wooden cup with a long handle, and he takes a long drink before handing it to Danit, who's looking up at him pathetically.

Violet searches the faces until she finds the old woman sitting in the shade of some elephant leaves. "Halmeonim!" she calls. The old woman looks surprised as Violet runs to her and kneels. Violet bows her head in greeting, pulls a small bag out of her pocket, and hands it to the old woman. The woman looks at her in confusion, and Violet gestures for her to take it. The old woman opens the bag and makes a joyful sound as she presses it to her chest before taking a piece of candy, unwrapping it, and popping it into her mouth. She croons as she pats Violet's cheek. "Yoojin told me they're your favorite," Violet laughs. The woman unwraps another and holds it to Violet's lips. "These are for you!" she replies, but the woman insists, so Violet opens her mouth. The rich coffee flavor floods her mouth as the chewy candy sticks to her teeth. "*Gamsahabnida.*" Violet's thankful she asked Dom to give her some phrases to use on the flight down.

The old woman laughs and nods her head. She looks at the rest of her group and asks Violet something in Korean, pointing at Danit. "Can you help me?" Violet asks back. "I want to spend time with Yoojin, but those people keep getting in the way. *Il-eul juda?*"

The woman frowns but nods in understanding before carefully getting to her feet and patting Violet on the arm. She starts grunting orders and everyone gets back to work. Yoojin watches curiously as she gathers Danit, Dom and Violet, leading them to one of the flooded tiers. She instructs them to take off their boots and roll up their cuffs. Danit is very confused and concerned as she's barked at in a language she doesn't understand. Yoojin snickers as he knows what she's up to. Dom doesn't argue when he sees Yoojin and Violet obeying without question. Halmeonim grabs a bushel of young rice plants and shows them how to plant them in the waterlogged field, spacing them out nicely. Yoojin, Dom and Violet get to work planting their bushels, but Danit gets special instructions as she refuses to put her feet in the muddy water without screaming like she's being stabbed. She gets hit on the arm and yelled at before Danit succumbs to her demands.

In time Violet and Yoojin run out of their rice seedlings and collect more before heading back out to the field again. Yoojin stops to watch Danit gripe at the old woman about her back aching, only to get a smack on her back and another scolding. Danit gets frustrated and kicks the water, splashing Halmeonim. It becomes a spectacle as the other helpers laugh at Danit's expense.

"Did you somehow plan this?" Yoojin snickers.

"Kind of? When I saw that you were avoiding me because of that woman, Halmeonim popped into my head. I wanted to explore more of this island anyway.

It's so stuffy up on that mountain," she giggles as she carefully steps into the muddy water. With each step, the mud squishes between her toes. "It's more fun down here, in my opinion."

"I agree. I used to come here every chance I got. I'd help in the fields or go fishing."

"Oh, can we go fishing next?"

Yoojin laughs. "Maybe if Danit doesn't break by the end of this."

"I think she's starting to get the hang of it." Violet watches as Danit starts getting a rhythm to her planting.

"About earlier," Yoojin starts. Violet stops walking and turns to give him her full attention. "I need to tell you something."

"Say it." Violet tries to sound encouraging.

"I want you to know. What my mother does is not a reflection of my feelings towards you."

"That's obvious."

"Let me finish." Violet bites down on her lips to hold them closed. "Arcadia is responsible for the destruction of Safe Haven. I overheard my mother receiving a report. They bombed it again. The underground facility is destroyed." Violet looks at him blankly. "Violet?"

"You think I didn't know? I recognized your airships from the first attack."

"Why didn't you say anything?"

"I wanted to see what you would tell me if I acted naïve." Violet shrugs.

Yoojin rubs the back of his head. "There's more." Violet presses her lips together. "My mother gave instructions to watch a shelter. I believe she means yours, because they intercepted a communication requesting you to check in with them."

Violet's nostrils flare as she takes in this information. "I'm sure you know I don't like your mother."

"Yes," Yoojin says solemnly.

Violet stands close to him in case others might overhear as she says in a low voice, "Then please understand, if anything happens to that shelter, to my family. If she threatens the safety of any of those people, know that I will burn her world to the ground." Violet's voice shakes as she struggles to contain her rage. "Your people don't have the right to choose who lives or dies." Yoojin's throat bobs as he nods once, looking down in shame. "Is that why I haven't heard from them? Because they intercept our communications?" Yoojin nods, incapable of looking her in the eye. "I thought we were just too far away to reach them." Violet sighs as she looks out at the rice paddies.

"I know this'll change things, but I'll do everything I can to ensure they're left alone. I never meant for anyone to get hurt."

"This changes nothing between us, Yoojin. The blood of Safe Haven has stained your mother's hands. You're not to be held accountable for her actions. I know you're a good man, and you'd never hurt innocent people."

Violet notices the glaze over Yoojin's eyes. Pulling her into his chest, he holds her tight. "Thank you. It means so much to hear you say that." Violet wraps her arms around him even though she can feel the sweat through their shirts unpleasantly sticking together. "I love you," he says into the crook of her neck.

At this moment, Violet's frozen in panic. Though she's been telling herself she's in love with both Yoojin and Killian, now that she hears those words from him, a wave of terror runs through her, and she realizes she can't return the sentiment. What if she lost Killian? She thinks of not only her feelings towards him but also how Nathan would feel. Nathan's never met Yoojin, and she'd never want to expose him to that woman Yoojin calls a mother. Violet hugs Yoojin awkwardly in return, and when someone clears their throat nearby, she is thankful for the interruption.

Danit's frowning, but she apologizes for interrupting regardless. "Might I have a word with Violet?" she asks. Yoojin releases her hesitantly, but Violet encourages him with a smile. He takes Violet's seedlings and joins Dom to finish planting. "Violet, I need to tell you something." Violet nods, waiting patiently. "I have a message from Killian Grey." Violet's mouth becomes dry at hearing his name come from this woman. "I've come here solely to relay this message."

"What's the message?" Violet barks.

Danit raises a brow as she answers. "Killian wants you to leave this place and return home. It would've been best if you'd never come here. You're putting yourself and others at risk."

Violet cocks her head and shakes it in confusion. "I'm sorry. How does Killian know where I am? He hasn't even contacted me."

"It'd be impossible for him to contact you."

False. Violet comes closer to Danit, narrowing her focus on her. "Who are you? How do you know Killian. And why would he send you all the way here from wherever the hell you came from to give me this message?"

"I'm a friend. I come from Stratos Development. He would've come himself if he were permitted. I came at his request."

"You're telling me that Killian would come all the way here to tell me to go home." Violet folds her arms over her chest.

"Yes. You have no idea what these people are capable of." Danit steps close, lowering her voice as she speaks. "You mustn't trust the Kims."

Violet's feeling somewhat manic and bursts into laughter. It draws the attention of their group as Yoojin and Dominic look on. She stretches out her fingers and balls them into a fist several times as she collects herself. "I'm here to find out exactly what they're capable of." She steps closer, causing Danit to step back. "If I were to trust anyone, it'd be Yoojin. Who are you to tell me whom I can and cannot trust? If Killian truly sent you, he knows better than to tell me what to do, especially through some random woman from high society."

"Violet, following his instructions is in your best interest. He told me to give this to you so that you'd know it was from him." Danit stands her ground, holding out a small picture from the last meal Violet had with her family. A picture of Nathan with his arms wrapped around her neck. She stared down at the photo. Stacy had told her that when they entered the Stratos, all their possessions were stripped from them.

Violet takes the photo, stuffing it into her pocket. "Consider your message received, but I'll decide for myself," she says as she walks past her.

"Have you no message for him? Or should I inform him of your engagement with Yoojin Kim?" Violet stops, blood beginning to boil. Turning on the spot, Danit faces her with a knowing smile.

Violet grabs hold of Danit's dirty tunic so she can't escape. Though Violet is shorter than Danit, she uses her strength to take control. "I think you've been misinformed. I don't like when strangers involve themselves in my personal affairs, but since you insist, you can inform that *husband* of mine that he needs to focus on his own goals. I will go home when I've done what I came to do."

Danit's eyes widen as she pulls at Violet's hands, but they don't budge. "Unhand me now," she demands.

"Violet?" Yoojin calls in alarm.

"You think you can threaten me into submission." Violet laughs. "You say I don't know what Arcadia is capable of. Do you know what I'm capable of? Look at yourself." Violet looks her over. "A couple of hours with me and you've yielded your colors, allowing me to outrank you. A privileged little princess who's never worked a day in her life, reduced to a mere peasant, covered in mud." Danit's features reflect her anger. In one swift movement, Violet grabs Danit by the throat and sweeps her legs out from under her. Danit lands on the rocky ground with a thud. Violet doesn't hear Dom or

Yoojin yelling her name as they run toward them. Danit gasps for air, scratching at Violet's arm drawing blood, but Violet doesn't feel a thing as she leans down with her lips close to her ear.

"If I hear more reports of you coming into physical contact with Killian, I will end you. Am I clear?" Violet pulls away to look her in the eye and tilts her head as Danit's eyes widen. "You don't think I'd send Killian off without having eyes on him, did you? Stay away from what's mine." Danit weakly slaps Violet's hand as Yoojin pulls her off. She inhales deeply and begins coughing. Violet laughs manically as Dom assists the helpless princess to her feet.

Chapter 30

DOMINIC

Roger has requested a follow-up visit with Violet. At Yoojin's request, he hadn't reported the incident from yesterday to Madam Kim. If Yoojin failed to smooth things over with Danit, that might be the basis for this visit. Dom watches Violet's back as he escorts her to the infirmary. Her muscles can be seen beneath her brown knit top with each movement. He questions whether he made the right choice to keep it to himself just how strong she is. She had taken him to the ground as if he were nothing but a ragdoll. Is the Kim family in danger? Is her presence here a threat to society? How much damage would she cause if she decided to attack before they could take her down?

For the past few days, she's made it clear that she wants his people to be treated as equals. Everything she stands for is good and for the good of everyone. Madam

Kim would never stand for Violet's ideas of equality. Until yesterday, there was no question of whose side he'd stand for. Though he doesn't know what was said, she attacked an unarmed innocent and laughed like a lunatic. Magistrate Danit Sinai was terrified. Violet's never looked more menacing. She hasn't been the same since. She refuses to answer his distracting questions and has been humming a tune that is, quite frankly, bone-chilling.

As they enter the infirmary, Aadhya greets them. Suddenly Violet seems herself again as she greets Aadhya in return. She's led to an exam room, and Dominique is instructed to stay in the lobby. Roger comes to meet him with his hand reaching out. Dom shakes it respectfully. "Dominic, thank you for bringing her."

"It's my duty," he says with a question in his tone.

"I'm surprised you didn't report the incident. We heard it from the Magistrate herself."

"Yoojin asked that I delay the report."

"You're a good friend to Yoojin, but don't put lives at risk for a friendship. You could lose your rank." Roger pats his shoulder kindly.

Dom's lips tighten into a thin line, and he nods in understanding. "What will happen to her?"

"Aadhya and I have worked tirelessly to find a cure for Violet's condition. Perhaps with this solution, she might live a normal life, and she'll be sent home to her son as requested by Magistrate Sinai. She'll be provided transport the morning after the 'soiree,' as Madam Kim calls it." Roger chuckles.

"You can cure her?" Dominic doesn't see the humor in this conversation and can't help but feel concerned for her.

"Not exactly. It'll neutralize the chemicals coursing through her body that give her inhuman strength. It will also affect how quickly she heals, so make sure she's careful. We'll need to give her another injection tonight. When Liam comes to relieve you, he'll administer the second dose while she sleeps."

"Did she agree to this?"

"We thought it best to let her think we're providing nutrients she was lacking in her bloodwork. Be discreet. She'll feel weak and somewhat tired. Take her straight back to her room to rest. Meals will be sent to you."

"Is this necessary, sir?"

"We wanted to ensure everyone's safety for the party tomorrow. If Yoojin wants her to be safe, this is the only way to protect the world from her and her from the world." Roger pats his shoulder again before turning on his heel and striding down the hall.

A moment later, Violet stumbles out of the exam room. Aadhya is at her side, catching her arm. "Are you all right?" Aadhya worries over her.

Violet giggles. "I think I got up too fast. I'm just a little lightheaded."

"Can I get you anything? Water or a snack?"

"No, thank you, Aadhya. You're so sweet. I look forward to seeing you tomorrow."

"Me too, Violet." Aadhya flashes her gleaming smile as she hands Violet off to Dom. She glances over her shoulder as she walks away.

"Are you feeling okay?" Dom asks.

"Yup, just a little dizzy. It'll pass." Violet beams up at him. He smiles weakly in return. She holds onto the crook of his elbow for stability as they return to her room. He can feel her relying on him more the longer it takes to get there. By the time they arrive in her hallway, she's stumbling like a drunk. Dom sighs in frustration when he sees Yoojin waiting outside her door. He wraps his arm around her waist and she does the same, hoping it doesn't look like he's dragging her along.

"What happened?" Yoojin asks.

"I'm so tired. I'm gonna go to bed. No time for play, Woof," Violet slurs, letting go of Dom to push past Yoojin and open the door.

"Is she drunk?" He glares at Dom accusingly.

"Nope, just shot up with Pop's Vitamins," Violet mumbles as she stumbles across the room. Dom pushes past Yoojin to assist her before she can fall and hurt herself. She collapses onto the bed, rolling onto her back. Dom unlaces her boots as she squints at him. "Dom dom dadom dom," Violet calls melodiously.

"Yes, Violet, what do you need?" Dom comes to stand beside her, dropping her boots bedside.

"You're a good boy," she says sleepily with her eyes closed.

"If you say so," Dom smirks, patting her limp hand before heading back to a glowering Yoojin.

"What is she talking about?" Yoojin demands.

Dom checks to ensure Violet's fast asleep before closing the bedroom door behind him. "Violet was injected with a serum to give her nutrients her bloodwork was lacking." He looks down at the floor, lips pressed together in frustration.

"Vitamins don't make people like that," Yoojin growls, getting into Dom's face. His face crumples in anger, meeting his friend's eyes.

"You're right. That's what they told her when they injected her with a poison that slows down her healing and weakens her. Where were you? You say you love her, but you abandon her for a couple of days and then let your father cure her, if you can even call it that. Do you even know what they're planning?" Dom pushes Yoojin and his eyes widen. "I've listened to you pine for this woman for years, and this is how you treat her? You can't even protect her from your own family. I thought you were different. You're no better than the rest of the nobles. You think only of yourselves and how to make yourselves happy without thinking of how your decisions affect humanity. I'm sick of it. I'm sick of you. Now get out of my face so I can do my job." Dom checks Yoojin's shoulder in passing before plopping down onto the sofa.

Yoojin comes to sit across from him. "What are they planning?"

"They're making sure she's no longer a threat before shipping her home the morning after your engagement party."

"Engagement party?"

Dom squeezes the bridge of his nose. "Yoojin, you can't keep living in ignorance. Your mother has been planning this since you broke your leg."

"To whom?"

"You're so thick. Do you think she'd allow a woman with a defect to become your wife? She was already on the fence when she heard about Nathan. When you returned wounded and lovesick over an unavailable sick woman, did you think she'd let it slide? What if your children inherit that defect? Did you even think before bringing her into a den of wolves? Think with the head on your shoulders for once."

Yoojin leans forward, rubbing the back of his neck. "You're right. I wasn't thinking rationally. I just wanted to control one thing in my life."

"With your mother on her throne, you'll never have that control."

"What am I supposed to do about that?"

"You figure it out. I have too much on my plate." Dom twists his body, lifting his feet onto the sofa so that he's reclining.

"Such as?" Yoojin bites.

"Deciding whose side I'm on. Do I carry on selfishly like the Kims, who let old women work themselves to death to provide for their families, only to be rewarded with bad healthcare and a lack of respect? Or do I keep Liam from administrating the second dose in her sleep, commit treason and help her escape Arcadia undetected, and likely lose the life I worked so hard to have?"

Yoojin nods, biting his bottom lip. "You won't lose your position." He gets to his feet and briskly leaves. Dom sighs, closing his eyes once more with his arms crossed over his chest.

Dom wakes to the sound of the door opening. Quickly he stands at attention. Liam walks in with a smirk. "Not hungry?" Liam snickers, pointing at the meal waiting in the hall.

"I was waiting for Violet to wake. I didn't want to disturb her," he lies.

Liam nods with a knowing grin as he crosses the room to Violet's bedroom door. He takes out the injection vessel and spins it in his hand. Dom meets him at the door, grabbing the handle. "I'll administer the serum," he says, holding his hand out for the vessel.

"I've got it. We've wasted our time serving this commoner while she disrespects Madam Kim and our way of life. Finally, she's being put in her place."

"I'm sure you've been warned of how dangerous she is. It'll be safer if someone she knows and trusts administers it."

"She's already been weakened."

"Yes, but why do you think there's a second dose? She doesn't know you, and if she wakes to a stranger standing over her, she might have enough strength to take you out or break the vessel. I'd rather not take that risk. Are you willing to take that chance?"

Liam shifts his weight from foot to foot with pursed lips. Shoving the vessel into Dom's hand, he folds his arms and leans against the wall. Dominic closes the door behind himself.

The room is dark, but the moon shines enough light through the windows to allow him to see her silhouette on the bed. He takes a couple of steps toward her but stops to look down at the vessel in his hand. Looking back at her sleeping form, he shakes his head and takes a step, but an arm wraps around his neck and something hard knocks into the back of his knees, dropping him to the floor. He holds his hands up in surrender.

Violet speaks low in his ear. "Turns out you're not a good boy after all. I'm disappointed in you, Dominic. Drop the serum." Dom places the serum down quietly and raises his hands in surrender. Violet's arm has a tight enough hold around his throat to make speaking difficult, but he can still take labored breaths. "Aadhya was kind enough to warn me of Kim's plan to cure me. Swapped it out with a tranquilizer. She said Liam would administer the second dose." She sighs. "What should I do with you? I can't kill you. That'd cause too many problems with Yoojin."

"Violet, I…Liam is out…side," Dom chokes out.

"I know. I was listening."

"What…are you…going to do?"

"I'm going to take Arcadia down."

"How?"

"I know what keeps your mountain afloat. I can take you out, then Liam. I can run like the maven and take down the mountain before Kim can sound the alarm. Down goes your hierarchy."

"You'd kill hundreds of thousands of people. Women…children." Violet tightens her hold. "The tidal wave…would wipe out everyone. Please."

"What would you suggest I do? You idiots have blindly killed innocents for decades," Violet grunts through her teeth.

"Please, I'm on your side. Let me help you."

"Are you? You told Yoojin you couldn't decide." Violet flexes her arm in warning. A knock at the door has them both flinching. "Poor the serum down the drain, and when Liam leaves, we'll hash out a plan together. Please, I have a family. I'm putting their lives in your hands." Violet releases him, snatching the vessel before he can blink. She drains the serum in her bathroom sink and tosses the empty vessel to him. She goes to her bed, shoving off the pillows from under her covers that had acted as her double.

"When he leaves, bring food. I'm starving," Violet says as she aggressively adjusts the blankets around her.

Dominic is quick to leave, handing the vessel back to Liam. "What took you so long?" Liam snatches the vessel out of his hand.

"Violet's a light sleeper. She woke up scared, as expected. She may be slower in reaction but still had some strength. Got me in the throat." He clears his throat and rubs it to emphasize.

Liam puffs air out his lips. "I can't wait for that trash to go back where it came from. Gives me the creeps."

"All the trash will be taken out in due time."

Liam cackles. "Go ahead and take your leave so I can get out of here."

Chapter 31

GARETH

Piper brings her meal to the table where Gareth's already waiting. She catches his eye and he cracks a smile as she takes her seat next to him. He wraps his arm around her neck, pulling her close to kiss her head. The affection naturally brings a curl to her lips, making his heart leap. Jasper sits across from them, as he has since being rebuked, with tissue stuffed up his nostril and dark circles forming under his eyes. They flick up to Piper and back to his tray. Looking back and forth between them, Gareth removes his arm from around her. "What happened to you?"

Jasper glances at Piper again and back to his tray as Piper glares him down while stuffing her face with bread. "I made a mistake," Jasper answers nasally.

"That's not like you." Gareth narrows his eyes on Jasper.

"He's fine," Piper says before filling her mouth with more food.

"Piper." Gareth turns his body to face her. Piper ignores him, continuing to eat. "He's been trying hard to make up for what he did. How many times does he need to apologize?" Piper cocks her head to the side, giving him a dry look.

"Just let it be, Gareth," Jasper interjects.

"Piper." Gareth's tone drops an octave, drawing her attention mid-bite. "Holding a grudge will only cause bitterness. He regrets what he did. Can my sweet Piper find it in herself to let this go and stop punishing him?" He wraps his arms around her, pressing her tight against him.

Piper watches Jasper as he awkwardly pushes his food around his tray. Taking smaller bites to avoid moving his nose, he winces each time. "Fine," she says. Jasper looks up at Piper with glossy eyes. "I won't give him false direction anymore." She taps Gareth's arm and he releases her so she can go back to eating.

Gareth leans in close. "Good girl," he whispers in her ear, sending shivers down her spine. Piper bites her lip to avoid grinning like an idiot. Jabbing her elbow into his side, he chuckles as he begins to eat, watching her out of the corner of his eye. Jasper lets out a breath as he avoids eye contact with them.

The speakers chime as an announcement begins. "*Tomorrow is Visitor Day. All trials will be rescheduled.*" There's an audible sigh of relief. Piper's chest tightens as she looks up at Gareth. He looks down at her with an encouraging grin. He can see the tension as her shoulders pull in. Glancing back at Jasper, he looks back and forth between them. Piper looks down at her tray, no longer having an appetite for the remainder of her meal.

Afterwards, Jasper follows them into the commons. Piper eyes him as he drapes himself across a chair nearby as Gareth turns on some music. He turns the volume up a little louder than necessary, but no one complains. Piper rubs her arms, looking around the room. Holding out his hand, Gareth pulls her attention back to him. Resting her delicate hand in his, he pulls her up against him, resting one hand on her lower back and the other delicately leading her as they sway in rhythm with the song.

He smiles down at her and blows at the wavy black hair that's fallen into his eyes, but it has a mind of its own. He notices how her face has changed over the months. Her cheeks have hollowed out, and the dark circles under her chocolate-brown eyes are evidence of her stress. Piper must think the same, as her free hand traces the darkness under his eye and tucks his unruly hair behind his ear. A long breath escapes him as he looks into her eyes. The sudden glaze over her eyes tugs on the string tied snuggly around his heart. He tilts his head to rest his cheek against hers as they move to the music. "What's wrong?" he asks with an undertone.

"I'm scared," she whispers.

"It'll be okay. I'm going to get you out of here."

"If we do escape, what about my aunt? What will happen to her?"

"I'll make sure both of you are well taken care of. I promise."

She moves her head to press her lips against his warm cheek. "Do you remember his instructions? It's been so long."

"We'll meet him at the edge of the woods on the highest cliff. He'll return my keys, and then we're on our own to follow the beach to the emergency door hidden under the natural bridge." Gareth turns her out and pulls her back in.

"Don't forget, we can't be followed," Piper adds. As he sways, turning their bodies to the tune, Jasper comes into view. His body language says he's bored, but his eyes watching them say they have his full attention. When he realizes Gareth's watching, he finds a hangnail on his thumb that needs his attention.

"We'll be careful," Gareth sighs.

"Okay." Piper closes her eyes, taking a deep breath.

Gareth presses his lips to her forehead. "Let's not think about it. We'll worry about tomorrow when it comes." He breathes against her forehead. Piper smiles up at him and nods. Gently he presses his lips to hers, and they part for him.

Gareth wakes with a start, his arms empty and his heart hammering against his chest. He sits up in the darkness, searching with his hands, his breath coming in short bursts. A bright light pierces the darkness, blinding him for a moment, and then it's back to dark. Then a hand reaches out to him, and he grabs her. Piper climbs back into the small bed and snuggles up to him. "Are you all right?" she whispers as her hand presses against his pounding chest.

"Where did you go?" Gareth pulls her in tight, breathing her in as if she may not be real. The panic of waking without her in his arms erases the memory of the dream that woke him.

"I just needed the restroom," Piper says sleepily, patting his cheek.

Gareth nuzzles up to her warm neck as she turns in her sleep. He can't be sure if he fell back asleep, but he doesn't feel rested in the morning. For a moment, he longs to lie there with her until the day's end. Grudgingly, he rises with the others, waking Piper as well. The morning seems to drag, and he can't find it in himself to feign a conversation. The tension rolls off Piper and flows into him, the longer it takes to finish breakfast. Jasper doesn't seem to notice as he glances around the room.

When they're finally led to the lobby, he tries to distract Piper with reading, but her bouncing knee gives her away. They're both anxious to leave, but must wait until they're the last so as not to draw attention. Gareth rests his hand on her knee to steady her. Slowly, one by one, their peers are called out. When the last person leaves, Piper watches wide-eyed and then glances back at Gareth. She looks like she might be sick, and Gareth takes her hand in his. Kissing her knuckles, he holds eye contact with her. "Let's go."

Piper nods determinedly to keep the contents of her stomach from spewing out. They clasp hands and walk out, greeting the attendant on their way. The attendant nods but carries on with their task. She looks around at all those mingling. Gareth leans in to whisper in her ear. "We're just strolling. Don't give them a reason to give us attention." She nods, trying to put on a smile. He squeezes her clammy hand.

As they pad through the pine, Gareth casually looks around as if admiring the scenery. As they draw closer to the cliffs, the crashing waves become louder, and he can almost taste the salt in the air. Adrenaline pulses through him, the closer they come. A crack echoes through the woods, dragging their attention behind them. Jasper's wispy blond hair catches his eye behind a tree. Gareth signals Piper to stay.

He quickly backtracks to meet Jasper, only to find him crouched over an unconscious Reese. "I didn't mean to knock her out," he gasps. "I only meant to question her."

"Take her back."

"Please, let me go with you. I know what you're doing. I overheard your conversation with Killian. I can help you. Please, I beg you. I can't stay here."

Gareth runs his hands through his hair, pacing. There's no time. As soon as she wakes, the plan is over.

Gareth grabs Jasper by the arm, dragging him along. "We need to move."

"What are you doing?" Piper is panic-stricken when she sees the two.

"There's no time. We have to hurry." Piper doesn't question further, and they begin running.

Gareth looks back, expecting anyone else to come after them, but there's no one. They finally reach the edge of the woods, spotting Killian in his white coat and gray suit, glowering. They stand before him, out of breath, at the cliff's edge. "I told you to make sure you weren't followed," Killian groans.

"Jasper ensured we weren't." Gareth stands his ground.

Killian looks around, reaching into his pocket. He pulls out Gareth's keys and shoves them into his hand. "Take them and run to the end of that beach. There's a door—"

"Hidden beneath the natural bridge," Piper finishes for him.

Gareth shoves the keys onto his wrist. "Go before someone notices you're missing," Killian says, shoving Gareth away. The others don't need to be told to follow.

"Go where?" another voice calls out to them from the woods. They turn to find Dr. Oric walking casually with a wide grin and his hands clasped behind his back.

"I told them to return. Before someone noticed they were missing."

"Well, I think it's a little late for that." He almost skips over to Killian's side. "I noticed." He keeps his eyes solely on Killian. Gareth pulls Piper to stand behind him and Jasper. "I see…everything." He shrugs with a chuckle, then releases his hands, revealing a gun. In one swift move, he aims and fires. Piper screams as the sound echoes out to the ocean. It feels to Gareth like his blood instantly drains from his body, and his mouth runs dry as he watches Killian stumble back. Killian's pristine coat is stained red as he places his hand over his heart. The shock in his eyes is haunting. Oric reaches out and pushes him off the cliff's edge. Killian tries to grab hold of Oric's hand but his fingers, wet with blood, slip. Piper cries out, but Gareth just stands there, silently stunned.

Oric turns his attention to them with a widening grin. "I don't like when people interfere with my plans," he reasons.

"You killed him," Piper cries.

"Killian stuck his nose where it didn't belong."

"You're vile," Gareth growls.

"What are you going to do about it, Nox?" Oric taunts as his smile melts away. "Are you going to kill me?"

Piper pulls on the back of Gareth's shirt, shocking his legs out of their frozen state. The two back away slowly as Oric watches them curiously. "Here." He throws the gun on the ground, halfway between him and Gareth. Staring between Oric and the gun, Gareth decides to go for it when a rustling in the woods draws his attention. Black suits are running in their direction, weapons drawn. Oric cackles, "Would you like to play a game of cat and mouse?"

Gareth turns, pulling Piper along with him. Oric's laughter fades behind them. They run as fast as they can down the path to the beach. The brush is an obstacle attempting to make them stumble, but they can leap over it with speed. He realizes their mistake as soon as they hit the sand, making it hard to keep their pace. The sand gives under their weight, working against each step. The closer to the water, the easier it is to run, but the less cover they have. Shots are fired. Piper screams. Jasper grunts. Gareth runs as hard as he can, weaving to avoid being hit, holding tightly to Piper's hand. They don't look back.

As the beach curves, the natural bridge comes into sight. It's still far off, but there's enough distance between their hunters that they may have enough time to get to the door before they can get more shots off. Their lungs burn, and there's a stabbing pain in Gareth's side, but he pushes through it. Piper begins to lose her momentum. "We're almost there!" he grunts. They continue pushing and finally reach the bridge, panting. Jasper searches for the door as Gareth releases Piper's hand and looks back to find that their assailants are far behind. Their gear slowed them down enough to give them a fighting chance.

"Gareth?" Piper's shaking voice rips through to get his attention. He looks for her eyes, but she's looking down. "Ungh," she groans. His eyes drop to her blood-stained hands. The sand at her feet is painted crimson. "Gareth." She gasps as she looks up at him with tears streaming down her cheeks.

"I found it!" Jasper yells, but all sound is muffled. He no longer hears the waves crashing or the panting of his breath. Piper reaches for him as she begins to fall. Gareth catches her in his arms, holding her upright as the assailants start to round the bend. "I found it!" Jasper yells again as he returns to them. A shot is fired and hits the bridge near Jasper's head, causing him to flinch away. Jasper pulls Gareth to the other side as he drags Piper with him. Gareth pulls his hand from her back, and sees that it's sticky with warm blood.

"Gareth," Piper cries.

"Shhh, you're okay," Gareth croons. "I'm going to get you out of here."

"No," Jasper breathes.

"Help me," Gareth demands. Jasper helps lift her as she groans, and they move to the door. Gareth scans one key after another until it finally opens. They fall into the elevator dragging sand along with them. Jasper rips his shirt and presses it against her wounds as she moans in pain. Gareth scans a random key and returns to Piper's side. The door slides closed and the car begins to move.

"Gareth," Piper says weakly.

"It's okay. You're okay," he croons, wiping her hair away and smearing blood across her forehead. His eyes blur, and he furiously wipes away the tears, obscuring his vision.

"Gareth, you have…to keep going," Piper gasps.

"We will, you and me. I won't let you go. I promise."

"I can't feel my legs." She tries to put on a brave face and smile, but her mask crumbles as she looks into his tearful eyes. She reaches her bloodied hand out to him and he catches it, pressing it against his face to warm her chilled fingers.

"I promised you the sun, remember?" Gareth's voice breaks. He can hear Jasper falling apart but refuses to take his eyes off her. Piper's teeth begin to chatter, and Gareth's unsure if it's nerves or chills, so he rips off his tunic, draping it over her. The elevator comes to a slow stop. Pulling her into his arms, he gets to his feet as Jasper tries to keep pressure on the wounds. The doors slide open, exposing them to an empty corridor. Gareth glances at the map in passing to get his bearings.

At the end of the hall is another set of elevators. He finds the key he needs and the doors close behind them. Gareth adjusts her in his arms as the elevator begins to move. "I'm so tired," she says.

"No, you need to stay awake, okay?" Gareth shakes her shoulder.

She widens her dilated eyes. "I'll try."

"Good girl." Gareth cries. "Please stay with me."

"I love you," Piper whispers. Gareth can feel her breaths becoming shallower.

"I love you too." Gareth showers her chilled face with kisses as her head goes slack. "Piper, stay with me." He sinks to the floor, pressing his cheek to hers. "Please stay with me. Please." He pulls away to look at her. "Piper." As she takes her final breath, a tear falls and wets her cheek. His shoulders shake as he presses his face into her chest.

Jasper checks her pulse. "Don't touch her!" Gareth growls. Jasper crouches into a ball, sobbing. Gareth wails as he tries to wake her up. "Please, Piper, please wake up!" he begs. Shaking her shoulder, he yells, "*Piper*, wake up, *now*! Wake up! Piper! *PIPER*!" His voice breaks as he yells her name repeatedly. He sharply presses his lips to hers; she doesn't return it. The elevator comes to a stop and the doors slide open. Jasper gently pulls Piper out of Gareth's arms and lays her on the floor with her head propped up on the remains of his shirt. Gareth holds onto her hand in desperation.

"We have to go," Jasper cries.

"I can't leave her like this."

"She's gone, Gareth. They're coming for us," Jasper says urgently.

"I can't let them take her," Gareth says, still pressing her hand to his face.

"They already did! We have to go!" he yells. Gareth shakes his head, sobbing into her hand. Jasper wraps his arms around Gareth, pulling him away. Gareth fights him, cursing him, but Jasper's stronger. He manages to pull Gareth away. Piper's hand drops and her lifeless eyes stare off to the side as the elevator doors close.

Chapter 32

VIOLET

Violet opens the blue satin box that had been delivered this morning. Unfolding the velvet wrapping, she reveals the gown Yoojin had tailored for her. She pulls the dress out and watches it change from mahogany to royal blue as it moves. A smirk comes to her lips as she yearns to see Madam Kim's reaction. It's a fabric created at Violet's request. The tailor initially looked at Yoojin nervously, but once he confirmed his approval he became elated. Violet knew this tailor was held back creatively, and she was obliged to free them of restrictions. They provided something unique that would catch everyone's eye.

While she prepares for the evening, she can't get Danit's words out of her mind. *Killian wants you to leave this place and return home.* Did this message indeed come from Killian? Did he want her to go home for Nathan? No, he thinks Nathan's dead. Is he still holding onto jealousy? What if the message didn't come from him? What if Danit knows she's a danger to Arcadia? Is Danit protecting Arcadia? What if it did, in fact, come from Killian? By telling her what to do, could he be trying to get her to do the opposite? What if Killian's in danger? What if he needs her help? How could she get to him? Or is he genuinely trying to protect her? So many unanswered questions, and no one she can trust to find the truth.

Violet opens her bedroom door to meet Dominic waiting to escort her to the ball. His eyes bulge as he twirls his finger in the air. Violet takes a turn, allowing him to see the entire ensemble. The iridescent gown looks modest from the front with a high neckline, and the subtle padding sharpens her dainty shoulders. The caped sleeves that drop to the floor match the hem length of the skirt train. The skirt has a top layer that almost acts as a bustle. The front of the skirt is cut away, revealing skintight merlot-colored pants and matching heeled boots. A tiny clasp is at the back of her neck as she turns. The backless gown reveals the black veins of lightning shooting down her back, reaching out to the dimples on her lower back. Her short curly hair is twisted upwards, providing a faux mohawk of curls sitting atop her head. A gold face chain is draped just under her eyes, crossing the ridge of her nose tucked behind her ears, with two-inch spears dangling at each end matching the seven-inch spear resting at her bosom.

"You're a force to be reckoned with."

"Thank you." Violet smiles wryly.

Dominic holds out his elbow. With a deep breath, she places her hand in the crook of his arm and allows him to escort her to the banquet hall. Putting all questions in the back of her mind, she needs to focus on getting through tonight first. They take an elevator to the very tip of the mountain. The cold air bites her bare skin as the doors open, raising bumps. They're currently open to the elements, but a large glass pyramid stands before them, glowing with imitation candlelight. Her skirt flows behind her as Dom leads her across the stone bridge lit with lamps. Guards greet them; music spills out of the entrance.

Violet questions her motives for arriving late as they enter the glass pyramid bustling with people dressed in royal blue and black suits and gowns. The white marble floors have been polished until you can see your reflection staring back at you. Pyramidic crystal chandeliers seem to hang from nothing overhead. Violet keeps a straight face as many eyes turn to gawk or scoff. "When Madam Kim said 'soiree,' I thought she meant a small gathering, not a full-on ball," Violet says through clenched teeth, feigning a smile. Dom snickers.

Wading through the crowd, they part and a familiar shining face greets her. Violet lets go of Dom to take Aadhya's outstretched hand. Violet's jaw drops, seeing her in her royal blue sari. The high-necked, sleeveless blouse is decorated so intricately with gold flora, geometric embroidery and beading that you can hardly see the blue silk beneath the design. The sheer blue silk wrapped heavily around her waist and draped over her shoulder is also beaded and embroidered on the hem. Her simple center-parted bun is adorned with a gold, geometric headpiece hanging from her hairline and matching earrings. The nose ring she typically wears has been replaced with a simple gold stud.

"Aadhya, I'm in awe. You look stunning!"

"Thank you so much, Violet, as do you. I've never seen a fabric like this before. You look beautiful."

"Thank you. Hopefully the designer won't lose his job for making it for me."

"Yoojin would never allow that to happen." Aadhya crinkles her nose, shining her bright smile. She tucks Violet's hand into the crook of her arm and leads her the rest of the way, Dom taking his place as her shadow.

"Who are all of these people?"

"Mostly family and highly esteemed personnel." Aadhya lowers her voice and leans close. "Were there any complications last night?"

"All is well, my friend."

Aadhya nods. "Please let me know if you need anything in the future."

"Thank you, Aadhya," Violet whispers. "There is one thing. Take care of him for me. We probably won't see each other again after tonight."

Aadhya smiles timidly and bows her head. "Good luck to you, Violet."

The crowd parts, revealing the Kims eating at a banquet table. Violet catches the eye of Madam Kim, and her eyes narrow. "I don't believe in luck," she responds to Aadhya.

"Then I wish you happiness."

"Likewise." Violet lets go, turning to face Aadhya. With a wink, she curtsies low, showing deep respect. Aadhya grabs her arm to stop her.

The sound of chairs screeching draws everyone's attention. Yoojin joins them on the floor, grabbing hold of Violet's elbow. "Oh dear." Violet feigns weakness. "I still feel a little tired from that serum you gave me."

"Violet." Aadhya shakes her head, subtly hiding the hint of humor.

Violet audibly gasps. "Yoojin! Look how handsome you are." She holds his arms as if she needs stability. Looking up at his attractive face, she's thankful to feel there's no longer any allure to him. She touches the gold embroidery on his lapel, distracting him. Swiftly she moves Yoojin next to Aadhya and covers her mouth. "You match!" Her voice comes louder than she expects, making a spectacle. "I suspect that was Madam Kim's doing." Aadhya blushes as Yoojin clears his throat, awkwardly adjusting his sleeve. Violet giggles as she takes Aadhya's hand and tucks it under Yoojin's arm. "Hold on to him for me, would you?"

Yoojin begins to pull away, but Aadhya places another hand over his arm, locking him in place. Violet winks as she turns to greet Yoojin's family. Dominic follows close behind her. Ms. Sinai is close by but surrounded by admiring guests. She catches her eye, but Danit glances away, showing more enthusiasm as she speaks with her group. Violet smirks in passing. "Roger." She nods, avoiding his eyes. "Madam Kim, you look as lovely as always."

Madam Kim raises her chin, noticing the slight. "Thank you, Ms. Odaire. I must say, that gown is something."

"Yes, well, I felt the need to represent my people. Your tailor did a magnificent job. Makes me look quite regal, don't you think?" Violet takes a turn, allowing the fabric to swirl and shift in color.

"Quite."

"Great. Well, as much as I love staring at your face, I'm starving, so I'm going to eat. Those vitamins you gave me, Roger, really take a lot out of you, don't they?" Violet puffs her cheeks and blows at one of the curls dangling on her forehead, and the chain across her face dances. She salutes them as she passes.

Several people in yellow suits walk about with trays of glittering liquid. As they roam around the room, the guests grab glasses, paying no mind to those serving them. "Excuse me," Violet says, stopping one of them with her hand on his arm.

"Yes?"

"May I have one?"

"Of course," he smiles, picking one off the tray and handing it to her.

"Thank you." She beams at him. She doesn't remove her hand, so he stays as she gulps the drink down. "Ack, that's gross. Why is it so spicy?"

The man snickers, trying to keep his composure. Violet looks at the empty glass and looks around. "I'll take the empty glass, miss."

"Thank you. May I have another? What's your name, by the way?" Violet asks, though she's still making a face from the bitterness of the first glass.

"What are you doing?" Dom comes to stand behind her.

Another glass is handed to her. "My name is Ander, miss," the server says.

"Oh, sorry. Can't forget Dom." Violet hands the glass over to Dom, and the server provides another. "Thank you, Ander."

"Violet, I can't drink on the job."

"Why not? I've been cured, remember?" Violet helps Dom lift his glass to his lips as she drinks from hers. He throws one back quickly. "Ack, it burns. Why is it like that?" She takes both empty glasses and trades them for another full glass. "Thank you, Ander. I hope you have a nice evening."

"Thank you, Miss O'daire."

Violet taps her chest and belches. Those nearest look at her in disgust. "Oh, pardon me." She raises her glass in passing.

"I don't think you should drink that one."

"It's fine. My body doesn't allow me to stay intoxicated long." Violet approaches a table towering with foods she's never seen before. A server in a brown suit provides her with a small plate. She thanks them and begins loading her dish, tasting as she goes as she juggles plate and glass.

Dom places a warm hand on her back and leans close to her ear. "This wasn't discussed in the plan."

"What better way to show my weakness than snacking and becoming intoxicated?" She glances back at the Kims' table. Aadhya's whispering to Yoojin, and Violet's heart swells seeing them together. They really are a beautiful couple. Aadhya is sweet and strong; she'll be good for him. Hopefully he'll show a backbone with her, though Aadhya seems like she can take care of herself. Madam Kim still has eyes on Violet, but Roger's out of sight.

She turns back to grazing when something cold touches her bare back. She turns to find Roger standing behind her. Dom has taken a step back out of reach. "Apologies for startling you."

"Roger, that's okay," Violet says, looking back at her food, though it no longer looks appetizing.

"I hope you're enjoying yourself."

"Very much, thank you." Violet throws back the drink and scrunches her face, though it's starting to go down easier.

"You should take it easy. Drinking too quickly never ends well."

"My body burns through it pretty quickly, Roger. It'll be fine." She grins.

"Of course." He smiles down at the floor. "Would you care for a dance?"

"A dance. Like that?" Violet points at the couples spinning about the floor in a waltz. "I can't dance like that."

"Nonsense. If you have the right partner and allow them to lead, I think you'll do well. You might even enjoy it." Roger holds out a hand to her. Violet looks at her plate and back at the spinning couples. With a sigh, she crams a morsel into her mouth and shoves the plate into Dom's chest. He takes it grudgingly as Roger leads her onto the floor.

Violet looks around the room. Aadhya slaps Yoojin on the arm to get his attention. Ignoring his glowering stare, she allows Roger to show her where to put her hands. "A quick pointer," he says. "Keep your elbows locked; that will allow me to lead you in any direction." Violet nods, licking her lips to check for crumbs.

Roger takes a step forward. Violet feels uneasy having to rely on him to not back into strangers. He smiles as he glides across the room with the other couples. Violet finds that he leads well, and she only stumbles when she looks down at his footwork. "Keep your eyes on your partner, my dear," he says.

Violet sighs, having trouble keeping up the façade of enjoyment. "You dance very well," she says, trying to distract herself.

"Thank you, Violet. How are you feeling?"

"A little tired."

"I'm sure you'll feel right as rain when your body acclimates to the boost of nutrients." Violet has nothing to say in response to his blatant lie, so she covers her frustration with a smile. "I'm sure Aadhya's filled you in on what this evening's in celebration of."

"She was kind enough to clue me in on your plans."

"I hope you have no hard feelings. This marriage has been planned for years. He agreed to it before he found out you were alive."

"I have no intention of throwing a wrench in your little marriage plans if that's your worry."

"Aadhya informed me of your feelings. I worry that they haven't been made clear to Yoojin."

"Oh?"

"I wonder if I might ask a favor."

"Ask away." *Prick*, Violet thinks to herself, growing tired of spinning around the room.

"Would you please urge Yoojin to proceed with this marriage arrangement?"

"Why does he need to marry at all?"

"He can't keep roaming about in cities full of dangers. One day his luck will run out. He almost lost his life once." Roger gets lost in his memories.

"I know. Lucky I was there to save him," Violet says curtly.

"Ah, yes." He laughs to himself.

"You're welcome."

"We're grateful, but had he not been searching for you, he never would've—"

"I was dead, remember? How could he be searching for me if I was dead? Perhaps it's you and your disgusting society that have your son running around in dangerous abandoned cities."

"I think you misinterpret our way of life. Our people are happy and safe."

"You work the elderly to the bone in the fields, providing you food and nourishment, while you sit pretty on your little mountain in the sky. They live in sheds amongst the dirt, while you walk on marble floors and sleep in silk."

"We provide them healthcare and protection. You shouldn't speak ill of things you know nothing about."

"Your healthcare... Tell you what. I'll tell your son to give up on me. I'll tell him how I feel about him and the world he lives in, if you keep your wife from murdering innocent people and bombing small colonies that hold no threat to you psychopaths."

"We don't kill the innocent."

Violet leans in, searching his eyes. "Do you really believe that?" She looks around as if lost in thought. "That would explain where Yoojin inherited his naivete. I wonder if Madam Kim's spine is hereditary. It seems your side of the family is lacking."

The spinning stops and a voice says, "May I cut in?" Violet looks over to Yoojin with a hand on his father's shoulder.

"Please do!" Violet exclaims. "Thank you for the dance, Roger." She dismisses him with a toothy grin. Roger's face has turned red, unable to utter a word as he fumes. He releases her and attempts to retain his dignity as he returns to his wife.

"There's no cure for a run at the mouth. Oops." Violet teases, patting her lips.

"Are you all right?"

"Of course, why wouldn't I be?"

"It seemed like your conversation was becoming heated."

"I know how to push people's buttons." Violet shrugs as she places her hand in his. Taking her waist, he begins spinning her around the room as gracefully as his father.

"Violet, about what I said the other day."

"Let me stop you there, Yoojin." Violet inhales deeply. "I can't return those feelings. I thought I could. I did at one point, but not anymore. I can't let go of Killian. I love him. It was always him. Even when my memories were taken away, it was him I was searching for all those years."

The song ends and another begins, but Yoojin drops his hands. "How can you still love him after he hurt you? After what he's said and done?"

"If what Stacy said is true, then it's not his true feelings toward me. He's being manipulated. We'll overcome it as we've overcome everything else." Yoojin shakes his head angrily. "Yoojin, please understand."

"What am I supposed to do, then?"

"Carry on with your marriage plans. Aadhya loves you. You must have feelings for her. Otherwise, you wouldn't have agreed to the marriage in the first place. Tell me I'm wrong," Violet challenges.

Yoojin's emotions seem to flip-flop on him as he takes a deep breath and ruminates over her words. "I just want you to be happy."

Violet smiles at him as tears fill her eyes. Wrapping her arms around his chest, she says, "I will be."

"How can you be so sure?"

"I have faith." She cements that sentiment in her heart. "I also have faith that you and Aadhya will be happy. So, enjoy your engagement party, and don't worry about me."

"I'll always worry about you. Reckless."

"Is that my new nickname?" Violet looks up at him with a chuckle.

Yoojin smiles in return. "It should be. I suppose I'll need a new one as well."

"I have the perfect name for you. Cowboy. Pew! Pew!" Violet shoots her finger pistols at him as she bursts into laughter.

Yoojin rolls his eyes to the ceiling. "I can't believe he told you that story."

"Really? You're surprised Dominic would humiliate you?"

"You're right. I should've expected it." Their laughter carries through the hall as they make their way toward the food. Violet spies Madam Kim's disapproving glare and a disgruntled Roger beside her.

Dom meets her with her plate filled with more items. She shoves one of the brown morsels into her mouth and the flavors explode. Never having tasted anything like it, she's enthralled and demands more. As Dom leads her to the dessert table, glasses chime and everyone's attention is drawn to Madam Kim. Announcing Yoojin and Aadhya's engagement has now become the main spectacle as Yoojin crosses the room to meet her. The audience cheers loudly for the couple. The pure joy on Aadhya's face as he reaches for her hand melts Violet's heart. The lights dim as Yoojin and Aadhya have their first dance as an official couple. Violet watches in awe as the most beautiful couple she's ever seen whirls along the floor.

Madam Kim smugly watches on until her attention is taken by one of her underlings whispering in her ear. Violet almost misses the interaction, watching her friends dance, when Dom nudges her. Madam Kim whispers over to Roger. He nods approval before she slips away to follow the man. Leaving the most important event of her son's life wouldn't make sense unless it was necessary. Violet tosses her plate on the table behind them, and they make their way through the crowd. Did they find the gift to Madam Kim too early?

Following Madam Kim and her lieutenant is easy enough, as they're in a hurry, too focused on getting to their destination to notice anyone around them. The corridors are empty and soon they arrive at the control tower. Dominic, having access to the building to report to Madam Kim, can sneak Violet in. The facility is tiered. The main floor has a multitude of panels with two black suits working on either side. There's a handful of people working in the tower, as there are those who are still coming and going from island to mountain. There's a small staircase in the center leading to the next tier where several hands are at work, all of them wearing an earpiece. Four expansive windows allow them to see out to the landing strip. Dominic guides her to a dark corner not often used but for breaks.

Madam Kim and her lieutenant stand at the top tier discussing the situation. "Have you identified the ship?" they hear her ask.

"It's the same ship the bioscout discovered in Safe Haven before it was destroyed."

"Have you made contact?"

"No, madam, we didn't want to give them a reason to believe the island is occupied."

"Patch us through."

The others get to work. The speakers buzz with static and then they hear, "This is Alan Andrews requesting permission to land." Violet's heart almost manages to leap out of her chest as his voice comes through.

"This is Arcadia air support. Permission denied." Madam Kim folds her arms. Violet lurches out, but Dominic pulls her back.

"I'd like to speak to Yoojin Kim. He's our friend. Please allow us to land."

"You are speaking with Madam Kim Eun-Ju, his mother. I do not permit you to land. It seems you're flying a stolen ship."

"The ship was abandoned, not stolen. Please, we're looking for our friend Violet O'daire. We need confirmation of her safety, and then we'll leave."

"It's imperative that the location of Arcadia remains secret. We cannot allow you to leave."

Kim taps the lieutenant's shoulder. He gives the command. "Lock onto the target." Without another thought, Violet sprints up the stairs, taking the length of her sleeve, wrapping it around the lieutenant's throat twice and holding tight while ripping the gold spear from her neck and aiming it at Kim's throat.

"What is that?" Alan says over the microphone. "Did you lock on to us? Please, we won't tell anyone. Just let us go home. Nova, turn us around. Please let us leave!"

"Let them go," Violet demands, holding the sharp end to Kim's neck.

"How did you get in here?" Kim hisses, then sees Dominic slowly climbs the stairs. "This is treason," she says in his direction.

"I've already come to terms with that."

"Have you thought about how this will affect your family?"

"They're the reason for all my actions. Hands away from the controls."

"Are they still locked onto us?" Nova's voice comes through.

"Awaiting your command," someone over the coms chimes in.

"Call your men off now, please," Violet again commands.

"You've ended your life here, Violet, and the life of everyone you love. There's no way out of this. You must've noticed by now that you aren't as strong as you were. That serum Roger gave you wasn't nutrients, you naïve little girl." Kim laughs.

"Was it now?" Violet tilts her head.

"Please, Ms. Kim, we're unarmed and mean you no harm," Alan begs over the coms. "Is that ship following us?"

Hearing him beg these disgusting people lights a fire in Violet's heart. Yanking her sleeve free, there's a loud crack, and the lieutenant's body goes limp. Madam Kim flinches. She can hear the other suits whimpering. "I won't ask again. Let them go."

"Violet!" Yoojin yells from the entrance, pulling her attention for an instant.

Kim touches her earpiece. "Fire at will."

"No!" Violet shrieks so loud that a crack forms in the glass in front of them. She lurches forward, ripping the earpiece along with some of Kim's hair, and tries to stop it, but she doesn't know how to work the device as she begs the man on the other end to stop.

"Rook, what are you—" Static. "Nova!" More static. From the window in the far distance, she sees a spark of light, then pieces of metal and fire falling and fading into the darkness of night. Violet stands at the window with her mouth open, as if silently screaming.

"Target destroyed. Returning to base." Dominic pulls one of the suits into a headlock before they can hit the panic button.

"What have you done?" Violet cries.

"I did what was necessary," Madam Kim says, backing away slowly.

Violet turns on her, wet eyes bulging. "Necessary."

"All of this could have been avoided. They'd be alive. The people of Safe Haven would be safe. None of this would have happened if you had died when that bomb was triggered."

"What are you talking about?"

"You think I didn't know what my son was doing out there? I saw you seducing him. I wouldn't have it then, and I won't have it now."

"You set off the bomb." Violet could see the truth in her eyes. She's so pleased with herself. "You tried to kill me."

"What?" Yoojin's voice comes from the entrance. Madam Kim looks shocked to see her son in the room. Before anyone can blink, Violet stabs two of the three people at the control desk in the neck before grabbing hold of Madam Kim and pressing her back into her. She yanks Kim's head back by the hair, and the glistening spear smears blood on her neck. "Violet, don't!" Yoojin begins to charge, but Aadhya pulls him back.

Violet whispers into her ear, "It must've been so disappointing to find out I survived."

"That will be remedied," Madam Kim hisses.

Violet scoffs. "I wish you could see what becomes of your precious Arcadia when I'm done with it, but…I must do what is *necessary*." She swipes her hand with such force that the spear hits bone. Madam Kim's body hits the floor. The screaming in her head numbs Violet as she limply turns to Dominic. He has a blank stare.

"Dominic," Violet calls over the screaming in her head. Releasing the woman from his headlock, he digs in his pocket for a device. She watches as the suit runs past Yoojin, crumpled on the floor, weeping in Aadhya's arms. That's when Violet realizes the screaming is not just in her head but is coming from Yoojin. She holds her hand out to Dominic, halting his actions, without taking her eyes off Yoojin and Aadhya, "Has the ship landed?" Violet says to the two suits left in the corner.

"Answer!" Dominic commands them.

They scramble to check. "He's landed, sir."

Flipping open the case from his pocket, Dominic waits for Violet. "Do it," she says. He presses the button, seconds later, the ground beneath them shakes and rumbles. The bombs Dominic had planted amongst every warship on the grounds while everyone slept light up the night sky. Sirens wail. Violet and Dominic watch out the windows as pods take off in every direction. They're evacuating the mountain. Violet steps out of the puddle of blood. Removing the train from her waist, she's left with the top bustle layer which she drapes over Yoojin's mother. Walking down the stairs, she leaves a path of blood with each step. She pauses next to Yoojin and Aadhya. "I'm sorry for your loss, Yoojin."

"You told me you feared Killian after he killed Charlie. You thought he had gone too far, became a monster." Aadhya rubs his arm consolingly while Yoojin seethes. "Look at the monster *you've* become. You deserve each other." He spits those words at her.

"If I have to become a monster to allow Arcadia a fresh start with equality, to save the lives of the innocent, to save my son...so be it."

"I never want to see you again."

"As long as things change here, you won't have to." Violet stares back at him.

"Are you threatening me?" Yoojin growls as he turns to glare at her feet.

"It's a warning." Violet looks down at Aadhya. She nods in understanding. Yoojin stares at the blood she leaves behind as she walks away. Dominic follows behind Violet, knowing there's nothing he can do or say to make this situation easier for Yoojin.

When they're alone in the corridor, they pick up their pace. "We need to get off this rock."

"Do you think he'll come for us?" Violet asks.

"I don't know, but I don't intend to stay and find out."

"Do you think there were many casualties?" They pick up the pace to a run. Running in heels isn't the easiest for Violet, but she manages.

"It should be minimal, as most were either working at the event or were guests."

They reach an elevator that will take them to ground level. The doors close behind them. Violet leans against the wall, tilting her head back. The skin of her hands feels strangely taut. "I hope he can forgive me one day," she says, looking down at her blood-stained hands.

The last words Alan spoke to Violet before they separated play in her mind repeatedly. *Remember who you are, Violet. When someone throws heat at your feet, walk through that fire. You aren't a survivor. You are a fighter. Come home to us.* She covers her face with her bloodied hands. A sob escapes her lips. Dominic turns to face her, resting his hands on her arms. "I should've stopped her sooner. I could've stopped her," she cries, shaking her head. "They died because of me. It's always me. Everyone I get close to gets hurt. I should have stopped her." She wails.

"Stop it."

"I could've saved them. Their blood is on my hands."

"Violet!" Dom shakes her by the shoulders, pulling her out of her head. "You did what you could. What's done is done. There's no benefit to hashing out what you could've done differently."

Violet blinks away the tears. "How will I explain this to Nova's people?"

"We'll worry about that later." The doors open and they step out. "First, we need to find a way off this mountain."

The fires have died down slightly after burning off all the fuel from the wreckage. While searching for a reliable vehicle that will get them out safely, they hear a gunshot. Violet ducks, covering her head. She looks up when she hears Dominic yell. Two people wrestle him to the ground. "Dom!" She moves forward and her surroundings spin. Another shot is fired, and Violet feels this one in her back. Reaching behind her, she rips out a tranquilizer dart. Her body becomes heavy as she tries to reach for Dom. "Dom." She crawls towards him and collapses.

"She's down. Take her to the shuttle," Roger demands.

"We agreed to send her home, Dr. Kim," Danit's panicked voice sounds distant.

"If you think I'm going to let this woman go free after the damage she's done, after what she did to my wife…" He chokes. "She leaves with you or she dies. It's your choice, but I don't think Dr. Oric would be very pleased if he lost this specimen. Now get her out of my sight." Two suits pull Violet to her feet, and she can't find the strength to lift a finger as her head lulls back. Roger comes to stand before her. "If they refuse her on the shuttle, execute her then and there."

"S'much for yur cure," Violet slurs. A heavy hand swipes her face, the force causing drool to dribble down her chin. They drag her away as everything turns dark.

Chapter 33

GARETH

She's gone.

Gareth and Jasper are crouched, holding their breath as a group of suits run past. They've finally made it to the 9th floor. They can avoid being seen by staying off the streets and passing through lush gardens and courtyards. Jasper peeks over the terrace wall as the suits' footsteps become more distant. It's all clear, so he hits Gareth on the shoulder to lead the way. When he doesn't make a move, Jasper looks back. Gareth's fingers are pressed into his forehead, and he grinds his teeth as his lips tremble. "Gareth, we can't stay here. I don't know the way," Jasper whispers in a rush.

Gareth presses his palms into his eyes. The pain distracts him from the ripping pain in his chest. He looks over the terrace. Wiping his nose on his bloodied arm, he pushes off. Jasper follows, crouched low as they make their way through a garden full of statues, flowers and shrubbery. "Two houses down," he says, nodding in that direction. As they move slowly through the next yard, the water features muffle the pattering of their bare feet on the path.

Creeping up to the next house, they see two suits leaving. They drop to the ground behind a hedge. "We appreciate your cooperation, Ms. Nox," one of them says as they're leaving. "Just let us know if you hear from them."

"Of course." Stacy stands in the doorway, waving off the suits.

They start moving when they're sure the suits have left and Stacy has gone back inside. They round the house and slip inside through the back door. Gareth holds his finger to his lips as they move through the house. He hopes the rest of the family isn't home. The only person he trusts is his cousin. He moves through the entertainment room and then upstairs where Stacy would be. Jasper looks around, distracted by the pristine home. They can hear Stacy in the kitchen as they climb the glass stairs.

Gareth motions Jasper to stay on the stairs as he silently makes his way down the hall. No sign of the rest of the family. He rounds the corner to the kitchen. Stacy turns and screams, nearly jumping out of her skin. He shushes her, clasping a hand over her mouth. "I'm sorry, it's just me."

Stacy shoves him away, wiping her mouth and spitting. "Is that blood?" she asks wide-eyed. Gareth looks down at the crusting, dried blood on his hands and abdomen. He's unable to recover his voice, so he nods. "Gareth, what have you done?"

"What have I done?" He repeats her question. He wonders what story Oric spun for her to question him. "We need your help, Stace."

"We?" Stacy throws her hands out in question. Jasper comes around the corner then. She jumps again but steps back until she has the countertop support.

"I know this looks bad," Gareth starts.

"You think? Both barefoot and shirtless, covered in blood? Suits coming to our door to tell us you've lost your mind and killed one of Oric's patients?"

Gareth's features darken as he steps closer to her. "Oric killed her, not me. I loved her." His voice breaks as the image of her lying on the elevator floor, pale and cold, cuts into his vision. He scrunches his eyes shut, trying to get rid of the image. "Do you even know what he's doing to those patients, to us?"

"That's none of my business. You shouldn't have even been down there! What were you thinking?"

"Please, Stace, he's been torturing us every day. We had to get out of there before he killed us." Stacy shakes her head in disbelief. Gareth closes the distance, grabbing her shoulder to get her attention. "Your friend Killian helped us escape."

Knocking his hands away in disgust, she asks, "Where is Killian now?"

Gareth opens his mouth to speak, but the words won't come. Jasper steps forward. "Oric shot him. He's dead." He shifts his weight from foot to foot, folding his arms over his chest.

Stacy glares him down. "Why would Oric kill him? They work together."

"I told you, he tried to help us escape."

"I don't believe you."

"What?" Gareth's eyes widen, filling with tears. Jasper runs his fingers through his blonde hair, nervously licking his lips.

"None of this makes any sense."

"Please, Stacy, you're my cousin. Please, please help me."

Stacy looks him up and down and glares at Jasper. Folding her arms over her chest, she bites the inside of her cheek. "Get cleaned up. I'll get you some clothes, and you'll start from the beginning." Jasper and Gareth let out a breath in unison. She leads them to the bathroom and goes down the hall to retrieve clothing.

"She died in my arms," Gareth says, staring down at his hands, tears spilling from his eyes as if he could still see her, pale and limp. Stacy pulls him into a hug. Jasper sits beside Gareth on the sofa, slouched low with his arms folded over his chest. Reliving the experience has tears streaking his cheeks. Covering his face with one hand, he hiccups, trying to hold in his sobs.

"You've gone through so much," Stacy says, rubbing Gareth's back as he grips her tightly while he weeps. She sighs as she waits for his breathing to settle. When she pulls him away, she holds his face, wiping the tears with her thumbs. "You know, this never would've happened if you'd stayed where you belong." Gareth's breath catches and his brow knits together as he stares into her blue eyes. "You wouldn't have met her and put yourself through all this pain."

Gareth pulls her hands away from his cheeks, pursing his lips. Jasper shifts uncomfortably. "I wouldn't have met her, but she would've been going through all that alone."

"That's true," Stacy says, pulling her hands out of his vicelike grip. "Why don't you both get some rest? We'll figure out a plan of action in the morning."

"What about Uncle John? Won't he be home soon?"

"No, my parents have retired. They won't be coming home. You know where the bedrooms are. Make yourselves comfortable." Stacy smiles down at them before withdrawing to her room.

"I thought you said she'd be sympathetic?" Jasper finally speaks up.

"So did I. This isn't like her."

"Are we safe here?" Jasper leans forward, resting his elbows on his thighs.

"She wouldn't turn us in. Stacy's the only person we can trust with this. She knows what's happening is wrong. I thought she'd be more upset about Killian."

"Why?"

"She was in love with him."

Jasper sighs, rustling his hair in frustration. "I'm going to sleep while I can." He lies down on the sofa, tucking his legs behind Gareth.

"Do you want a bed?"

"I'd rather have multiple escape routes if things go south here."

Gareth nods, moving himself to the floor to give Jasper space. He leans his head back and takes a shaky breath. Jasper's hand lands on Gareth's head. "I'm sorry."

"For what?"

"What happened today with Piper. I can't help but feel like it was my fault. Maybe they saw me following you."

"It wasn't your fault. They would've come for us whether you had come or not."

"Then I'm sorry she's not with us."

"Me too." Gareth tilts his head forward, curling into a ball. Jasper pats him on the shoulder before turning away from him.

Gareth reminisces in memories of Piper, keeping her alive in his mind. His head lulls back against the sofa, and he begins to dream of her. The dream takes a turn when he hears her call his name: "Gareth, we have to get out of here." He jolts awake. His heart pounds in his chest. Jasper is still sleeping behind him, and it's become very dark. Gareth's neck is stiff from sleeping in such an awkward position. "Gareth." Piper's voice comes in a whisper. Adrenaline pulses through him, setting his veins on fire. "Gareth, wake up! It's not real!

Gareth!" Piper's voice comes louder as if it's right in his ear.

Gareth turns to Jasper, ripping him out of sleep. "Do you hear that?"

Jasper holds his breath, listening. Silence. "What was it?"

"I heard Piper yelling."

"Gareth, you need rest. She's gone. They took her from us."

"I know I heard her," he argues.

"No—"

They're interrupted by the front door crashing open. Jasper and Gareth run for it as the house floods with suits.

Chapter 34

VIOLET

Screaming in the distance has Violet opening her heavy lids. The lights are too bright. Blinking, her watery eyes slowly adjust as she focuses on the whitewashed tiled walls and floor. Before her lies a table with a pile of clothing and two different communicators.

"No! Wake up! It's not real! It's not real! Let go of me! Gareth! Wake up!" the voice screams.

Violet turns her head to the sound. An open door leads out of the room, and a young girl with chestnut hair thrashes against two men in grey suits, dragging her away. Violet reaches up, but something is restricting her. Her breath catches as she looks down at her body. Gone is the tailored gown, replaced with a loose white piece of clothing. Her arms and legs are strapped to a bed angled upward, so it almost feels like she's standing vertically.

Trying to wriggle free of the restraints, she realizes the effect of the tranquilizers hasn't worn off. How long had she been out? Looking around, she notices a needle in her arm. Following the dark line of the tube, she spots a machine. Panic strikes as she realizes what's happening. Another voice cries out, a man's voice, and she remembers Dom being taken down. "Dom?" The cries continue. "Dom!" Violet shouts louder. It becomes silent once more.

Hearing footsteps in the hall, she tries harder to free herself of the restraints. She grunts from the exertion. The thick metal cuffs bite at her wrists and ankles. The footsteps draw nearer. Putting all focus on releasing her hand, she pulls and wriggles, biting back the pain as the bones bend unnaturally. It's too late. They're here. She turns her head to find Killian standing there as the door closes behind him. A mixture of a cry and laugh slips out when she sees him.

Killian looks so different. His hair is cropped shorter and slicked back neatly. He's grown out a short, maintained beard. The arm they gave him would almost look human if it weren't for the joints. For an instant, she thinks she sees the smirk she had always been fond of, but with a blink it's replaced with a blank look. His dark eyes barely reflect light, looking so severe and cold.

"Violet." His voice rumbles in greeting as he approaches her. Violet's breaths become uneven as she observes him remove the needle in her arm and patch her up. Hope starts to grow in her chest. "You should have gone home as I told you," he says with his back turned to her, removing the bags of blood drained from her. He moves out of sight.

"You shouldn't have sent your whore to deliver the message. I probably wouldn't be here if she hadn't come."

"No, you'd be dead." His voice sounds closer. "I'd be careful of what you say about the magistrate. She has more power here than you think. Besides, she was nice enough to bring your belongings." Killian moves about the room behind her. She looks at the pile of clothing and recognizes it as what was left of the custom-made gown and her communicators.

"I would've killed them all," Violet snarls.

Killian comes into sight, slamming his hands down on the frame behind her. "You are not invincible!" he yells viciously, inches from her face. The anger melts away from his face, his brows curving upward. "You shouldn't have come here," he whispers, seemingly looking through her.

Violet yearns to touch his face. Yanking on her restraints, she leans her head forward. "Killian." His eyes focus back on her glistening ones. "Set me free. I can get us out of here."

He moves back, dropping his hands. Reaching over, he drags a table around. "They took too much blood from you, Violet. You're too weak to do anything."

"Why are they taking my blood?" Violet's voice shakes, knowing he's right.

"The people here have a sickness. You're not the only one with mutated genes. They call it *mortemossa*. The mutated genes attach to the bones and begin eating away at them. Their bones become brittle. It's excruciating."

"What does that have to do with me?" Violet watches as he distracts himself with a task.

"The blood samples sent from Arcadia counteract that mutated gene, killing it instantly. It doesn't reverse the effect but stops it from progressing. Your blood will save thousands of people." He pauses, looking down at the table.

"Killian, let me out of this. Help me." Killian turns to her again. He gently tucks a curl behind her ear and presses his hand against her face. Violet leans into the warmth. Something's left behind when he takes his hand away, stuck to her temple. "Killian?" He does the same to the other side. The way he touches her shows love and affection, while the look on his face screams the opposite. Her chest constricts. Her breaths come short and shallow as she tries to yank free of her restraints. "Killian, please, I love you. Please!" she begs as he pulls the collar of her clothing down.

He places round sticky pads with wires hanging from them onto her chest. His fingers leave a lingering touch on her skin. "I can't help you now," Killian finally answers her with a chilling calm in his voice. "You're in Dr. Oric's care now."

"Oric? What then? What happens now?" Violet's voice comes out weak and frightened.

"He wants to test your limits." Killian collects another item from the table and looks back at her with an unreadable expression. He gently takes her chin.

"What does that mean?" Killian doesn't answer as he holds a rubber mouthguard to her lips. Violet shakes her head. "Please," she begs. Her vision goes blurry as her eyes fill with tears. Killian gently pulls her chin down. She searches his eyes, weeping as she complies, allowing him to slip the mouthguard into place. Killian stares at her lips, and his expression subtly changes as if battling conflicting feelings. His thumb caresses her bottom lip before he steps back. Violet whimpers as she tries to yank free. Killian avoids her eyes as he turns his attention to a device in his hands.

There's a click, and every muscle in Violet's body tenses. It feels as though her brain is rattling like dried beans in a jar. Her body convulses as lightning pulses through her. After what seems like an eternity, it stops. She cries out, gasping for air, moaning between breaths. She begs Killian, though her words come in mumbled slurs with the obstruction of the mouthguard. He watches her with a neutral expression. She thrashes, trying to break free again, though this attempt is much weaker. He looks back down at the device, and she knows what's coming. The static echoes through the room, and Killian glances at the table with her belongings.

"Mama?" Killian and Violet freeze, both holding their breath. "Mama, where are you?" Violet's heart jumps up her throat. He's awake, and she wasn't there for him...again. *Again.* She goes cold as she watches Killian lift the communicator, but he hesitates.

"Where are you, Mama?" Nathan begins to sound worried.

"Amfer it." Violet spits out the mouthguard. "Answer it." Spit dribbles down her chin. Tears stream down Killian's face as he brings it closer to him.

"Mama! Why aren't you answering?"

"Answer it!" Violet screams. The metal restraints moan at her attempt to reach for him. She pants from the exertion as she uses up the adrenaline's energy.

"Nathan?" he responds.

"Dad? Where's Mom?" Nathan's voice is almost a whisper. Killian closes his eyes tightly, fresh tears spilling down. He briskly closes the distance between him and Violet. Holding the communicator near her mouth, she takes a deep, steadying breath, and he presses the button. She stares into his cold eyes. "I'm sorry I wasn't there when you woke up, my love," she chokes out into the mouthpiece.

"Where are you?" Nathan cries.

Something changes in Killian's expression when he hears the emotion in Nathan's voice. Violet narrows her eyes on him. "I'm coming, baby."

About the Author

Ashley Ashforth, a devoted wife and mother of two, hails from the lush Pacific Northwest. Her ability to conjure vivid dreams and a wide array of hobbies have shaped her storytelling. Writing is her true passion, offering endless joy. She's committed to sharing her narratives with fellow book enthusiasts. *Arcadia: Fallen Colonies II* showcases her knack for crafting immersive worlds, complex characters, and compelling tales. Dive into her post-apocalyptic universe, where suspense and unbreakable bonds unfold amidst the ruins of the future.